ST. MARTIN'S

MINOTAUR
MYSTERIES

"OUT OF THE CORNER OF HER EYE, JANE THOUGHT SHE SAW THE REAR DOOR OF THE VAN MOVE . . ."

A warm breeze slid through the open side door, a leaf skittered across the cement floor. Jane froze. The breeze was warm, she knew that, so why did she feel a chill, such a cold blast that the hair stood up on the back of her neck. Her short haircut threatened to betray her panic. *I've become a character in a cheap horror movie*, she thought, and in the next second, all humor, all hope drained out of her. "I'm going to find another body," she said aloud.

She felt the weight on her shoulder and the back of her neck before she felt any pain. She fell forward, one arm grazing the potting table, the other reaching toward the van. The passenger door was unlatched and she grabbed the corner of it, swinging forward, staggering with it as it moved, as she went down. She was spinning; she was mumbling as she hit the floor.

"Not my body. I'm not supposed to find my body."

Also by Sharon Fiffer

DEAD GUY'S STUFF

Available in hardcover from St. Martin's Minotaur

Killer
STUFF

Sharon Fiffer

St. Martin's Paperbacks

KILLER STUFF

Copyright © 2001 by Sharon Fiffer.
Excerpt from *Dead Guy's Stuff* © 2002 by Sharon Fiffer.

Cover photograph © Herman Estevez.

ISBN: 0-312-98370-0

Printed in the United States of America

St. Martin's Press hardcover edition / September 2001
St. Martin's Paperbacks edition / September 2002

St. Martin's Paperbacks are published by St. Martin's Press, 175 Fifth Avenue, New York, NY 10010.

10 9 8 7 6 5 4 3 2 1

To, for, but not about Steve

ACKNOWLEDGMENTS

I am most grateful to Steve Fiffer, who always knows when to offer both personal and professional support, and to our three wise and patient children, Kate, Nora, and Rob. Thank you to the powers that be at Ragdale, an artist's colony where I discovered, among other things, architectural artifacts in their most exquisite natural habitat. Thanks to Alice Sebold and Thom Bishop, who read early drafts and portions of the manuscript and gave sage advice and unconditional encouragement. Thanks to Gail Hochman, who found the book a house, and Kelley Ragland, who made the house a home. Thank you, also, Chuck and Lynn Shotwell, Ellen Morgan, Sheldon Zenner, Ben Sevier, and Marcy Hargan.

And special thanks to the people at the EZ Way Inn with whom and in front of whom I grew up. A real place with a real life for more than thirty years, Don and Nellie's EZ Way Inn was as much my home as any other house our family lived in. Although I've loaned my parents and the tavern to Jane Wheel for her story, the real EZ Way Inn and the real Don and Nellie remain my own. Their fictional counterparts are just that—fiction—but I will always be grateful to the originals for providing me with so much inspiration.

1

If she hadn't spent an hour sorting through the postcards and theater programs under the workbench, if she hadn't held each slope-shouldered pale blue jar up to the window searching for chips and cracks, if she hadn't pretended to be Nancy Drew, sniffing out an early copy of *The Hidden Staircase*, complete with book jacket, page-by-weathered-page checking for mildew, Jane might have been the scout, the picker, the shopper, the collector who found the small dull-green vase—maybe it was even Grueby, just maybe it was the real thing—in a box of oh so desirable vintage flowerpots, each of which were marked one dollar.

Instead, it was some neighbor who dragged the box right out from under Jane's nose and chatted incessantly in the check-out line to anyone who would listen about her African violets and how poor Hettie's sweet little pots would brighten them up. This woman, this violet farmer, paid seven dollars and walked outside, not even aware of what she was carrying. Jane, tapping her foot in line, watched the woman from the large picture window and saw a man approach her. He kept his back to the house, but Jane saw him hold out his hand and the woman nod. He apparently made an acceptable offer, since Jane watched him walk away with the entire box, leaving the silly woman shaking her head and holding a twenty-dollar bill. Jane had only glimpsed the matte green glaze of the vase nestled in with the flowerpots, and could have talked herself out of believing it was a valuable find if she hadn't seen that picker sniff it out and disappear.

"I don't even collect ephemera!" she screamed at the four hand-tinted postcards spread out on the driver's seat. *Greetings from Carlsbad Caverns. Mount Baldy. Painted Canyon at Sunrise. Badlands Sunset.* "I don't even travel!"

Jane, driving her neighbor's Suburban, a bus of a car that might accommodate the Hoosier cabinet she had hoped to find that morning, tried to merge into unusually heavy traffic on Interstate 94. "It's Saturday morning. Go home and sleep."

She thought the approaching blue pickup was slowing down for her, so she gunned the engine and gritted her teeth. The vehicle had the power, but she didn't have the feel for its size; she lost control and nearly went across two lanes as she slid into the traffic. She saw the driver of the pickup snarl and twist his mouth. Through her rolled-down windows, she heard the swearing that was required when a driver made a dumb mistake. She thought she even heard dogs barking and growling. There was another flurry of horns, two swerves, one squeal, as she straightened out the car and stayed in the middle lane. No real damage. She thought she saw a few fingers raised in her direction. "Yeah, peace to you, too."

Nine A.M. Already 82 degrees. Humidity rising. Jane felt herself melting down at the core. It wasn't even August yet. She cranked the temperature up to frigid, then rubbed her bare arms as the arctic air blasted her elbows.

It was too hot to go to another sale, especially an architectural sale where she would have to haul out her crowbar, hammer, and screwdriver and help dismantle a graceful old beauty so that new money yups could build a six-thousand-square-foot mausoleum with a family room and attached three-car garage. But she was after doorknobs. Not just the crystal prisms that she was scouting for Miriam in Ohio, but small closet knobs, solid brass ovals that could be mounted either vertically or horizontally. They felt like cool metal eggs in your hand. Just below the knob, another plate was mounted, the keyhole, waiting for its skeleton, cleverly concealed by another brass oval that hung vertically. Cunning little doorknobs. When you looked at them dead on, they looked like the punctuation mark of a new language.

Jane glanced down at the map. She exited the expressway, beginning to like the feel of a truck. She was tall behind the wheel, powerful. *Maybe this will be my career change,* she thought. *Maybe I can go to the famous trucker's school. Or maybe I'll let Charley have the house back and move into a van with Nicky.*

Two more turns, down a quarter-mile private lane, and she was there. A large circle drive was already filled with pickups, vans, and a fleet of Range Rovers and their relatives like the Suburban she drove. More cars were parked on the lawn. A man in a bright orange vest waved her into a spot between the rose garden and a rusted fountain. There were three people on their knees in the garden carefully digging up the roses as well as the hostas and dwarf lilacs. There was no line at the door, which was good and bad. Good because the heat wouldn't kill her as she waited to get her crack at the inch-by-inch destruction of this arts and crafts masterpiece. Bad because she was late, maybe too late to locate and claim her doorknobs and any other pane of leaded glass, unusual door hinge, or drawer pull she had to have. Jane didn't always know what she wanted, what she needed, what she craved until she saw it.

It had started with flowerpots. Two years ago while at her parents' house in Kankakee for Thanksgiving, she'd gone into the basement to find the extra gravy boat and spotted a maroon, ceramic flowerpot with an attached saucer. The deep color, the raised design, the hefty utility of it pleased her. She'd brought it upstairs. Her husband, Charley, took it from her, turned it over, and read, "McCoy. My sister collects these." He took one of Jane's mother's plastic pots of ivy and stuck it into the flowerpot and both plant and pot were transformed. Shiny, dark green leaves curled themselves around the wine-colored pottery. Nature nested into man-made object. Family and guests looked up. It created a moment. Even Nicky had looked up from his Gameboy and nodded.

After dinner, packages of turkey and stuffing, green beans and pie, were neatly wrapped and packed into a box for their drive back to Evanston. Jane tucked in the flowerpot. In her own house, on a kitchen shelf next to her cookbooks, it looked lonely. A few months later, when her neighbor's mother died, Sandy had a garage sale and Jane helped her unpack boxes of salt and pepper shakers, animal figurines, souvenir pillows.

"I can't believe my mother, who couldn't even kiss you good-bye when you left for college, could hang on to all this junk. Not a sentimental bone in her body, but she never threw one crummy thing away," Sandy muttered, unpacking carton after taped carton.

When Jane discovered four small flowerpots, green, yellow, pink, and maroon, raised designs, saucers attached, she asked Sandy if she could buy them. "Take 'em. I want this junk out of my sight."

Five flowerpots on a sunny kitchen shelf made a statement. *We are a collection,* they said. Jane added collector to her list of titles, along with wife, mother, and advertising executive. She also added stoneware jugs and bowls to the top of her cabinet, pottery vases to the bookcases, and fifties kitchenware to her open cabinets over the sink. She collected slim, elegant cigarette boxes for Charley and ceramic dogs for Nick. Sal at the office mentioned she liked flower frogs, and Jane found her dozens; metal, glass, even a ceramic come-hither mermaid. Mickey collected walking sticks, and Jane presented her with a hand-carved, black walnut, bird head beauty on her fortieth birthday.

Friends of friends, acquaintances began calling her, describing the items that would make their lives complete, giving her a top price, and, often, offering her a commission. At first she refused to make a profit, but after picking up an unusual stork nursery planter, cold paint on the beak intact, at a rummage sale for twenty-five cents that she knew was listed in a McCoy price guide for ninety-five dollars, she allowed Miriam, her secretary's cousin, to give her twenty dollars for it. Miriam, who was a collector and dealer with a small shop in southern Ohio, now regularly supplied her with lists of her own and her customers' hearts' desires.

When Charley had moved out last spring, he'd cleared his books off the bedroom shelves and emptied his closet of blue workshirts and khaki pants. Sighing, he'd touched her cheek and told her now, at last, she would have room for the mechanical banks she had begun bringing home. "On that top shelf over there, don't you think," he'd said, taking out his handkerchief and wiping her eyes gently. "I'll just collect these rare tears, if you don't mind." He slipped the square back into his pocket, picked up his few cases, and left for South Dakota.

Two weeks later Jane's agency lost two large accounts and decided they should eliminate Jane and her entire department.

Jane could have protested that only one of the lost accounts had been hers and the client was notoriously fickle, moving his business around every few years to "keep things fresh," but she didn't have the heart. She regretted that her assistants, creative staff and secretary, were only given three days to clear out and was guiltily embarrassed that she, by virtue of title and time served, was paid more than a half year's salary, barely enough to make the mortgage on the sweet, stucco, four-bedroom with front and back porches and fruit trees in the yard, but more, she thought, than she deserved.

Nicky had planned to spend the summer with his dad at the dig, so Jane told Nicky that she hadn't been fired, she had been given an opportunity then proceeded to pack him up as quickly and efficiently as she had her office files and photos.

"I'm going to find a T. rex, Mom," Nicky had told her as he'd stuffed batteries into the pocket of his suitcase.

"Not if you don't look up from your Gameboy."

"Dad said I could bring it. They have radios and little TVs at the campsite. Dad said just not to count on going into town for batteries all the time."

"This'll be a good summer for you, Nicky. A real camp, not some wussy little storefront YMCA deal."

"Yeah, Dad says we'll pee outside all the time."

"Fabulous."

"And when I come home, I'll bring Dad and you guys don't have to get the divorce."

Jane stopped rolling socks and underwear and T-shirts and hugged her ten-year-old son.

"Just bring home the T. rex, honey."

"Look out, lady." Jane jumped back, but not far enough. The heavy piece of carved oak molding crashed down, grazing her left shoulder and knocking her back into several people on their knees actually prying up floorboards.

Several men, shirtless and sweating in the morning heat, looked up and swore, ready to say more until they saw that it was just a woman—five-three, bobbed brown hair tied back with a scarf, good-looking in her jeans and tank top, big eyes spilling over with tears from the pain in her shoulder. Nah, she wasn't worth a fight. But not so great looking that she was worth losing the boards for either.

Jane staggered away from them into the open and empty dining room, bare wires hanging from the ceiling where a chandelier had hung, wires protruding from walls where, she imagined, etched bronze sconces had been mounted.

"Hey, lady, I am so sorry. I didn't think that molding would give with just one pull. You okay?"

Jane rotated her left shoulder, dropped her wrist, then slowly raised her arm. Painful, a bad bruise, but no break. "I'm okay."

"Let me make it up to you, what'd you come for?"

Jane studied this eager clumsy stranger. He couldn't be

a regular or he never would have left that piece of molding in the hallway.

"First you better collect your weapon."

"The boys'll get it. Those guys prying up the floor are my crew."

"What's so great about that floor?"

"It's the nails. There are some hand-forged roseheads in there. Some early cut nails, too. Way earlier than the house. The carpenter who laid the floor must have hoarded nails like crazy. Some of them aren't even nails that should go in a floor. Bitch to get out so Bill, the sale director, said I could have them for free as long as I bought enough other stuff and hauled away the floorboards. You look pretty pale. I'll get you a Coke from my truck." He turned, then turned back. "I'm Richard."

"Jane."

Jane's shoulder throbbed. She leaned against the wall, trying to get her bearings. Through the dining room doorway, she saw what must be a butler's pantry. It was the only spot that offered a counter where she might be able to have a seat, if she had the strength to boost herself up. No one seemed to be hammering or sawing in there. She walked slowly over, figuring it must already be gutted.

The glass doors of the pantry had been removed, which gave her more space for a seat on the counter. As soon as she drew her knees up to her chest on the counter, she spotted them. Lovely brass oval knobs with keyholes beneath. There were two miniatures on the small, built-in cabinet high above the now doorless china cupboard. Slowly she stretched herself out and turned and stood on the counter. She could reach the knobs, but her leverage wasn't perfect. She pulled a small screwdriver out of her back pocket. They weren't going to budge. She'd have to take the doors off. She scooted sideways to check the hinges. Her heart racing with discovery, she momentarily forgot the throbbing in her shoulder. When she wedged herself into the corner, she rammed her left side directly into the china cupboard and recoiled like a broken spring. Her weight, now thrown too far back, she began teetering on the lip of the counter, a cartoon character on a cliff.

"Help!"

"Jane!" Richard ran in, braced her from the back while she steadied herself; then he lifted her down from the counter.

"How about that?" Jane said. "I yelled help and somebody came."

"Drink this." Richard called out to Louie, one of the floorboard crew, and asked him to take the cupboard doors off for the lady.

Jane drained the Coke. "First you try to kill me; then you save my neck."

"Yeah, all in a day's work. Thanks, Louie."

"Boss, there's a . . ."

"Is that a box up there?" Jane asked.

Treasure. Jane loved nothing more than a mystery box, something everyone else had missed. No dealers here, except for the architectural artifacts guys like Richard. No grabby, bitchy women looking to pay a dime and charge a dollar at their own little flea market tables, no grizzled old prospectors bumping her out of line waiting for numbers at dawn at a northshore estate. It was just Jane and Richard and one heavy cardboard box that clinked when Louie set it down.

Louie looked from Richard to Jane and saw that she had the goofy, glazed look that the real junk junkies get when they are excited.

"You want me to take it out to the truck, boss?"

"Shouldn't we see what's inside?" Jane asked, trying to keep her hands from tearing at the cardboard.

"We bought this part of the house already, so we own it, right, boss? I'll take it out to Braver's truck."

Richard put his hand on the box and shook his head at Louie. "Let's guess what's inside," Richard said. "You go first."

"Okay, a signed Tiffany light fixture," said Jane.

"Waterford, decanter and cordial glasses, a forgotten wedding gift," said Richard.

Together they opened the flaps of the box.

"Shit, boss, it's just flowerpots," Louie said. "I'll put 'em in the truck for Doris."

"These are cool, though." Richard held one up to the light.

Jane laughed out loud. "Cool?" Six vintage flowerpots, one McCoy in a pale blue, diamond quilt pattern, the only pattern she didn't own. It was garage sale karma. What's lost is found. "Oh, yes, they are cool."

"So you take 'em. Bill isn't going to want them. Come on," Richard said, "we'll put them in a sturdier box for you."

"What about Doris?" Louie asked.

Richard shook his head. "What my stepmother doesn't know won't hurt her."

Jane let Richard carry her cupboard doors and her box of flowerpots to the table set up by the kitchen door.

"Ten dollars," Bill said, barely looking up, "for the whole thing."

Jane started to reach into her jeans pocket, but Richard grabbed her wrist hard.

"Bill, this is a box of flowerpots that somebody left behind, even the estate sale coven, and two cupboard doors that are off standard. She uses them to paint on."

"Five dollars."

"Better."

Jane mouthed thanks. Louie called out from the hall that there were some fancy hinges upstairs, but Rich was going to have to hurry up to claim them.

"Bill, look up. This woman almost got killed at this underinsured deathtrap. Get one of your goons to carry this stuff out for her."

A stringy teenager, bored and mean, trying desperately to look like the outlaw he desperately wanted to be, grabbed the box with one hand, the doors with the other and stared hard at Jane, daring her to tell him to be careful.

"Wait," Richard said, stopping him, "there's paper here to wrap these babies up and I'll get you a better box. This one's falling apart."

"No, it's fine," she said. She was pleased that he recognized the importance and care of these flowerpots but didn't want him to go to anymore trouble. Truth was, she wasn't used to the attention or the intensity of Richard's eyes as he watched her fumble with her wallet. She was getting flustered. She tossed her keys to the stringy scowler and before Richard could protest further, she told the teenager her car was a blue Suburban with a license plate SMB.

"Thanks, really, you've done enough. You've made my day," Jane said, thinking, *Was that the stupidest thing I could say or what?*

"Me, too. Here's my card. Call me. Tell me how your shoulder is." As an afterthought, he smiled.

Good teeth, she thought.

"Are you married?" he asked.

"Separated. You?"

"Confirmed bachelor."

It had been so long since she had talked to a single man as a single woman, she had no idea what she was supposed to say.

"I date though. You?"

"Oh yeah, sure," said Jane.

"Call me. Sue me," Richard said, patted her unhurt shoulder, and hurried off.

"Of course, I date. Why wouldn't I date?" she yelled after him.

"I don't date, Ma! You know I don't date!" she yelled into the phone.

"I still can't hear you, Jane. Your dad and the boys just got back from golfing and the bar's full. Can you call me about this later?" shouted her mother.

"You called me. I'm returning *your* call, Ma, so you call me back." Jane fished for her shoes under the bed, holding the receiver several inches from her ear.

"Yeah, well, it's something your dad really should talk to you about so he'll call you tonight. Unless you're going out with this junk collector."

"I'll be home."

Jane's mother's phone message:

Yeah, okay. This is Nellie. Your mother. Jane, call me. Call your mother. It's Saturday. Morning. You're probably out buying junk. Christ. Call me later, Jane. It's Nellie. Your mother.

Jane had unpacked the car and propped the postcards up on the kitchen table. Whenever she brought home something new, something foreign to the collections of glass and metal flower frogs, McCoy vases, flowerpots, old textbooks, poetry chapbooks, Bakelite buttons, marbles, Pyrex mixing bowls, water pitchers, English ivorex tourist plaques, old manual typewriters, she set it out to see if it took.

The flowerpots had started in the kitchen but had moved to an old teacher's desk in the dining room, then a bedroom shelf, and now finally rested comfortably on a piecrust table nestled into the curve of the bay window in the living room. Clustered together, Jane thought of them as a family. At first, when she would place a new, pale green, basket-weave pot in among the others, they'd seemed reluctant to accept a new member. An unusual pattern, a different shape, a new color, the pot stuck out, didn't blend. A few days later, Jane would glance over and it seemed to her that the old familiar pots had circled round, taken in the stranger, championed its place in their natural order.

But what of the new six? They were beauties: pink, green, yellow, black, celery, and pale blue. Not a chip, not a crack. Jane placed them in a sinkful of soapy water and considered new locations. There wasn't a spot left on the family table.

While the pots soaked, Jane went upstairs to shower off the heat and dust of one estate sale, two garage sales, and the salvage sale where, for the first time since Charley had moved out, someone had asked her if she dated. "What a stupid concept," she said out loud as she stood under the steamy

13

water. At her wedding fifteen years ago, her friend Tim had whispered in her ear, "Just think, Janie, now you have a date every night," and she had almost fainted.

Jane pulled on tan shorts and rummaged for a T-shirt in her nearly empty dresser. After Charley left, she had all the drawer space in the bedroom, but she couldn't bring herself to spread out, to occupy what she still thought of as Charley's territory. Her things were normally still crowded into the old dresser on her side of the bed, "her side" being another concept she hadn't been able to erase. Her drawers were almost empty now, she realized, because she hadn't done laundry in two weeks. Nicky wasn't here to keep her domestically honest. No soccer socks or baseball pants or basketball shorts to turn over quickly for the next day's practice, the next night's game. And it was only the end of July. If Charley's dig went as scheduled, he wouldn't be bringing Nick back for another month.

I'll be buried alive in my own filth by then, Jane thought, not entirely horrified. As much as she missed her son, she didn't mind being alone as much as she had feared, and she loved throwing towels on the floor, hanging her socks from the handlebars of Charley's exercise bike.

When she pulled on a white T-shirt, she was surprised at the pain in her shoulder. She had forgotten getting clobbered by the molding, but now as she explored her left shoulder and upper back with her right hand, she could feel the swelling; she could make herself wince with every poke into the spreading bruise. *Richard has a way with women,* she thought. *He makes himself unforgettable.*

She had told her mother about him without a second thought. Filler. Just something new to say. Her parents called her almost every day now with one excuse or another. She knew they were thinking she could end up as some kind of statistic. Downsized, divorced, no, Ma, separated. *Yeah right, what the hell's the difference?* Nellie always asked. Nicky gone for the summer. They were patiently waiting for her to confess that she had become alcoholic, diet pill dependent, depressed, sedated, suicidal. She could hear the ring of disappointment in her mother's voice when she answered that everything was fine; and yes, she'd thought about selling her big house but not yet; and yes, summer was a good time to put things on the market; and yes, indeed, summer was almost gone; and no, she didn't think she'd come home this weekend, there was a rummage sale she had been looking forward to; and yes, she was still buying junk on the weekends; and no, not yet, she hadn't spent all her money yet. Now her mother would ask her every day about the "junk collector" who'd almost killed her until Jane could think of a new distraction.

Clean and cool, she grabbed a bottle of wine to bring to Sandy as thanks for loaning her the Suburban. Sandy hated the car. It had been her husband Jack's idea to get a Suburban assault vehicle. He wanted to show the neighbors how much money he was making now, that's all, claimed Sandy, and she loved loaning it to Jane. The more she got it out of her sight, out of the garage, the happier it made her.

"You can have Jack, too, for that matter." Sandy had smiled directly into Jane's eyes as she tossed her the keys last night. Jane didn't know whether this was a simple joke or a complicated one. Last March there had been a party, a neighborhood progressive dinner. Jane hated these forced occasions, but Charley had thought they seemed like snobs if they didn't go.

"Yeah, so?" Jane had asked.

"It's rude, it's mean, it's small . . ." Charley had stopped.

"It's small town? Charley? It's small town, like me?" Jane was bent over, underbrushing her short hair, and she snapped her head up. Her lips were lightly lined in pink, but the rest of her face glowed with no makeup. She was wearing a simple black T-shirt dress. The neck was scooped low, showing off her beautiful collarbones, her fine neck. All Charley had wanted to do was take her small, perfect face in his hands and cradle her skull as carefully as he would the two-hundred-million-year-old bones of a baby duckbill.

"Jane, I didn't mean anything."

"Look, pal, every day I spend millions of my clients' dollars persuading people to drink this beer instead of that beer. It will make them smarter and cooler and happier and richer. It will make them laugh and look like twenty-one-year-old studs and studdesses. I may come from saloon keepers in Kankakee, and I just may be small town, but I know artificial attempts at friendship and happy camaraderie when I see them."

"You know I didn't—"

"Like a fucking neighborhood progressive fucking dinner is an uptown night at the fucking opera. Like this isn't small fucking town." Jane jabbed gold hoops recklessly through her earlobes.

Charley nodded at the doorway where Nicky stood, his Gameboy temporarily at his side.

"So you guys aren't going?"

"Oh yes, Nick, we're going. We are most definitely going to do the neighborly thing." Jane went over and hugged her son. "Sorry for the swearing, pal."

"You sounded just like Grandma Nellie."

At the party, Jane, still angry, was restless. She drank too many vodka tonics poured by too many heavy-handed husbands, who also knew that the only way this collection of lawyers and doctors and traders and professors and executives were going to get neighborly was to get drunk. When she went into Sandy's kitchen to refill a breadbasket—they were finally past cocktails and appetizers at the Graylords' house— Jack had been carving a second butterflied leg of lamb. She had leaned over him to inhale the smell of rosemary and garlic; and he had turned his head, kept his eyes wide open, and kissed her on the mouth. She had stayed perfectly still, her eyes locked on his, accepting the kiss without encouraging it. They both heard someone come into the kitchen and quickly leave; neither had looked up, neither had moved.

Jane still didn't know who had come in that night: Sandy, Charley, Nosey Noreen, Blond Barbara. But the rumor flew through the block. Jane felt it. It was a palpable breeze that blew through every open screen door that warm spring.

When she and Charley separated two months later, everyone assumed it was because of Jack. People spoke to her less and less. Fewer and fewer kids gathered on their drive-way. Nick spent more and more time at friends' houses.

Sandy was the only neighbor who had never changed her behavior toward her. They weren't close; they weren't pals. All of Jane's best friends were still down home, back in Kankakee. Except for Charley and acquaintances from work, Jane didn't really talk to anyone. She and Sandy joked, they baked each other cookies in December, they traded plant cut-tings. They hadn't quite gotten to friendship; but until the kiss, they could almost see it from where they were. Jane hadn't been uncomfortable about borrowing the truck; she needed it and Sandy didn't. But after the remark last night, Jane knew she wouldn't borrow it again.

She knocked on the side kitchen door and walked in, jingling the car keys and calling out. "Sandy, are you home?"

The air-conditioning was cranking. Jane began shivering. It was 60 degrees, tops. She heard the television on in the living room and walked through the kitchen and front hall. "Sandy? Jack? Are you home?"

She could see that the front door was ajar, and she thought one of them might be out in the front yard or on the porch getting the mail. She went over to the door, preparing a smart-ass comment about how they were letting the air-conditioning escape, that it was an oven in there. She opened the door and looked out, but no one was there. The mail was still in the box; the *Chicago Tribune* was on the step. Jane stepped out and fetched both, stepped in, and closed the door.

"Sandy, what are you doing? Yoga?"

Sandy's feet were on the couch, but the rest of her body was out of sight, presumably on the floor, probably, Jane figured, in deep meditation, since she still hadn't answered.

Her bare feet were pale, almost blue from the cold, Jane thought, until she got closer. Sandy's body was on the floor, her arms stretched out at her side, her torso straight. Her eyes were closed. Her mouth was pursed in a circle; quite possibly her lips were forming Ohm, a mantra Jane could hear and recognize if Sandy had been able to chant, if she had been able to talk, if her throat hadn't been cut, slashed so deeply that her vocal cords recoiled like rubber bands.

Jane went back to the front door and opened it. She was surprised when neighbors began running toward the door, pushing past her, slamming her into the doorway until she slid down the wall and sat on the floor, still.

How did they know, she wondered, unaware that she had been standing, staring straight ahead out the door screaming steadily for five minutes before Barbara Graylord had finally looked up from her roses.

2

The crew was noisy; the lights were bright. Certain personalities asserted themselves—loud protests, sarcastic epithets, slow, whiny complaints. It was like any beer commercial and every beer commercial Jane had ever produced. No matter how pretty the actors or loud the music or catchy the banter, the star was product. Is the bottle sweating just enough? Does it gleam? Does it shimmer? Does it pour out like the nectar that will turn you into someone else, anyone else, turn your world into his world or her world? Product. The best work, the work that worked, was when the crew followed directions, the only ones Jane ever gave. Love the product. Worship the product.

This time the product was Sandy. Placement? Body on the floor, arms outstretched, feet on couch. Dressed in blue shorts, white T-shirt, a colorful vest, blood-soaked to black. Skin, blue. Attitude, dead. Jane watched from the floor in the front hall. *The lighting is overdone,* she thought. *They're going to wash everything out. The prints will be too harsh, too stark. The product will not look loved.*

The police crew took photographs, taped off the room, dusted, scraped, tweezed, measured, bottled, and bagged. The neighbors who had come running, Barbara Graylord, Noreen something and her husband whoever, the heavyweights from across the street, were all gone. They had spoken in quiet, scared voices to the police and walked out the front door, each clutching the railing as they stepped down off the porch.

Jane had heard her name whispered. People nodded in her direction. Somebody gave her a blanket, and she sat huddled under it still. Other neighbors, as they heard the news, saw the police cars, the hastily parked black sedans, came to the door, but were met by the greeter/bouncer policeman, who shook his head and said something Jane couldn't hear. She thought this was like those neighborhood parties, those block picnics, those damn progressive dinners, but it was the "club" version: the studio 54, the country club block party—to get in you've got to know somebody or be dressed a certain way. Or be dead.

"Mrs. Wheel?"

Jane raised her head, surprised at how much effort it took. Her head, each arm, each leg seemed to have a separate weight, a separate life. Her head was a heavy burden. To lift it was painful, such hard work.

"I am Detective Oh."

This is where I wake up, thought Jane. *I wake up and the TV is still on and a Pink Panther movie is playing and I get up and pee and drink some water and go back to sleep.* "Clousseau?" she asked hopefully.

"I am Detective Bruce Oh."

Jane stared hard at this man, who was staring equally hard at her. She desperately tried to remember how to speak English.

The photographers, dusters, tapers, and baggers seemed to be leaving all at once. Oh asked them something about the kitchen and the phone and the sink, and they answered. He smiled, satisfied, and held out his hand to Jane. "Please let me help you to your feet. Let's sit in the kitchen if you don't mind."

Jane hesitated, not wanting to come out from under her blanket, not convinced her legs would work.

"The officers will be removing the body now, and I think we should go into the other part of the house, don't you, Mrs. Wheel?"

Jane accepted his hand, clutched the blanket with the other, and rose, her legs working exactly as they had before when she had lived a much simpler life—an hour earlier.

At Sandy's kitchen table, Jane brushed crumbs off the place mat in front of her and tried to concentrate on Detective Oh.

"Your tie is wonderful," Jane said.

"Yes, my wife shops for vintage clothes. She buys me many ridiculous things to wear. I keep only the ties."

This tie was covered with bowling pins, each pin hand painted with a different pattern and number.

"Mrs. Balance, Sandy, was your close friend?"

"Friend." Jane nodded. "Acquaintance, maybe? We weren't terribly close, but we were friends, the way neighbors are."

"Can you tell me what happened today from the time you saw her this morning until the time you came in and found her this afternoon."

"I didn't see her this morning."

"Mrs. Barbara Graylord said she saw you driving Mrs. Balance's Suburban early this morning, and over coffee at approximately nine this morning, Mrs. Balance told her she had loaned it to you as she often does on Saturdays."

"Yes, but I picked up the car last night. I leave early. This morning I left at six-fifteen, and I didn't want to wake Sandy."

"You left at six-fifteen for work?"

"No, I go to estate sales, garage sales."

"You and my wife." Detective Oh shook his head.

"May I have some water?" Jane tried to remember if she had eaten anything.

Detective Oh nodded at an assistant, whom Jane had not even noticed before. He, too, was taking notes. There was also a uniformed female police office sitting in the corner with a small notebook. The assistant brought her a glass that Jane drank at once. He refilled it.

"So you went to sales. You perhaps later can give us the addresses, you know, tell us your route for the morning. Then you came here to return the car?"

"Not right away." Jane took a deep breath, decided to get through all this as quickly as possible. "I went first to an estate sale and waited in line for a number. After I got my number, twenty-three, which was pretty good, it meant I'd get in during the first wave, I drove to a Starbucks and picked up coffee. I had an hour before the actual sale would start. I read the paper and went over my list, things I was looking for. Sometimes in the excitement of all the stuff, you forget what you really want and spend too much time on what might be interesting, but you don't want. You lose a lot that way. Am I telling you too much? Is this what you want to know?"

Detective Oh nodded. "Everything, please."

"After my coffee, I went back to the sale in Northfield, still a half hour early so parking wouldn't be impossible, but it was sort of already. I stood in line, got into the house, and it was magnificent. Overwhelming. So full of stuff it was unbelievable. The basement and garage were full of unopened boxes so I spent a lot of time going through them, went to the attic and went through postcards. Found a few pieces, went downstairs, and saw someone leaving with a box of flowerpots, mostly Shawnee and Morton, I think, but there was a little vase in there that might have been really valuable. The whole box was under ten dollars, and I was mad at myself for getting lost up there in the attic. I broke all my own rules."

"Then you came home?"

"No, two more garage sales, then a quick walk-through of an estate sale in a newish subdivision, then I drove out to an architectural salvage sale in Lake Forest."

"What's that, a salvage sale?"

"Before a house is torn down to make way for new construction, it's sold for parts. We go out there with our tools and take doors and windows, hinges, doorknobs, molding, mantelpieces. People even dig up plants and bushes and trees."

"You, Mrs. Wheel, go out there with your tools?" Detective Oh looked skeptical. "What do you tear down and use?"

"Right now, I'm after doorknobs. I buy for myself and a few others. I'm sort of a freelance scavenger, a picker. I find things that others I know might want. It started as a hobby, I guess, and now I'm trying to make it pay. I always bring tools with me these days. I once found a mantelpiece that no one else had discovered. It was left in an upstairs bedroom, very small, off size. Exquisite carvings, though. I needed a saw and a crowbar in addition to the hammer and screwdriver I had with me, so I couldn't get it. As far as I know, it got buried when the house got bulldozed." Jane felt tears coming and realized how silly it would be to cry over a mantelpiece when a friend and neighbor had been killed in the next room. Even sillier in front of a police detective.

"So now I always carry an assortment of saws and a crowbar with everything else."

"So you went to this demolition derby then came home?"

"Yes, I got home around two."

"But you didn't come here first to drop off the Suburban?"

"No. I was hot and filthy, so I went home and showered and changed and grabbed a bottle of wine to bring Sandy to thank her for the car."

"You parked it in the garage? Is that how you usually returned the car?"

"Yes. The side door was unlocked, so I came in and called out."

Oh looked directly at her when she answered, his face blank, his head still. Even when he wrote something down, his eyes barely left hers.

"Did your friend Sandy ever talk to you about her husband? About Jack? Did she confide in you about marital problems?"

"No. Well. No."

"You seem hesitant, Mrs. Wheel. It's important that we know everything. Even something that might not seem important might be vital. Even if something was confidential, private, it might be important now to tell us."

"Last night, when Sandy gave me the keys to the car, she said I could have it and I could have Jack, too."

"Was she joking?"

"I assumed she was."

"Did you ask her what she meant? Why she would say such a thing?"

"No."

"You didn't question your friend when she said something so unusual? You didn't ask her if anything was the matter or if anything was bothering her?"

"As I said, we really weren't that close."

Detective Oh consulted his notebook. "I've spoken to some other neighbors. Let's see, you frequently had coffee together in the morning on her deck or your porch. You had a garage sale together. You attended neighborhood parties together; you brought each other casseroles. You baked cookies for her at Christmas. You purchased dishes for her at auctions; you completed her set of dinnerware, her Lu-Ray Pastels, when you found some soup bowls in Sharon Pink. You borrowed her Suburban on weekends, and you kissed her husband, Jack, at parties."

"Once."

"Which?"

"I kissed Jack once. At one party."

"Yes."

"I know there are rumors about Jack and me, but they're not true."

"What kind of rumors, Mrs. Wheel?"

"You know, Detective, neighbors always talk, gossip, about kissing at parties, those kinds of rumors."

"True rumors?"

Jane shook her head, the one that had grown so heavy in the last few hours.

"But you did say that you kissed Jack Balance at a neighborhood party this summer."

"Last spring. I haven't been to any parties this summer."

"You've dropped out of the social scene?"

"My husband and I separated. He's in South Dakota on a dig. He's a geology professor. Our son is with him. I lost my job in May. I haven't felt like socializing."

"Your husband believed these rumors about you and Mr. Balance?"

"My husband believed *me*."

Detective Oh stood up, looked out the window, put his two forefingers on his lips, then motioned to the other police in the kitchen. "Would you excuse us please for just a moment, Mrs. Wheel. We have to check something. We'll need to ask you about finding Mrs. Balance. We'll be right back."

Jane stood up and took her glass to the sink and turned on the cold water. She didn't hear the back door open, but she felt footsteps and turned quickly toward them.

Jack Balance, tan and handsome, wearing a white Polo shirt and elegant checked golf pants, hurried in the door.

"Jane, what's happened? Where's Sandy?" Jack walked directly to Jane and put his arms around her.

Over his shoulder Jane could see Detective Oh standing in the kitchen doorway watching her. Behind him, each peering over his shoulders, were the other two police officers who had listened so far to her statement.

Jane tried to pull away and answer him, but Jack held her tighter. What had begun as a welcoming hug now felt like the grip of a man fallen overboard, clutching a life preserver. Before Jane could disengage his arms and protest that she was a pretty leaky vessel to put his hopes in, the police reentered the kitchen.

"Mr. Balance? I am Detective Oh. These are my associates, Officer Tripp and Officer Mile. We are here because your wife, Mrs. Sandy Balance, was found dead at approximately 4:15 P.M. by Mrs. Wheel."

"Oh, my god!" Jack staggered back into a chair. "Was it her heart? She always suspected a problem with her heart, and I didn't believe her. I didn't take her seriously."

"No, Mr. Balance, your wife did not die of a heart attack." Detective Oh came over to the table. "Mrs. Wheel, are you ill?"

Jane, still standing at the sink, had grown more and more light-headed. A dull ache thudding in the top of her skull was beginning to relieve itself in tiny bursts of pain and pinpoints of light directly in front of her eyes. She felt the room spin; then she felt herself spin to catch it. Detective Oh's voice was farther and farther away, drowned out first by the crashing of waves, then by the loud, incessant buzz at the core of a machine.

She woke on the floor. Officer Mile was putting a wet cloth on her head and trying to apply one to the back of her neck. Oh, Tripp, and Jack Balance were staring down at her.

"You fainted, Mrs. Wheel," Detective Oh said.

"I'm hungry, Detective." Jane sat up slowly but stayed sitting on the floor.

The police huddled together by the sink for less than a minute, and Officer Mile came over and offered her hand to Jane while Detective Oh spoke.

"Officer Mile will escort you home, Mrs. Wheel. We are

not finished with your statement, but we can let you rest and eat something then finish up later."

Jane nodded. "I'm sorry, Jack, about Sandy. Let me know if there's anything."

She looked over at Jack, who was staring at her. The corners of his mouth worked oddly against each other, and for a moment, she thought he was going to blow her a kiss.

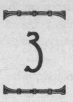

3

"Sorry for the heat. I only have an air conditioner up in the bedroom," Jane said, not at all sure if Officer Mile was going to be staying with her until Detective Oh and the rest got done with Jack. Then what? Would they come over and sit at her kitchen table, drinking iced tea and solving the crime? Or would they ask her if she'd like to grab a sweater and give her statement *downtown*. In Evanston, *downtown* would simply be Elmwood and Dempster, five minutes away from her house, so would it even be called *downtown*?

Jane also did not know whether or not to offer Officer Mile some dinner. Was she going to stay and watch Jane eat, keep an eye on her? Was she under surveillance? Was she a suspect?

"Gazpacho?" she asked, pouring from a heavy pressed glass pitcher she had picked up a few weeks ago. She had found three at garage sales this summer and shipped off two of them to Miriam. She had liked the heft and weight of this one enough to hang on to it awhile.

"No, I shouldn't, thanks." Officer Mile ran her hand over the outside of the pitcher. "Is that Heisey glass?"

"Yes," said Jane, cutting some bread and rummaging for cheese in the refrigerator. "It's a beauty, isn't it?"

"Yeah, my mom collected it and I kind of caught the bug. You've really got some killer stuff here," Mile said, not noticing when Jane winced at her choice of words. Mile walked around the kitchen admiring the fifties mixing bowls and ceramic shaker tops that were used to cap bottles of water for dampening clothes.

"God, my grandma sprinkled her ironing with one of these."

"Yes, I'm packing those up tomorrow to send to a dealer in Ohio."

"This what you do? Shop old stuff and sell it?"

"Sort of, I guess. I lost my job at an ad agency a few months ago; so while I'm deciding what next, I'm picking."

"Picking?"

"Yeah. Searching out stuff that I think a collector or dealer might want. I'm just an amateur. I get too caught up in looking at stuff, at wanting stuff myself."

"Can you make a living at this picking?"

"I don't know. My husband has our son with him this summer. I haven't had a lot of obligations so I've gotten into this pretty heavily. I've been able to scout furniture, get bigger pieces with Sandy's truck . . ."

Officer Mile straightened up. She seemed to remember that she wasn't supposed to be socializing.

"Would you mind if I checked my phone messages?" Jane asked, as she rubbed her hands with a napkin.

"Not at all. I'll just sit here in the kitchen."

Jane went into the study across the hall and pressed the answering machine.

Jane's mother's phone message:

Yeah. This is Nellie. Your mother. Are you out with the junk collector? Your dad wants to talk to you. Call him. Or me. Your mother. Good-bye. This is Nellie.

Jane decided to wait on returning that one.

Two more nonmessages, eventual hang ups. They must have thought about leaving messages since the tape had run to the end.

She returned to the kitchen and noticed that Officer Mile was writing down what appeared to be lists of what she had on her shelves.

"Am I under house arrest or anything?"

"Oh no, I'm just sort of practicing, you know. Being an investigator. Detective Oh says you learn something from every object that surrounds a person. He says a house is full of stories."

"I think Detective Oh is right about that."

"I let your dog in. She looked so hot out on the porch. I gave her a pan of water. I didn't see her bowl."

Jane looked down at the floor and saw her best copper saucepan half full of water sitting in a puddle by the back screen door.

"My dog?"

Officer Mile nodded toward the dining room. Curled up asleep on a hand-braided rag rug from the thirties was what appeared to be a shepherd/collie mix sporting a red bandana around its huge neck.

Officer Mile smiled at the dog then at Jane. "She's a sweetie. So friendly and happy. She makes a good watchdog for you, huh?"

Jane had nursed the feeling all day that she was lost in some kind of bizarre wonderland. She tried to remember if she had seen a bottle marked "Drink me" and actually swallowed something. She took a deep breath and mentally ticked off her list. Lost a box of flowerpots, almost creamed on the highway, clobbered by a doorframe, found a box of flowerpots, found Sandy Balance murdered, now entertaining a police officer, who is sharpening her powers of observation by letting a strange dog sleep in my house.

"It's not my dog." She stared at Officer Mile, whose smile faded to zero.

"The absence of a dog dish on the floor should have been a clue, Officer Mile," said Detective Oh, standing outside the screen door. "Officer Tripp, please remove the dog from Mrs. Wheel's house."

The police officers entered the house.

"Here, doggy; here, pooch." Tripp awkwardly held out two fingers.

"Oh, for heaven's sake," said Mile. "I'm sorry, Mrs. Wheel, she just looked like she belonged here. Come here, sweetie." Mile walked over and roused the dog, who rose lazily and licked her hand. The dog then shook herself and walked over to the kitchen table and put her head in Jane's lap.

"You're quite sure you don't have a dog?" Detective Oh asked, almost smiling.

Jane patted the dog and shook her head. "I've never seen her before. Unless . . ."

"Yes?"

"She looks like a lot of dogs I've seen at sales. Almost every truck has a big mutt sitting in the front seat. Most of them are mean, trained to guard stuff. There's supposed to be one friendly dog; I've heard some of the regulars joking about her. But she couldn't have followed me home from Lake Forest. Besides, I didn't see her there today." Jane took the dog's face in her hands. "She is a sweetie. No tag either. Hmm. Let's put you outside, darling; somebody's looking for you."

Jane put her out on the back porch with a bowl of water. Charley had made the entrance to the screened porch a swinging door that opened either way. If the dog heard her name called, she could nudge the door open.

"Iced tea? Gazpacho?" Jane, somewhat revived by food, was aware of how late it was getting. Maybe they would finish this tomorrow.

"No, thank you, Mrs. Wheel." Detective Oh sat down at the kitchen table, nodded to Tripp and Mile, and all sat and stood at the ready with notebooks and pencils. "We will take only what we need tonight, and if there's anything else, and there always is, tomorrow is another day.

"Tell us about entering the Balance house and finding Mrs. Balance."

"I came in through the side door with the car key in one hand and a bottle of wine in the other. I set the bottle down in the kitchen and called out. I walked into the center hall and noticed the front door open so I stepped out on the porch, picked up the paper and mail, set it down on the hall table, and looked into the living room.

"The TV was on and I saw Sandy's feet up on the couch. I thought for a minute she was exercising, doing yoga or something." Jane stopped, remembering the map of veins covering Sandy's bare feet. "They looked blue, her feet. It was cold, freezing. Then I went around the couch and saw her with . . . saw her. I think I went back to the front door, and that's about all I remember."

Jane finished the story calmly and efficiently; but in her head, a refrain was chanting, *Sandy's dead, Sandy's dead,* and the incessant beating was beginning to hurt her eyes, her ears.

Oh asked her to recall once more everything she'd touched in the house. He asked her if Sandy had ever expressed any worries, any fears. Had she confided that Jack might be unfaithful?

"Just the remark to me last night. But . . ."

"Yes?"

"After that party, after I assumed the rumors were flying, Sandy and I actually got a little closer. I mean we still weren't great friends, but there was certainly no real tension. I mean the rest of the neighbors treated me like sh-—a pariah, but Sandy seemed at ease, like she knew better, knew I had no interest in Jack."

"Because you didn't?"

"I did not."

"You just like kissing."

"Detective Oh, it was a warm spring night. I had had a few drinks. I was restless. No one but Charley had kissed me for the past fifteen years. Jack and I were friendly enough, but I wasn't attracted to him. I was just . . . I don't know . . . startled. And curious, I guess."

"You and your husband were having some problems."

"No. Not really."

"No?"

"Not until then."

Jane fought the urge to put her head down in her arms on the table.

"We'll leave you for tonight, Mrs. Wheel." Detective Oh stood up. "A few things though. Lock everything up tonight.

We'll have additional cars in the area, but I'm advising everyone to be extra careful. Also, do you shop sales with a partner, a friend?"

"No."

"Did you see anyone who knows you at the sales?"

"No."

"Can anyone vouch for your whereabouts between eleven and one?"

"I was at the salvage sale around then."

"They will remember you?"

"I bought something." Jane thought about Bill, who hadn't even looked up when he'd taken her money and the sullen teenager who'd carried the box to the car. She rubbed her shoulder, now truly swollen.

"There was a man who dropped a doorframe on me. Richard. He gave me his card." Jane walked over to the refrigerator and took the card from under a T. rex magnet. "I think he'll remember me."

"May I have this?" Detective Oh took the card.

RICHARD ROSE, SALVAGE SUPREME.

Jane saw the police to the door and noted that her new best friend was still dozing on the screened porch. She scrounged some cold cuts and cheese, mixed some Cheerios for fiber and B vitamins into a blue McCoy dog dish that had been stashed in the cupboard, holding odd keys and sticks of gum, and put it on the porch floor.

"Hope I see you in the morning, pal."

She locked up the house and went upstairs to bed. It was only ten, but felt later, a year or two later, than this morning.

She brushed her teeth, put on one of Charley's old

T-shirts, and got under her quilt. This was the only cool room in the house, and she realized she didn't want to be cool. She switched off the air conditioner and opened a window. If someone was out there prowling around, she might as well give herself a chance to hear it sooner rather than later.

She took the phone into bed with her just as she had done every night since Charley left. She longed to talk to Charley right now. He wouldn't be able to make sense of it any more than she could, but his voice would be reassuring, a calming presence. Charley was kind, after all, and that was all she wanted right now.

A breeze made its way through the window. She was a mile from Lake Michigan, so by the time any cool air arrived it was considerably thinner than the lake breezes that were supposed to make Chicago summers livable. Still, this air made Jane shiver and she huddled deeper under the quilts. Cocooned in her covers, she felt calmer and began to feel each muscle and tendon relax, to give in to bed and blanket and exhaustion. Because she believed she was now back in control, she was quite surprised to hear herself scream when the phone next to her ear rang out.

"Hello?" She was breathless.

"Janie, you okay?"

"Dad?"

"Your mom's been trying to get you, honey, but she keeps getting the machine. Sorry it's so late. Were you sleeping?"

"No. You okay, Daddy?"

"Yes, hon, but I need to talk to you about something— serious."

"Seems to be my day for serious."

"What's the matter, honey? Did something happen with that junk collector?"

"No." Jane wanted to explain her day to her father, but realized there is no vocabulary, no language in which you can convey, don't worry about me, but I found my neighbor with her throat cut, and I might even be a suspect, but really, I'm okay, to your father or mother.

"What's on the docket for tomorrow? Sunday?"

"Well, no flea market tomorrow, so I guess I've got no plans."

"You do now, honey. Come home. I want to run something by you."

"Okay, Dad."

"Really? That's all it takes. Your mother wrote out a list of reasons I was supposed to use to convince you."

"Tell her they worked."

At 5 A.M. she sat straight up in bed, shuddering over a dream she couldn't remember. A few hours later, driving to Kankakee in her old Nissan, she saw the final image of the still elusive dream. It was Sandy, standing on a boat that came nearer and nearer to shore, where Jane was standing. Sandy was waving, bobbing her head and smiling; and Jane waved and smiled back until she realized that Sandy's smile was not a smile. It was a curved slash through her neck that nearly severed her bobbing head from her body.

"Mom, I'm calling from the car. I'm on my way home."

"Where are you?"

"Just passing the exit for Lincoln Mall."

"You're at Lincoln Mall?"

"No, Ma, I'm driving. I'm already past it. I'm about forty-five minutes from you. Will you still be at home or at the tavern?"

"You mean to tell me you're in your car?"

"Yes, Mom, I'm in my car, getting closer to you every minute."

"Don, she's in the car, driving while she's talking on the phone."

"Mom, I might be getting a call from a Detective Oh. I left your numbers for him."

"Who?"

"Oh, just take a message."

"What?"

"If Detective Oh calls, tell him I'll call him back. Are you going to be home or should I drive to the tavern?"

"Tavern. Christ, you get off that phone now. And don't be calling anybody else."

Jane rubbed the fingertips of her right hand on her jeans, then the fingertips of her left. There was no ink from the fingerprinting at the police station earlier that morning, but her fingers still felt sticky. On her way out, Oh had walked in and asked her if she'd be available all day. He'd frowned when she said she was going to Kankakee for the day.

"Am I not allowed to leave town?" she asked.

"Well, during an investigation, it's usually not advisable, but . . ."

"Detective Oh, I found Sandy dead. I didn't kill her. If I need a lawyer, you'd better tell me now."

"No, Jane, go visit your parents. May I have their number, though? Just in case something comes up?"

It would serve him right, Jane thought, to have to try

to get through *Who's on First, Oh's on the Phone* with Nellie.

She should have warned her parents about the murder, the mess, but she couldn't bring herself to do it. It would have to be face-to-face.

When Jane was in fifth grade, her family lived in a subdivision west of town. It had been her father's dream to build that new ranch house, every appliance in it shiny and waiting for them to use it first. Jane resisted the move. She liked the old house on the old street in the old neighborhood. She could walk to school, to the park by the river, to the drugstore that had a soda fountain. Out in Heil Estates, no one walked anywhere. People drove out of garages with their remote-controlled doors in the morning and rolled back into them at night. Sidewalks were unnecessary since human feet never touched pavement.

Jane rode a yellow school bus for thirty minutes through rolling farmland to get to her new school out in the country. There the transient subdivision kids and the steady farm kids made a fragile peace for seven hours a day.

One Friday when Jane was running to her house from the school bus, rummaging for her key, the paper delivery boy, Jim Maxwell, came running down the street with an unrolled copy of the *Kankakee Daily Journal*. "Extra! Extra!" he was yelling, coming straight at Jane. When she looked up, she saw a picture of her mother, Nellie, on the front page, her eyes huge and angry, holding up a wad of tape. Behind her stood Jane's father, looking startled. The headline proclaimed, "Daring Daylight Robbery." Three men with sawed-off shotguns had robbed the EZ Way Inn of the thousands of dollars Don had picked up from the bank to cash payroll checks.

One of the robbers knew that he picked up the money on Fridays at ten, and the Roper Stove boys started coming over around 11:15 for lunch. During that window of time, three men had entered, forced the bartender Carl and the bread delivery man Francis into the backroom, then forced Jane's mother and father to take all the cash out of hiding.

After Jane saw the headline and read the story, she called the tavern crying. "Is it true, Mom?"

"Of course it's true; it's in the paper, isn't it? Call me back after the rush."

During the robbery, Nellie had kept up a constant chatter.

"There's a guard from across the street who comes in early on Friday; he's got a gun, too. Can I stir my soup? Come on, it's chowder; it's gonna stick."

She had even eyed one of their guns that had been placed on the kitchen counter while others were being bound with tape. The leader saw her, grabbed the gun, and told Nellie he'd like to silence her for good. Don probably saved all their lives when he'd shouted, "For Christ's sake, Nellie, just shut up!"

Now Jane had her own crime, her own horror. Her father had told her he thought about that robbery every day of his life. Now she could tell him she understood. Or maybe she shouldn't tell them at all, just wait a few days, then send them the newspaper clippings.

She drove past the exit for Peotone and Wilmington. She'd have to make another trip down this way soon. There were little shops here that might have some old fishing lures and a creel that Lucy from the office had wanted her to find. Maybe she'd have time to buzz through the antique mall in

Kankakee today. Not her favorite kind of shopping, but in an old river town like this she just might find it at the right price for a Chicago shopper like Lucy.

Jane decided to exit through downtown Kankakee. She drove down Court Street, past the post office and the Masonic Temple, past the gray, imposing courthouse, the remnants of stores, now closed or transformed: Jack and Jill Shoes, now a cosmetics outlet; Matt's Toy and Hobby, now a currency exchange; Bon Marche; and Hecht's, now a beauty school; Roger's Dress Shop, now a discount computer outlet. Most of the old stores, though, were simply closed. "For Rent" storefronts outnumbered the going concerns. It was like every other medium-size town that depended on big factories. When Roper Stove closed, the town suffered, tossed and turned with too much time on its citizens' idle hands, too many taverns, too little money, and too few resources.

The EZ Way Inn was still open for business, but there was no more weekday lunchtime rush, no 3:30 after-work rush, no check cashing on Fridays, and no euchre tournaments on Saturday nights. Still, business wasn't so bad, Jane's father kept telling her. It was now a quiet neighborhood bar that still attracted the retired Roper Stove workers who had once eaten Nellie's chili on Mondays and Polish sausage on Thursday and cashed their payroll checks on Fridays.

When Jane turned into the tavern's parking lot, she pulled her Nissan next to her father's pale yellow Buick. There were no other cars. She walked in through the kitchen door. She had entered that tavern thousands of times in her life, maybe three times through the front, the rest through this wooden screened door with its spring that would accept no adjustment, would just resoundingly bang every time it closed. Jane was forty and her parents had bought the EZ Way Inn when she was three. A rough estimate, but she figured this might be right around her thirteen thousandth time walking through her mother's kitchen with the huge iron stove and grill, the double-door refrigerator, and the wooden countertops crosshatched with thousands of knife marks from the thousands of onions peeled and chopped for cubed steaks and barbecue.

The tavern wasn't open yet. Don was sweeping the "dining room," the open space on one side where there were eight chrome and wood-grain formica tables, with their padded, chrome chairs still resting upside down on top of them. Nellie was wiping down the huge wooden bar that ran around the entire expanse of the other half of the room. It was almost a complete rectangle with one break through which Don and Nellie entered their sacred space. The side that faced the front door, the entrance to the bar, did take a corner, made a small L where it attached to the far wall. It was behind the bar in that little alcove north of the bottled beer coolers where Don kept his desk, his adding machine, his book of Hoyle, a sports trivia paperback, a world almanac, and his account books. It was that corner in which he stood to cash checks, in which he sat to write up the orders for the whiskey salesmen, the beer distributors, the cigarette machine and jukebox services, and to count up the days receipts.

Her father rested his broom by the pay phone and came over with a big smile. "How's my girl?" he asked, giving her a hug.

Nellie looked up from the bar, cocked her head, frowned, and said, "Did you go and get your hair cut again?"

Jane was home.

"Do you want a sandwich?"

"Ma, it's only ten-thirty in the morning."

"Did you have breakfast?"

"As a matter of fact I did."

"Yeah, what?"

"Nellie, for Christ's sake, she just got here. Leave her alone. You want coffee, honey?"

"Coffee's fine. Thanks. You guys don't have to work today, do you?"

"No," Don said, handing her a thick, green glass mug. "Carl's coming in to open up at noon, but I was just too tired to clean up last night."

"You closed last night, Dad?" Jane asked, turning the mug in her hands, wondering what Martha Stewart would do if she saw the hundreds of pieces of collectable Fire-King Jade-ite her mother had stashed in the cupboards of the EZ Way Inn.

"I came in from golfing and Dwight had called in. Your mother had been working all day. Carl's doing as many nights for me as he can, but hell, he's a year older than me. We're too damn old for this."

Don had been saying he was too old to run the tavern since Jane was in high school. She had turned forty last winter, and she was beginning, only this year, to believe what her father was saying.

"Where's the Windex? I'll get the jukebox and cigarette machine." *And then I'll tell you all about the body I found,* she thought.

Nellie handed her the spray bottle and a thick, white, bar towel, and Jane got busy cleaning and polishing. She didn't recognize any of the newer songs. F14 was still "Happy Birthday" and Don always made sure he kept Tony Bennett singing "I Left My Heart in San Francisco" and Sinatra singing "My Way." Now Jane noticed some country songs and rock 'n' roll by groups she assumed were closer to Nicky's age than hers.

"Mom, do you still have any of those old records we had from the jukebox?"

"Threw 'em out years ago."

"Even Michael's seventy-eights?"

"He didn't want them. Can't play 'em anymore; nobody has the right kind of record player. Don't tell me you collect those things, too."

"No," Jane said, "but there's a restaurant that opened up in Wilmette, a fifties nostalgia place that uses a lot of props."

"When we moved, I threw out everything."

Jane nodded. She knew. Her stuffed bears, her autograph hound, her Nancy Drew books, her brother Michael's Superman comic books and baseball cards, the first sweater Jane knit when she was eight years old . . .

"Well, it didn't fit you anymore," had been her mother's explanation at the time.

Don and Nellie finished their cleaning and polishing, collected the rags and supplies, and the three of them locked up and left. Carl Wilson, who had worked for them for thirty years, would let himself in at one and open up. The Cubs were playing St. Louis, the beer would be cold, and there was a euchre deck and scoreboard on every table.

At her parents' house, Jane poured herself some more coffee and sat in the small kitchen. She prepared to tell them her story and was choosing between guess what and you're not going to believe this as openers when the phone rang.

Jane went white and dropped her cup back into its saucer.

Her dad studied her as he moved to answer.

"Okay, Carl, sure. We'll be here." Don hung up and looked at Nellie. "Carl's bursitis is acting up. He'll open, but he's afraid he can only last a few hours."

Their lives had always circled around that bar. When Michael and Jane protested that they never went on vacations or that their parents never showed up for school events, both Don and Nellie would claim they couldn't close the tavern; they couldn't leave the bar in anyone else's hands.

"We have to think about our customers, Janie," Don would say.

"I hate those people," Jane would answer.

"They're your bread and butter, young lady," Don always answered, and that would be the end of that.

"You expecting a call today, Jane?" Don asked, pouring more coffee.

"Mom, look what I found for you. On the counter."

A pair of salt and peppers sat by the sink. The salt was a circus ringmaster with an animal trainer's hoop and the pepper was a roaring lion.

"They're from the thirties, I think. Cute, huh?"

"Yeah, I guess so." Nellie barely looked over as she prepared a plate of fruit and cheese and sausage and saltines, the lunch she served every Sunday after cleanup.

"Ma?"

"Jane, I don't collect salt and pepper shakers."

"You had them when I was a kid."

"Couple pair, maybe."

46

"Look at this shelf, Ma, you must have fifty pair there."

"Forty-eight came from you. They might be cute, but we just don't want so much stuff."

"We? You, too, Dad?"

"Go ahead, Don, tell her. I'm going to change out of these shoes. You two eat."

"Dad? Don't you want those Zane Grey books I find for you?"

"You know better than to pay attention to her, honey. You're jumpy as hell. What's going on?"

"My neighbor was murdered yesterday, Dad. I found her."

Don put his large hand on his daughter's trembling one.

"Now I have to see it for the rest of my life."

"That why the police might call?"

"It's a long story, Dad, but I think they think I might be involved."

"Let's call Dennis right now."

Jane laughed for the first time in days. "Dennis is your accountant, Dad."

"Yes, but I'm pretty sure he went to law school, too."

"Dad, thanks, but I have a lawyer. Charley's college roommate is at a big firm in Chicago. I'll be fine."

"What about Charley and Nicky? Told them?"

"I talk to Nick every Sunday night when they go into town for supplies and showers. I'll tell him and Charley tonight."

Jane got up and rinsed out her coffee cup in the sink. "So you're going to have to go to work today after all?"

"I don't think so. Carl calls every Sunday to tell us about

his condition—bursitis, lumbago, gout—just to prepare us. But he makes it through until ten. We close up real early on Sundays now."

"What did you want to see me about, Dad? You said serious."

"Now's not the time. You've got enough on your mind. Wait until they nail her husband."

"What are you talking about?"

"It's always the husband, Jane. Don't you watch TV anymore?"

Jack? Jane tried to remember the last time she had seen Sandy and Jack together. Late spring. After Charley left but before putting Nick on the plane, so it must have been May. She had divided some hostas in the backyard and walked the extras around the corner to Sandy; she and Jack were sitting on their deck. Jack was asking her to sign some papers and Sandy was refusing. She wasn't arguing, just calmly shaking her head. Jane thought she remembered Sandy saying something matter-of-factly about the terms not being right. Jack hadn't seemed angry either. In fact, he'd laughed as he'd gathered the pages up and gone back to the jumble puzzle on the comics pages of the *Tribune*. Neither seemed disturbed when Jane walked up the steps. She looked over Jack's shoulder at *ecaamrm* and immediately offered, "Macramé?"

"You win, Jane, you always do," Jack said, putting down the paper and standing.

"What do I win?" she asked, remembering that Sandy had begun to tease Jack then, told him he would have to move down to doing the *TV Guide* crosswords if Jane ever stopped helping him with the tough ones.

Jack told her she had won a cup of coffee and went inside

to fetch it. Sandy, in her lazy, half-amused drawl, looked at Jane's basket and said, "Oh no, not more hostages."

"Hostas, Sandy. Can you use them?"

"Oh, Jack'll plant them somewhere. Just tell him they're rare and expensive. More important than Barbara's fucking Lady-Kiss-My-Ass rosebushes. The two of them are in some kind of horticultural pissing match."

"I don't think Sandy's husband murdered her, Dad," Jane said, once again rubbing Jack's months-old kiss off her lips.

Jack was pompous. He was a show-off. He was the kind of new money she recognized. He came from a small town in South Dakota, not that far from Charley's dig, but he wanted no Badlands dust clinging to his Gucci loafers. When Charley had asked him about roads out of Keystone, Jack had shook his head. "Haven't been back since I was eighteen. Don't know a thing about it."

Jane knew from Sandy that Jack had worked from the time he was ten years old, saved every dime, gotten college advice from the high-school librarian, applied to five eastern schools without telling his parents, and with work-study, loans, and fee waivers gotten what amounted to a full ride to three.

In Boston, according to Sandy, he had reinvented himself. Made himself into a cowboy orphan and ingratiated himself with the families of his classmates. Mothers and fathers fought over who got to have Jack for Christmas, for spring break. He was rugged, he was handsome, he was smart, he was homeless. Graduated with honors. Harvard Business School for an M.B.A. Then he went to work for Sandy's father as an investment banker for a few years.

"After he left Daddy to start his own company, he really

raked it in. He made Daddy so much money in his first year that any hard feelings have been forgotten." Sandy told Jane this the day she helped with the garage sale. Jack had been against the idea. He thought having a garage sale was pure trailer court.

"He wants us to move out of this neighborhood altogether, out of Evanston. Wants to go farther north: more property, pool, tennis court, the works. Thinks it's mighty working class around here now."

"Charley and I have lived on this block the longest, ever since we got married. It used to be all underpaid professors and housewives. I was the first mom to truck off to the train in tennis shoes, and now you can't throw a rock without hitting a Coach briefcase in the morning."

"Yeah, it's changing around here, but not fast enough or in the right direction for Jack. He's bored with yuppies, you know, been there and done that. He's had his fortune for at least ten years so now he considers himself old money. He wants to move into a manor house and hang a family crest over the door, anything to bleach out the real roots."

"I'm surprised Jack lets you talk to Charley and me."

"Jack identifies with you. Secretly, of course. Small town, always talking about being a saloon-keeper's daughter, but successful advertising executive. He might not want to talk about his past, but he likes it that you do. And he likes it that you've left it all behind. Charley's an intellectual: absent-minded professor. The kind of old tweed jacket type who looks good parked in your living room during a dinner party."

Jane considered the presentation she and Charley made as a couple.

"Face it, Jane," Sandy had said, "you and Charley are the only content providers on this block."

Jane watched her father clean up the kitchen. He moved more slowly, was more deliberate in his swipes at the counter, his rinsing of cups. *He looks like a man with something on his mind,* she thought. *He looks his age.* But even with all his experience and wisdom showing, even though she knew her father watched every police and lawyer show on television and his knowledge was considerable, she didn't believe Detective Oh would be nailing this husband anytime soon.

"What did you want to talk to me about? Come on, Dad, that's why I came down today."

Her father hesitated only a few seconds. "I was hoping you might be able to come and help us out for a week or two."

"What?" Jane was sure she had misheard. From the time she could talk, and she was sure that even in her crib as an infant, her father had repeated again and again to her that he didn't want Michael or her in the tavern business. "Educate yourselves. Don't end up in a saloon."

When Jane had developed a reputation for the beer commercials she had created, the world of "yuppie brew" as the article in *Advertising Age* called it, she had joked to her father that she had ended up selling beer after all. He tacked the newspaper article about her up on the EZ Way Inn bulletin board just as he had done her report cards and drawings, Michael's ERA in Little League and his graduation picture from the Air Force Academy.

"No, Jane, you're working with your brain, not your back," he'd said.

"What's this about, Dad?"

Her father settled himself in the chair next to her. He

spoke quietly, she assumed so Nellie would not hear him.

"I'm going over to the hospital for a few tests next week. Probably outpatient, but Doc won't promise me anything. Your mother works like a dog, but she can't do everything and she can't keep the books and the orders straight. Dwight isn't reliable; I never know if he's going to show up or not. Carl's too damn old.

"I've decided to sell the place this fall, but I can't let business fall apart before I put it on the market. There's talk that something big is going in across the street in the Roper Stove Building. The place might be worth something. It's all I have to give you and Michael and your mother; I want to get as much as I can for it."

"What tests, Dad?"

"Janie, I've been in the tavern business for thirty-five years and I smoked cigarettes for forty years. That's a lot of smoke in these lungs. Doc thought he saw a spot there at my last checkup."

"No, Dad." Jane stood up and began to pace the length of the kitchen. "I can get you in to see great doctors at Northwestern. You've got to come home with me."

"No, honey. If you want to help, you have to come home to me. Michael can't leave his job and his family right now, and he's too far away out in California.

"You're between jobs and Nicky won't be back for another month. If you can help me through this, your mother won't get screwed on the sale. If the new airport comes in or a new factory across the street, this place'll get a price. If I'm sick and laid up, sharks'll smell blood and your mother will end up giving it away."

Don patted Jane's hand and stood up, nodding as if all were explained, all understood. "Think about it. Don't tell your mother all the details, okay?"

Jane calmed her swimming head by raiding her mother's stash of potato chips. "Salt calms me down; what can I do?" her mother used to say, shrugging off warnings of high blood pressure. Every night, after dishes were dried and counters wiped, homework finished, baths taken, Nellie waved good night to Michael and Jane, measured out the water and coffee grounds so Don could plug in the pot as soon as he came downstairs in the morning, then pulled out a giant bag of chips, poured a Pepsi over ice, and sat in her comfortable chair with the *Kankakee Daily Journal*. Her health was perfect, her figure trim, and her energy boundless. Eating chips made her happy, as happy as she allowed herself to be, so Nellie continued to fill a shopping cart with her favorite brand twice a week. Jane knew at least two of her hiding places and ripped open a bag as soon as her father went outside to turn on the lawn sprinkler.

"Eating my chips?" Nellie called in from the bedroom.

Jane walked in, holding the bag and licking salt off her fingers.

Her mother sat on the edge of the double bed. She had put on baggy white pants and a blue T-shirt decorated with embroidered flowers. She wore little socks with pompoms on their heels that stuck out of the backs of her Keds. She held something in her hand that Jane couldn't see in the dark bedroom. Her mother believed in privacy and thrift: closed blinds and fifteen-watt lightbulbs.

"What are you doing sitting here in the dark?"

"Listening. It's the only way I find out anything around this house."

"So what did you find out?"

"That you're in some kind of trouble with the police; and after forty years of marriage, your dad doesn't think I can add two and two."

"Why don't you tell him you can?"

"I cook, I tend bar, I clean, I fill the coolers. You think I want him to make me do the books, too?"

"Do you know what's wrong with Daddy?"

"Not a goddamn thing. Doctors can charge a lot of money for those extra tests."

"Okay."

"You want to come and help out a few days, we'll pay you. You're out of work, right? You've got a murderer running around your fancy neighborhood, right? You want to come home; we can make room."

"Thanks, I appreciate that." Jane marveled at her mother's skill, turning another's actions into her own grudging favor. "What have you got in your hand anyway?"

"Nothing. Just saying my goddamn rosary."

While her parents haggled over the care of their lawn, a Sunday ritual from as far back as Jane could remember, she decided to pay a call. Several close friends still lived in Kankakee, had returned there after college, found satisfying jobs, reasonably priced houses on the river, and seemed to Jane to be happy. She had scoffed at them, tried to pry them out of their small and dying town, reveled in her city life, tried to persuade them to join her. She had been so certain that she was doing the right thing, that she was happy, not them. "It's not a contest, Jane," her friend Tim had once said; "if I'm happy here, it doesn't mean you can't be happy there."

Jane was not convinced that it wasn't a contest. The more she saw people around her content, fulfilled, the more she hated her job. Producing these glittering slices of life to sell beer or soda or tires or canned soup grew sillier and sillier. Charley was so deeply involved in his work, so satisfied, so filled with it that he seemed to be growing farther and farther away from her. She knew one morning she would wake up and discover him fossilized, embedded in tangled stone sheets. Even Nick needed her less and less. Capable, funny, independent, he condescended to her mothering. He allowed her to cook meals, drive carpools, ask about schoolwork, but he seemed bemused, already listening to music she could no longer hear.

In the past, when she visited a friend who was happy, like Tim, she felt that he might be holding some useful piece of information, a key she needed. But her pride wouldn't allow her to ask directly, she merely stayed alert for clues. Now, with a murder hanging over her head and her father's terrible news, she thought she might demand that he give up the answer.

Jane drove a few blocks out of her way so she could take the lucky route, the one that took her past her favorite childhood haunts. She drove down River Street, honked at the root beer stand, then turned left to pass Saint Patrick's Grade School, a square brick building that still reminded her of a miniature maximum security prison, complete with a concrete exercise yard. *Nothing like Nick's school*, she thought, *with its grassy, well-equipped playground, baseball diamond, and prairie garden.* Jane waved at the lions guarding the public library a block down from Saint Pat's, then zigzagged back to pass the building where Weiner's store used to be. She and Tim had stopped most days after school for a seven-cent popsicle or a frozen Bonomo's Turkish Taffy. Weiner's was long gone, replaced first by a KFC, then a host of other businesses, none lasting for more than a year. *None of them had Mr. Weiner's touch, the knack of combining an excellent butcher counter with reasonably priced after-school snacks,* Jane thought; then she turned back toward downtown Kankakee and parked in front of a brick storefront, with 1897 cut ornately into the stone of the arching doorway.

Jane loved the front of Tim's shop. Cut flowers spilled out of their containers, ivy cascaded from planters, every possible space was filled with something lush green or blooming and bursting with color. Inside, two antique armoires stood open with their shelves crammed with flowerpots and vases, mostly pottery from the 1920s and '30s, but a careful inventory showed every color, every glaze, every era, every design represented. Tim had talked his way into every kitchen in Kankakee at one time or another and bought all that was now pricey and collectible for dimes and quarters as he helped widows and retirees dispose of their households. T & T Sales had made enough money so that Tim could open this Paris flower market in Kankakee. Although he hadn't yet persuaded all the locals to spend twenty dollars on a bouquet from the metal bucket by the front door, he had persuaded enough doctors and lawyers to hire him for weddings and parties. His big decorating assignments and an occasional T & T sale kept his profit margin high. Tim liked to say he wasn't just a pretty face; he was a businessman.

"Jane, my love, what are you doing here on a weekend?

No rummage, no flea?" Tim hurried over to kiss her cheek and approve her latest haircut. When Charley had left, she had asked Greg to cut all her hair off. He had insisted on a more moderate approach. For the past few months she had, half-inch by half-inch, gone shorter and shorter. Now her hair was the shortest it had been since kindergarten. Since she had first met Tim there, where they were seated side by side at the blue table, he recognized the look immediately. "Ah, if you could only fit into that little yellow romper you wore on the first day of school," he said, and sighed.

"I'm ready to just buzz it, but Greg won't let me. He still insists it's a go-slow process." Jane smiled. "But what does he know? His hair's all retro seventy one, down to his butt."

"Just keep wearing lipstick and big earrings, honey, or everybody's going to think Charley left for the wrong reasons."

"Or that I kicked him out."

"I thought you did."

"Not exactly." Out of habit, Jane began turning over the flowerpots and vases in the armoire, studying their bottoms.

"I've never seen this Weller mark before."

Tim, at his desk, checking his calendar and copying a phone number, said, "There are over twenty-five Weller marks, probably thirty. Aren't you studying the books I loaned you?"

"When I have the—"

"The reason you've never seen this Weller mark is that it's not Weller." Tim came over and took the green vase out of her hands and replaced it on the shelf. "W. J. Walley, Sterling, Massachusetts. This is probably from around 1890."

Jane picked up two large metal flower frogs, weighing them in her hands.

"Tell me you and Charley are reconciling. Then I can rest easy about Nick." Tim was Nick's godfather and took his position as seriously as Jane knew he would when she'd asked him.

"Oh, Timmy, I still care about Charley. I'm just too confused and screwed up and lonely to be a happily married woman right now."

"So be an unhappily married woman. Who in the world told you that you were supposed to be happy?" Tim was combining snapdragons, zinnias, and something wonderfully blue to make country bouquets. "As a child of divorce, I know something about what it's doing to Nick."

"Tim, your parents got divorced last year. You hadn't been to Florida to visit them in eight years."

"Never mind. I'm going these days. Three days at Mom's assisted-living village, then three days at Dad's senior bachelor pad. It's hell having a broken home, even if it's a broken nursing home. As soon as their memories get a little worse, I'm putting them back together. Hell, I'm too old to remember two Boca phone numbers."

"Timmy, I'm in a little trouble, I think," Jane began.

"Of course you are, doll. Your rugged and smart husband is out in the desert somewhere cradling old animal bones and you are out picking through broken tea sets and brush rollers at rummage sales," Timmy said, glancing at her clothes. "And you are starting to dress like some kind of grunge mama with a badass haircut. . . ."

"Tim, please," Jane said.

He stopped arranging the bouquets and looked at her face. He saw she was crying. Silently and apologetically, she set down the flower frogs and rubbed her right forefinger where she had pricked it on one of the sharp metal spikes. Even in kindergarten when Greg Abels had thrown a dodge ball as hard as he could at her and knocked out a tooth, she'd apologized to Sister Ann for crying. He knew this must be serious.

"I'm sorry, Jane." He came over and sat on the wooden bench twined with ivy. "I get so into playing this 'local gay boy makes good' bit that I forget I don't have to run and put on a Streisand record when you come in the shop. That movie with Kevin Kline ruined a lot of pleasures. Now if I'm not listening to Judy Garland or dialing up Liza's home page, no one takes me seriously as a florist or an antique dealer. I almost lost the Farlander wedding because I was listening to James Taylor when the mother came in to pick out table arrangements. Everybody wants Martin Short doing Frank in *Father of the Bride*."

"Instead of a regular guy like you?" Jane asked, wiping tears.

"What can I say? I'm a man's man kind of man's man. Sorry for going Capote on you. What's up?"

Jane took a deep breath. "Remember my neighbors, Jack and Sandy? You met them when you came up for the modernism show?"

"Tough woman, expensive highlights, two-hundred-dollar T-shirt. Sure. And Jack? The illustration from a GQ article on how to get into a country club? Oh, yeah, I know Jack. 'Could you find me a desk like that?' 'An armoire like this?' Then he was shocked when I found it, and it cost m-o-n-e-y. That's why the rich get richer, babe; they don't want to spend—"

Jane picked up Tim's hand. "Sandy was murdered yesterday."

"No."

The phone rang and Tim loyally sat still.

"Go ahead, answer. I'm not going anywhere."

Tim went behind the turn-of-the-century partner's desk he had so lovingly restored and answered the phone. When it stopped midring, the door to the shop opened, ringing a higher-pitched entry bell.

A handsome young man, thirtyish, came in, snapped off the head of a magenta snapdragon, and stuck it in his top buttonhole. He looked straight ahead at Tim, and Jane felt a twinge of jealousy. Tim's life seemed to be one long, romantic adventure with, so far, no unfortunate consequences, none that he would ever let her know about. They had a curiously protective and protected friendship. Maybe murder was going to change that. Change all of her relationships.

"Jane?" said Tim, hitting the mute button.

The young man who hadn't noticed anyone but Tim now looked at her disapprovingly and managed a sulky wave in her direction.

"It's for you." Tim shrugged, shook his head, and handed her the phone.

"Mrs. Wheel, I'm sorry to have to call you at your friend's place of business."

"It's all right, Detective Oh. I'm glad you have the opportunity to see how easy I am to find."

"Easy? Your mother gave me a list of fifteen places you liked to go when you are in Kankakee. Three have been out of business for more than a year."

Jane smiled. If she ever did commit a crime, she would definitely use her mother as a front.

"Sorry."

"Mrs. Wheel, we have a question you might be able to help us with. We are looking for the murder weapon, trying to determine the murder weapon I should say, and I wonder if you were familiar with the Balance kitchen?"

"Somewhat."

"There were two homes for knives. A magnetic strip along the wall next to the sink and a block with six places for blades. Only four knives were in the block. Do you have any memory of seeing that knife block full?"

"I don't know. I've sliced bread in that kitchen, but I think I used a bread knife from the strip by the sink because the cutting board was right there. I don't even remember the knife block."

"Long shot. Some people are in a house once, and they know exactly how many pictures are on the wall. Some people have a visual memory, you know, they don't know how many knives they own, not in numbers, but can picture the knife block full or with empty slots. You have a keen eye as a collector so I thought you might have a picture."

"Jack did most of the cooking when they ate at home. I mean they usually went out, I think. I know Jack liked to grill food, and he always loved to carve . . ." Jane stopped. She was going to say how much he relished carving. She had watched him expertly dismantle a turkey one Christmas and a roast on New Year's Eve.

Last spring, just before the kiss, she had watched him sharpen the blade of his carved, horn-handled knife on a steel with a matching handle. She had been impressed with his skill. She had been more impressed with the gorgeous handle of the knife. Now she remembered why she had gone over to Jack carving the lamb. It wasn't just the smell of the rosemary and the garlic; she had wanted to feel the handle of the knife, hold the carved horn, worn and warm to the touch, solid, curved to the palm. She had anticipated its sensual feel. Jack had seen her, thought the look in her eyes—what Charley called her finder's passionate stare—was for him. He thought she was asking to be kissed. What if he thought she . . .

"Mrs. Wheel, we are thinking primarily about a bread knife, a serrated blade."

"Yes?"

"Is anything wrong?"

Jane watched Tim toss a set of keys to the handsome man, who clearly was hoping for more than the casual wave Tim gave him. He shrugged, blew Tim a kiss, and left the store. Tim rolled his eyes and smiled at Jane.

"No, I was just trying to remember their kitchen, the knives, but . . ."

"Yes?"

"Like I said, I've sliced bread there; they had a bread knife, maybe two of them, but I can't tell you where they were placed or where they belonged. I only used them as company when the kitchen was being used; nothing was put away. I didn't pay attention any other times."

"Okay. Will you be back at your home tonight?"

"I may stay over, Detective. My parents want me to." Jane saw that Tim, who had been listening as closely as possible, was nodding vigorously, pantomiming something she didn't get. He seemed to be raising his hand forcefully like a child who knows the answer in his third-grade classroom.

"So I can reach you at your parents?"

"Yes."

"Oh, one other thing you might want to know. You still have a dog."

"What?"

"We've been walking the neighborhood, looking through trash, checking in bushes, you know, and Officer Mile says that the dog is on your porch, seems to be guarding your house."

"I didn't leave any food, just water."

"With your permission, Officer Mile would like to put some dog food out. She has several dogs and said she could bring over food and a collar, just for the time being."

"It's fine, but shouldn't I call the pound or somewhere, try to find the owner? I like her, but she's not mine."

"Yes, we'll take care of that; but for the time being, we'd like her to stay at your house. She could be a lead in this."

"Do you think she's a witness?" Jane couldn't resist asking. "A seeing-eye dog?"

Detective Oh tried to laugh politely, but it came out as a clearing of his throat.

"Exactly. Have a good visit with your family."

She hung up.

"Tim, what's the hand raising? Do you have to go to the bathroom?"

"No, honey. Auction today. Bidding. Hand waving. I want that, you know. Starts at four. I gave young David my truck and a list of things he's to bid on, but I plan on going myself. Can you think of a better way to relieve stress?"

"Any pottery?"

"Too rich for your blood. Two vases I've got to have. Grueby. I'm not sure how they ended up here. I thought it was some mistake at first, but I'm certain they're the real thing. This is a couple of estates put together, so who knows. Haven't had a chance to talk to Amos about it."

"You do a lot of business with him?"

"Yeah, I usually get in for an early preview, but he hadn't had time to even sort out all the stuff. Should be some interesting box lots—might find a flowerpot or two, some of that cheap stuff that I wish you'd grow out of."

"Yeah, yeah. I met David before, right? Last winter? He looks different."

"Better haircut. Another me-in-training. He's of the school: If I'm gay, I must have great taste. He's got a fair eye but not too original. You know, a subscriber to *Martha Stewart Living*, so he's two weeks ahead of the newsstand tastemakers, but not exactly a trendsetter. Phil met him somewhere and he came in and asked us for work. I hired him to assist at a couple of big parties. I send him to auctions, strictly freelance."

"He seems to like you."

Tim dropped his voice and said flatly, "I'm not involved with him or anyone. Since Phil left, I'm officially asexual. I'll swish and sway for fun around here when it gets dull and the doctors' wives are bored, but frankly, nothing interests me. He was the one."

"Any word from Phil?"

"Nope."

"Any guess?"

"Yup. Here's my scenario. Get ready, because it's really bad. I think he was sick, and he loved me too much to make me take care of him."

"So he just disappeared?"

"Yeah. He left eight months ago. I've gotten two tests."

He stuck the last bouquet in the bucket, crossed out twenty dollars and wrote ten, and placed it outside the front door. He smiled and shook his head when he saw Jane's eyes. "No, don't worry—negative. But here's the sick part. I keep thinking, if it comes back positive, I'll know he loved me. He couldn't face our dying together."

"Timmy . . ."

"Jane, don't even think about giving advice to the lovelorn. You send a perfectly wonderful guy whom you love and who's crazy about you out to the Badlands with your incredibly wonderful son then mope around in some kind of lonely angst. Who says the midlife crisis belongs to men. You perimenopausal women are pieces of work yourself."

"Tim!"

"It's true and if you don't button it, I'm not going to show you the boxes where your cheap-ass pottery is hiding at the auction."

Tim turned a ring of keys over to a pretty high school girl, who had come in quietly during his tirade. She smiled sympathetically, if a touch condescendingly, at Jane, who did not smile back. *Someday you'll be perimenopausal, too, sweetheart,* she thought. *Whatever that means.*

4

Tim drove fast. *He's still a maniac,* Jane thought, as she followed him to the auction house west of Kankakee. She lost him after two blocks. He wove his red Mustang in and out of traffic, waving and honking, nodding and smiling. In high school, Tim had talked his way out of speeding tickets as easily as he'd talked his teachers into reading his ideas for papers and grading them instead of the required twenty pages. He still maneuvered through life doing exactly what he wanted. Jane was going to learn how to do that as soon as she decided what she wanted—or what she didn't want.

At Amos Auction she wanted everything. The lust began low in her body and rose up, giving her arms a prickly, itchy sensation and reddening her cheeks. She ran her hand over a rosewood marimba, the wood warm to the touch. She lifted up chunky pottery vases, checking for the comforting stamp of U.S.A. on the bottom. She fingered each sharply cut prism in a box filled with lamp parts. She caught sight of Tim talking to a large man with a steel gray ponytail at the cashier's table. She went over and registered, showing her driver's license, a credit card, and receiving a cardboard number, eighty-seven.

"Janie, this is Amos Melton, the biggest junk runner in

downstate Illinois," said Tim, patting Amos on the shoulder.

"Second only to Timmy here." Amos shook her hand with an enormous paw. "Understand you're getting in the business."

"Flirting with it. Still buying too much for myself."

"Yeah, it's a disease all right."

Hundreds of people milled through the hall, filing past tables of ceramic statues, framed prints, and box after box of, well, stuff. One box contained a collapsible umbrella, a cast-iron matchholder that could easily be a reproduction, two unmarked saucers that looked like Bauer Ringware but were unmarked, and two bud vases, one a pale pink glass with etched stalks of wheat. Jane might pick up every item in here for a quarter, maybe even a dollar for the bud vases, at a rummage sale, but would she bid five dollars for the box here?

Auctions were testing grounds, reality checks. At a rummage sale, she filled bags with twenty-five-cent items that she thought might be worth more or that she might like to look at later, place in the perfect spot. She could always use one more Pez dispenser that could perch on the edge of a pot of ivy. At an auction, buying a box of someone else's junk was a public event, the price driven by the greed and frenzy of the crowd rather than anything that had to do with an object's value. A 100 percent profit on a five-dollar box was still only five dollars. Tim had been working on Jane to stop nickel-and-diming herself into a junk-filled house. "Step up," he advised, "to the next plateau."

She was turning over a cheaply made figure of an angel that seemed out of place in a box of old kitchen utensils when David came up behind her.

"If you like that, you'll love the box of Hummel knock-offs over in aisle two," he purred.

"I don't—"

"Of course not," he said, holding up an old eggbeater with a misshapen, melted plastic handle. "Besides, it's not true what Timmy says . . . 'We are what we buy.'" He dropped the beater back into the box. "Or is it?"

Jane watched him slither through the crowd toward furniture. "Yeah, go buy yourself an asshole," she muttered.

Jane bent down to search a table filled with more kitchenware, no colored Pyrex, which she loved, or pale blue or green Fire-King, which everyone else seemed to love, so she dragged out the box underneath, which instead of bowls held pictures.

"Didn't anyone love them enough to want these?" she whispered.

The box was filled with wedding pictures. The groom, a man with big ears, grinned straight at the camera while a small blond bride looked at her husband adoringly. The date on the back of the pale oak frame was 1937. There were ten, eleven more pictures that Jane thumbed through, most in cardboard folders with the name of the photographer, Bill Doobie. This was "Uncle Billy," a friend of her dad's who had photographed her as a baby. So these people were local. The couple in traveling suits, the bride wearing a corsage, a family photo dated five years later with one of their parents with them and a baby on the groom's knee, 1942. Why didn't he have to go to war? What was wrong? Or was he home on leave before shipping out, wearing civilian clothes and holding his baby for the last time? A few other wedding poses, one with the wedding party, two bridesmaids in sheer organdy with picture hats, and two groomsmen, both taller than the groom, looking dapper and proud in their tuxedos. Jane wrote down the box lot number in her notebook and placed everything back carefully. She wiped away tears with the back of her hand, knowing her face would soon have that dirty, streaky look and Tim would come after her with his monogrammed handkerchief, shaking his head over what a sentimental fool she was.

"Ouch!" Jane's tears changed from those of foolish sentiment to those of indignant pain. Someone big, judging from the crushing of her instep, had stepped on her kneeling foot. Because kneeling placed her foot sole up, her toes were being smashed bottom to top into the ground.

"Oh, man, I'm so sorry, lady. I didn't see you. I am so sorry." The voice was familiar. The apology was familiar.

"Richard?" Jane turned around slowly, trying to stumble her way into standing.

Richard Rose helped Jane stand, and she stared at him in wonderment. *What did this guy collect anyway? Bruises?*

"Jane?"

Despite the throbbing of her foot, Jane was actually happy to see him. Maybe, she thought, it's because he was the last person to see her before everything changed. She stumbled getting up, and he was quick to hold out his hand,

"I'm really sorry. Man, you must think I'm some kind of clumsy idiot."

"It's just my foot. No problem, I've got another one."

"Listen, I'm sorry. I'll see you around." Richard held up one hand, a wave or warding off evil, and kept his eyes aimed at the floor.

"Okay," Jane said, puzzled.

"I'm not a rich man, you know? The business is mortgaged up to the neck."

"Oh?" Jane answered politely.

"So if you think going after me is any kind of sure thing, you are wrong."

"Okay."

"My second cousin is one hell of a lawyer, too. Has his own commercials on all the time."

"Ah, really?" *'Curiouser and curiouser,'* Jane thought.

"Besides, I've got witnesses who will say they shouted at you to watch it. Those sales are at your own risk; you can't—"

"I'm sorry, but I have no idea—"

"When I said you should call me, I meant for a date, not . . ."

"Well, I've been busy, you see . . ."

"When I said 'sue me' I was just—"

"Richard"—Jane held up her hand—"what are you talking about?"

"This policeman called yesterday to see if I was the guy you talked to at the sale. He asked me the time and where we were and how long we talked. You know."

"You thought it was because I was suing you?"

"Yeah."

"Because of my shoulder?"

"Look, I'm truly sorry, but it was an accident and accidents just happen sometimes."

"Richard, rest easy. You're not my ticket to the good life. . . ."

"Yeah?"

"You're my alibi."

For the first time, Richard looked up and met her eyes.

"My neighbor was murdered yesterday. I gave Detective Oh your card because you could verify that I was where I said I was. I found the body, see, so I had to answer all these . . ."

"You're not suing me?"

"I'm not litigious."

"Great."

"I'm a murder suspect."

"Terrific."

"Ain't it?"

"Listen, maybe we can go out sometime."

"Bowling and dancing are out of the question." Jane limped forward a bit, testing her foot.

"How are your toes?"

"I can wiggle. I think that's the test."

"Depends what you're testing," Tim said, coming up behind her and slipping his hand under her elbow. "Find a flowerpot?"

Jane introduced them. Tim shook hands with Richard, eyeing him suspiciously. Richard, happier to be an alibi than a defendant, was beaming. Jane felt momentarily elated. Tim called these blips on her usually angst-ridden mood radar her "giddies." They occurred whenever she felt something formerly misunderstood was clarified. When she and Tim were in second grade, Sister Elizabeth explained the end of the world as a time when everyone would rise up and come together and everyone's life would be revealed. Jane imagined an infinite array of drive-in movie theaters where everyone's life would be playing around the celestial clock.

"There'll be no more secrets, Tim," Jane had whispered, giggling, having her first public giddy.

"There'll always be secrets, Janie, even in heaven," Tim had whispered back.

"What are you buying, Richard?" Tim asked, looking down at his own list.

"Against that wall over there, see those pillars, those carved shutters and doors? I might try for them." He dug out one of his cards and handed it to Tim. "I was south of here, down to Watseka with my crew, taking down a barn. I saw the sign and decided to stop in and cool off."

"Those aren't shutters." Tim dug out one of his own cards and passed it to Richard. T & T CONDUCTED SALES/ ESTATES AND SPECIAL COLLECTIONS. "They're doors."

"Yeah? Pretty small for doors."

"Those carved panels are the top sections of the doors to a horse-drawn hearse. That's why they're carved on both sides. Open up, pay your respects, and admire the detail and the wood grain."

The auctioneer, Billy Joiner Jr., banged his gavel.

"Good afternoon, ladies and gentlemen. Are we ready? Do we have our numbers?"

Billy was a showman. Not as good as his father, Big Bill, who even after his first stroke, could talk faster than anyone could listen, but still an auctioneer to admire. This wasn't a suited, suave, fine art showroom auctioneer who raised his eyebrows and spoke in hushed and reverent tones about the "piece" being offered. This was Billy, who wanted to move out these boxes of junk, these three-legged tables, these loose-wired lamps as fast and furiously as he could.

"Humina, humina, five, five, five'll get you ten, ten ten, ten'll get you, ten'll get you fifteen, fifteen, do I hear it fifteen?" His eyes moved as quickly as his tongue, roving over the bidders, the buyers, sizing up those who were in for the long haul. He read the need and the greed and the want and the got-to-have in their eyes, in the desperate wave of their hands.

Two hours after the first bang of Billy's gavel, Richard owned two plaster pillars and three boxes of miscellaneous hardware, door pulls, and doorknobs. Jane owned one box of family photographs, including wedding pictures; two braided rag rugs; one box of old sewing notions, including four Ziploc bags of old buttons; and a box that contained two moldy Tupperware containers, more buttons, a wooden box with bad costume jewelry, and what Jane thought from her spot on the bidding floor looked like a pink basket-weave McCoy flowerpot, but turned out to be a cheap plastic floral planter.

"That's why we preview, dear, so you won't end up with these boxes of junk." Tim was looking over Jane's shoulder as she sifted through some rhinestone pins.

"Not so bad. More buttons. I love buttons."

"Janie, that's five dollars you'll never have again."

"Oh, but I'll have twenty-five just for these. Look at these sweeties." Jane held up a handful of small, two-tone Bakelite buttons. "Look at these 'cookies.' Miriam has a button collector who'll give me two or three dollars apiece for them."

Tim was nodding to David's hand signals across the floor.

"Ready to split, 'cookie'?"

Richard looked from Tim to Jane. "I was wondering if you might like to get a drink or dinner, but maybe you're ..."

Jane explained that she was visiting home, that her parents expected her for dinner, and Tim was an old friend. Tim rolled his eyes and drifted off to give her privacy to make a date.

"Sorry you didn't get the doors."

"I wasn't as interested when I found out what they were. Too morbid, don't you think? Besides, I gave my guy a top price, and I didn't give him the signal to top it."

"You had a guy here?"

"Sure, some of my guys from the barn job came with me. I got this one guy, friend of my dad's, who loves these things. He's usually unbeatable. Gives anyone else bidding the evil eye and scares him or her off."

"You and Tim both have 'guys?' Man, if I'm serious, I'm going to have to get myself some 'people.'"

"How about your phone number? You seem to have given my card away to the cops."

Jane wrote down her home number. Richard helped her carry her boxes out to her car.

"Didn't bring your truck today?"

"It was borrowed."

"See ya. Take care of your toes. Don't sue me."

Tim yelled from his car parked a few spaces over. "I'll be at your parents in a few minutes. David's bidding on a few big pieces that are going up after the break. I forgot . . ."

Jane didn't hear what Tim forgot. *It was borrowed.* Yesterday she'd borrowed a truck from Sandy, today Sandy was dead and she was out picking through boxes of junk and giving out her phone number. Yesterday, her father was the strongest man she knew, and today his age and his fear told her that he could be that no longer, and she answered by going out and bidding on a stranger's wedding photographs. She pulled out the flimsy pink plastic flowerpot. It was cracked down the middle. *"You are what you buy,"* she thought.

*   *   *

"So, Nellie, when are you going to give me your recipe for vegetable soup?" Tim asked, holding out his glass for more iced tea.

"When you stop bullshitting me about wanting it." Nellie passed the sliced lemons over to him with her left hand. "Everybody in town knows you just want my stove and pots and pans. You don't give a damn about my soup."

Tim shrugged. He had been trying to sweet-talk Nellie out of her EZ Way Inn kitchen for years. He knew Jane was after it, too; and after all, the EZ Way Inn was her second home. Don and Nellie were her parents, but one of these days she was going to piss Nellie off enough so that she'd call Tim and let him go through all the old restaurant dishes and bowls, crocks, and Bakelite-handled utensils that were stored in the backroom. He would, of course, give Jane a peek, might let her have a spoon or two.

"Stop it, Tim," Jane snapped from the living room where she was unpacking her boxes. "When my mother gets ready to break down the kitchen, I'll be there packing it up." She went back to laying out buttons in neat rows on the coffee table.

"Tim, you really make money on all this old stuff?" Don asked, pushing his chair away from the table.

"I do. I've gotten good at spotting quality, and I'm even better at spotting what people will spend money on, which, sad to say, is not always quality." Tim stirred his tea. "I mean there are always those who will spend good money on quantity . . . boxes of photos, big bags-o-buttons . . ."

"Aha!" Jane came in and pulled out the chair next to her father. "Look, Dad," she said, ignoring Tim. "I spent twenty-three dollars today. Tomorrow I'll send these five buttons off to a dealer in Ohio and invoice her twenty-five dollars. These have paid for all the other stuff and when I go through the rest of the buttons and the photos, I'll easily clear another fifty. Maybe more."

Tim picked up one of the Bakelite "cookies" and rubbed it between his fingers. "Not bad, but it's still chump change. I think you ought to move up to the majors. . . ."

Jane looked at her watch. "I've got to call Nick and Charley now. They only stay at the storefront for an hour on Sundays," Jane said, looking at her father who, much to Tim's amusement and Nellie's disgust, was sorting through the buttons with more interest.

"Daddy, why don't you take Tim down to the basement and let him look at that old glassware you found in the basement at the tavern? He might be able to tell you what it is and price it for you."

"What a bunch of baloney." Nellie folded her dish towel over the sink, went into the living room, and turned on the television.

"The thing is, Mom, I found it. I'm the one who saw it. Everyone was getting ready to leave the site for the day and I'm the one who saw it. . . ."

Was his voice deeper?

"It might not turn out to be a whole skeleton, but Dad's sure there's a lot more there. It's not like it's a T. rex, but it's still something important. . . ."

Did he sound taller?

"There's a CNN camera crew up here, too, and they're filming lots of stuff for a feature they might do. I mean, if this turns out to be something, I'll be in a documentary. . . ."

Every week Nick was older and smarter and more enthusiastic. He hadn't asked for updates on any of his friends or *X-Files* reruns or more batteries since his first phone call.

Jane heard Charley's voice in the background.

"How about you, Mom? What'd you do this week? Find any skeletons in the backyard?"

"Better let me talk to Dad for a minute; you shouldn't be wasting your hour of electricity and plumbing talking to me."

"It's okay. Cindy said we're staying in town tonight. She wants a shower and a real bed and Dad said he did, too."

"Cindy?"

Jane heard more mumbling in the background.

"She's one of Dad's assistants. She's real nice and knows a million card games. Here's Dad. I love you, Mom."

"Me, too, Nick. I love you."

"Thank you, Jane." Charley sounded taller, too. In fact, he sounded tan and rugged and kind and safe.

"Nick sounds wonderful."

"He's thriving. I thought it would be a good experience, but I never dreamed he'd take to it like this. And he's truly a member of the team. Has a great eye . . ."

"Charley, keep a straight face in front of Nick while I tell you this, okay? Sandy Balance was murdered yesterday. At home. I found her when I returned the Suburban."

"Jane, I want you to stay away from Jack. Don't let him near you."

"Nick?"

"Out of the room. Listen, I don't trust Jack."

"You sound like my dad. I don't think the police think it was Jack. He was playing golf. A thirty-six-hole alibi."

"Who then?"

"Well, there's me. Every woman on the block was happy to tell the police I kissed Jack at a party and that I liked driving Sandy's truck."

"Do you want me to come home? I could be there by Tuesday."

"Thanks, Charley. No. I'm going to be coming back here for at least a few days. Dad has to have some medical tests, and I'm going to help out at the bar. I'll ask Tim to drive home with me to get my stuff."

"Stay away from Jack."

"Who's Cindy?"

Don and Tim were washing glasses in the kitchen sink when Jane came in from her old bedroom. "Find something good?"

"I like these old shot glasses and old-fashioneds. They're not fancy, just twenties and thirties commercial glassware."

"You're not ripping off my dad, are you, Tim?"

"Don't worry, honey, I told Tim he could have them if you didn't want them. You have first choice."

"What the hell is that?" Nellie jumped up and looked at the kitchen phone that wasn't ringing. They heard another ring, far away and tinny.

Tim walked over to the canvas bag he had parked at the door and pulled out a sleek, forest green flip phone.

"Yes? Okay, good work. I'll bring Jane."

Tim handed the phone to Nellie, who held it between two fingers, disgusted. "You ought to get one of these, keep you in touch with the world." He motioned to Jane. "Come on, let's go see what David brought home."

Jane begged her mother not to touch the piles of buttons sorted on the coffee table and made her promise not to wash or dust anything else in the boxes.

"Will you two be up when I get back? About an hour?"

"Yes," said Don, pulling another glass out of the soapy water.

"No," said Nellie, returning to the television.

Jane pulled her car up next to Tim's, and they walked through the back door of the shop together. All the lights were on in the backroom and one small flood in the front of the store illuminated three ivy topiaries.

In front of the big flower cooler, David had unloaded the treasures of the day. A small legal bookcase, its glass doors closed. On top of it several books on gardening and flower arranging from the late 1940s, several watercolors, botanicals, simply framed, stunning in their delicacy. Jane studied them.

"How much? They're exquisite."

"Janie, look at these." Tim pointed to a pile of rugs, not so neatly piled in the center of the room.

Jane saw that Tim was looking beyond the large hooked rugs to the carved panels that Richard had pointed out.

"You snake, you knew Richard wanted those."

"Richard had no idea what they were. Come look at this carving. Gorgeous work."

Tim and Jane were on opposite sides of the rugs and both reached down to run their hands over the oak carvings of vines and leaves, birds and flowers. Together, they took the carved knobs and each lifted a door to see the interior work. The inside of the panels mirrored the outside. Just as intricately carved, just as perfect.

"Why do you think they worked so hard on the inside of these doors? For a hearse?" Jane asked.

"I don't know, respect for the dead?" Tim lifted the heavy half door away from the rug. "You know the doors would stand open, too, for the viewing, so the inside needed to be as elegant as the outside. . . . What's this gunk all over the bottom here?"

Jane and Tim both looked down and under the doors. At first Jane thought it was part of the design of the rug underneath. Earthy grays, dark browns, and maroons that somehow looked, at first, like the pattern of a human face. She even reached down to touch what she thought looked like eyes, a nose, but Tim grabbed her wrist. Jane looked at the long fingers surrounding her thin wrist then just beyond. Under the carved doors, she saw that Tim had stopped her just before she stuck her fingers straight into the blood oozing out of the hundreds of pinpoint holes in David's face and neck.

5

David was dead before he was bled. That's what Jane thought she heard the coroner's assistant tell the uniformed police officer with glasses. He passed that information along to a plainclothes officer who was assisting the detective who now sat across from Tim at a metal table covered with ribbon scraps and bits of green florist's clay. Jane had given her statement to this same detective while Tim had thrown up repeatedly in the small bathroom next to the back door.

What was his name? He had mumbled something when he shook her hand. It was easier to focus on simple questions like what was this detective's name rather than think about bigger issues. For example, should she mention that this was the second dead body she had found in thirty-six hours? It certainly seemed relevant. Jane felt certain that if this were a news story, the anchor would say it was ironic. "Ironically, this is the same Jane Wheel who discovered the murdered body of her neighbor less than thirty-six hours ago." But it was not ironic. Not at all. Coincidental, yes. Quite coincidental. She looked at her watch. It wasn't quite ten o'clock.

"May I use the telephone?" Jane asked the uniformed policeman who had been speaking to the coroner.

"I don't think the lab guys are finished going over everything."

Jane pulled her cellular phone out of her leather backpack. "May I use my telephone?"

"I guess it'd be okay." The officer looked around but everyone looked busy; and when they looked busy, he knew he should be busy, too; and if he asked a silly question, it would call attention to the fact that he had nothing to do. His first murder.

Jane found the card she was looking for in her wallet and dialed the Evanston number.

"Detective Oh, I'm sorry to bother you at home. This is Jane Wheel. I'm still in Kankakee and I . . ." I what? Jane was trying out how to explain she had found another body, and she wondered whether she should tell the Kankakee police or whether it would simply be misleading and confusing. How does one put that?

"Mrs. Wheel, could you join us over here?" Detective Mumbles was calling her over to the table where he and Tim sat.

"Detective Oh, I seem to have found another body here and I'm not sure what the protocol, not the protocol exactly, but whether or not I should bring up—"

"Mrs. Wheel?" Mumbles was speaking loudly and clearly now.

"Would you like to talk to the detective here?"

Jane passed the phone over Tim's head. "This is Detective Oh in Evanston, Illinois. He wants to talk to you."

While the police talked on the phone, Jane took Tim's hand.

"Feeling any better?"

"No. You're staying pretty calm, I must say. Two bodies in two days and you're cool as a cucumber."

"Oh no, I'm not cool, I'm just on to this now. Sandy's murder took me off guard, I admit, but now I know this is a dream. It's a bad one and a long one, but this isn't real, Timmy. Don't worry."

"She's in shock," Tim explained to one of the uniformed officers at his side.

"Detective Munson, can I talk to you over here please?" the coroner said, not looking up from David's body, which Tim and Jane had avoided looking at for the past thirty minutes.

Munson, that's it, Jane thought, as he handed her back her phone.

"You've had quite a weekend, Mrs. Wheel."

"Detective Oh explained?"

"He's on his way." Munson went over to the coroner.

People either got it or they didn't. She and Tim told their story to three different police officers in quick succession. They had gone to the auction, they'd looked at stuff, they'd bid on stuff, they'd bought stuff, and they'd brought it home. This is what they had done today. It's what they did every weekend. Only one of their listeners got it. One of the uniforms got a glazed look when Tim gestured toward a box of old wooden-handled garden tools that David had successfully bid on.

"My wife picked me up a beautiful spade at a house sale. Made in England. Pleasure to dig with, too. One dollar," he said, and sighed.

Munson gave him a look. "Very interesting, Officer Boskey, but let's stick with the details of today's auction."

"Is there anything here that you didn't instruct Mr. Gattreaux to bid on? Any surprises?"

Tim shook his head.

"Anything missing from the store?"

They had already determined that the cash box, which had fifty dollars in small bills to make up Monday morning's bank, sat undisturbed under the counter.

Tim looked around vacantly.

"Did you have a computer in the backroom? CD system? Television? Anything that could be sold quickly on the street?"

Tim said no, then stood slowly and walked over to the pine armoire that held his art pottery collection. Methodically he shifted his eyes left to right, shelf by shelf, studying, no, reading the vases and planters that lined the piece of furniture.

"One frog," he said as he turned back to the police.

"Pardon?"

"One glass frog is missing. About this big." He used all of his fingers to make a three-inch circle, then closed them into a prayer. "It was carnival glass. Thirty-dollar price tag."

"Thirty?" Jane asked. "I've found those at rummage sales for a buck. The most I've ever paid was five."

"That's a new one, junkie selling carnival glass on the street for a fix," sneered one of the uniforms.

"I didn't really want to sell it. I liked it," Tim explained to Jane.

"Excuse us for a moment." Munson took his officers and huddled once again near the carved doors that still partially screened David's body from their view.

"Timmy, they asked me about your relationship with David, and I told them that as far as I know it was business."

"True. They asked me, too. God." Tim sat down and rubbed his eyes. He couldn't rub out what he had seen, and when he opened them again, they contained the same look of horrified surprise.

"What did they do to his face? Why was it . . ."

"Ventilated?"

Jane and Tim looked up. Detective Oh was wearing jeans and a pale blue cotton sweater. He carried a sport coat.

"I'm sorry to be so casual. I didn't take time to change. Hello, Mrs. Wheel."

Jane was shocked at Oh's speedy arrival. Of course he'd had a uniformed police officer drive him, sirens blasting. She asked him how fast they had driven. He smiled and suggested she check her watch. She was shocked at how much time had actually passed.

"Murders throw off the clock. All rhythms become confused. Sometimes everything begins moving in slow motion, and other times your life becomes a cartoon, or an old-time movie, all speeded up.

"I'm Detective Bruce Oh." He reached his hand toward Tim.

"Tim Lowry."

"You were Mr. Gattreaux's employer? You're the owner of this shop?"

Tim nodded. "This past year he worked for me part-time: attended auctions and sales; bought things for me."

"Ah, he was a picker? Like Mrs. Wheel?"

"Not exactly," Tim said, smiling slightly, the first softening of expression he'd allowed himself since finding David. "I told David what to buy and what price to pay. Mrs. Wheel follows her own heart."

"And what did Mr. Gattreaux buy for you today?"

Tim waved his hand toward the boxes piled at the back door. "All that and the rugs and the doors." Tim pointed at the oak panels still opened near David's body.

Oh handed over a notebook. "If you could put it in writing, please?"

Tim began listing from memory items he had instructed David to bid on at Amos Auction.

"Mr. Lowry, if possible, could you look over the boxes and see if you remember something that you asked for that is not here?"

Jane watched Tim walk hesitantly over to the boxes. It brought him close to the body, and Tim walked awkwardly sideways so he would not have to look in David's direction.

"Mrs. Wheel, this is a terrible coincidence for you, yes?"

"Is it okay for you to just come to another town like this and ask questions? I mean, I'm glad to see a familiar face, but Detective Munson might not like . . ."

"Let me assure you, Mrs. Wheel, that I will not interfere with Detective Munson's authority. I am with a team of detectives who work with the university criminologists and we often cross city and community lines when we have what might be . . . ah . . . linked criminal activity."

"Why would these two murders be linked? Sandy and David didn't know each other."

"Mrs. Wheel? You, remember, called me."

"I'm the link?" Jane raised her voice enough to startle Tim from his rummaging through boxes.

"Jane?"

She shook her head and waved Tim off.

"Detective Oh, I was just here. I was visiting my parents and my friend Tim. I went to an auction. This is, like you said, a big coincidence. I called you because it seemed like I ought to mention what happened to Sandy; and quite frankly, I just didn't know how to bring it up, but I never thought these murders were linked to each other. They're just both appearing in my particular nightmare."

"That is such a common belief, you know, that it is your personal nightmare."

Jane stared at Oh.

"What if we put ourselves in the shoes of Mrs. Balance or Mr. Gattreaux? Their nightmares have worse endings, yes? Who were the players in their nightmares? Everyone thinks they are the stars of their own movies and all the rest of the people they see or they know are just supporting players. You, Mrs. Wheel, were a supporting player in Mrs. Balance's life? And maybe just a cameo player, a walk-on player in Mr. Gattreaux's life? Well, for a moment I'll ask you to stop thinking like the star in your own life—"

"Nightmare," Jane corrected.

"Whatever and become the stage manager for the other stars. Bring people on and bring people off. Think about who else was appearing. Who did you see on the last day of Mrs. Balance's life? Who did you see today who appeared on the last day of Mr. Gattreaux's life?"

"Today at the auction I noticed a lot of familiar faces, although I don't know any names. Kankakee is only an hour out of Chicago. The same buyers and dealers travel back and forth. I'm sure some of the book guys were there. And Debby."

"Debby who?"

"Oh, I don't know. Debby isn't even her name. She just looks like a Debby. She always snatches things out of my hands at estate sales. She's a talker. Always wants to know what you're going to do with the buttons or the yarn or the quilt scraps you're carrying. She points out the tarnish and the rips and hopes you'll put something down for a minute. She's always pulling out a jeweler's loupe to look at costume jewelry and a magnet to test metal . . ."

"You don't like her thoroughness?"

"She's cold-blooded. Once she told me she'd been at a great house sale and gave me the address. Wild goose chase. A vacant lot. I hate her."

"Did you see her yesterday at any sales?"

"Sure, she's always around."

"What about these book guys? Anything special about them?"

"First in line. Zoom to the books. Stand in the middle of the shelf and guard both ends with their arms waving everyone away. I've seen them gather up fifty books off a table at a rummage sale and pile them in a corner like they're buying them, then go through them and take two. Just leave all their rejects in the corner so no one sees them and they go unsold. Book guys are the most ruthless."

"Really?" Detective Oh was actually making notes.

"Yeah, I hate the book guys. They don't even look like they know how to read."

"You seem to be quite passionate about these sales and the people who attend them. My wife attends and she, too, talks this way sometimes."

"All you have to do is stand in line once on a Saturday

morning. Most estate-sale organizers give out numbers a half hour before the sale so the house doesn't get trashed by letting everyone in at once. People push and shove just to get their number. And if they don't give out numbers, somebody tries to organize a line. . . . There's this one guy who always brings his own notepad and makes people sign up, then he lines them up and makes people count off."

"Book guy?"

"Furniture guy. Book guys try to budge in ahead, pretending it's their first sale and they don't know that there's a line. The more illiterate a guy acts, the more likely he's a book guy."

Detective Oh looked toward the door where two men were bringing in the stretcher. He excused himself to go look again at David's body before they removed it from the scene.

Tim came over to Jane and threw Oh's notebook on the table. "He got everything I asked for." Tim rubbed his eyes. "He did a good job today." Tim sat on the table. "Goddamn him, why'd he have to get killed in my shop."

"Timmy!"

"Oh, I'm sorry, Jane, and I'm sorry for the guy, but do you know what this is now? Young, pretty-boy fag gets murdered in middle-aged, pretty-boy's flower shop? In fucking Kankakee? We've got ourselves 'Midnight in the Garden of Good and Stupid' and guess who's going to make the perfect suspect? No matter what I say or do, this is somehow going to come off as a cat fight." Tim was rubbing his eyes again. "Did you see what they did to his face?" He shook his head. "That was personal."

What had they done to his face? According to the preliminary report from the coroner, who'd spoken loud enough for everyone in the shop to hear, David Gattreaux, probably after carrying in the last box from the truck, was rendered unconscious by strangulation, his body dragged from the back door ten to fifteen feet and placed in the middle of the rugs he had purchased and unloaded. His face and neck were then perforated by a sharp metal object or objects. The top half of his body was then covered by two carved, wooden, half-size doors that were originally made to serve as the doors to a horse-drawn hearse.

Ironically, Jane thought. The television anchor would say, in a detailed report, that the "wooden, half-size doors were, ironically, the antique doors to a horse-drawn hearse."

It was almost midnight. The body had been removed. Jane had called her father and told him that something had come up at the store and they would be late. Tim still sat at one of the flower-arranging tables, idly braiding floral wire and shaking his head. Jane had made coffee, found a tin of shortbread, and served Oh and the Kankakee police cookies.

Oh and Munson were deep in conversation. The uniformed police officers were the only people who looked tired, who occasionally stifled yawns.

"You won't be able to open the store for a while."

Tim looked up, startled.

Jane put her hand on top of his. "It's a crime scene. I don't think they'll let you open for business."

Tim got up and went over to his desk. An old, cast-iron spindle held current orders. There were only three. He set the spindle on the table and unthreaded the papers. Two hospital bouquets and an arrangement for Dr. Farlander's wife, who ordered fresh flowers delivered weekly.

Tim asked a yawning uniform if he could fill an order for delivery. "I'll use supplies from the front of the store."

The officer interrupted Munson and Oh to ask, and they glanced at Tim and Jane then looked over the store. The evidence technicians were long gone. The area where David had been found and the corridor between the back door and the alcove with Tim's antique partners' desk remained taped off. Oh said something to Munson, who shrugged and said, "Just avoid the taped-off areas."

Tim walked purposefully over to the armoire, happy to have a task, and asked Jane to select twelve irises from the cooler. "Just slightly beyond bud," he called, "and bring some of the white freesia and," he stopped talking as he reached for a creamy white McCoy planter, "maybe a few yellow freesia and salmon foxglove."

"Do you have a compass, Mr. Lowry?" Detective Oh asked.

Tim looked at him, lost.

"Not a 'Let's take a hike, got your compass?' compass, Tim. The kind you draw circles with," Jane said. She had been watching Oh twirling his fingers for Munson, pantomiming using a compass.

"I don't think so."

Jane, gathering up the flowers Tim had asked for, chimed in. "He wouldn't have had time to make all those punctures, so evenly spaced like that, with a compass. I mean, that would take time and care and . . ."

Munson, Oh, and Tim all stared at her.

"Isn't that why you were asking? Aren't you trying to figure out the weapon?"

She thought Oh started to smile at her, but neither detective spoke and both went back to their soft conversation, the level now turned down to a whisper.

"Aren't these stems too long for that planter?" Jane asked.

"No, Nancy Drew, not if you have the right equipment," Tim said, laying out each flower carefully and cutting the bottom half inch of stem diagonally with a sharp knife. "When did you join the force?"

"Come on, it's my second crime scene in two days. I'm allowed to think, aren't I?"

"You're allowed. I'd rather do the mindless right now." Tim laid the irises six on top of six, then placed freesia on either side. He picked up one stem of foxglove and placed it first in the middle, then moved it to the side before handing it back to Jane.

"Put these back, will you? I always want to use them, but they're such show-offs. It's like they always think it's a costume party."

When Jane turned back from the cooler, Tim was placing the stems in the planter and they leaned out at odd angles.

"See, I told you that planter was too low."

"My dear, don't you buy boxes of flower frogs for all your little collectors? Some of us actually take them out of the display cases and use them."

Jane stepped over to the armoire and opened one of the doors. "Does it matter what color? There are green and clear here, and blue? I've never seen blue . . ."

"No, those are the ones for the display case. I need a big metal one. The back table has a couple and the middle drawer in the built-in hutch."

"Oh, yeah." Jane remembered picking one up earlier and pricking her finger. She opened the drawer in the hutch and saw dozens of spikey frogs. The circular ones ranged from half-inch diameters to six-inch. There were ovals and squares, diamonds and rectangles, and one that was a flexible chain of small spikes that could be shaped into a heart as well as a traditional geometrical. "What shape, Tim?"

"Rectangle. Four or five inches long."

Jane reached into the drawer as carefully as she could and still pricked two of her fingers on the needle-pointed frogs. "Oh," she said softly, then louder, "Oh, oh, oh."

"Are you calling me, Mrs. Wheel, or exclaiming?" Detective Oh had just closed his notebook and was nodding at something Munson was saying when he heard Jane.

"I'm solving crimes, Detective."

In her left hand Jane held a four-inch, rectangular, metal flower frog. Its spikes, close together, regularly spaced, stuck out of the base approximately two inches. With her right hand, she pointed toward two oval frogs with equally long spikes. They were flaking off a dark green paint on their bases, but the spikes were clotted with a thicker substance, dark and sticky-looking.

"Call back your evidence boys, Munson," Detective Oh said softly; "Mrs. Wheel is on the case."

6

By the time the technicians returned and removed the flower frogs, inspected the hutch, dusted all the furniture once again for fingerprints, and taped off even more of Tim's store, the sun was minutes away from rising. Tim's arrangement for Mrs. Farlander lay unfinished, and the irises and freesia were wilted beyond resuscitation. Tim had removed his silver address book and leather calendar planner from his desk and started writing a phone list to cancel orders and appointments.

Jane listened as unobtrusively as possible as Munson and Oh discussed how the investigation would proceed. Munson and his officers would continue to canvas the neighborhood, questioning residents about any activity or noise the night before. Oh and Munson would share lab reports as soon as they came back. Until they had that information, it was impossible to link these crimes. Except, of course, through Jane.

Munson stood up to leave. "Mr. Lowry, your store will have to remain closed for the time being. An officer will remain here around the clock. You're sure no one else has a key? No part-time clerks to alert?"

"No. David didn't even keep a key. I gave him an extra this afternoon so he could unload tonight." Tim nodded at the single key on a DON AND NELLIE'S EZ WAY INN key ring that Munson held up. "That's the one. Jennifer Grant is my only part-time clerk. She's a senior at McNamara. I'll call her parents."

"And no 'friends' have keys?"

"No."

Jane watched Tim size up Munson and Munson's raised eyebrows at the word "friends."

"Detective Munson, did you have a brother who went to McNamara? Terry Munson?"

"Yeah. Terry's my kid brother. Why?"

"We were pretty close friends in high school." Tim smiled.

"Really?"

"Yes. We were on the football team together." Tim turned to Jane. "Remember Terry, Jane?"

Jane shrugged. "Not really."

"Lives in Michigan now," Munson said from the door, "with his wife and kids."

"Please give him my very best." Tim held up two fingers pressed closely together. "I mean, we were tight."

Jane watched Munson drive away.

"Couldn't you resist? He might go home and call up his brother and find out you never played football."

"Freshman year. Look it up in your yearbook," Tim said, and switched off the floor lamp by the armoire. "I can't stand the damn phobes. No, I can't resist."

"Mr. Lowry, after you've had some rest, maybe we could talk some more about Mr. Gattreaux and some of the other jobs he's done for you. I'm particularly interested in the kinds of things he's purchased for you at auctions and at estate sales." Detective Oh walked with them toward the front door.

"Could one of you drop me please at the Holiday Inn? I'm going to sleep for a few hours before returning to Evanston."

"No car? Didn't you come here in a police car?"

"I called for a driver. My wife needed our car and I thought I might be able to persuade Mrs. Wheel to give me a ride back on Monday, so I sent my driver back. I knew it would be a late night." He turned to Jane. "Of course, I can call for an officer to come back if that's inconvenient."

"It sounds fine to me. I'd like to sleep and head back between one and two?"

"Yes, perfect." Detective Oh nodded to Jane, who told him she'd drop him at the motel. "Mr. Lowry, what did you say was missing from your case earlier?"

"A flower frog. Carnival glass."

"Yes."

Monday afternoon was sunny, clear. Cooler than the week-end. No humidity. The break in the weather made Jane feel oddly hopeful as she threw her coffee-colored leather duffle into the backseat.

"New luggage?" her father asked.

"Estate sale. A dollar-fifty."

Don reached in and rubbed the side of the bag, smiled, then leaned against the car, facing Jane. They spoke at the same time.

"Janie, why don't you call Charley and Nick home?"

"Daddy, I don't want you to add me to your worries."

They tried again.

"I'll come back on Thursday and work the weekend."

"If you need to stay up there and get this settled, it's fine."

Jane held up her hand. "See you Thursday."

"Call when you get home."

Jane nodded.

"Have that detective check your house out before you even go in."

"Okay."

"And stay away from that neighbor's husband."

Jack. Was it always the husband? Her dad was certain. Charley was, too. "Stay away from Jack," he had said, when she told him. Not "Poor Sandy" or even "Oh, my god," but, "Stay away from Jack." Why did they both jump to the same conclusion? Did all men secretly want to kill their wives?

Nellie came outside with a grocery bag. "Here's some soup."

Jane thanked her mother. Nellie had not looked even slightly surprised when Jane arrived home at sunrise. She didn't blink when Jane told them that David had been murdered in Tim's store.

"He overcharges."

Jane and Don had both stared at her.

"Two dollars a daisy? That's robbery."

Nellie set the bag in the backseat.

"See you on Thursday, Mom."

"Whatever you want."

Detective Oh was standing outside looking at his watch when she pulled into the circular drive of the Holiday Inn. Although he had been casually dressed in a sweater the night before, he now wore a white shirt and tie. The tie was wide silk with hand-painted geometrics. Thirties? Forties? Where did his wife find them? He put his small gym bag and briefcase next to Nellie's soup and folded himself into the small front seat.

"Am I late?"

"You are amazingly punctual, Mrs. Wheel. I was looking at my watch to confirm my admiration. So few people are on time. The younger officers I work with are always late and don't even see it as a problem."

"I hate being late," Jane said, merging into the light afternoon traffic. "My parents were late for everything. Something was always coming up. Bartender wouldn't show or Dad would have to wait until a late delivery came in or something. Usually they didn't show up at all for things at school; and when they did get there, my part was over or my group had already performed our song." Jane passed a truck, forgetting to signal until she was almost completely back in the right lane.

"So now I'm always early. Good for garage sales, but bad form for cocktail parties."

Detective Oh smiled, pretending not to notice her moving violation. He seemed relaxed, content to hitch a ride and make small talk.

"Are garage sales your favorite? Or do you like those demolition derbies best?"

"My real favorite, I think, is a good rummage sale. Not too big, not run like a collection of boutiques by blondes who fancy themselves shopkeepers for a day. You know, like the big sale in Kenilworth?"

Oh shook his head.

"People are lined up hours before they open, book guys

trying to budge their way in first. Eight A.M. the front doors open and they hand you a map as you storm in. Linens, clothes, housewares, toys, books, records, hardware, lamps, garden, treasures. They're all in different rooms. And the people in charge of each room have all this power. Some are okay; they'll let you fill a bag and then charge you a quarter. Fair prices. Or they'll let you bargain with them as they write up a ticket. But the blondes with manicures . . . they make you wait in ridiculously long lines just to tell you a dictionary with a broken binding is a 'good' one and it should be four dollars. You put that back, but find one paperback you want for fifty cents, even though you know that's too much. Then you have to wait in line all over again to have your bag stapled so you won't be able to wedge anything into the bag after it's been marked paid.

"One sale at a Greek Orthodox Church was so filled with paranoia they had women marking twenty-dollar bills with special pens. Checking for counterfeits? Thwarting thieves?" Jane asked, laughing. "It made me want to steal something really badly."

Oh cleared his throat. Or laughed. Jane couldn't tell which. "So why is rummage your favorite?"

"It's the last stop for things. At a garage sale, if a pretty nice vase is marked five dollars and they won't come down, it's because they'd rather take it back into the house than sell it cheaper. Maybe they'll give it away to a daughter with her first apartment or a neighbor who admires it but is too embarrassed to bargain for it. When people really don't want stuff, though, they give it to a church rummage sale. When it's rummage, it's one step away from the garbage. It can't go home again. So if you find a crocheted napkin holder for a dime, you're its last chance. No one who remembers who made it is going to come to the rescue. It's all up to you to decide which thing goes on being loved and protected."

"You don't sound much like a picker, Mrs. Wheel. My wife says they're ruthless. They just grab whatever they think they can make a profit on."

"I usually make a profit. A small one, but I'm getting better." Jane ran her fingers through her short hair. "I'd make more if I could stop myself from *wanting* the stuff. Greedy, I guess."

"More like sentimental, I think."

"I just keep falling in love." She sighed. "At least..."

"Yes?"

Jane had been going to say that at least that's what Charley had said. Charley thought she loved her stuff, her finds, more than she loved him. Jane had laughed when he'd accused her, thinking he was joking.

"I mean it, Jane," he had said quietly but with steel in his voice. "You are in a different world when you come home and sort through those buttons."

"Like you, Charley, on a dig, or piecing together a skeleton or writing up your research."

"No, Jane, with me it's science, but with you it's romance."

"Mrs. Wheel? At least?"

"Nothing. I forgot what I was going to say."

They were entering Chicago's city limits. Jane was surprised how quickly the drive had passed. She was surprised, too, at feeling the first gnawing regret and fear about driving down her street, entering her house.

"Anything new on Sandy's murder?"

"There are a few things you might be able to help me with. A few things we found."

Jane realized that she was going to have to ask twice for an answer from Oh. He would never just offer anything up. *It's probably part of being a detective,* she thought. *The more he makes me work for information, the more I have to reveal.*

"Yes?" said Jane.

"Yes," said Oh.

But I have nothing to reveal, thought Jane, *so why am I trying to be coy?*

"Hmm," said Jane.

"Hmm," said Oh.

It's to prove I'm tougher than he thinks, she decided, *that I'm smarter than he thinks.*

"Interesting," said Jane.

"Very," said Oh.

Jane navigated the Dan Ryan Expressway easily in the light midafternoon traffic. She began her Monday mental checklist, a work habit from the agency that had served her well on commercial shoots. She could actually visualize a list of duties and whether or not they had been checked off. While others ran around with clipboards and designer pens tucked behind their ears, she had always been able to remain cool and unencumbered. "Take off your Rolex, Tommy, you weren't wearing it in the first take," she would remind an actor playing a beer-drinking steelworker, embarrassing the continuity person on the crew. Jane had once been the only one to notice a missing button on an actor's blazer. She had saved the client two hours and thousands of dollars by ripping off her own jacket button, an almost perfect match, whipping out a tiny, vintage Bakelite cylinder that housed a needle, thread, and thimble, and sewing the button on the talent's sport coat in two minutes.

Now her checklist revolved around packaging and mailing out her finds from the weekend, typing up her invoices, recording sales information, putting together a weekly package for Nick, and all the household duties she had taken on since letting the cleaning crew and lawn service go. Charley had insisted he would still pay for them, but she had refused. She liked the cut grass sticking to her bare legs when she mowed; she liked the closure of a well-scrubbed floor. It was cleansing, the penance for losing her job, the payback for letting the rest of her life run to chaos.

"Wait a minute," Jane said out loud.

"Mrs. Wheel?" Oh opened his eyes.

"I remember something," Jane said, forgetting that she was going to be as coy a detective as Oh.

"Yes?"

"The house was freezing. Sandy kept the air-conditioning high because she always liked wearing long sleeves. She hated her elbows." Jane looked at Oh apologetically. "I don't know why; she just didn't like the way they looked."

"I understand," said Oh, encouraging Jane to go on.

"When I went into the house on Saturday, I remember thinking how cold it was. I was going to tease Sandy about it; and when I saw her feet on the couch, they looked blue from the cold. That's why I thought they looked blue." Jane paused. "But before I realized her neck, before I realized she was dead, I noticed that she wasn't only wearing a long-sleeved T-shirt, she was wearing a vest over it."

"Okay." Oh continued to sound encouraging, but he began flexing and stretching his fingers as if to channel his own impatience.

Jane exited the expressway and began the ten-block drive to her own house, forgetting to ask Oh where he wanted to be dropped off.

"I remember the vest because I was going to say something about it being ninety degrees outside and Sandy was making it winter indoors and she was wearing this vest."

"It was a special vest?"

"It was a Gourguechon." Jane looked over at Oh as she pulled up in front of her house and turned off the car. He shrugged and lifted his hands.

"Come in and I'll show you."

Jane unlocked the front door. Out of habit she walked left through the dining room and into the kitchen to look around. The kitchen was always her first stop. She needed to see the Pez above the windows, the vases perched on top of the cabinets, the Pyrex mixing bowls and ball jug pitchers lined up in front of the windows. She looked blankly for a moment at the tinted postcards against the sugar bowl, then remembered she had picked them up on Saturday. They had not made themselves at home and still looked strange and awkward there. She moved them to a small bookshelf and propped them up against the cookbooks. "Just for now," she whispered.

"Mrs. Wheel, you were going to . . ."

"Yes, come upstairs."

Oh followed Jane into her bedroom, where she opened a closet, took out a jacket, and spread it out on top of the navy-and-maroon Amish quilt on her bed. The chocolate brown wool of the jacket looked at first like it might be part of the quilt, the rich, dark colors complimenting each other. Jane turned on her bedside lamp and pointed to the jacket.

"That's a Gourguechon."

Oh looked at the garment. It looked like a high-quality, man's tailored sport coat. Possibly from the forties. The lining, however, was something else entirely: purple silk with hand-painted geometrics, not unlike his own tie, showed at the cuffs as well as at the collar.

"Gourguechon is the name of two sisters or sisters-in-law, I always forget. Diana and Francine. They took men's vintage coats and relined them with fabulous fabrics and trimmed them out with vintage beads and buttons. See?"

Jane pointed to the intricately carved mother-of-pearl buttons, each one a different shape.

"They made vests, too. They took old bartender's vests and trimmed them with collars made of vintage ties. Like yours. And they used the same kind of antique buttons and beads."

Oh fingered the cuff of Jane's jacket. "Beautiful work."

"Very expensive. Each one is unique, a work of art. I bought this jacket two years ago when I got a bonus on a big account and it was still a stretch. Sandy had three jackets and two vests."

"And she was wearing one on Saturday."

"Yes, the best one. It had four Bakelite buttons. All cookies."

Oh raised his eyebrows.

"Two colors in a pattern, like you'd get in rolled cookie dough. I'll show you downstairs. But this vest had four large ones, all different shapes, colors, and patterns. I wanted the second button so badly. I kept offering trades. I have lots of cookies that would have looked good in its place."

"Mrs. Balance didn't want to trade?"

"No. She said that button was why she'd bought the vest. She said it was the Jack-and-Sandy button. It was a black-and-cream yin/yang circle. It was what I noticed on Saturday when I saw Sandy, before I noticed everything else. I just remembered it in the car."

"You remember seeing the button?"

Jane shook her head.

"I remember *not* seeing the button."

7

Jane poured herself a glass of iced tea while Detective Oh made two phone calls. The first was to his office. Jane heard him requesting photographs and asking for a driver to pick him up. The second call was to Munson in Kankakee.

"It's Oh. Would you please ask Mr. Lowry to give you a description of the missing flower frog, the glass one. Yes, that would be better; I'm sure he can find . . ."

Jane held up her hands, interrupting and mouthing an apology for interrupting at the same time. She reached up to a glass shelf that stretched across the top of one of the kitchen windows and pulled down an amber iridescent glass cylinder. Although solid and heavy as a paperweight, this object was riddled with large holes in its convex top.

Oh nodded appreciatively at Jane. "Yes, Detective, that will be fine. Not tomorrow. Wednesday or Thursday, perhaps." He hung up and turned to Jane. "So this is a carnival glass frog?"

"Yes, although Tim's might have been a different size, this is the basic shape and it's what the glass would look like."

"Expensive?"

"I found this one for fifty cents at a rummage sale, but

I saw one for ten dollars at an estate sale and one in an antique mall marked thirty."

"So not that expensive?"

"Tim had vases in the store worth thousands. The pottery on the top shelf is American Art Pottery, some that's really hard to find and very expensive. In fact, he had other flower frogs in the cabinet that were fancier: Roseville pottery frogs in some really rare patterns, and I know he had a Rookwood, gorgeous pink, marked on the bottom."

"How about that button? That yin/yang cookie. Expensive and rare?"

"Five or six dollars, maybe? Probably not rare; I've never tried to get one from a button dealer."

"But you liked it so much?"

"I like finding things, discovering the treasure," Jane said, sipping her iced tea, "not shopping at a treasure store."

"May I?" Detective Oh gestured toward the tea pitcher and Jane poured him a glass and passed him a bright blue bowl of cut lemons.

They sat down together at Jane's kitchen table. She smoothed the cheery forties cloth, printed with impossibly ripe cherry clusters, blueberries bursting juice, happy, dancing peaches. Oh, too, looked at the cloth. He pointed to a smiling lemon winking at a grapefruit.

"I believe I have this on a tie."

Jane began to laugh. It was absurd, this serious detective seeing all of her finds, her stuff, her junk, her rummage, and recognizing something familiar.

Oh, too, looked as if he might laugh. When the phone rang, he sobered up and sat politely, watching Jane.

She picked it up with a smile still in her voice.

"Jack?" Oh watched her smile vanish. "Of course. I'm glad you called . . . I don't think I could . . . Yes, I'll think about it."

Jane hung up. "Sandy's memorial service is Wednesday."

"Yes, I know." Oh sipped his tea and waited for her to tell him what else Jack had said.

"He asked me if I could come over and go through some of her things, help him decide what to do."

Oh raised his left eyebrow.

"It's too soon, don't you think? Besides, Sandy must have someone closer to her, a family member who can do that. It wouldn't be . . . I could just hear Barbara and the rest of them if I go in that house."

"Mrs. Balance was an only child. Her mother passed away a few years ago, and her father has been quite ill. You may be the only friend."

Jane's eyes filled with tears. Oh awkwardly patted her shoulder then walked back and forth between her sink and the back door. He stopped and seemed to be staring at the hand-embroidered tea towels stacked on the counter, but instead he reached beyond them, picked up the knife Jane had used to cut the lemons. He looked at its serrated edge, then laid it on the counter. A sturdy, wooden yardstick hung next to the pantry cupboard. Oh looked at it then back at the knife. Jane watched him measure it with his eyes.

Jane came over to him, grabbed a towel embroidered in blue and red, a dish running away with a spoon, and wiped her eyes.

"Is it too short or too long? Or is it just right?" Jane opened a drawer and threw a box of Ziploc bags on the counter. "Shouldn't you bag it and take it downtown, Detective?"

"Too small, I think," Oh said softly.

"So that eliminates me as the killer?"

"Not at all. It eliminates a bread knife, this bread knife, as the murder weapon."

"I could have killed her, come home, washed the knife, and put it back in the knife block before I went back to discover the body?"

"Of course, but the wounds in Mrs. Balance's neck were made by a bigger, heavier blade, one that could saw through . . ."

Jane flinched, and Oh hesitated. He looked behind her shoulder and nodded. Jane turned at the loud knock at the kitchen door.

When Jane opened it, Officer Mile entered and gestured to the dog by her side. The shepherd looked lovingly at Jane but obeyed the hand command and continued to sit outside the door.

"She obeys me, but her heart belongs to you."

The three watched the dog stare at Jane, her tail wagging impatiently as she sat. Jane asked Mile how to release her from the position. Mile quickly gave her the hand commands she was using for come, sit, and down-stay, but advised her to practice them.

"Training a dog is really training yourself. Lots of practicing, so you learn to read each other's minds."

"She's such a wonderful dog; somebody's missing her," Jane said, burying her face in the dog's neck. "Have you put an ad in the paper?"

"Not exactly."

"I'll do it today."

"No, Mrs. Wheel, not yet," Oh said, shaking his head and replacing the knife in the wooden block. "Did you bring it?"

Mile handed Oh a large manila envelope and a pair of white cotton gloves.

Oh sat down at the table and indicated that Jane should sit.

"You are interested in solving this case, Mrs. Wheel?"

"I thought I was the suspect."

"Not at the top of the list. But even if you were, all the more reason to solve the crime as quickly as possible, yes?" Oh asked, putting on the gloves.

From the large envelope Oh removed a smaller brown envelope and four photographs. It took a moment for Jane to focus and figure out that they were pictures of Sandy. Not Sandy. They were pictures of Sandy's vest on Sandy's dead body. Extreme close-ups, narrowing the field to Sandy's midsection, to her blood-spattered vest, and to the empty space where a button should have been. One of the photographs had been so enlarged and focused that Jane could see a tiny tear in the fabric next to a thread hanging loose. The photo reminded Jane of those in children's magazines, close-up pictures of one part or area of a familiar object. The child had to figure out that the pebbly surface and dashed lines were really a close-up on the sewn seam of a football. Nick would always bring the pages to Jane, try to stump her, but she could always get them: the holes in a saltshaker, the handle of a faucet, one blade of an eggbeater.

"Important to see the big picture, Nick; but like those architects said, God is in the details."

Officer Mile was mightily impressed by the missing button observation. Jane could tell by the nod and smile and encouraging looks she kept giving her. Oh, however, kept looking at the photo, fingering the ordinary buttons on his own oxford cloth shirt with his gloved hand.

"The button does appear to have been ripped from the vest. They are checking the vest itself right now, but it doesn't quite make . . ." Oh looked around the kitchen. His eyes went from the new old flowerpots to brightly colored mixing bowls to ball jugs to pressed glass pitchers. He stopped at the shelf of vintage cookbooks and went over and removed the book that didn't belong. Jane had tucked *The Hidden Staircase* between a first edition of *The Settlement Cookbook* and a wartime pamphlet on making desserts with less—*Coping Competently with Rationing*. He moved over to the shelf and picked up the book. "You collect mysteries, too?"

"When I find a Nancy Drew, I take it. They're very popular. The book guys usually get to them first."

"If you go to a sale looking for those pots," and he waved his hand toward the flowerpots, "you still look at the books?"

"Of course. I look at everything. That's part of the problem. Successful dealers usually go right to their area and get the best stuff. I'm all over the place. Trying to be a picker, I'm looking to find everything; and when I see something I grab it."

"Like a bakery cookie?" Oh pointed to the loose thread in the photo.

"Bakelite cookie, Detective Oh," Jane corrected. "Yes, if I saw one, I'd grab it. At a rummage sale or in a sewing box at a house sale, but not off someone's clothes." She hesitated, looking at the photo. "Even if they were dead."

Jane, it's Richard. The guy you're not going to sue, remember? Um, I could take you out to dinner or something this week. There's a huge sale this weekend in Lake Bluff, a presale on Thursday. I got an invitation . . . If you're up for it, we could go and grab a bite after. I promise not to hurt you . . . I mean, step on your foot or drop anything on you. Anyway, it's Tuesday. I'll just call back later. Bye.

Jane, her hair still damp from her shower, sat down next to her phone machine. She contemplated ripping its wires out. *It's got too much power,* she was thinking, *way too much power. It lets people right into your house. Their voices come right into the room and then they stay there, echoing, settling into your brain on little lawn chairs, making themselves comfortable.*

She was separated; she could go on a date if she wanted to. Charley had packed up his stuff and moved out two weeks before he left for South Dakota. That's a separation. Who the hell was this Cindy Charley was working with? The one Nick said who knew so many card games? If Charley was playing hearts around the campfire, she could go out for a bite with Richard. He wasn't unpleasant to look at, if you liked those big papa bear types. He was a picker, knew his way around a sale; they had things in common. She didn't really like pickers, though, did she, even though she wanted to be one?

"At least he's not a book guy," she said aloud.

When the phone rang, she jumped, wondering if she was willing machinery into action, but she stopped herself from answering. If it was Richard calling back, should she go? She knew about this sale. It was the Hendershott house. A gold mine. Pickers and diggers had been staking it out for months. The perennials planted on the north lawn of the property alone would bring thousands. And there was a presale for which she did not have an invitation.

Jane, hi, it's Jack again. Call me. I really must talk to you.

Jane knew she couldn't avoid Jack forever. There was, after all, a funeral to attend. Oh hadn't exactly advised her to go over to Jack's and help him with Sandy's things, but he hadn't warned her against it. He'd hinted that with her eye for detail she might pick up a clue, a key, a tidbit that might help the police get to the bottom of this. Or had he been trying to trick her? Send her into the arms of Jack, her lover, with whom she had plotted the murder of his wife. Then he, Oh, could spring out of the closet and catch them. One minute Jane was sure of Oh's belief in her innocence; the next she was certain he was ready to handcuff her and take her away.

"Oh, god, please don't let me start thinking of him as inscrutable," she moaned softly.

What did Oh really think of Jack? Was he in the same camp with her father and Charley? Do all husbands want to kill their wives? Absolutely not. Couldn't be true. It wasn't that Jane was exactly a fan of Jack's. She liked doing crosswords and jumbles with him. He seemed to appreciate her best finds. He had looked at her so appreciatively, so warmly, that night as she had leaned in to inhale the lamb, admire the knife, like he had been waiting for her. He was the only man other than Charley she had kissed in fifteen years.

"I *would* pick the frog instead of the prince," she said out loud.

She tried to remember everything she knew about Jack. Why was she having such a hard time believing he was a liar and a murderer. He might be a liar. He had wiped out his entire past. He was a snob. He was a reproduction, and Jane only appreciated originals, fading, peeling paint, and all. He was a reinvention, a reconstruction, a fake, a forgery. According to Sandy, Jack had spent a small fortune filling in the gap in his front teeth, perming and coloring his hair.

"Shoot, honey, that man has had more manicures this month than I've had in my life," Sandy had told her just last week over blueberry muffins.

Jane's new best friend wandered into the study and nuzzled her knee. "Okay, let's try out names on you," Jane said, scratching the dog's ears. "Mimi? Roverina? Muttsy? Helen? Rita? Bernice?"

The huge dog wagged her tail at each name, seemingly happy enough just to be spoken to, to be taken seriously for a moment.

"Let's go with Rita. 'Lovely Rita, Meter Maid.' Yes. Oh, Nicky's going to love you. I think even Charley might like you, even if you are still alive. We'll tell him you're descended from a wooly mammoth."

Jane filled Rita's water bowl and made sure the outside

porch door was latched. Dragging a cardboard file box out of the study closet and setting it on the kitchen table, she grabbed tape, pen, yellow highlighter, pink highlighter, and her canvas "shopping" bag, whose contents she dumped out on the kitchen table.

Mondays and Tuesdays, even after weekends where bodies were found, along with the buttons and mixing bowls, were filing days.

Jane spread out last Thursday's *Tribune* and weekly *Evanston Review* classifieds. These were her second copies. She had used her first newspapers to make her map on sale day and these clean copies were for her filing system.

Ripping off an inch or so of clear tape, she pressed it directly over an ad for a sale she had attended on Friday. After pressing down on the center of the piece of tape that covered the sale information, she carefully lifted up each end, the tape now pulling off the classified neatly from the paper. She carefully applied the tape, with its four lines of sales information, to a file card from the box: Scotch tape lamination.

Jane checked her notebook and wrote down on the card what she'd bought at that particular sale, the price . . . asking and selling, interesting pieces she'd missed, other bits of information. On this card, she wrote that she had talked to the woman who was selling her mother's belongings and noted that the house would soon be for sale. The daughter was pretty sure it would be a teardown, so Jane flagged the card to remind herself to drive by and take more photographs of the house and property. She had snapped one, but had been short on film so she would have to return. Photos helped her prioritize sales, gave clues to where she'd have the most luck, especially helpful on days when five or six promising ads vied for her attention.

Once a month when she drove to Ohio to visit Miriam's shop, she brought these scrapbook files, and Miriam sat with her over tea and taught her about window frames and cornices, mantelpieces, and doorknobs.

Miriam. She had given Jane her first crowbar. Two years ago, when Jane and her assistant had been scouting locations in Ohio, Lucy had suggested they drop in on Cousin Miriam. Her shop, in the middle of Nowhere, Ohio, just outside of Where the Hell Am I? as Miriam described it on her business card, did most of her selling by Internet and mail order. Her shop, however, was the experience of a lifetime for anyone who had ever picked up a piece of yellow ware and turned it over to study its bottom. Shelves of vases, pots, planters, and jardinieres; tins of buttons; crocks of rolling pins; baskets of cookie cutters; cases of jewelry; and dowel rods laden with carved Bakelite bracelets: paradise. But it was Miriam who was the treasure.

"This is the tip of the iceberg." She smiled. "Just the tourist stuff."

Miriam owned a farm and the two original barns were filled to the rafters. One held architectural pieces, the other, furniture. Since Miriam had stopped her annual buying trips to Europe when she hit sixty-five, she carried mostly American pieces. Quilts hung on every wall, and even though her wares were crammed into every corner, they were arranged into the kind of still lifes that make the casual browser pause and say, "That's just what I want to see in my home every day."

Jane had wandered through Miriam's acres of stuff in a

daze; and when she came to a small, carved mantel, she told Miriam the story of leaving a similar one at a demolition sale because she didn't have the proper tools. When she and Lucy reluctantly walked to their rented van to go back to Chicago, Miriam called them back to the porch. She gestured to a large wooden box with rope handles. Although the red paint on the box had faded to a pale hint of color, the black stenciled letters were still bold: A. M. MARTIN.

"Take it, Jane," Miriam ordered, "it's got your name on it"—she lit a Camel with a vintage Zippo—"metaphorically, of course."

Inside the box were three saws, a large and small crowbar, a regular hammer, pliers, a wrench, a wedge, and a small sledge. Resting on top was a list of items, crude but accurate sketches of pottery marks, descriptions of pressed glass patterns and colors, and a variety of specifications on hardware and period decoration.

"Don't leave home without it," Miriam cautioned.

Jane never did.

It was that toolbox that made her pick up the phone, stab at the numbers, take a deep breath.

"Jack Balance here." Jane thought she heard him inhale deeply after answering. *Is he smoking? In the house?*

"It's Jane. I haven't had a chance to tell you how truly sorry . . ."

"Yes, I know. Can you come over? I'm lost here. I have no idea what to do with anything. I . . ."

Jack did sound distraught.

"I'm not sure I can go through Sandy's things with you, Jack. Isn't there anyone else? An old school friend? Family?"

"She was an only child. She had two cousins she hated.

I called her college roommate, but she's out of the country until the end of the summer. You're the only friend who can do this."

"Are you sure you're supposed to go through her things? Have the police . . . ?"

"They've been through everything. Those bastards threw her stuff around like, like she was trying to hide something and they were going to find it."

"I'll help you put things away, Jack." *But first*, she thought, *I have to get my toolbox out of the truck.*

Jane hung up. She considered calling Oh and telling him she was going over to Sandy's but quickly decided against it. If she was right about the button on Sandy's vest, maybe there was something else she could see at the house. Or not see. If she was really going to be absolved of Sandy's murder, she might have to find out who did it. She actually felt better for a minute. Thinking of Sandy brought an image of the smiling, wisecracking Sandy instead of the lifeless corpse she had last seen. Then she remembered David, bloodied under those damned carved doors, his face riddled with those tiny holes; Tim, pale and shaken.

"One murder at a time; we'll solve this crime by crime," Jane muttered to herself.

Approaching from the west side of the house, Jane could see yellow police tape torn and wadded up at the back door. Had Jack ripped it down? The front door, however, seemed accessible. In fact, the scene was idyllic. A cardinal sang in the evergreen next to the front porch; the *Chicago Tribune*, folded open to the crossword and jumble, was tossed onto a small teak table; half a cigar rested in an amber glass ashtray; and a cup of coffee grew cold next to the twig chair.

"Mistake," Jane said, looking at the blank space next to KESMAIT. "Jesus, Jack, you are slipping."

Jane halted on the porch. She always went in through the back door off the garage, up the three stairs, through the side door into the kitchen. She felt her legs go stiff and heavy when she tried to make them march through the front. Her throat thickened and she felt her stomach turn, the way it might if the cigar were still lit and smoking. She could taste the cold coffee, bitter in her mouth.

She turned away. *I'll just stop in the garage first and pick up my toolbox,* she thought. She knew the warmth of its wooden handle; the worn fit of the wood in her hand would give her the comfort and the strength she needed to go in and face Jack. *He didn't do it, I know he didn't do it,* she repeated to herself. *Dad's wrong. Charley's wrong. It's not always the husband. This is just a big "kesmait."*

She opened the side door to the garage, unlocked as usual. The Suburban was parked on the east side, where she had left it on Saturday. The potting table was the same, stacked terra-cotta flowerpots, a container of pea gravel with a wooden-handled flour scoop sticking up. Jane smiled at it. Sandy was going to sell it at her garage sale; it had been in her mother's kitchen and Jane had told her to save it. "It'll come in handy potting plants," Jane had said. Sandy, one lip curled up in a kind of hopeless smile, said, "I might as well scoop fertilizer with it. My mother wasn't much of a baker."

Jane walked over to it, wanting to touch the faded red handle. Out of the corner of one eye, she thought she saw the rear door of the van move. A warm breeze slid through the open side door, and a leaf skittered across the cement floor. She froze. The breeze was warm, she knew that, the sun was hot, high in the cloudless sky, so why did she feel a chill, such a cold blast that the hair stood up on the back of her neck. Her short haircut threatened to betray her panic. *I've become a character in a cheap horror movie,* she thought, and in the next second, all humor, all hope drained out of her. "I'm going to find another body," she said aloud.

She felt a weight on her shoulder and the back of her neck before she felt any pain. She fell forward, one arm grazing the potting table, the other reaching toward the Suburban. The passenger door was unlatched and she grabbed the corner of it, swinging forward, staggering forward with it as it moved, and she saw the empty front seat, the dirty rubber floor mat, as she went down. She was spinning; she was mumbling as she hit the floor.

"Not my body. I'm not supposed to find my body."

9

Bruce Oh stared at the ties hanging from pale ash dowel rods attached to the molding in his closet. His wife, Claire, had installed the dowel herself because, she explained, the ties needed to be together, to overlap, pattern upon pattern. The fabrics and colors and playful designs of the twenties, thirties, forties, and fifties needed to commune, to mingle. She was a nut, his wife.

He chose a pattern with large and small squares scattered over a navy background. It almost looked ordinary, contemporary. It was one of the ties Claire had tried to spirit away for a church donation, but he had missed it immediately and discovered it in a bag marked "Saint Perpetua."

"Oh, Bruce, it's too plain. Totally undistinguished," she'd whined, as he'd brushed it off and replaced it in his closet. "I shouldn't have bought it. It looks"—she searched for a word horrible enough—"it looks retail."

What was it with these people? These people and also his wife? These collectors. He had known thieves and gamblers, extortionists and murderers. Were any of them as obsessive as these collectors? These rummagers? What did Jane Wheel call herself? Picker? These pickers?

Poor Mrs. Wheel. She seemed to be so lonely, so sad.

He knew how weak it was to think about suspects, witnesses, even victims in this personal way, but he didn't care. Now that he was working with the university, it was okay to philosophize, to ruminate. His students asked him all the time about personalities, about psychology. He could raise all the questions he wanted to about why people behaved the way they did. Students loved to talk, to think. There were no smirking sergeants to shrug and say, Who cares why he did it? We've got the freaking knife in his hand and his prints all over the freaking house. Now that Oh spent part of his time as a professor, he felt more at peace with the time he spent as a detective. It suited him, these two jobs put together. *Yin and yang*, he thought, *like a Bakelite cookie.*

Flipping the tail of his almost "retail" tie over, securing the knot and checking himself seriously in the mirror, Oh smiled. Leaning in close to the mirror, he checked his teeth, clicked them together twice, and wiped off the sink and counter with a tissue and threw it into the vintage "New Era" potato chip can that Claire had chosen for their wastebasket. Oh sighed and stroked an errant hair at his temple.

Breakfast was simple and consistent. One carton of lemon yogurt, one bowl of Cheerios, one cup of English Breakfast tea, brewed from leaves in a cobalt blue pot that Claire had found buried in someone's basement. The tea ball into which he loosely packed leaves was shaped liked a small country church, spire and all. Claire had eleven unusual tea strainers, all in different sizes and shapes lined up on a handmade shelf, the shelf itself placed into a folk art teapot shape, hanging to the left of the kitchen sink.

As his wife's passion for collecting the odd object here or there had grown into an obsession, Oh had finally convinced her to turn her hobby into a career. Claire had opened a hugely successful stall in an antique mart in downtown Chicago. Since her opening last year, the confusion in the house had lessened considerably. Now the objects that remained were the ones used by them or, in the case of Detective Oh's ties, worn by him. He offered on several occasions to allow her to sell the truly outrageous pieces, but she always laughed and insisted that the right occasion would soon come along.

Now as he poured his Cheerios, he noticed that Claire had inked in an "H" after the "O" on the box. He gave in to a genuine smile and shook his head. *She's a nut, my wife,* he thought.

When after a few bites into breakfast the phone rang, he quickly swallowed and answered efficiently, "Oh speaking." A pause, and then, "I'm going to the university later this morning. Want to drop them off here?" Oh hugged the phone to his ear while he cleared his yogurt carton and spoon, stopping to pour himself another cup of tea. "Fine, I'll expect you soon."

Officer Mile was a fine young officer. She had a good sense of people as well as duty, and she seemed to be especially interested in clearing suspicion from Mrs. Wheel. Some superior officers would have tried to erase the personal quality in Mile, but Oh saw it as a plus. Personal feelings were a plus, at least to an honest person. If something made you care about finding someone guilty or innocent, it made you work harder. As long as it didn't cloud your vision, as long as the truth was at the top of your list, feelings were fine with Detective Oh. And, of course, as long as you could hide them.

Oh spooned coffee into the pot so he could offer some to Mile and Tripp when they arrived with the paperwork they wanted to show him. He took out a small bowl from the cupboard that Claire had put sugar and sugar substitute packets in. The bowl was a bright blue-and-white spatter, a substantial weight plastic of some sort. What had Claire called it? Oh fingered the bowl. Picking up the phone he dialed Claire's cellular.

When she answered, he could barely hear her. "Claire, it's Bruce," he shouted.

"Speak up, darling, there are ten other people digging through this basement. Hard to hear."

"The bowl we keep sugar packets in? What is it?"

"It's an English jelly mold. You know, jelly, Jell-O. Jell-O mold. Called Beetleware, 1930."

"Yes, but what's it made of?" Oh shouted.

"Bakelite," Claire answered. "Why? It's hard to find; I don't think I want to sell it. It's functional enough for us to keep, isn't it?"

"How do you know? How can you tell when something's Bakelite?"

"Rub it hard with your thumb."

"What?"

"Rub it hard with your thumb. Or dip it into some hot water if you're near the sink."

"Okay, I'm rubbing."

"Smell it, Bruce."

"Oh, yes, I smell it." Oh wrinkled his nose at the bitter odor.

"Carbolic, right? Why? I didn't think you cared about such things."

"Just curious. Subject came up in a case. Is it really valuable?"

"Not heart stopping. But collectors can be kind of fanatic so you can get a pretty good price if it's in good condition. Can't restore it, so you have to find it perfect. No, I'm not." Claire's voice drifted from the mouthpiece. "I'm not finished with this box. Right. That it, Bruce? I've got to get back to business here."

Oh tapped his short, immaculate nails on the jelly mold. The clicking sound was satisfying, rhythmic. He almost didn't recognize the first soft rapping on the screen door when Mile arrived, thinking it some kind of echo of his own noisemaking.

"I have different reports here. And I brought the faxes we got from Kankakee. Look at these photos. I hope they mean something's wrong with the fax machine."

Oh shook his head and stared at the photo of David's dead body. "Those marks, those dark pinpoints, aren't the machine's fault. He was hit from behind, then strangled, his throat was practically crushed, maybe like this." Oh got down on his knees still looking hard at the photo, pretending to put one knee on something. Mile understood it to be the victim's throat.

"Then the murderer grabbed this sharp flower frog from a shelf and started his tattooing of the face, but it only made these little marks, these flyspecks, because Mr. Gattreaux was almost dead. Not much blood pumping. The flower frog was not the murder weapon, just a . . ."

"Finishing touch?" offered Mile.

"Yes, but more. A souvenir, a . . . what do my wife and Mrs. Wheel say? A collectible."

"But he didn't collect it. He left it there."

"He, Officer Mile?"

"Probably. The victim was a slim but well-built man. He

was knocked down, choked to death by someone strong enough, big enough to hold him down. I think a man."

"A flower frog–collecting man?"

"Detective Oh, he left the frog."

"On the last page of the report you'll notice that Mr. Lowry reports one item missing from his shop: a flower frog. Circus glass."

"Carnival glass," Mile said softly.

"Yes."

Oh aligned the first set of papers and placed them on the kitchen table. He poured more tea for himself and offered Mile a cup of coffee that she accepted and sat down to open a much larger file folder.

"Some good news in here, Susan?"

She took a packet of sweetener from the Beetleware bowl, tapping her own finger on the rim, and shook her head.

"Looks like Jack Balance was having an affair, not trying that hard to cover it up either. A hotel concierge in New York even remembers him introducing a female friend, who he happened to run into in the lobby, as a neighbor. Then the guy said he saw the same woman coming out of Balance's room later."

"Description?"

"She wore a scarf, covered her hair, average to tall, medium build, could have been a lot of women."

"Could have been Jane Wheel?"

Mile stirred her coffee. "Could have been. We've sent photos to him for possible positive identification.

"He charged some jewelry at an antique store, fancy handwrought silver pieces—none of it found in Sandy Balance's room. He also wanted to sell some parts of his business, but his wife was a co-owner and wouldn't sign off on any of the deals. His secretary told us that, said it wasn't a secret, that Balance talked about his wife all the time as the 'fly in the ointment.' She said it was affectionate, that he referred to her as a small-town girl scared of his success."

"Looks like she also said he was a liar." Oh pointed to the center of a typewritten transcript. "He instructed the office staff to say he was in meetings when he left early several afternoons a month. Supposed to say it even to his wife?"

"Secretary said he was taking off to play golf; he was obsessed, and he just said his days were *his* business."

"Business in the black? Books okay?"

"Nothing funny has turned up so far. He seems to have converted a lot into cash lately, but not enough to send up any real flags. His wife was listed as a partner on a lot of real estate deals. He needed her cooperation for a lot of transactions. Now everything is under his control."

"He hasn't got all that much cash, according to this."

"Yeah, as soon as he converted, he seemed to tie it up again. He owns every kind of property imaginable. Apartments and office buildings, pieces of shopping malls, farms, breweries, golf courses; he even owns a huge antique mall."

"Antique mall?" Oh shuffled the papers until he got to a list of holdings. "It's in Bourbonnais, Illinois? Where is Bourbonnais? That name looks so familiar. One of those big multidealer places like the one Claire's in?"

"It's pronounced Bur-bo-nay. French. It's right next to Kankakee, Detective Oh."

"These people with their collections, their stuff, all their old things . . . ," Oh grumbled as he wrote down addresses in a small pocket notebook. Looking up, he tilted his head. "Susan, where is Tripp?"

"Waiting for a few more reports to come in. Thought we might have something more on whatever was used on Mrs. Balance."

Oh stood and began clearing his breakfast things, muttering softly. "Something's missing, something's always missing." He picked up the Beetleware bowl and turned it in his hands. "What connects this David with Sandy Balance?"

Susan Mile looked up. "Jane Wheel?"

"What else?"

"Antiques? Collectibles?"

"Not really. Mrs. Balance didn't collect. David was just an agent for Tim Lowry. In fact, why not Tim Lowry as the connection? He knew David and he had met the Balances before. He'd consulted with Jack Balance on some furniture purchases."

"Just conversation over dinner though. He never actually did any purchasing." Susan ruffled through the larger of the files. "Jack Balance purchased an antique desk through a Chicago dealer and some other valuable furniture through the decorator who did his office. Nothing in here through Lowry. Nothing through any of the stalls in that Bourbonnais mall either, according to these receipts."

"Get the name of every dealer in that mall. Then look through canceled checks. Make sure you've got all his cash withdrawals, too. Might have bought some pieces off the truck, so to speak."

Susan wrote down the order on a small spiral pad then looked back up at Oh expectantly.

"Maybe there was a fight over a valuable piece. Lowry was a competitive dealer; Balance had the money to outbid him on anything he wanted. Lowry goes to talk to Balance, finds Sandy instead, somehow David finds out, so . . ." Susan stopped and shook her head. "That doesn't work."

"Why not?" Oh asked quietly.

"Tim Lowry and Jane Wheel have been best friends since kindergarten. He wouldn't drag her into this. Besides, two murders over a piece of furniture . . ."

"Susan, you know better. People murder over a cup of coffee. 'She made it weak, Detective, and she knew I liked it strong.' You've heard things like that, so these picker people would certainly murder each other over buttons and sugar bowls"—Oh gestured toward the jelly mold holding sugar packets—"but that's not it."

"What's not it?" Susan Mile spread out the photographs of murdered Sandy Balance. She took out another envelope and began laying out the police photos of David Gattreaux.

"Susan, what did you say before? That what connected them was collectible?"

"Collectibles or antiques, but," Susan hesitated, shifting the photographs, "you were right; Mrs. Balance didn't collect."

"Exactly." Oh rose quickly and dialed his office at the university. "Would you please, Mrs. Dubner, get the message to my seminar students to open packet thirty-seven and discuss? I may not be able to be there to monitor, so I'd like each student to write a report of the discussion for me. They should be very specific, yes. Very big case. Yes."

Oh hung up the phone just as Claire came through the back door carrying a broken cardboard box. She waved and struggled to balance the box on a chair while she disentangled the strap of her huge shopping bag and set it on the floor.

"Bruce, I found the greatest little cocktail shaker. Shall we keep it or sell it?" Claire held up a hammered silver cylinder with handles in the shape of two mermaids, their hair flowing down the back of the shaker in silver rivulets.

Oh nodded. "Charming. Sell, please."

Claire frowned slightly. "If I found a place for it on the bar?"

"We don't have a bar. We don't even drink."

Claire shrugged. "I've got to run upstairs to my office and check some auctions online." She rummaged in her bag. "Here, Susan, this is for you."

"Thank you, Mrs. Oh." Susan studied the glass swizzle stick, admiring the Scottie dog on top. "I love it."

"Well, there wasn't a set, but I know how you like those dogs, so I . . ." Claire's voice drifted off upstairs and out of their hearing.

Bruce Oh took the swizzle stick out of Susan's hand and examined it, then gave it back. "It's not that they were collectors; it's that they are *not* collectors. They are connected to the sales, friends, acquaintances of buyers."

"But why would that—"

Oh held up his hand. "Ask yourself first, Susan,"

"Okay." Mile nodded. Oh was a great teacher and always entertained questions, celebrated questions in fact. But he always liked them to be internal, self-directed. He believed if you learned to phrase your thoughts into questions to yourself, you would eventually be able to answer them. "Why would anyone want these two people dead? They're connected by people who know them both—Jane Wheel, Tim Lowry. Neither of *them* could have killed David because they were both having dinner with Jane's parents. It appears that Lowry was in Kankakee when Sandy Balance was murdered. Jane Wheel might have had the time, but the method makes it unlikely . . ."

Oh cleared his throat, but Susan held up her hand before he could speak.

"Jane Wheel is a much smaller woman than Sandy Balance. Even though there was a blow to the head before her throat was cut, it did not necessarily render her unconscious. Her throat wasn't merely slashed, it was . . ." Susan took out a photograph from a fat manila envelope and stared at it, frowning. "This cut goes through skin, tendon, cartilage, bone . . ."

Oh nodded as he picked up the ringing phone. "Yes, Tripp. I think Susan was just about to tell me that. Hang on. Yes, Susan?"

"Her throat wasn't cut, it was . . . sawed."

"Tripp, why don't you start over there and we'll meet you?"

Susan stood up and began gathering the photos. "Mrs. Wheel's toolbox?"

"Yes."

"Okay, maybe there's a saw there, but we still don't have a connection with the sales and the collectors."

"Why not?"

"Mrs. Wheel and her toolbox were at the Saturday sales, and Tim Lowry and David were at the auction with her."

"Yes?"

"Sandy Balance didn't go to any sales."

"No," Oh said, pocketing his keys and opening the door for Officer Mile, "but her Suburban did."

10

Jane felt herself being carried and carried badly. In the movies, a strong hero lifted a woman into his arms, making her feel protected, safe. Jane felt like whoever was carrying her was breathing heavily and in need of medication. *I only weigh a hundred and twenty, you wimp,* she was thinking. Her wheezing hero also had her face jammed into his shoulder so hard, she could barely breathe herself. *What an idiot,* she was thinking, until she realized that her not breathing might be the whole point. Someone had hit her with something, a shovel maybe, and hadn't killed her. This loser was taking her somewhere to finish the job.

Despite the pain in the back of her head and the new bruise forming on her left shoulder and the ringing in her ears, she decided she could still fight. *I'll pretend to still be out and as soon as we get where we're going, I'll give him something to gasp about.* She felt adrenaline masking her aches and pains. She felt the steely spine of Nancy Drew replace her silly suburban backbone. She was ready to save herself and solve the crime. She was Nancy Drew and Emma Peel. She was Annie Oakley and Miss Marple. Why couldn't she think of any other strong women avengers, detectives, tough girls?

As she was lamenting her lack of female role models, Jane was dropped onto a bed. She opened one eye and saw the broad back of a man going out the door. The shades were pulled, the room daytime dark. She thought the man was wearing a black or dark blue T-shirt and blue jeans. Almost six feet, maybe. She was terrible with estimates unless they involved height and width of furniture or yardage of vintage fabric. If she could hold a piece of cloth from her nose to her outstretched fingertips, as her grandmother had taught her, she could tell you if you could make curtains for your bedroom. Now she lifted her hands in front of her face. *I'm not even tied up,* she thought. *Sloppy killers. Underestimating me, are they? They think I can't get away.* She sat up, dizzy and sore, but found she could stay upright. This room seemed familiar. Where had she seen that wallpaper before?

The door opened gently and she forgot to pretend she was still unconscious. She realized as soon as she hit the bed that it hadn't been such a great idea anyway. The wheezer might have been dropping her into a lake or a concrete overcoat. *Concrete shoes, you idiot,* corrected Nancy Drew or Miss Marple or someone now living where her brain used to be.

"Jane, thank god you're awake. The paramedics and police are on their way." Jack set a Chase Chrome tray with iced tea and water and a bottle of Old Bushmill's on the table next to the bed. Jane was surprised by the tray for two reasons. First, the red Bakelite handle was in excellent condition, not a chip or crack, and those were hard to find. Second, Sandy disliked Art Deco.

"Is this the guest room?"

"Yeah. You helped Sandy pick stuff out for it, remember?"

Jane nodded. She pointed to the souvenir pillows piled on the chaise in the corner. "I had a feeling Sandy hated those."

"She did," Jack said, "but she also hated most of the people who stayed in the guest room."

Jane looked at Jack, who was smiling. He was handsome in the slick way that so many businessmen seemed handsome to her. Expensive haircuts, even tans, well-fitting clothes, their teeth fixed, their stomachs taut, their backs straight, they smelled good. They knew what to say, when to take your elbow, when to lean forward, when to laugh. It wasn't that it was phony; it was real enough. It was just too much of the same. It was regimented, uniform. It was machine made; the mold marks showed.

Charley was always scruffy, always distracted while shaving so you could see a shadowy patch of beard where one thought began and another started. Jane loved that about Charley, but she knew she also had been curious about the confident ones, the men who always had smooth faces and well-trimmed sideburns. What made them tick anyway? Was that why she'd leaned into Jack's kiss?

They both heard the sirens. Jane sat up straighter. "I don't need paramedics. I'm used to being bruised these days."

"You could have a concussion; I—"

"Who tried to kill me?"

"Who . . . Oh, my god. No, Jane, that wasn't . . ." Jack moved to the doorway and called down, "We're up here, come up."

The next thirty minutes Jane spent arguing with Melvin Samelsom, the conscientious paramedic who insisted Jane needed to go to the hospital. Jane fought back, wore him

...own with promises to call her internist and to invite a friend ...o spend the night with her and wake her every few hours. ...No, she wouldn't be alone; no, she wouldn't ignore swelling; ...o, she wouldn't go to sleep now. Finally Melvin gave up, ...vatched her sign the waiver, stood and shrugged his shoul-...ers. He had done what he could. His partner, a silent young ...oman who seemed neither brave, noble, or sympathetic—...he qualities Jane presumed to be required for the career—...imply stood, winked, and patted Jane's feet on her way out.

When Melvin and partner exited, Detective Oh and Of-...cer Mile entered. "How are you feeling, Mrs. Wheel? May ...e sit?" Detective Oh waited for her to answer, and when ...he nodded he pulled chairs from the small table by the win-...ow closer to the bed. "Would you mind if I opened the ...hade a bit? Would the light bother you?"

"We'll see," said Jane, and when she realized daylight ...ouldn't blind her, she gestured that all the shades be raised.

"Let there be," she said, pouring some water from Jack's ...ay.

"Mrs. Wheel, what were you doing in Mr. Balance's ga-...ge?"

"I came over to help Jack with Sandy's things. He asked ...e to. I remembered I had left my toolbox in the Suburban, ... I decided to get it first and put it on the steps so I wouldn't ...rget it when I left."

"You didn't tell Mr. Balance you would be entering ...rough the garage?"

"No." Jane looked up to the doorway. "I was just going ... get the toolbox then go around to the front."

Jack stood in the doorway. He stared at Jane as he spoke. ...heard something in the garage and when I went out, it was

135

dark in there. The windows are shaded and I saw a figure by the workbench and I picked up the shovel and swung. I figured it might be the killer, Sandy's killer. I just didn't think."

"Mr. Balance, it was so dark that you couldn't recognize your neighbor, Mrs. Wheel?"

"It was dark, but it wasn't just that. I've been jumpy and I think my eyes were playing tricks on me. It seemed like a bigger person, just a stranger who didn't belong there, so I acted on impulse."

Jack stepped into the room. "Please forgive me, Jane. I am so sorry."

"What did you do after you swung the shovel?" Oh asked, almost whispering.

"I saw that it was Jane. I had my phone in my pocket and dialed nine-one-one and gave them the address. Then I picked Jane up and brought her up here."

"Mrs. Wheel was unconscious?"

"Yes."

"Mr. Balance, we'd like to talk to you further, but right now, may we have some time with Mrs. Wheel?"

Jack nodded. He had not let his eyes leave Jane for the entire time he stood in the doorway. He put his hand over his heart, massaging the little man riding the polo pony on his pale yellow golf shirt. Once again, Jane had the strange sensation that he was trying to send her a message. He left and they all listened to his footsteps descending the stairs.

"Mrs. Wheel, where in the Suburban was your toolbox?"

"Passenger side, front seat, floor."

"You're certain?"

"That's where I left it. That's where I always keep it."

"Susan, ask Tripp to bring up the toolbox." Oh leaned

in closer to Jane. "Still feeling up to answering questions, Mrs. Wheel?"

"It's not there."

"Pardon?"

"That's where I kept the toolbox. In the front seat. But it wasn't there. The front door was open. I saw into the van as I fell."

"You're certain?"

"Yes. And Jack's lying."

"Yes?" Oh seemed mildly interested at best.

"I don't know who hit me or with what, but Jack didn't carry me up here."

"No?"

"I was pretending to be out, but I watched him leave the room. He was wearing a dark T-shirt."

"Mr. Balance might have changed his shirt?"

"It wasn't Jack."

"No?"

Jane wondered how much longer Oh could get her to talk with his one-word questions. He was one of those patient men, unafraid of silence. He could wait. And Jane was one of those whose duty in life, it seemed, was to fill in the silences. She sat up farther in bed. She tested her head, her neck, by moving it slowly, side to side. Charley used to come home, shake his head absentmindedly about his day, and say, "Same old bones, you?" and she'd entertain him for hours with stories of clients and commercial shoots, actors and stylists. Her father, with his cocked head and welcoming smile, would set up a drink for her at the bar and let her ramble. He would nod and she would talk. That was the pattern. And Jack, Jack had just looked at her over a butterflied leg of lamb, and when no one talked, she kissed, filling in the silence. Now here she was, bruised and dizzy, much too involved in two murders.

"Jack wasn't the one who carried me up here," she repeated, not adding just yet that the man who had carried her, although strong enough, struggled with his breathing, wheezed the whole way.

Tripp appeared at the door, carrying her toolbox.

"Where did you find it?" she asked.

"Front seat, passenger side. Right where you said, Mrs. Wheel."

"See?" she whispered to Oh.

He shook his head slightly.

"There had to be someone else to put the toolbox back." She patted the bed and asked Tripp to set the old wooden chest by her.

Oh shook his head almost imperceptibly. Jane saw it, looked at Tripp who, she now noted, was wearing gloves.

"What's happened to them?"

Oh nodded to Tripp, who opened the box.

"Is everything here, Mrs. Wheel? Anything missing?"

Jane rested her eyes on each well-worn tool for a moment. She so desperately wanted to hold that hammer, that screwdriver in her hand. Her inventory took less than a minute.

"Can you get me out of this house?" Jane swung her feet onto the floor but knew she'd fall if she tried to stand alone.

Oh continued to look at her. She felt the tears coming, but it wasn't until she glanced over at Susan Mile, who clearly looked as miserable as a police officer could, that Jane began to cry.

"My saw," she said, and curled her right hand around its

imaginary handle and held it in front of her. "My saw is gone."

When no one rose to help her, Jane stood alone and fell back on the bed. Susan and Oh rose at the same time and took positions on either side of her. Although Jane hadn't seen anything, Oh must have given Tripp a signal to disappear with the toolbox.

They walked with her slowly down the hall, Jane insisting that she felt stronger with every step. They approached the master suite, which was to their right, at the top of the stairs.

Jane noticed something through the open door. "Wait."

Susan began to hold her back, but Oh let go and simply watched her walk into Sandy Balance's bedroom. Boxes were piled high, sealed and labeled. The boxes were the kind you purchased flat, three to a package. When folded into shape, they were sturdy with tight-fitting lids. These had a green-and-white English ivy pattern covering them. The plastic they had been wrapped in was in the wastebasket next to the dresser. There were still a few garments hanging in the closet, but dresser drawers stood open and empty. No Clinique lipstick on the dressing table, no little dish with chains and rings and Sandy's grandmother's Bulova watch that she wore every day, no Elizabeth Arden nail polish on the bathroom vanity.

"What time is it?" Jane asked.

"Five past four," Susan answered.

"When was Jack allowed to move things in the house?"

"Midmorning he was allowed to go upstairs," Susan answered again. Oh watched Jane.

Jane opened her mouth, but stopped when she looked at Oh. *Damn him. I will not talk for him,* she thought. *I will count to ten before I say anything. I will bite my tongue. I will not* ask how Jack could possibly have done all this by himself in five hours. I will not question whether or not Jack could have been organized enough to have bought these boxes or labeled them so neatly or cleared the cosmetics and everyday artifacts so completely. I will not ask aloud why Jack asked for my help, why he pretended to need it, why he leaves plaintive messages on my answering machine or gives me that cow-eyed stare whenever anyone is watching. I will not ruminate on why he wanted me here and why he hit me with a shovel and why he's lying about carrying me up here.

"Fast worker," Jane said.

11

Jane accepted a ride from Detective Oh back to her house, even though it was less than two blocks, just around the corner. She didn't want to run into any of the neighbors, particularly Barbara Graylord, who would broadcast Jane's visit to the house and her unsteady walk home.

She remained closemouthed, began to appreciate the silence riding next to Oh. It wasn't uncomfortable; it wasn't even her job to care if it was. When Oh parked in back of her house, she looked out to see Rita's nose pressed against the screen of the porch. Outside the screened-in area, sitting on the steps, was Tim. He was reading a paperback and drinking from a large travel mug.

"Mr. Lowry's come for a visit?"

Jane shrugged. It was a game now, and she was winning. Maybe she could actually get through the rest of her life, or at least this messiest chapter so far, without saying a word.

Jane got out and walked right into Tim's loose-limbed hug.

"What's happened? No more murders?" Tim looked at Detective Oh over Jane's shaking shoulders.

"No, but Mrs. Wheel was hit on the head. Mr. Balance

seems to have mistaken her for an intruder. If you're staying, you might want this."

Jane was touched to see Oh hand Tim the paramedic's written instructions. *Melvin really cared,* she thought.

"Standard procedure. You're watching for a concussion, but I think she's okay. Very big bruises tomorrow though."

"Anything new on Sandy? Or David for that matter? Kankakee police said I could come up here as long as I checked in with you, stayed available."

"There is always something new, Mr. Lowry; sometimes it just adds to the confusion." Oh looked at Jane. "Mrs. Wheel, ever travel to New York on business?"

Jane nodded.

"Ever stay at the Hotel Elycee?"

Jane shook her head no, but she was too scrupulous not to add, "But I've had drinks at the Monkey Bar."

Oh looked blankly at her, then glanced at the medical instructions in Tim's hand, as if checking to see if blurting out non sequiturs was a symptom for which they were supposed to be watching.

"It's in the Hotel Elycee," she said, remembering the martinis she and Charley had ordered. Charley had come with her to New York for business, and they'd stayed over the weekend, gone to museums and galleries, seen a show. That Saturday night, mild and warm, they had walked for blocks and blocks discussing whether they were ready to have a child.

"Just one more martini," Jane had said, "then I'll be ready." Nick was born almost exactly nine months later.

"Ah," Oh nodded. "One more thing, then I'll let you get some rest. Do you collect jewelry? Silver jewelry?"

"Can't afford anything that I'd like to collect. I like Bakelite bracelets, I have a few, but they've gotten too expensive. What I really want is Kalo silver. Hand-hammered bangles. Impossible to find."

"Out of your price range, too, pal," Tim added.

Jane shrugged and forgot all about her vow of silence.

"Kalo was a silver shop in Chicago in the early 1900s. Beautiful work of all kinds—not just jewelry, but beautiful tea sets, trays, serving pieces, everything. I have a small money clip that I found at a house sale, but it's the only piece I've ever found. Dealers are usually called in to appraise silver and jewelry from an estate before the public sale, and they scoop it up."

"Did Mrs. Balance have any Kalo?"

"Not that I know of. She knew I loved it, so she would have told me about it, shown me if she had some. Jack knew, too."

"Knew what?"

"I liked Kalo. He asked me to recommend a gift once for Sandy's birthday, something unique. I told him about the bracelets. Money was no object for him, so I thought he might find it through a dealer. We talked about it one night on their porch, too, because I'd found a book at a rummage sale, *Chicago Metalsmiths*. The book's out of print; it's worth over two hundred itself."

"How much?" Tim asked.

"One dollar," Jane said, with her biggest grin of the day.

"You da man," Tim said.

"Yes?" Oh prompted.

"I brought the book over and showed it to them one evening. Charley and I were there for drinks. It was last spring, early though, before . . ."

"Before?"

"Before I kissed Jack."

"Get some rest, Mrs. Wheel." Oh climbed into his car. "But not solid sleeping, remember. Wake her every few hours, Mr. Lowry."

Tim waved good-bye with Melvin's sheet of instructions.

Jane introduced Rita to Tim. She put two milk bones on a Lu-Ray, Sharon Pink dessert plate and set it down for the dog and filled two pressed glass tumblers with ice and set them in front of Tim and the bottle of Grey Goose vodka he took out of his leather backpack.

"One for me," Tim said, filling one glass, "and none for you." He walked over to the bottled water cooler and filled Jane's glass to the top.

"I'm supposed to keep you awake and look into your open eyes, not liquor you up and put you to bed," Tim said, rummaging through the refrigerator. "Got any vintage lemons in here? Collectible limes?"

Jane joined him at the door and pulled out a jar of salsa, a plastic container of humus, another container of something that might have been spinach dip, and a jar she waved in front of his face. "Antique olives."

They rustled chips and crackers from the cupboard and spread out the food on the table and Tim surveyed the kitchen. He pointed out the pitchers and water jugs that were new, sitting on top of the cabinets. "What's the one with strawberries?"

"Don't know. U.S.A. mark incised; took a picture and I'll show it to Miriam."

"Okay." Tim stood, sipping his glass of vodka. "Here's what I'd buy out of this kitchen." He pointed to a Yellow Ware bowl in the hutch, the embroidered Mother Goose dish towels hanging near the window, and a pair of Roseville pottery candlesticks in the Apple Blossom pattern. "And those," he said, jabbing his finger at the candlesticks, "would be just for old time's sake. I'd turn around and sell them in a week."

"I've had that bowl over twenty-five years, Timmy. I got it for fifty cents at an auction when I was in college. You can have the dish towel as a present, I have two sets I got at an estate sale for under ten, and the candlesticks were Grandma's," Jane said, finishing her water. "Now tell me why you're so mad at all my finds."

"I just want you to sell up, dearie. Take your junk pottery, the McCoy planters and pots, the unmarked stuff, the *Haeger* for god's sake," Tim said, choking on the name *Haeger*, "and sell it all, every bit of it and buy one good piece. A Hampshire vase from around 1910 would be lovely. That green matte glaze that everybody thinks is all Grueby was used by Hampshire at least four years earlier." Tim closed his eyes in rapture for a moment then came back to consciousness.

"You're filling up this house, sweetie, with all the wrong stuff."

Jane put her head down on her hands and sighed.

"Don't go to sleep."

"I'm not. Just hiding from you."

"Honey, you've done filled up your house with everything you can find. Look at that stack of embroidered tablecloths, for god's sake. Why do you think you're doing that?"

Jane held up her hands in mock despair. "Tell me, Doc; tell me please."

"You are looking for love in all the wrong places, Jane."

"Ooh, jukebox psychology, I love it. Maybe I just like this stuff, these embroidered tablecloths. By the way, some are napkins and dresser scarves."

" 'Material Girl.' "

"Stop."

" 'In the Name of Love.' What the hell is this?"

"It's an Osbourne ivorex plaque, tourist souvenir from England, 1908. See, it's a scene from Dickens, *The Old Curiosity Shop*."

Tim poured another drink and threw in three olives. "And this? What are you going to do with this tin cake thing?"

"Carry my homemade devil's food to the ice-cream social?" Jane stood up and stretched, testing which part of her hurt the most. Shoulders, definitely. Richard's doorframe and Jack's shovel had made a lasting impression. "Timmy, look into my eyes."

" 'Brown Eyed Girl.' "

"It's been more than two hours, my pupils are not dilated, I'm having a drink."

"No." Tim moved the bottle away from Jane.

"Yes, Tim, and you can't stop me," she said, slapping his hand away from the Grey Goose and spearing two olives with a fork.

"Man, you are a mean sober."

Jane poured an inch of vodka, led Tim away from his appraisal of kitchen items, and sat him down facing her.

"Why were you on my doorstep, Tim?"

" 'You've Got a Friend'?"

"More like 'Bridge Over Troubled Water' right now, don't you think?"

"You're getting it. I just figured you didn't need to be alone right now. Weekly calls from Charley and Nick do not a happy household make."

"I've got a date with Richard."

"I don't trust him."

"Why? He's clumsy, but . . ."

"I've seen him around for years. His father was in the business, too. He's got a posse that would make a rapper jealous. Big thuggons who do the work."

"Thuggons?"

"Crossbreeding. Thugs plus morons."

"I'm just going to have dinner with him. No animal husbandry experiments."

"That's what the seedless cucumber's mother said."

"Timmy, I'm going to solve the murder."

"Which one?"

"First Sandy's, then David's." Jane refilled her glass.

"You're going to get drunk, Nancy Drew, then you'll be no good to anyone."

"I've been clubbed and beaten over the last few days. This is the Darvon I didn't take."

"You are so old-fashioned."

"Yeah, like Nick and Nora Charles: no pills, just booze."

"Nobody takes Darvon anymore."

"Gonna help me or not?"

"Yes, Nancy, but I'm not going to play that tomboy George. Who was her other sidekick?"

"Bess Marvin? Blond and plump?"

"No, I'll be Helen, the one who showed up in a few.

She was Nancy's real love. Ned Nickerson was just the beard for those two."

"Don't start."

"Come on. Feminine Bess and her cousin, Tomboy George. Those weren't telling us some kind of yin and yang thing about Nancy? Grow up."

"I'm taking a hot shower then going to bed."

Tim rinsed their glasses, put the bottle of Grey Goose in the refrigerator, and gathered up all the food on the table.

"What are you doing?" Jane asked, watching Tim toss everything down the disposal.

"Sorry, babe, this stuff should have been thrown out weeks ago. Detective Oh'll put you on top of the suspect list if he sees this stuff. Lucrezia Borgia ain't got nothing on you."

Jane stood unsteadily. "Timmy, maybe you ought to help me up the stairs. You can have Nicky's room. Or you can sleep with me. We can cuddle." Jane looked up into Tim's open, freckled face.

Tim nodded. Melvin's instructions cautioned that Jane should be checked every two hours for the first twenty-four.

"Yes, honey, we'll pretend it's summer camp. I'll be your counselor and you be homesick."

"Tim, we're really going to solve the murders, aren't we? You're serious about that, right?"

" 'For Once in My Life.' "

12

Jane woke up and slipped out of bed without waking Tim. She brushed her teeth, went downstairs and made coffee, sent Rita out for a quick trip around the backyard, and fixed a tray with coffee and toasted bagels.

"Surprise, Timmy."

"Flowers," Tim groaned, squinting at the tray through one eye.

"What?"

"Flowers on the tray. A little bouquet of sweet peas would be nice."

"Guess what, Sweet Pea? You have to *really* sleep with me, you know, not just *sleep* with me, to get flowers on your damn tray." Jane backhanded his leg.

"I guess you don't have a concussion, huh? Or anything broken?" Tim had both eyes open now, studying her.

"No concussion and I broke down and took ibuprofen for the aches and pains, so I'm feeling fine."

When Jane turned away from him to put the tray on the dresser, Tim could see the fresh coloring on her right shoulder, the older purple fading on her left.

"You look like a topographical map, honey."

"Did you bring a suit?"

"I always carry a sport coat. It's hanging in the car. Why?"

"Sandy's memorial's at ten."

Jane owned four black dresses, none of which she or Tim deemed appropriate for the service. Too skimpy, too tight, too sheer, too wooly. Tim pushed hanger after hanger to the side, muttering about her taste, her fashion sense.

"Here you go, Goldilocks; this one should be just right."

"What's happening at the store?" Jane walked behind her grandmother's three-paneled screen to slip out of her robe and into the forest green linen sheath Tim had selected.

"As far as I can tell, the police will keep me closed until they're done with the investigation; and from what I've seen of their police work, I might as well scout a new location."

"Details?"

"They're fixated on this as a crime of passion. Ex-lover, spurned lover, jealous lover, that's what they're looking for."

"Maybe they're right. Charley and my dad, both without knowing any details at all, said that Jack killed Sandy, and I thought they were being ridiculous. Too much TV detecting, you know, but now I'm not so sure."

"You think it could be Jack? I'm not saying I think the man's a straight shooter exactly, but a murderer?" asked Tim.

"You don't even know the half of it. The lies he's told. The secrets he's kept. He's lived a made-up life, for god's sake. I don't know. He doesn't seem like a murderer to me either; but everybody thinks the husband's the obvious choice, and I don't know whether we should keep fighting the obvious," Jane said, zipping up her dress carefully, trying to protect her sore shoulder.

"What's the obvious with David? He wasn't in a relationship that I know of, played the field a bit, I guess. Was planning to move to California as soon as he got the money. Flirted with me, but really was more interested in building a career."

"What career?" asked Jane.

"Decorator? Designer? He just liked buying nice things with other people's money," Tim said, sorting the beaded necklaces hanging next to Jane's dresser.

"Did he buy for anybody besides you?"

"Yeah, probably. He didn't make enough working for me. He still lived at home though. With his parents. Wouldn't have a whole lot of expenses, but . . ."

"But?" Jane asked, slipping gold hoops through her ears.

"Expensive taste. Wore an Armani tie a few weeks ago and some Gucci loafers. I asked him where he'd gotten the money. . . ."

"And?" Jane ran her fingers through her still damp hair and shook her head. Her short, short hair fell into shape around her face. "Stop drifting off and making me dig for everything."

"I hadn't really thought of this stuff before. You know, I was too busy thinking *Why me, why does this happen in my shop?* I hadn't really thought about *Why David?* that much. I always assume serendipity. Someone crazy murders someone unlucky."

"What? Wrong place at wrong time?"

"Something like that."

"Well, Timmy, let's just figure that anyone who gets murdered is at the wrong place at the wrong time. On the other hand, let's also figure that people mostly make their own luck, bad or good. So what did David say when you asked him where he got the money to dress like that?"

"That I wasn't the only starfish in the sea."

Sandy's memorial was not well attended. Her father was escorted by a large woman who, although she wore a navy blue suit, tastefully accessorized with a pale yellow print scarf, could not camouflage her position as his attendant, ready to manhandle him at any moment. She kept a firm grip on his arm and never took her eyes off his face. When he opened his mouth to speak, she raised her chin and parted her own lips slightly, a ventriloquist making sure her patient didn't say the wrong thing at the inappropriate moment. The patient, Sandy's father, seemed compliant enough, but clearly confused about what he was doing at the Wyman Funeral Home on a sunny Wednesday morning. Occasionally he whispered to the navy suit, "When will Sandy be here?"

Jane counted up the neighbors. Barbara and her husband, Michael, or Matthew, Jane could never remember, but she knew the monograms on the towels in their guest bath had an M and a B surrounding a gothic G. Why could she remember details like that? Jane had been in the Graylords' powder room once, during that damn progressive dinner. She'd drunk too much that night and still remembered all the decorating decisions, successes, and glitches of all the neighbors in whose homes she munched and sipped.

She remembered that the Hoovers, sitting now in the second row, had a gorgeous arts and crafts lamp in their living room. She had to pinch both her arms and bite her tongue not to ask permission to carefully remove the glass shade and look for signatures and marks on the base. Charley had seen her mutilating herself, had read the curiosity, no, lust, in her eyes, and had hissed in her ear, "You're not shopping here. This is a party, not some flea sale."

"Flea market, rummage sale, Charley. For god's sake, I thought you could name the deadly sins."

They smiled hard at each other, and Jane remembered fluttering her eyelashes at her husband as she walked over to refresh her drink, purposely eyeballing the crystal decanter to make Charley squirm.

Why was I so mean to poor Charley? Jane thought. Tim squeezed her arm; and for a moment, Jane thought he was reading her mind, emphatically agreeing, yeah, why were you so damn mean to sweet Charley? But Tim was nodding toward the other side of the funeral home. "Do you know who that is?" he whispered.

A tall, thin, middle-aged man, rather ordinary looking except for his walking stick, which had elaborate carving on its handle, had slid into a seat across the aisle.

Jane shook her head.

"He's a dealer in fine antiques. Has a small shop in the city, but travels all over the world as an appraiser and consultant. Horace Cutler. I sold some silver through him once from Doc Plotkin's estate."

"I was at that sale. I just remember some old plate."

"Yeah, I took the really good stuff out and sold it separately. Better deal for the family."

"Better deal for T & T, too, Tiny Tim?"

"Sure. But an open sale is always a crap shoot, no matter how many dealers sleep in their trucks outside the night before. This was A-1 stuff that could get much more at auction, and through a Horace Cutler it could get to the right people in the right places."

"He reminds me of somebody," said Jane.

"I wouldn't mind working for him myself, freelance, of course."

"That's who he reminds me of," said Jane.

"Who?" asked Tim.

"David."

"He's thirty years older than David," said Tim.

"But they wear the same ties."

Tim studied the elegant Cutler and shrugged. "Same build, same Gucci loafers." At that moment, Cutler, his eyes circling the room, stared briefly at Tim and Jane. He looked away with the slightest raise of an eyebrow. Simultaneously, Tim and Jane spoke.

"Same sneer."

"Same affectation."

Detective Oh and Officer Mile sat in the back of the room and nodded slightly when Jane turned around to see who might have come in after them. She recognized a handful of neighbors, none of whom even nodded in her direction.

"Friendly group of folks," Tim said.

"Remind me to move."

The service was brief. As far as Jane could tell, no members of Jack's family attended. Sandy's father left on the arm of the attendant without speaking to Jack, with the same clouded look on his face, his eyes frantically scanning the crowd, most probably for his daughter. The neighbors exited quickly. Horace Cutler nodded slightly to Jack but didn't stop. There were no tears, Jane observed sadly. Barbara Graylord stabbed at her eyes with a tissue, but Jane was sure it was only for effect.

Tim noticed that Oh and Mile were waiting around in the parking lot and took Jane's hand to lead her over to them.

"In a minute. Tell them I have to do something that will take two minutes and thirty-six seconds. Or just stall for that long. I don't care."

Jane watched Tim detour over to Jack to pay his respects. Jack nodded at everything Tim was saying; then he shrugged and turned away.

"What could they have to say to each other?" Jane muttered. She hoped Tim wasn't trying to protect her, acting as Charlie's surrogate and warning Jack away. She wanted to take care of Jack herself.

Jane got in her car, shut the door, and despite the heat did not open any windows or turn on the engine for the air conditioner. Tim thought he heard music playing inside the car, shrugged, and approached Oh.

"Is it procedure to attend murder victims' funerals?" Tim asked.

"Sometimes. There are always things to be learned."

"Can you say what you learned here? Seemed like a curiously frozen group of mourners in there."

"Yes, but with surprises. Why would Horace Cutler be there?"

"You know him?" Tim asked.

"My wife is an antique dealer of sorts. Occasionally she'll

drag me to a show or a reception, and she's pointed him out before."

"I was with Jack and Sandy a few times up here visiting Jane and Charley, and I never got the impression they were collectors in Cutler's league."

"I didn't think they collected at all," said Oh.

"That's what I . . ."

Jane opened her car door and Oh, Mile, and Tim all watched her as she emerged from her Nissan.

She wiped her perspiring face with a blue-and-white dotted handkerchief, shook her head, and came over to their group.

"A terrible service, wasn't it?" Jane asked, not expecting an answer. "Jack couldn't even pick out a song? Left it to the funeral director to put on that canned organ music?"

Tim saw that Jane was shaking all over, ready to explode.

"That asshole probably did kill her."

"Jane." Tim tried to give her a silencing glance, the pleading kind he saw in movies all the time, the one that said, not in front of a police detective. Please don't lose your mind here.

"Oh, shut up, Tim. I didn't do it and Detective Oh knows it. Jack isn't even trying to fake it. Sandy talked about music all the time, always had a CD on. I heard her say a million times what she wanted played at her funeral. So did Jack."

Tim looked over at Jane's car.

"Yeah, I had the tape in the car so I went and listened to 'Ring Them Bells.' Joan Baez." Jane swallowed hard and looked at Oh. "I take back everything I said that first night about not knowing Sandy very well." Jane looked at the parking lot, all the cars of the neighbors gone except for the Gray-lords, who were still inside with Jack.

Jane let the tears slide down her cheeks. "I think maybe I was her best friend."

13

Jack didn't invite anyone to a luncheon. No one would be receiving visitors at the house; no restaurant was named where funeral guests might gather. There was no procession to a cemetery, since Sandy's body, murdered once, then violated a hundred times over by the coroner and his staff, would eventually be cremated. He left with the Graylords and, as far as Jane and Tim could tell, drove home. They followed the Graylords' dark town car for most of the way; then Tim turned into a convenience store a few blocks from Jane's house.

"I'm picking up a few things for lunch. Wait here." Tim patted her knee and slid out from the driver's side,

Jane's anger hadn't stopped. It was growing exponentially. The more she thought about the generic service, the obvious lack of thought and care, the more she fumed. The minister, one whom Jack had pulled out of someone's hat since the Balances had no church affiliation, had read from two index cards, reciting Sandy's achievements and activities like so many lines under a senior picture in a high-school yearbook. Oh had said he was stopping at his office then coming by with some pictures he wanted Jane to look at. She would give him a piece of her mind; she would let him know that it was time to solve this. Sandy had been murdered long enough.

Leaning back in her seat, she stretched and tested out her neck, her shoulders. *That ibuprofen stuff really works,* she thought, *I ought to start making my life a little easier and take a pill more often.* Everyone said that when you hit forty everything hurt. She had noticed stiffness some mornings, a little ache in her elbow after working on the computer or carrying props around a set all day. Occasionally, her lower back felt vaguely out of synch with the rest of her body. Her father had warned her that it was hell to get old. He'd doctored his own arthritis for years, taking Tylenol all day long.

"Oh, god," Jane said out loud and sat up straight. Her father was going in for his test. Her mother had called and left a message while Jane was out in the yard with the dog that morning. She had been away from the house only two minutes, but her mother's radar had, of course, known which two minutes. Jane ran to the answering machine and jammed the start button and got her mother's typical nongreeting.

Yeah? It's Nellie. Your mother. Your dad got a call that there was an opening for him today, so Dwight is driving him to Urbana for that CT scan. CT scam, if you ask me. We're leaving right now, so don't call. I'll be at the bar. Where are you anyway? Call at three.

Jane had called then anyway and listened to the phone ring over and over. Her dad might have cancer. Why not? He was a saloon keeper and lung cancer was a saloon-keeper's disease. He had always expected it, waited for it. Now it was here. Jane would have to care for him; Michael was too busy. Bigger job, bigger family. He was too far away anyway. Nellie wouldn't be able to do anything. Oh yeah, she was hell on wheels with a bar rag and could dish up soup and sandwiches and Miller's on tap all day long, but she had never learned to drive. She had no idea how to keep the books, pay the bills. As far as Jane knew, her mother had never even written a check.

Jane started when Tim opened the car door. "I'm going to dazzle you with lunch. You haven't eaten in about a year. Then we're going to make some plans," Tim said, taking charge.

Jane nodded, even though she had no interest in lunch or plans. She just needed to get home and do something before total paralysis took over. She had three hours before her father would be home from his test. For three hours he could just be Dad, her healthy dad.

Tim shooed her off to go change and wash her face. Jane heard Tim rummaging through drawers. "Christ, you got a can opener made after 1950 in here?"

"The one mounted on the wall by the door works." She couldn't resist adding, "I guess I just don't cook from cans."

She could hear Tim muttering, but she cut him off. "I'm taking Rita out for a quick walk."

Jane should have felt at home in her own neighborhood, but in the bright, midday sunshine, walking a dog that wasn't really hers around a block where no one looked her in the eye made her feel like a tourist in an unfamiliar layer of hell. She was used to the ninth circle, reserved for flatterers. She had, after all, been in advertising. But now she was meandering around the eighth with the psychopaths and was having trouble negotiating the turns.

Rita, used to running around the backyard, seemed delighted to be accompanying Jane on a walk, a normal dog thing to do. Jane looked down at her wagging tail, trying not to feel guilty.

"You're not really mine, you know. Charley and Nick should be able to make me feel guilty, but you need to let me off with a warning," she said, trying not to move her lips. No reason to let the neighbors, who she was sure were all peeking out from tipped blinds, note that she was now talking to a strange dog.

Jane led Rita toward Sandy's, she would never call it Jack's, not after today, and turned into the alley behind the house. Rita stopped. Finishing her business, she looked up expectantly at Jane, who realized she hadn't brought a plastic bag. Oh man, one more thing they can say about me. She's a snob, she's a bitch, she's a tramp, she's a killer, and, did you know, she doesn't pick up after her dog? Jane kicked leaves in the direction of Rita's proud little mess and glanced over at the recycling bin behind Sandy's house. Maybe there was a bag she could use in there.

No bag on top and she didn't really want to dig too deeply. She took a piece of newspaper off the top. Switching the leash from her hand to her wrist so she could wad up the paper into a scoop, Jane noticed the section of the paper she was holding. The classifieds. Not that strange. The section that most people toss into the recycling bin first. But this paper looked familiar to her. She shook out the paper so inner pages fluttered to the ground and she was holding a single sheet. Tiny rectangles of sunlight shone through the paper, and danced over the ground. She held the paper up closer to her face. The small three- and six-line ads for garage sales and estate sales had been lifted from the paper. Someone had used the tape method on this paper to organize their weekend shopping, to make their map through the suburban rummage and trash and treasures. This is the way her classified section looked every Thursday. In fact, checking the date, Jane verified that this was last Thursday's paper. She had the mundane thought that Jack hadn't gotten his recycling out in time, since their neighborhood pickup was on Friday. Since she had been out of regular work, Jane had rigidly stuck to her weekend picking routine. She pulled out the promising ads in the paper on Thursday, made her map, and readied her file cards. She checked Miriam's wants-and-needs list, filling in her own clients' requests. Then, as compulsively neat and clean on the first floor as she was unorganized and messy on the second, since Charley and Nick had left, she tossed all the recycling, including the skeleton classifieds, into the bin and carried it into the alley before going up to bed.

Why did Sandy and Jack have a picker's paper?

"What on earth are you doing?"

Jane turned to face Barbara Graylord. She had a garbage bag in her hands, but carried it awkwardly away from her body, to protect her black Dana Buchman suit. A passerby might think she was shielding herself from Jane with a Hefty bag. That or offering it to her for approval.

Jane was surprised to see the fear in Barbara's eyes. Yes, this woman was silly, a gossip, a woman who hung monogrammed towels in her guest powder room next to overpriced designer bath accessories, who filled new-but-distressed-to-look-antique porcelain bowls with expensive potpourri. This was a woman who spent tens of thousands of dollars on rooms of Early American furniture reproductions matched to machine-made rugs fashioned to look handwoven. But despite her love of affectation and disrespect for the real and true, Barbara Graylord could not be entirely stupid. Surely she did not think Jane had taken a small hacksaw to Sandy Balance's throat. Even if it turned out to be, god forbid, Jane's hacksaw.

"Barbara, I . . ." Jane had nothing to say, no explanation.

"On the day of the woman's funeral, you come over here?" Barbara kept the garbage bag between them. "You paw through the woman's trash before her ashes are in the urn? What on earth are you hoping to find? Her clothes? Her jewelry? Some goddamn pottery?"

Barbara's voice grew louder and louder, as if she was calling on all the neighbors to join her.

"You are a vulture!" she screamed. "A scavenger! A rat!" Barbara threw down the bag, a bulging reeking gauntlet, and it hit the metal can with such force that the plastic ripped and grapefruit rinds, diet Coke, and Slim-Fast cans rolled out into the alley.

"Wasn't Jack enough? Now you want her . . ." Barbara looked at the wooden platform that held the Balance garbage cans and recycling bin, but there were no bundles, no objects except the newspapers in the red plastic crate. Her tirade had alerted at least three other neighbors plus Barbara's husband, M for monogram, who had come out into the alley. She looked around at her audience wildly and shrieked, "Now you want her recycling?"

M came and took Barbara's arm and turned her back into her own yard, but she continued to scream about the tramp, the home wrecker. Jane never heard her say murderer,

163

killer, but she looked around at the few people who stood rooted to their own little garbage nests in the alley and read that disturbing message in their eyes.

Jane stared back at those watching her, judging her. Jane had either been crying or fainting since Saturday. She had been floundering since losing her job. She had been unmoored since Charley and Nick left. What the hell, she had been damned confused since turning forty. Now she cleared her throat. Jane had been looking in all the wrong mirrors to find out what she looked like, who she was. Who were all these people to judge her anyway?

"I was just walking my dog," she said evenly.

Dean Valder, a seventyish retired banker who lived three doors east of the Balances, walked over and nodded to Jane.

"What is she?"

"I'm not sure, but she cheats on her recycling," Jane said, pointing to all the cans rolling around the alley.

Dean reached down to pet Rita. "I meant your dog."

Jane nodded an "I know" and smiled.

"Just a bitch," she said.

Jane turned toward the street, toward her home. One by one she met the eyes of the neighbors who lingered in their backyards. "This confidence might not last," she whispered to Rita, "but it sure beats feeling beat."

Rita, on the other paw, had lost all the fire and energy Jane had gained. At the Balance garbage cans, as soon as Barbara began berating her mistress, Rita had hung her head. Now she half-heartedly sniffed at the garbage can and recycling bin, then backed away, continuing to hang her head and moan.

"What is it?" Jane stopped and stooped to stroke Rita's head, but the dog quickly ducked and turned away.

Dean Valder, still taking stock of Rita, nodded again. "That dog's been beat. You get her from a shelter?"

"She just showed up at my door."

"Dogs are smart enough. They'll find someone good to take care of them, if they get the chance," Valder said, smiling at Jane. "Then their confidence comes back. I don't think that Graylord woman has any pets." He waved and shuffled back to his own back gate, humming under his breath.

Why didn't the Valders ever come to those damn progressive dinners? Them I might have liked, Jane thought, coaxing the dog to get up and move. She couldn't remember any of Mile's hand signals, so she rubbed Rita's head and ears and talked to her. She could feel the big animal tremble under her touch.

"I will never hurt you, Rita," Jane promised, as they walked out into the street.

Whether it was Jane's words or the distance they put between themselves and the Balance alley, Rita perked up. By the time they got home, dog and owner had a bounce and wag in their steps.

"Took you long enough," Tim said, arranging sprouts on top of Romaine. He had used her favorite platter, oversized off-white Buffalo china, with what Jane assumed was a club or restaurant monogram, wGc, in green script. The platter seemed too thick, too heavy for home use.

"This plate weighs five pounds empty. How practical is that?" Tim complained, as he crumbled bacon and hard-boiled egg over the salad.

"Keeps me out of the gym."

Jane surveyed the food, which, to her surprise, looked like the best meal she had ever seen. But it was the presentation that truly dazzled. Tim had made thick sandwiches with what he had found at the deli counter at the White Hen: salami, turkey, cheese, pickles, and built them higher with tomato and lettuce. Rummaging through her vintage utensils, he had found cocktail skewers with Bakelite squirrels and bunnies perched on their tops. He used them to fasten the monster Dagwoods, so the platter of sandwiches, the salad, and the Fiesta-ware-clad table looked like a picnic out of the pages of *Better Homes and Gardens*, circa 1956. He had dragged down a bright red ball jug from above her refrigerator and made fresh lemonade. Jane had forgotten that the depression glass reamers could actually be used for squeezing lemons. Perfectly pulled through Bakelite Scottie napkin rings—the originals, not the Restoration Hardware reproductions—were cloth napkins that matched the tablecloth, a bright blue cotton covered with red ripe cherries and golden peaches.

"Is it lunch or an illustration for one of your sales brochures?"

"I would like a picture before we start, if you don't mind."

Both Tim and Jane always carried cameras. It was important to not only photograph what you had—all the better to compare your stuff with the dealers' stuff at the mall, my dear—but also to photograph what you wanted. Tim had taught her that. If you love it, take a picture. If it calls out to you in the night, demands its own silver frame and a place by your bed, if you find the photo in your wallet next to your sons' and daughters' school pictures, you might have to go back and get the object itself. Tim kept a photo album in his car that held pictures of china patterns, lace curtain panels, hundreds of pieces of silver, Van Briggle vases. Miriam had also taught Jane to take photographs but had been less dramatic.

"You think you'll remember the color of a plate or the pattern of a quilt forever, but after the fourth hour at a decent flea market, you won't remember your Cross and Crown from your Heart and Gizzard."

When Jane had stared blankly, Miriam had given an impromptu lecture on nineteenth-century American quilt patterns. She had then handed her a disposable camera from her seemingly endless stash of them and warned her never to leave home without one or two in her pockets. She would need them to find her way back to whatever she wanted to buy as well as to learn fair pricing. It also helped that Jane could bring photos to Miriam, who had never once been stumped over the use, name, or history of an object no matter how old, how tarnished, how obscure, or how corrupted.

Tim's camera was a tiny, silver Olympus that fit unobtrusively in the pocket of his sport coat. The latest model. He pulled it out and shot the table from two angles.

"Remember, Tim, none of this is for sale," Jane said, placing her napkin on her lap and digging into the salad.

"Not until you get an offer," Tim said, biting into one of the sandwiches and, after some difficulty chewing the two-inch-high creation, managing to swallow. "That's the fun of it. Sell it and find something better."

"I'm working on the letting go part."

"Heard from Charley and Nick?"

Jane squinted her eyes at Tim and growled. "I'm not going to bite. I've got detective news."

"Ah, Nancy, let Helen pour you some lemonade while . . ."

"Was that a knock?" Jane asked. Both Jane and Tim cocked their heads. A faint rapping came from the front of the house.

When she got to the front door, Detective Oh was trying to fix Jane's hand-carved folk art door knocker.

"I'm so sorry; I've broken your bird's neck."

After pulling the leather string attached to the woodpecker's tail and seeing that no part of the bird moved or made a noise, Oh had pushed on the head itself, causing the bird to peck at the striking plate, making a half-hearted knock.

"It's okay, I just have to fish out the rubber band and hook it like so," Jane said, attaching the loop to a small hook under the wooden beak. "See?" Jane pulled gently on the string and the woodpecker's head bobbed back and forth, striking the metal plate, sounding a definitive knock.

"Charming," Oh said. "Collectible door knockers, too?"

Officer Mile carried a large envelope, but Oh kept his hands carefully in his pockets as they walked back to the kitchen. He noted all the displays, the still lifes that filled the living room on one side of the front hall and the dining room on the other. Stacks of old books used as pedestals, one for a tangle of vintage reading glasses, one for three brown fish bottles, their corked mouths stretching up to the ceiling. They might have been angling for the old fishing lures that hung from an antique silver chandelier, unwired, but glowing in its faded glory. An old fishing creel leaned up against the mantel next to a large twig frame. The photograph was circa 1930, fishermen with huge cigars hanging from their mouths, their arms draped over each other's shoulders.

"I hope you're here because you've solved the crime."

"We have something we'd like you to look at." Oh stopped when he saw the lunch laid out on the table. "I'm sorry, we're interrupting."

Tim stood. "We have so much; please join us."

"No, but . . ." Oh seemed overcome at the sight of the table.

Officer Mile didn't try to hide her pleasure. She looked ready to clap her hands in delight.

"It's like my mother made a table." Oh revealed the trace of an accent, the first Jane had heard. His speech, she now realized, was formal but seemed natural enough for a police officer, a reserved one at that. Now she heard the slight hesitation of someone who spoke or perhaps listened in more than one language.

"My mother was determined to make my father and me very American. She read every magazine and watched every show. We displayed flags and had backyard picnics and everything was bright, red, white, and blue. None of my all-American friends had homes that looked like the ones on television programs. We did."

"Where was your mother born?" Jane asked.

"Cleveland, Ohio."

"No wonder she wanted to assimilate," Tim said.

"My father was born in Japan, but immigrated here when he was quite young."

He indicated to Mile that they should sit, but shook his head at the offer of food. "Nothing for me, thank you. Officer Mile?"

Mile accepted a glass of lemonade and set the envelope on the table.

For a moment they were all silent, staring at it.

"I hope that's the warrant for Jack's arrest," Jane said finally.

"You call yourself a detective, Nancy?" Tim scowled. "They don't carry arrest warrants around in big envelopes like that. They take them out of their inside jacket pockets, like so." Tim demonstrated with a folded napkin, holding it over his heart. He then flashed it in Jane's face, clapped it back to his heart, then shook it out and placed it on his lap. "Right, Detective Oh?"

"Sometimes we let them read a few lines before we whisk it away."

"Yeah, but you don't put it on the table like the eight-hundred-pound gorilla, right?"

They all returned their eyes to the envelope.

"I'm afraid it's not the solution to the crime, Mrs. Wheel. It's just a sketch."

Officer Mile removed the papers from the envelope and set out two sketches of what appeared to be a smartly dressed woman. She placed them in front of Jane, and Tim leaned over so their heads touched, studying the drawings.

"It looks like me, doesn't it, Tim?"

"The hair. Or lack thereof."

"I think it looks a lot like me, except . . ."

"Yes?" Oh leaned forward slightly.

Tim finished, "Except the suit." He looked at Jane. "That's the suit."

Tim and Jane both started laughing.

Oh and Mile sat patiently still, although Mile's expression showed clearly that she wanted to be let in on the joke.

"Do you believe it? That's the very suit."

"Your suit, Mrs. Wheel?" Mile couldn't resist asking, even though Oh sat without revealing any curiosity.

"The suit I should have," Jane said. "This morning Tim was despairing at my wardrobe and told me that I really needed to have a well-tailored, grown-up suit like this. This is the one he described. 'Boxy, yet tailored jacket, three buttons, slim skirt, fitted, but not slinky, in a charcoal or black, just below the knee.' Look, Timmy, she's even wearing the right sensible pumps."

"What? No Birkenstocks with her Donna Karan?"

"I don't do that," Jane said.

"You don't wear the wrong shoes with Donna because you don't own Donna. What in the world did you wear to work?" asked Tim.

"It was advertising, Timmy, and most of the time I was considered a creative type."

Oh cleared his throat. "Anything else strike you about the sketch, Mrs. Wheel?"

"Well, it's me wearing a suit I should own, but I would never wear that bracelet with it, no matter what he advised." She nodded her head toward Tim. "I have a carved red Bakelite bangle, about an inch and a half wide, that I'd wear with this."

"That'd be okay," Tim said. "You know, classic with a touch of whimsy. I like it. But this looks like a nice little hammered metal number. Too bad we don't have more color and details here, Detective."

"You could probably tell who made the bracelet then, right?" Detective Oh asked.

Jane leaned closer to the sketch. "Actually this looks like a Kalo bangle, doesn't it, Timmy? The detail of the little marks here?"

"That's a stretch—you're seeing what you want to see." Tim looked up at Oh.

"Picker's disease," he explained. "They want to find something so badly; then they get home and their Bakelite turns out to be painted wood or plain old plastic, their Kalo turns out to be a hippie-made bent spoon handle turned into a bracelet."

"The gentleman who directed the sketch was quite particular about the bracelet. He remembered it because he said she touched it all the time and seemed to admire it. Called attention to it," Oh said.

Jane excused herself and went into the living room. When she returned with a hefty coffee-table book, Tim's eyes lit up. "I want one of those."

"I'll keep my eyes open," Jane said, paging through *Chicago Metalsmiths: An Illustrated History*, until she reached the section on the Kalo shop. "See, it's got this look to it, the way it's sketched."

She pointed to a small arts-and-crafts-style pitcher where the metal showed tiny hammer marks, giving the piece texture.

"You don't have a Kalo braclet like this though?"

"No bracelet like this." Jane sighed.

"Mrs. Balance had no bracelet like this?"

Jane shook her head. "If Jack had found one for her, she would have called me right away."

"You know who this looks like, kind of?" Tim was still staring at the sketch.

Mile and Oh said together, "Who?"

"Audrey Hepburn."

Mile raised her eyebrows. Oh did not change expression. "Do you really think I look like Audrey Hepburn?"

"No, dear. This sketch looks a bit like you, but it looks more like Audrey Hepburn, like someone sort of gussied up for a part. It's like an Edith Head costume sketch or something."

Mile explained to Oh, "A Hollywood costume designer. Nineteen-fifties mostly, right?" She looked at Tim, who nodded.

"She looks costumed, that's all. There's something about the way she's holding her head, her body."

"Like she's afraid something's going to rip," Jane added.

"Or fall off."

"So who did it?" Jane asked, standing to pour more lemonade.

Oh looked at Mile, who seemed to have no popular culture translation for this.

Tim waved the thin, photocopied sketch at the police officers. "If we're going to appraise it, we have to know more about the materials used and what you know about it, the artist, if the original is signed, numbered, if there's any writing on the back . . ." Tim stopped as the silence grew heavy in the room. "Oh, fuck me, I forgot what we were doing here. This is a police sketch, isn't it?"

"Timmy, you're blushing. 'Dealers' Disease,' " she said to the police officers. "Much worse than 'Pickers.' What are we looking at?"

"This is a sketch of the woman who met Mr. Balance at the Hotel Elysee in New York last May," said Officer Mile.

"She was introduced to one of the clerks as a neighbor, and they seemed surprised to meet. Later, she was seen coming and going from his suite."

"Your police artist has a nice touch," Tim murmured, back to studying the sketch. "But do you think her nervous sort of posture is from the description or the attitude of the artist? You know, sketching a suspect, giving a little guilty flick of the wrist here, a hunted look to the eyes there?"

"You see all that, Mr. Lowry?"

"I'm afraid I do," Tim said, shrugging. "Maybe it *is* a disease."

"Perhaps I have your disease, too. I see a kind of nervousness in this woman, too."

"It's definitely not me," Jane said.

"You're never nervous, Mrs. Wheel?" asked Oh.

"I wouldn't be if I were dressed in that outfit. Wearing that, I'd feel like a million bucks. Nerves aside, I've never been to the Elycee except to have a drink in the bar there many years ago. I'd be happy to meet the hotel clerk in person."

"No need. Since school wasn't yet dismissed for the summer, your son was still at home. It would be easy enough to prove you were right here during that weekend. We also took the liberty of sending the clerk your picture, and he said he didn't believe the woman was you, although he thought there was a resemblance."

"So what are we playing here?" asked Jane.

"I thought you and Mr. Lowry might have some interesting insights, and you most certainly did. The designer suit, the bracelet, the posture of the woman, her fears of something falling. Most interesting was your impression that the woman in the sketch looked like you. Good insights. A lot to think about."

"Sandy was laid to unrest today with a generic memorial that could have been ordered through a Sears catalogue. I want to stop just having thoughts and solve this."

"Yes."

"So I'll present you with some real proof."

Jane picked up the page of cut-out classified ads that she had found in Jack's recycling bin. She put it on the table in front of Oh and stepped back with her arms folded.

"Mrs. Wheel, I don't quite understand what your proof proves."

"Those holes in the paper are ads for interesting sales. The contents, the addresses, times. They've been pulled out with tape and made into a master list by someone who shops the sales."

"Ah."

"So that proves ... that proves that Jack could have ... known ..."

"Where the good sales were?"

"It proves that Jack knew where I was, so he could ..."

"Why would it matter, Mrs. Wheel?"

Jane was stumped. She knew it mattered, knew it was key. She just didn't know which of Pandora's boxes it might unlock. Sandy was murdered while Jane was at these sales. If Jack was following her around, then he wasn't home murdering Sandy. Oh had told her that Jack's golf alibi had an hour-long hole in it. Alone on the back nine, so he said, while his partners went into lunch. He could have raced home, killed Sandy, and dashed back to the club. That didn't explain why he would need the classifieds.

"Maybe Jack wanted to make sure I wouldn't be walking in on him."

"Mrs. Wheel, he could have locked the door and murdered his wife. If you had returned the car and the door had been locked, what would you have done?"

"Thrown the keys on the floor of the front seat and left."

"Yes."

"He didn't need to know where I was to murder her," Jane said.

"No, I don't think so," said Oh.

"What about your saw?" Tim asked.

Everyone looked at Tim, who was still sitting at the table with the sketch in front of his plate.

"What about Jane's saw?" Tim asked again. "She said it's missing, that it might be the murder weapon. Maybe Jack needed to follow her and steal her saw out of the car."

"Take the chance of being at the right sale at the right time to sneak into the van? Maybe be seen by Mrs. Wheel?" Oh cocked his head to one side and looked at Tim.

Jane shook her head. The funeral had done more than make her angry. It had cleared her head. "If Jack planned on using that saw, he could have taken it anytime. I've left it in the van before. Sandy's borrowed my toolbox before. Jack never wanted her touching the tools he had in the garage. Very expensive, hung on their own little pegs, never used."

"If they were never used, no one would notice if one new saw was replaced with another new saw," Mile said.

"As long as it was replaced on the right peg. The tools were outlined on the board so they could be hung back in the right spot," Jane said.

"Hey, Jack has more than a little Martha S. in him," Tim said, raising one eyebrow, "outlining the tools and all."

Oh promised to call as soon as something turned up. At the front door, he turned to Tim. "Your employee, your friend, Mr. David Gattreaux, he was a picker, too, yes?"

Tim nodded.

"Perhaps he used tape on his newspaper, too?"

"Maybe, but he didn't kill Sandy. The sharpest weapon he would have been able to handle would have been the serrated edge on the tape dispenser. I couldn't send him to a demo sale; he didn't know how to use tools. Claimed he couldn't even pull out a nail."

Tim and Jane didn't speak after Oh and Mile left. Jane filled the dishpan with soapy water to wash the plates and cups by hand. Tim tied one of the several vintage aprons she had hung on wooden pegs near the kitchen window around her waist and stepped back to admire her standing at the sink.

"Beautiful, Jane. You look as good as Mrs. Cleaver. Maybe you would have been happier as a housewife instead of Ms. Career Woman."

"Yeah, and maybe you would have been happier as Mr. Cleaver, instead of . . ."

"Mr. Cleaver's boy toy?"

The phone rang. Jane and Tim both looked up at the giant wall clock over the sink.

Three o'clock.

"Dad?" Jane answered.

"Hello?" Her father sounded confused. "Janie, what happened to hello when you answer the phone? I can't be the only one who ever calls."

"Three o'clock. Mom left a message you'd be home at three."

"No, I'm still at the hospital ..."

"Where exactly, Dad? I'll leave now."

"Honey, calm down. I'm fine."

Jane looked at Tim, who was sliding paper and pen in front of her and gesturing for her to write everything down.

"Fine how? Fine because you can cope, fine because you're a sport, or fine fine?"

"How fine? Fine fine." Don began to chuckle, a bass rumble. "Sounds like a song, doesn't it?

"What did they do exactly? What did they find?"

"They did a scan of the lungs and what Bernard thought he saw on the X ray is just some scar tissue. Breathe, Jane, I don't hear you breathing."

"So, it's not"—Jane hesitated—"it's not serious."

"It's nothing, honey. Just a big scare. Your mother says it was a trick to get me to take the test, a scam."

"You'll never convince her otherwise. The only thing that would have shaken her theory is—"

"If I actually had cancer," Don finished her sentence for her. "She still would have thought they'd doctored up the picture to keep me coming back."

"Nellie's the original conspiracy theorist," Jane said.

"What's that, honey? I couldn't hear; your mom's talking."

Jane could hear her mother saying that they had you coming and going; it was all a scam.

"Are you and Mom going out to celebrate?"

"Yeah, I thought we'd go over to Blue's Café and have dinner, then close up together tonight."

"You're a real romantic, Dad."

After Jane hung up, she smiled at Tim, who was now in his patiently waiting pose, hands folded in front of him on the table like a schoolboy after filling both their lemonade glasses with a few inches of Grey Goose and a splash of lemonade.

"I should be elated instead of exhausted," Jane said, sipping at her drink, "but I feel like collapsing. What's wrong with me?"

Surely she couldn't be disappointed that Don was fine and healthy. Jane loved her father. No, better than that, she liked him. He was strong and quiet and amused by the world. When Jane was a child and came home outraged at the school bully or an unfair teacher, Don would place his big hand over hers and say, "Kill 'em with kindness, honey; it gets 'em every time."

"You geared up for the worst," Tim explained, "and there's something about the worst that brings out the best in us. Would have put everything in perspective. Cancer does that. Terminal illness. AIDS. Nothing more important, nothing gets in the way of the right thing to do, the only thing to do," Tim said, draining his lemonade. He looked at Jane but seemed to be looking beyond her as well. "If you know you're going to die soon, you don't worry about your credit rating or shopping for groceries or getting nailed for a tax audit."

"But, Timmy, I should be happy, delirious. This is my dad we're talking about."

"You will be. Euphoria will kick in, but right now you've got the anxiety letdown, the exhale thing going. That was a worry that could kick the ass out of all your other worries.

Adrenaline's adrenaline, babe, and you had some going on and now it's draining out of your system."

Jane sat at the kitchen table, head in hands, and watched Tim finish the dishes. He talked about American glass companies as he held up tumblers to the light and described an upcoming wedding he was designing with all vintage tableware. He was chronicling his hunt for Bakelite-handled forks, describing it with as much drama as he could muster when he turned to see her reaction and saw that she had fallen asleep at the table. Her head rested on her arms, and she smiled slightly. In first grade they had had a teacher, Sister Rose, who used to let them have a rest time after lunch. Jane looked just the same now as she had at six, her head resting on her arms, her arms resting on a well-worn oak desktop. Tim hung up the dishtowel and softly pulled out the chair across from her and sat down.

How did we get here? he asked himself, resting his chin in his own hands. *How the hell did we ever get here?*

14

Bruce Oh did not know if he looked his age. He was forty-nine and felt neither happy nor unhappy about it. It was what it was. When people made remarks about feeling young or old, he had no idea what they were talking about. People who struggled to appear younger, to knock off five years by punishing themselves in a gym or a tanning salon, either amused or annoyed him, depending on their zeal and vanity. He believed in a moderate diet, exercise for health, and daily meditation.

He walked early in the morning, just as the sun was rising, wearing a Walkman and listening to the news or shutting it off and simply wearing it so none of his neighbors, also walkers, would suggest they chat. He needed the isolation, the mindless activity in which he could immerse himself and sort out the day.

Since he kept track of his exercise by the clock and not by the mile, he couldn't tell anyone how much distance he covered. He only knew that when he laced his shoes and slipped on his Walkman, he checked his watch, and after striding purposefully for thirty minutes away from his prairie-style bungalow on the south side of Evanston, he turned around and walked just as briskly back home.

Claire kept buying him journals in which to record his mileage. For his last birthday, she had given him a pedometer. He could not convince her that he didn't care about the distance. That wasn't his measurement.

"My dear," he would say, "I don't wish to acquire miles, to count them up."

Oh knew that Claire did not understand this. Her life was gathering things, stuff. Just like Mrs. Wheel. She believed that the story of their lives came from the things people saved, while he believed that a life story began only after all the stuff was stripped away. Once, when Claire was especially frustrated with him, she'd told him that he only cared about those who were murdered. Not true, of course, but perhaps he did listen more carefully to the story of a person's life after they were gone. Death made an eloquent storyteller, if one had the patience to listen.

Because of the memorial service and a lengthy call with Munson, he had missed his sunrise walk this Wednesday morning and was now walking, late afternoon, toward a setting sun, thinking about Jane Wheel or, more specifically, Jane Wheel's neighbors, Jack and Sandy Balance. He let his mind drift to Kankakee and David Gattreaux. He and Detective Munson had put up the proper front, an amiable working relationship, two departments cooperating to solve two murders that might be linked. But Munson had resented Oh's involvement and had made it clear that he felt this was a crime of passion, that it was a home-grown crime of passion at that, and it had nothing to do with the Balance murder.

"Gattreaux lived what we would call a pretty risky life style," Munson had told Oh, "lots of partying, lots of sex partners, lots of people, some of them not so nice, who didn't like him much."

"Not being well liked doesn't necessarily lead directly to being a murder victim," Oh had remarked.

"Maybe not, but he was a real asshole, this guy. Used his good looks to play people for suckers. Bartender at a gay bar downtown called him a real user."

"Drugs?"

"Probably. Weed, cocaine, you know, party snacks; but that isn't what he meant. Used people. After he got what he wanted from somebody, he didn't know him anymore."

"So you're looking for a jilted lover?" asked Oh.

"Man, you sure sound like a romantic. Yeah, we're looking for somebody who spent a little quality time with Mr. Gattreaux and was unhappy when he broke it up."

Oh wasn't happy with Munson's one-track approach. He couldn't get him interested in the auction scene, the collectors who might have been bidding against him. Munson assured him he was investigating anyone who might have had contact with Gattreaux there, since the murderer might have followed him to the store, but clearly he felt the auction and bidders themselves were a dead end.

Oh was certain that Munson wanted to expose a love triangle with Gattreaux, Tim Lowry, and the murderer and would be just as pleased if he could prove Lowry himself was the instigator; tie the whole dirty little crime up with a floral ribbon and send it away. Munson didn't even want to know about the Balance murder. Couldn't see why anyone would make the connection except for Jane Wheel and that, Munson assured Oh, would prove to be just a coincidence.

Maybe Lowry was more involved with Gattreaux than he wanted anyone to believe. Oh checked his watch. Fifteen minutes before turning back toward home. Maybe Lowry saw his opportunity to link Gattreaux's murder to Sandy Balance's through Jane. Get rid of Gattreaux and conveniently throw everyone off, send them searching for some serial collector killer. Jane shows up at the flower shop and tells him her story, and he sees the opportunity, invites her to the auction to cheer her up. He slips away during the bidding to tell Mr. X to follow Gattreaux to the shop and make the hit while he's having an alibi for dinner with Jane's family.

Jilted lovers or unhappy spouses or greedy exes. Isn't that always what it was in the mystery books or the television shows? But if Jack Balance was trying to get away with murdering his wife, why didn't he bother to play the bereaved spouse? He seemed intent on shoving his affair in everyone's face. He practically blew kisses at Mrs. Wheel every time she came into view. Gattreaux had lots of "sex partners" according to Munson. He was promiscuous. So far, nothing they'd turned up proved that Lowry was a playboy. No one could link him to anyone since his partner Phil had vanished last year. And Jane Wheel wasn't anyone's mistress; she was too involved with all that stuff she was addicted to. Like his wife, Oh thought, smiling. Claire was too involved with her finds to ever have an affair. He was lucky, he supposed, to have only inanimate objects as rivals.

All these collectors are married to their work. Oh checked his watch and turned around. Pretending to make love to their spouses, their partners, but looking around the room, wondering what those old movie posters would look like over the dresser, thinking about the chenille bedspread they had just missed snatching up at the last house sale. Claire used to tell him he was distracted by cases, but his absorption had nothing over her reading of the classifieds, her laser beam–scanning technique when she walked down the aisles at a flea market. He could still reel her back in. He made her laugh when he took her face in his hands, brought it close to his, and demanded, "Check out my patina, baby."

But really, he thought, *they should be partnered up with other finders, other pickers and dealers, so they could actually understand each other.* Being partners with somebody who doesn't see the same beauty, the same potential, who doesn't feel the same passion can be lonely. For both maybe. Claire had her stuff; Oh had his murders. That worked. That gave them a common language. What worked for Jack and Sandy Balance? What quit working? Gattreaux . . . did he even *have* a partner? What about Lowry and his ex-partner, Phillip? Munson had told him that grim story only a few hours ago. What would that do to Tim Lowry?

Oh stopped so quickly that he almost tripped over his own feet. He looked up at the street sign to figure out where he was. If Gattreaux was a player, a user like Munson said, maybe he had used the wrong person. Maybe someone didn't want to be in his little black book. As Oh was turning that thought over in his mind, an unmarked police car pulled alongside him.

Mile reached across the front seat and opened the door. "A man called the station looking for you, Detective."

"Yes?" Oh asked, sliding into the car.

"Says he knows who killed Sandy Balance."

"Fine. At the station?"

"Wants to meet you tonight after an estate sale," Mile said.

Oh sighed. "A sale. Of course."

15

"I am not going to horn in on your date, Janie, so stop whining." Tim pulled out a red tank top and a black-and-red-checked shirt from Jane's closet. "Try this, the shirt over the tank."

"We're going to preview a sale. It's not dinner and dancing. You should just come along." Jane inserted a red, carved Bakelite hoop in her ear and turned her head to check it in the mirror. "It's not just a demo sale; the whole basement and first floor need to be emptied out. Not those tan pants, Timmy, I'll get filthy. Just jeans. And it's by invitation only; that's why it'll be so cool. My first chance to get in the door in the first wave."

"This guy sounds like a real romantic"—Tim swung his legs up on the bed and reclined against the pillows—"a real keeper."

"Charley took me to a digging site on our third date, and I remember you thought that was pretty cool."

"It was a chartered plane to South America."

"I had to pay my own fare," Jane said.

"You made more money; he was a lowly teacher."

"Assistant professor. I always made more money. Until now, that is. Okay, what do you think?"

"A bit studied. Clean and pressed grunge, the vintage plastic on the ear, illustration for a weekend antiquing article in *Country Living,* but okay," said Tim, nodding. "Yeah, okay."

"No, if I was in one of those articles, I'd be wearing this," Jane said, holding up a khaki fishing vest with multiple pockets.

"You don't really wear that?"

"Sure I do. Receipts in this pocket, cash in this one, checkbook, charge card, and driver's license here. And in this one, index cards, two pens, Miriam's list, my list, small screwdriver, magnet, flashlight, and magnifier. Tissues and Wash 'n Dries. Disposable camera here."

"You are such a tourist," Tim said, hanging up the rejected shirts and pants that Jane had thrown on the bed.

"It works. No one should be afraid of how they look, if how they look works."

"You sound like an advice columnist."

"Richard is picking me up in fifteen minutes. Won't you come, Tim? You know you want to."

"I know it's been awhile, dear, but this is called a date. X asks Y to go somewhere. Y does not bring Z."

Jane stuffed a lipstick into her jeans pocket. "Why do I have to be Y and you get to be Z. I'm the question mark and you're the mark of Zorro."

"And Richard, you'll note, is Brand X. What do I say if Charley calls tonight?"

"They only call from town," Jane said, "on Sundays."

Richard pulled up in a dark blue pickup truck at 6:30. Jane watched him finish his cell-phone conversation then bound up her front steps. He was tall; a large man in a plaid shirt. Bigger than she remembered. He, too, was dressed for an illustration. An article about Rich, the rehabber, or Richard, the king of renovation? He wore a baseball cap that barely contained his curly brown hair. He was square-jawed, bearlike, Jane thought, then she remembered her bruised shoulder and her smashed foot. Oxlike, she revised. Or maybe a bull in a china shop. He was rubbing his big hands together when she walked to the door.

Peeking out the window, Tim said, "He looks like he's going to make a meal of you, for god's sake."

Jane shot Tim a look before she opened the door all the way.

"I don't want to rush you, but we should get there," Richard said, ducking his head instinctively as he came in.

"I'll just grab my bag. I don't need to be bringing tools, do I? You remember my friend, Tim? From the auction in Kankakee?"

Richard nodded and shook Tim's hand. "Sure, you're the dealer who knew about those doors, right?"

Tim nodded. "Is this the Hendershott preview tonight?"

"Yeah, I'd like to invite you, but they sent out flyers to their customers and I had my guys over there getting numbers this afternoon, and I only got one for Jane and me. Sorry."

Richard shrugged and held up the two numbers, seven and eight, that he had fished from his pocket while talking.

"Oh, that's okay. I just burst in on Janie unexpectedly to keep her company while her son and—"

"I'm ready," Jane cut Tim off, smiling hard at him. "Would you feed Rita, please, and lock up if you're going out?"

"Surely," Tim said evenly, returning her smile.

"Can I grab a glass of water? Kitchen through here?" Richard headed off when Jane nodded.

"Man, you got some killer stuff here," Richard called from the kitchen.

"Thanks," Jane answered, then whispered to Tim, "Behave yourself, please."

"Ready?" Richard opened the door and ushered Jane through it.

Tim watched them walk out to the pickup, watched Richard open the door, Jane boost herself in. He shook his head sadly. She had worn that silly vest after all. He quickly poured food into Rita's bowl, calling out to her.

"Sleeping under the couch, Rita? Cooler under there, baby?" Rita walked in from the den, immediately to her water bowl, then back out the swinging door to the screened back porch.

"Guard the house, Sweetie," Tim called, locked the door, and walked quickly out to his van. If he took the shortcut that Trudy had told him about, he'd still beat Richard and Jane to the Hendershott place. He took the index card with the directions out of his pocket, along with his sale invitation and his number. Written on the small blue ticket was a note from one of the partners running the sale. *I pulled some strings, Tim. Is this number good enough for you?* It was ticket number 1.

"So this is where we do that dating small talk." Richard glanced over at Jane and flicked on the turn signal. "You want to start?"

"You, please."

"Okay. I went to college in Colorado for a few years, but liked skiing more than Rhetoric 101, so my dad hauled me home and suggested I work for him awhile. He figured I'd hate the business and go back to school a new man, committed to an education and not ending up like him. But I liked the business. Heck, I liked the old man and how he ended up."

"How'd he end up?" Jane asked, content to bounce along in this pickup and listen to somebody new talk, somebody she never would have met at the agency or on a commercial shoot or at a neighborhood progressive dinner.

"Filthy rich. He had an eye and was ripping off mantels and molding before anyone realized what a market there might be for architectural salvage. All the rehabbers and renovators in the city went through my dad. If he didn't have it, he knew where to find it.

"Even if people didn't think they were selling something, my dad would talk to them; and before they knew what hit them, he and Louie and the rest of his guys were taking out the old wrought-iron garden gate that he assured them would spike their kids or not keep the dog in the yard. People would beg him to take stuff. Sometimes he would just offer to take it out for free then turn it around and sell it for a thousand. Sometimes, he actually got people to pay him to haul it away."

"Sounds pretty"—Jane tried to think of a way to say dishonest without offending Richard—"shrewd."

"He was spectacular. Retired to Florida now and left me in charge."

"Are you as shrewd as your dad?" Jane asked.

"Nah. Everybody's caught on. Now if you tell somebody

they got a nice rock formation on their property, they want to excavate it and haul it into the *Antiques Roadshow*. Then some guy in a three-piece suit'll say, 'Oh, yes, this is one of the stone tablets Moses brought back. See how you can barely make out *Thou shalt not covet?*' Everybody thinks everything's a damn collectible. Look at your kitchen, for god's sake."

"Yes?"

"I bet you didn't pay over five bucks for any one item in there. You just got the eye and the dedication, right?"

"Maybe, but . . ."

"Those little embroidered towels of yours, they go so high at an auction now. They used to be junk. A box lot of old kitchen stuff. Now everybody's a 'collector'; everybody's pawing through old utensils and looking for Bakelite handles or bringing in loupes to study hallmarks," Richard said, shaking his shaggy head. "They're a riot, these 'collectors,' strolling through the flea markets, wearing their big sun hats and those thirty-pocket fishing vests."

Jane was interested to note that Richard could step on her toes even when he was driving. Possibly not the best beginning to a first date. She patted down her pockets.

"Did you or your dad ever feel that it was unfair to pay so little for items and then make such a huge profit?" she asked.

"Oh yeah, we lost a lot of sleep," Richard said with a laugh. "You're kidding, right?" He glanced over at her, looking at her for the first time since they had gotten into the car.

"Not really. I mean, sometimes I think if there's such a market for an object, then why not enough for everybody to . . ."

"You're in the business, aren't you?"

"On a small scale."

"You make a living thinking like that?" asked Richard.

"I just started thinking about doing this full-time, I just left my day job."

"Doing?"

"I was in advertising," Jane said softly.

"So that would account for your high moral sensibility on matters of commerce."

"I didn't mean to suggest anything about you personally, but I've seen dealers talk to people about their stuff, trying to get a better deal and . . ." Jane let her thought trail off. Hadn't she tried to get the same better deals? Just not as a successful dealer?

"What about that box of flowerpots?" Richard asked.

"What about them?"

"How much you gonna sell them for?"

"Oh, I love those; I don't want to sell them," Jane said.

"But if you did want to sell them, what would they go for?"

"Oh, a couple of bucks apiece," Jane said unconvincingly.

"Come on, Jane, I know one of them was McCoy," said Richard, "and there were no cracks, no crazing; they were mint, for Christ's sake."

"Fifteen for the McCoy, five or ten for the others."

"At least. But you didn't stop me when I got Bill to sell you the whole box for five bucks?"

"He wasn't the actual owner, he was a dealer; he didn't . . ."

"Why wasn't he the real owner? He had either bought everything as salvage and was reselling it or he was representing the owner of the property. Either way, he was the voice of the owner."

"Yes, but he didn't . . . ," Jane started.

"Have a sweet old lady face? Or look like a bereaved family member too distraught to know what he was doing? Still the owner. Still the person you took advantage of. Still the person you made a profit off."

Jane wasn't sure she wanted to finish her thought. This felt like an old argument. Richard talked faster and faster, and she could see he wasn't the listening type. What would he say about her moral sensibility if he knew she was wondering if a number seven or eight at a preview sale was enough reason to be in a truck with him.

"Look, you're sentimental, that's all. It gives you a good eye. You just need the voice of reason to make you a profit. You'll get it"—Richard said, as he parked the truck behind a line of trucks already lined up in front of a sprawling Victorian house, its shaky porch crowded with people in jeans and old shirts, men with shaggy ponytails, and women wearing no makeup, no jewelry, and carrying canvas bags—"or you won't," he said, opening the door and jumping down out of the truck.

"Maybe you're right," she said out loud, thinking, *They might own it, but they don't love it.*

"Sorry about what I said about the vests," said Richard. "On you, a vest looks really good."

There was still fifteen minutes before the house opened. Even though this was a preview sale, which meant there would be primarily dealers waiting for the doors to open, there was still a mix of experience and innocence, savvy and wide-eyed excitement. Jane recognized three book guys. One, a tall, Elvishaired man in his thirties, was the one she most despised. He had the widest arm span and could sweep off bookshelves and block off more volumes than most of the others. They were all grabbers and pushers, but he had the physical qualities to make him the king. He reminded Jane of a basketball center, the lug in the middle whose job it was to set the screen, standing solidly planted and deflecting all comers, while his little partner dodged behind him, scanned titles, flipping them out from their shelves into a canvas bag to go through in a corner at their leisure. Their discards would end up all over the house as they went through, grabbing here, blocking there. They were masters at planting themselves in a kitchen, ostensibly looking through the cookbooks, but effectively blocking anyone from getting into the silverware drawers or into the cabinets for the pressed glass tumblers. They knew their stuff, so that while the little one was going through the cookbooks, knocking them all over the counter, Big Elvis would use those long arms to grab the Bakelite salt and peppers, the Androck potato masher, the wooden-handled, Indestructo Number 4 ice-cream scoop.

Jane hoped they didn't have numbers five and six. She wanted to be ahead of them for once in her life: ahead of Elvis and Little Elvis; ahead of Stony, the rock-faced blonde who collected embroidery and delicate cutwork tablecloths for her shop in Wilmette; ahead of Country Joe and Fish, the tall, bony, sixty-something in a cowboy hat with his long-faced wife, whose outstanding physical characteristic was her abilty to suck her cheeks in and out like a trout while canvasing a sale. She carried sold stickers in her pocket and slapped them on all legal bookcases, wardrobes, and sewing cabinets as she wriggled through houses, elbows flapping.

Jane wondered what her own tell was, what tic she exhibited to those standing around her. Did she have any movement, any feature that would give her a nickname with this crowd? Yes, she loved Bakelite and buttons and sewing boxes, but if Granny Buttons had a lower number at a sale, she'd clean out the place and be gone before Jane got in the door. Ghost Gardener was a young woman, pale as ivory, who looked like she might faint at any moment; but she was as strong as a bull, carrying boxes full of pottery, mostly planters and vases, out to her truck with the meticulously lettered sign, THE SECRET GARDEN, OLD AND NEW OUTDOOR ARTIFACTS. Jane had never beaten her to a flowerpot.

What Jane found, loved, and finally bought, were the discards. A book that Elvis had tossed into a corner, *Bee's Ways*, a history of bee-keeping, published in 1948, very nonmint condition, worn and well-read, would find its way into Jane's canvas bag. The rejected wedding photos of plain people, wearing unspectacular bridal garb would find their home with her. The box of buttons under the mildewed rags on the basement floor would be tossed aside by Granny since she knew the plastics and the glass and the metal had all been stored together in a damp, rusty tin. Jane would scoop it up, hoping to salvage a few glass paperweights, a tiny, overlooked Bakelite cookie, maybe a sterling silver thimble in the bottom.

Standing on the front lawn of the Hendershott place gave her the shivers. Begun in the 1830s, the house had been passed down through the Hendershott family of Lake Bluff generation after generation. Old newspaper photos showed that the construction was not completed until 1904. It was eccentric, as the family was rumored to be, with odd rooms added on, a tower and a turret here and there for good measure. It most closely resembled a massive Victorian, one reflected in a fun-house mirror. It was rumored to have hidden rooms and secret passages, stairways that led nowhere, doors that opened into solid walls instead of rooms.

Preservationists in River Heights, a neighboring suburb, claimed it had housed presidents, senators, governors, insisted that its grounds harbored botanical treasures, but could never provide any documentation. The Hendershotts had never cooperated with the local historical society or newspaper feature writers who begged to get inside and write about the house and its history. With no facts to interfere, its legend and glory had blossomed. It had evolved into a destination sight, the kind of place you drove to when out-of-town guests were visiting, a low-rent tourist attraction.

When Mildred Hendershott died six months ago, she was the last of the line. She had left her entire estate to the town of Lake Bluff, stipulating that the house was to be torn down completely, leveled, and the land almost six acres— given over to public use. The personal effects of the house were to be disposed of as the town saw fit, sold if necessary to make the improvements needed on the land for whatever the town decided to build. The fear, of course, was that the gift would be more costly than the town could bear. Even sculpting a park out of the land could run into the millions, not to mention the public Shakespearean theater, the new library, the ice-hockey arena that had all been seriously proposed for the site.

The town need not have worried. The Hendershott art collection alone was sold at auction for well over the sum that any first-rate theater and public garden would cost to build and maintain. Many of the furniture pieces were being held in storage so they could be displayed in the theater lobby, the project that had finally won out.

The ceramics, art, glassware, jewelry had all been evaluated by experts and had been sold or displayed. But the sheer amount of stuff the house held was overwhelming. The boxes and crates and wardrobes and cabinets in the basement and cellars were now to be scavenged by the second team. The dealers and pickers and rummagers, who were the foot soldiers of the collecting world, would now have their chance. And for once no one was complaining that the house had been picked clean already. The usual grousing heard while standing in line in the 5 A.M. dark and damp—about how so-and-so had said that Country Joe's cousin had known the estate buyer and had picked over the house already or that the estate sale team was really a group of dealers from Wisconsin and they had replaced the valuable stuff with rejects from their other sales—was absent today.

Jane was so busy scanning the crowd and shivering in her presale delight that she forgot about Richard. She preferred shopping alone or with Tim, who understood how to leave a wide space between them when they entered a house or market. Now when she felt a hand on her elbow pushing her toward the front porch, she instinctively jumped.

"We need to get up there in line. Louie and Braver are waving to us, see?"

Jane recognized Louie as the worker who had retrieved the box of flowerpots at the sale last weekend. Braver was slightly smaller than Louie, but with the same massive forearms and scowling eyes.

"Are they brothers?"

"Cousins. They worked for my dad and now they work for me. Loyal as pups."

Jane said nothing, but thought that puppy was the last animal to which she'd compare these two. Braver's head darted back and forth like a snake, and Louie stood pounding one fist into his other hand as if waiting for the fight bell to signal round one. They held numbers five and six.

"This is Jane, guys. Jane, Louie and Braver."

Braver poked his head at her and Louie nodded in her direction.

"They're only letting twenty in at first, boss, in this big old place. You believe that?"

"Doesn't bother me a bit. Not with our numbers."

"Yeah, but you're not going to like this, Richie," said Braver; "they sent out special numbered tickets with some of the invites."

"What the fuck are you talking about?"

Jane felt Richard's hand on her elbow convulsively tighten.

"Our numbers are in order *after* the mailed-out numbers. People are plenty pissed off. This downstate rinky-dink estate sale team sent out numbers to their special customers. About twenty. So they'll go in the first wave, then us."

A thin woman in a blue-and-white-striped apron came out the front door holding a clipboard. She cleared her throat and looked out over the crowd pushing and shoving their way into a sort of line.

"Those of you with blue tickets, please line up on the left according to your numbers. Those of you with white tickets, please line up on the right. Blue numbers one through twenty will be admitted first; then when we see how the group disperses, we will be calling in the next groups from this line." She indicated the white ticket line, whose members were beginning to catch on that they had been tricked into a false sense of superiority.

"What's the big idea, mailing out numbers?" someone yelled.

"Who do I have to sleep with to get on the mailing list?" another woman called out sarcastically.

The aproned woman stared back at the hecklers coolly. "You may subscribe to our newsletter for a fee when you get inside. Although the entire house is open, items are mostly on the first floor, attic, and basement. Those of you here scouting for architectural pieces, you will be able to do some work on the second floor and the third-floor ballroom and mark off places in the rest of the house to return to tomorrow. You should see the people in green 'Trenton Sales' T-shirts. Do not begin using tools or removing anything until you have found a green T-shirt to work with you."

Jane felt that the second twenty was still a wonderful place to be, but she could see how sour Richard had grown.

"Look, no tools. Doesn't look like salvage people in that line, so you're still in a great position."

"Yeah, but I don't like hanky-panky. Look at her shmoozing all of her subscribers over there."

Jane was beginning to wonder if she was ready to date. She had thought she had sensed a bearlike sweetness in Richard. Maybe she had just sensed that he was bearlike. Still, he did have invitations to sales; he had guys who would pry off doors for her; and he understood stuff. He loved and appreciated stuff. He had seemed genuinely kind and funny and certainly apologetic when he'd injured her.

Sure, tonight he was acting like any picker she might have avoided because of his ruthlessness and temper, but hadn't he pointed out to her that she was a picker, too? An aspiring picker? He and Louie and Braver were swearing and gesturing as if she weren't even there. Maybe they were just treating her like one of their own.

Jane looked over at the blue ticket line. No familiar faces. None of the usual suspects from Chicago or suburban sales.

"This company is from downstate," Jane said, determined to be the peaceful picker with a heart of gold. "They probably sent numbers to dealers too far away to come in and get numbers this morning. They just leveled the playing field for their regular customers."

Jane was on her tiptoes trying to see the front of the blue line, where the woman in charge was talking animatedly with someone.

Richard, hearing Jane's voice, seemed to remember her and remember he had brought her to this dance.

"Damnit, Jane, I'm sorry. Sorry for my language and all, but this kind of shit makes me so mad. Just seems unfair to all of us locals who managed to get out here this morning for the numbers."

"What would you be saying if you had a blue ticket?"

"That life ain't fair," said Richard, with a smile.

Jane and the three men watched the first twenty go into the house. She didn't mind so much. Numbers seven and eight still put her well ahead of the local dealers she recognized, the ones who most often beat her to the goods. If she could just focus when she went in there, she'd be fine—if she didn't get too distracted to move quickly and grab first, ask questions later.

"You got a cat, Jane?" Richard roughly brushed off the back of her vest. "You're covered in hair."

"Dog. A stray that wandered in the day . . . a shepherd that I found."

"I like cats," Braver said with a sneer. "I don't give a damn what you say, dogs can't be trusted like cats. I don't give a damn what Louie says, fucking dogs are so needy . . ."

Louie stared straight ahead, his lips clamped tightly together.

"Shut up, Braver," Richard said sharply. "We've disrespected Jane enough tonight."

"I was talking about dogs, Richie."

"I was talking about your filthy mouth," said Richard, smiling to undercut his words. He then turned his back and planted himself between Jane and Louie and Braver.

"Not such a great idea for a first date. I'm sorry."

"Don't be sorry for my sake," Jane said, hoping Louie and Braver realized she was including them, hoping for peace. "I'm thrilled to be at this sale, thrilled to be this far up in line. Look behind us."

They all turned and stared back at the line that snaked down the porch steps, down the stone path to the entrance gate, and realized that from where they stood, even with the advantage of the height of the porch, they could not be sure where the line ended, as it worked its way around the parked cars in the west meadow.

"See that person in the red shirt; see that glint of red next to that station wagon out there?"

"Yeah," said Richard, squinting into the lowering sun.

"If I weren't here with you guys, that would be me."

The front door opened and all four turned again to face

the Hendershott house, Braver and Louie rocking back and forth on the balls of their feet, Richard squaring his shoulders, and Jane taking a deep breath.

The same woman who had faced the lines of customers before appeared in front of them. "Before I let in the next ten people, let me remind you. Do not start using tools on the property until you've paired up with one of our workers. Look for the green T-shirts. Household and linens are back in the kitchen and sunporch, tools in the coach house and shed out back, but you can only get there by entering here first. Clothes and miscellaneous in the attic; boxes and boxes of god knows what in the basement. Books in the front parlor. Some furniture and smalls throughout the first floor. China and crystal in the dining room. Plants and pottery in the conservatory."

"Mr. Green, with the candlestick, in the billiard room," said Richard.

Jane felt the push. Even though it would be only ten people going through the door, the crowd sensed movement and from the very end of that line vibrated the "me next, me now, me too," excitement and impatience of these pickers.

"Meet you in the kitchen in an hour," Richard said to Jane, then instructed Louie to head up to the ballroom and Braver to check the coach house and shed.

Jane walked through the door and saw Richard, Louie, and Braver disperse and disappear. Poof. Gone. She was alone and tingling with excitement. Her hands shook a bit, and she felt chilly despite the heat in the old place. Focus, focus, focus.

She walked past the front parlor and the book people, straight back to the kitchen and back porch. In the pantry, she picked up a small butter crock, started to read the inscription, stopped, and stuck it into her bag. She wasn't going to be stopped. She saw an old ceramic brewery mug and thought she saw Kankakee written on it and nestled it into the bubble wrap in her other tote. She'd sort this stuff out later. Back to the sunporch and linens. A sewing basket. Yes, it was full and marked five dollars. She picked it up and glanced through it. The usual suspects, old fasteners on cards, seam binding gray with dust, an old crochet hook, was it bone? Tracing wheel with Bakelite handle. Some advertising thimbles. Nothing much, but the basket was worth five. No buttons though. She signaled the green shirt on duty to begin writing her ticket.

"Any buttons?"

"Two big tins and a box, but somebody got them right away."

"I've got this crock and mug." Jane pulled them out of her bags.

"Five each?"

Jane hesitated. These weren't rummage sale prices, but she was sure they were worth at least ten each to Miriam, so she nodded.

"Any ideas about what's in the basement?"

"You name it. Costumes, old puppets, printing equipment. I saw rock collections and shells. This family was a more than a little nuts, if you ask me. Papers and account books from the turn of the century. The last one. Maybe the one before that. Here," she said, tearing off the invoice, "keep adding to this. We're keeping a claim check in the side porch if you want to check things, like at a rummage sale."

"Nice touch."

"Yeah, well better than having somebody pick up somebody else's bag and have a fistfight break out. Seen that happen, believe it or not."

"I believe it," said Jane, and headed down to the basement, still carrying her bags and basket.

If only thirty people were in the house, it felt like twenty were in the basement. They had spread out and were going through boxes, some wearing gloves, holding tiny flashlights between their teeth as they unloaded papers and notebooks, sifted through letters, photographs, and crumbling books.

Jane found a corner and a promising box. No water stains on the bottom, but clearly old, creased with grime. She opened the top flap and shined her flashlight in, hoping to scare away any critters who might have moved in.

Jane breathed in sharply. She had struck gold: photo albums. No, better than that: photo albums and postcard albums and scrapbooks. She lifted out a small Victorian postcard album and untied the mauve ribbon that held it closed. Its cover was worn and soft. Warm to the touch. The buttery leather fitted her hands. She opened it to a photo postcard of a church. Written in spidery, faded ink on the undivided back was, "This is where Lem married Belle."

Gently paging through, she saw that every page held a card. Another album beneath it was also filled. She stuck her face into the box and inhaled deeply. No mildew. Jane felt her pulse race.

She lifted the box. Heavy, but she had a picker's superhuman strength. Like the Incredible Hulk, or some other comic book hero that Nicky could tell her about, she was always strong enough to drag out a treasure box. Carrying the box in her arms, with the handles of her canvas bags over one wrist and the sewing basket handle over the other, she staggered to the green shirt stationed at the basement steps.

"How much for the whole box? I haven't gone through it all, but it seems to be all old postcards and photo albums. Maybe seven or eight." Jane lowered the box to the ground without taking her hands off of it, shielding it from the others with her body. She was almost whispering.

The green shirt peered into the box, but Jane could see she was not interested in actually sticking her hands in. She hesitated.

"I'm usually in jewelry," she apologized.

Jane's heart soared. This was not the iron blonde of the sales team, "Sisters Three," who priced things in exact proportion to how much desire she read in your eyes. This was a sweet, sincere, young person from downstate Illinois who had a heart of gold and naive blue eyes. Jane swallowed hard, hoping to remove the tremor from her voice.

"They're pretty crumbly, but I'm willing to buy them for one price and go through them later."

"Let me see." The woman gingerly lifted the corner of one of the albums. "Feels like nice leather."

Jane's heart dropped. Worse than the iron blonde, she was the gray-haired blank stare of "End of the Line," who figured that if anyone wanted to buy something, it must be worth twice as much as she'd originally priced it. She'd pull things out of the box you carried and say, "Oh, I made a mistake; the family didn't want me to sell that" and stick it under her feet at the checkout table. This idiot from downstate Illinois had the timid soul of a know-nothing and would overprice; Jane could tell by looking into her vacant blue eyes.

"Seventy for the box?"

Jane had feared a hundred, maybe two, hoped for fifty,

and now was so overcome she stared for a moment, waiting for her to repeat the figure.

"That's about ten each, probably the bargain of the night."

"Fine," Jane said, handing her the invoice.

People were thundering down the steps, and Jane knew how lucky she was. They were probably allowing larger groups in now, as they saw how everyone dispersed. The basement would soon be polluted with greed and dust. Someone would have gotten to this box and ripped out individual cards, a photo here and there. Jane had rescued it intact. She carried the box of history up the stairs.

Jane decided to pay for her first wave of finds and check them. She could begin again with free arms and the euphoria of knowing she had already gotten more than she had hoped for. Of course, when her arms were once again empty and when she counted up her cash, her greed would return. She had missed the buttons and who knows what else was in that basement or what was in the attic. There was a coach house. A shed. She forgot everything but the physical joy of the hunt that coursed through her. Her fingers and toes tingled.

Jamming her receipt stamped PAID and her package check ticket deep into her jeans pocket, she thought of Charley. She realized he had known what he was up against, seeing her euphoria when she returned from sales and unloaded dusty object after dusty object on the kitchen table. Once he had shaken his head and sighed, "How can I compete with this," holding up an old Bakelite bowling trophy inscribed, VERONICA LAVELLA, 1941.

Jane decided to shop the front parlor next. Nearly an hour had passed. In the parlor, she could check out the books and sheet music and still keep one eye on the hall that led into the pantry and kitchen to catch Richard.

Richard. Her first date in fifteen years. And not the perfect match. How was she going to escape from this?

Nellie had never offered much dating advice, just a crusty, "They only want one thing, boys, and you'd better not be the one to give it to them," or the more congenial, "They're all animals so what's the difference who you go out with." Her blanket condemnations were often punctuated with arbitrary rules, which she insisted were essential but didn't know why.

"You got to come home with who brought you," she always told Jane when she left on a date.

Once, when Jane asked, "What if the guy who brought me turns out to be a drunk or an ax murderer?" her mother had shrugged and retreated into the general canon. "I told you, they're all animals." As happened in most conversations with her mother, they never quite reached a finish line or concluded; they just ran around the same circles until, tired and beat, they slowed to a stop.

Elvis was standing in front of one of the bookcases with his arms spread out. Little Elvis darted in under his wingspan and pulled out volume after volume. Jane didn't want the aggravation, so she walked into the hall and peeked into the pantry. No Richard and it was ten minutes past their rendezvous.

He's tearing up a floor somewhere, she thought, and headed for the coach house. There was a back porch, curiously peaceful in the midst of people pushing on the wicker rockers and emptying baskets of old periodicals onto the plank floor. The sun was setting and the porch would not be shaken from its time, its purpose. On three sides one could look out from this hill and see the fields stretch out, purple and brown. No amount of shrill, "I don't want the magazines; how much for the basket?" "You got to be kidding, this wicker's falling apart" remarks could penetrate the ghosts of this space. The Hendershotts remained on this porch. It was original to the house, the great-great-great-great grandparents had wanted a view and gotten a beauty. Jane hoped they were all peaceful ghosts and didn't have to wander around seeing this mess. The familiar guilt about being part of the problem of the greedy scavengers threatened to creep in and ruin her excitement over being one of the smart pickers, so she stepped off the porch into the yard.

The shed was a modest name for a barn that rested just beyond the northwest corner of the cultivated lawn. Past the shed the property extended into heavily wooded fields where night seemed to have already fallen. Jane could see light coming from inside the shed and noted the familiar silhouettes of pickers on their knees, sifting through boxes and crates. Two men, unable to suppress grins, were pushing a wooden wheelbarrow filled with old farm implements around the house into the front yard. Jane wasn't the only one blissfully pleased with the array of goods and the reasonable prices and attitudes of this downstate sales team. *I've got to remember to get on their mailing list and subscribe to their newsletter before I leave here*, she thought.

The coach house was opposite the shed, but situated on the land so that the living space faced out into the wooded field. Although she could see light from the high windows,

Jane couldn't tell if there was much of a crowd. She walked around to what she expected would be the open carriage doors. They were closed, however. The only entrance seemed to be a regular door leading up a flight of stairs to the living space above the stable. Jane heard voices and the sound of boxes being dragged across the floor. She began climbing, keeping to the right side as a man in a work shirt and chinos, holding a box over his head, made his way down the narrow passage. "Sorry," he said, as he brushed against her.

"It's okay," she said. "What's up there?"

"Everything," he answered, disappearing out of the door.

About five steps from the top, she heard a loud thud and shouting, "no OA meeting." Or was it "AA meeting"? She couldn't distinguish the words exactly. Was someone not attending to their twelve steps and fighting it out here? She hugged the rail on her right hard with both hands, hearing footsteps heading for the doorway at the top. She expected to be pushed and elbowed, figuring that at least two people were more likely fighting over some object of desire and that any second one or both would be barreling down the stairs to find a green shirt to settle the argument.

She was not expecting what did happen. One more thud, stone silence, then sudden and complete darkness. The entire building went black. Jane continued to hug the railing as a small, fine beam of light started down the stairs. She could not see who held the flashlight but felt the heavy step. The stairway was too narrow for blind passage.

"Be careful, there's someone here," she said, trying to become part of the wall as she felt the steps thunder closer. The flashlight swung up and the beam caught her directly in the eyes. The light was as blinding as the darkness.

The person descending said nothing. She felt his bulky shape pass her, brush her roughly, and she heard heavy, rasping breath. At the bottom of the stairs she heard the door bang and the phantom gasp for air.

Jane heard rustling movement upstairs and people beginning to call to one another. She heard flashlights being clicked on and saw beams dancing around the room. She pulled out her own and made her way up the stairs as carefully and quickly as she could. She did not want to be caught in that passage again, especially if some picker tried to take advantage of the darkness and make off with a trunk or a heavy chair, dragging it off to their truck in the convenient darkness. Better to stay off the stairs until someone got the power back on.

At the top of the stairs, she entered a large room with furniture piled against one wall. Rugs were piled on top of each other on one side of the floor. In the crisscrossing beams, she could see boxes all over the floor, some with people huddled over them, protecting their finds until the lights went on. In one corner a woman was calmly continuing to go through a box of pamphlets and what looked liked road maps, directing her flashlight into the box and not bothering to check out the rest of the room.

Jane called out, "Is everyone okay up here?"

There were a few murmured "Yeahs," and one, "What the hell's going on?" a question posed, she assumed, because someone thought she was a green shirt coming to check out things in the coach house. Another man, also assuming she worked for Trenton Sales, told her to check out the backroom.

"A couple of guys were fighting in there when the lights went out."

Jane didn't particularly want to check out a brawl, but she liked being mistaken for management. She was hoping she'd have the guts to actually price things if anyone asked her before the lights came back on and people noticed her shirt was red, not green. She picked her way through the rubble, directing her flashlight over the boxes and piles of magazines.

In the backroom, probably once used as a small bedroom, she saw only more boxes and a pile of rugs and blankets in the corner. She heard more steps behind her coming up the stairs and saw out of the corner of her eye that more powerful flashlights and lanterns were illuminating the main room.

So much for my short career with Trenton, she thought. A loud hum started from outside. Within seconds, the generator that powered the property and the lights came on in the main house which Jane could see from the small window on the opposite wall, and in the coach house. Eyes had adjusted from light to dark to flashlights, and now people blinked their way back into the moderate light of the living space. Jane heard people come into the bedroom behind her, but she didn't turn. There was something about that pile of rugs, the shape of those blankets. Jane, despite the illumination from the overhead fixture and the two floor lamps in the corners, kept her flashlight on the piles in the corner. She froze when the blankets began to move. And moan.

Three steps closer and she could see the man's face, a bruise spreading under one eye and a bump growing above it. She fell to her knees and dropped the flashlight. Just as she reached out, she heard a familiar voice behind her.

"Stop, Mrs. Wheel, do not touch anyone, anything," Detective Oh said, kneeling beside her and speaking into a small radio.

"But I have to, it's"—Jane said, hearing her own voice sounding very far away—"it's Tim."

"Yes, I see who it is. I've ordered an ambulance. I am wondering, however, who this other gentleman might be."

Jane glanced over and coolly assessed the bloodied face of the man partially covered by a frayed Persian rug. "That's Braver," she said. She watched as Oh felt for a pulse. When he laid Braver's wrist down gently, she knew he was dead.

"My head, please help my head," Tim said, and moaned again.

Jane again reached out and was once more restrained by Detective Oh. "I hear the paramedics on the stairs now."

Jane noticed Oh had put on gloves and was removing objects from around the men, taking something from Tim's hand. When he turned away to place it out of the way, Jane leaned over to be face-to-face with her best friend.

"Timmy, what happened?"

"A fight, I guess. I didn't see . . . Janie . . ." Tim fought for breath and Jane leaned in closer.

"In my pocket, take care of it," Tim whispered.

Jane checked to see if Oh was still busy with all the uniforms that had come upstairs. He was directing them to escort pickers and shoppers downstairs into the stable area and hold them there. The paramedics were a few feet away. Jane quietly put her hand over Tim's chest and pulled out the pieces of paper from his shirt pocket and folded her fingers around them.

"Got 'em, love."

"Buttons are yours."

"Whatever you say, Timmy."

Oh was in the eye of the storm of activity that lasted ten minutes at most; then the coach house was quiet. Tim was taken by the paramedics to Highland Park Hospital where Jane arranged to meet him later. She noticed that Oh sent a police officer to accompany him. Everyone who had been upstairs when the lights went out was now in the stable giving statements.

Oh had allowed Jane to remain and led her out into the living room area while investigators continued to bag and collect around Braver's body. He motioned for her to sit on an old leather sofa and he pulled up a crate to be opposite her.

"Tell me how you always happen to be at the wrong place at the wrong time."

"Detective, there are one hundred and two shoppers here and thirty-eight employees of Trenton Sales," Officer Mile said, reading from a small notebook as she entered the room. "Everyone's being checked out through the front sale table in the main house."

"Good. How about the line waiting to get in? Names taken and dismissed?"

"In the process," Officer Mile answered, nodding to Jane. "Anything else?"

"Make sure the woods are checked out. I want a walk-through now and at dawn. Someone could have been parked on the other side of the county line road if they knew how to get through the woods on foot," said Oh.

Mile nodded, spoke into her own walkie-talkie, then turned back to Detective Oh and said, "There's a Richard Rose in the main house who insists on knowing what happened. Says his date and one of his employees are missing."

"I'm the date, and Braver's the ..." Jane nodded toward the door to the backroom.

"Give us fifteen minutes, then bring him up." Oh adjusted his crate, then called to Officer Mile, who had started down the stairs, "Please tell my wife to go on home. I'll get a ride."

Jane, puzzled, looked up at him.

"I was here with my wife. She was invited to the sale, and I just came along for ..." Oh hesitated.

"That's how you got here so fast."

"And you, how did you get here so fast? To where another murder was committed?"

Jane shook her head. She wanted to say something casual, flippant. She couldn't think of anything. She hadn't liked Braver much, but she didn't like knowing he was dead in the next room. And it could have been Timmy, too, if the lights hadn't gone out.

"Who did it? Why Braver? Why Timmy? There was just junk up here."

"You think someone killed Braver and tried to kill Mr. Lowry in a fight over something? Some object?"

"I heard a fight on my way up. Men were yelling, and I heard a thud."

"Was it Mr. Lowry yelling? Did you recognize his voice?"

Jane shook her head.

"Could you hear any words? Any idea what the argument was about?"

"I thought I heard someone say something about AA or OA or something like that. Letters, not words."

"Did you recognize anyone up here? Any dealers or pickers you're familiar with? That you know from other sales?"

"No. I think most of the low numbers who got in early were from downstate. Trenton Sales isn't a Chicago company."

"Did you and Mr. Lowry come together?"

"No. I came with Richard Rose. Braver works for him. Worked for him," Jane said, correcting herself. "I asked Tim to come with us, but . . ."

"Yes?"

Jane felt in her pocket for the pieces of paper Tim had asked her to take from him. She took them out and pretended to be nervous and distracted, just fingering the scraps and continuing to talk to Oh.

"I didn't even know Tim was coming. He . . ." Jane stopped talking and smiled when she saw the blue square. "I invited him to come along with Richard and me, bragging that we'd have low numbers and would get in early." Jane held out the blue ticket to Oh. "Tim gave me this before the ambulance took him away."

Oh read the invitation and asked if he could keep the number one blue ticket.

Jane nodded.

"Did he give you anything else or say anything that might help us piece together what happened?"

Jane was not totally comfortable lying to Detective Oh, but she didn't want to give up the other ticket that she had taken from Tim's pocket. She recognized it as a claim check for merchandise he had already purchased. He trusted her to pick it up before she left the house.

"No."

Oh stood up and walked over to the window. Although there were lights set up on the property, the woods were dark. Jane wondered about his night vision. Could he see something in those trees, in that cloudless sky?

"Detective, may I . . . ?"

Oh held up his hand, not in a strong and defiant gesture, but gently, as if shushing a child. She might have made the same motion to Nick if he was questioning her about dinner while she was trying to think, trying to figure out her hours on a shoot or remember how much paprika she used in the stew.

He walked back over to her and sat back down on the same crate. "Did you notice what Mr. Lowry had in his right hand?"

"No."

"He was holding a small ax. I can't tell for sure yet, but I believe it might be the weapon that killed Mr. Braver."

"Did you see Tim's head? If he hit Braver, it was after Braver hit him. Self-defense," Jane said loudly, standing up.

"Do you think he could have struck a killing blow after that bump on the head?"

Jane shook her head. "I don't think Tim could ever strike a killing blow."

"Think about the voices you heard, the argument. You said you didn't hear Lowry's voice? Did you hear two different men?"

"I think so."

They both turned toward the door, hearing footsteps. Officer Mile was speaking soothingly to Richard, who was loud and blustery.

Oh walked to the door and called down. "Please wait a

few more minutes down in the stable. I'll call you on the radio, Officer Mile, when we're ready."

Jane heard Richard protest; then the voices faded as they clumped back down the stairs.

"Would you recognize the voices if you heard them again?"

"I don't think so. They were muffled, just raised, masculine voices. I didn't make out any words, didn't hear anything clearly."

"No one jumped out of the window in that room, that's for sure," Oh said. "It's a thirty-foot drop straight down into those raspberry brambles."

"Someone ran down the stairs though," Jane said, remembering how she had hugged the railing and almost been knocked over.

Oh leaned forward.

"When the lights went out, I was on the stairs. I squeezed up against the wall because I thought someone might be coming down after the argument. Someone flashed a light in my face and ran down past me."

"Say anything?"

Jane shook her head. "Nothing. He was breathing hard, though, like . . ."

"He? You're sure it was a man?"

"I think so. Yes, I'm sure."

"Why?"

"Well, size. The flashlight shone down at me."

"You were on a lower step, yes?"

"Yes, but I could just feel that it was someone big. And the breathing was a man."

"Something special about the breathing?"

"Heavy. Gasping. I'm sure it was a man."

"Yes."

"So find this man; he did it. He fought with Braver, Tim walked in and saw them, so he knocked Tim out and ran."

"And put the ax in Mr. Lowry's hand?"

"Why not?" Jane asked. "Somebody's killing people and doesn't want to get caught. Why not put a weapon in somebody else's hand? Anybody who watches television would know enough to do that."

Oh nodded and continued to pace around the room. An officer from the smaller room poked his head in and told them they were about to finish up and wanted to take the body out. Oh asked the man stationed at the door to clear both the stairs and the exit from the stable out to the waiting ambulance.

Before the officer could turn around, they heard footsteps and a loud, protesting voice.

"You can't keep me away from there. I've got to know who . . ." Richard entered the room and stared at Jane. "You?"

"Me what?" Jane asked.

Three uniformed policemen surrounded Richard, but Oh waved them back.

"I heard that Braver . . . You didn't kill Braver?"

Jane was a serious person at heart. She knew that there was a dead man in the next room, was completely aware that Braver was the third victim she had encountered in less than a week, was perfectly aware of the horror, the suspicion, the nightmare that showed no sign of ending. Instead of numbing her, sending her into a blank shock, the immensity of the past week gave her monkey brain. Thoughts, images, half-finished phrases skated through her consciousness. The total absurdity of the situation was growing unbearable. All she had wanted to do this week was find a flowerpot, pick up a button or two, discover an unidentified Bakelite dangle pin and pick it up for a song. She felt an overwhelming desire to drive to Kankakee and hug her father. She wanted Oh's tie. She wanted Tim beside her. She wanted Charley and Nick to be at home waiting for her with a hot meal.

"Does this mean there won't be a second date?" Jane asked.

"Braver was like an uncle to me . . . Can I see him?" Richard was looking at Oh, seemingly unaware that Jane had spoken. Maybe she hadn't. Her brain and voice were playing tricks on her, and she wasn't sure what she was saying aloud.

Jane heard Oh ask Richard about Braver's family. None. Only his father and him. Braver had been with them for forty years.

"Louie," said Jane.

She knew she had said that one aloud because both men turned and faced her.

"You told me that Louie and Braver were cousins. On the porch, remember?"

"Yeah, oh yeah, of course, Louie. We've taken care of both of them so long, I forgot. Yeah, Louie and Braver are first cousins."

Oh asked Richard to page Louie's beeper and turned to Jane. "Feeling all right, Mrs. Wheel?"

"I'd like to get to the hospital to check on Tim."

"Yes, why doesn't Officer Mile drive you and we'll be in touch later?"

Jane was surprised that it was so easy. She asked and she received. Richard stared at her, but Jane couldn't read anything in his eyes.

"Richard?"

He cocked his head slightly, listening.

"Thanks for bringing me."

He nodded.

"And I'm so sorry about Braver," she added.

Richard reached into his pocket and drew out a handkerchief. As he raised it to mop his face, a white plastic object trapped in its folds clattered onto the floor. Richard quickly retrieved it and jammed it back into his pocket.

Oh looked quickly at Jane and back to Richard.

"Albuterol," said Richard, patting the bulge in his pocket, "for my asthma."

16

Jane asked Officer Mile's permission to pick up her purchases before they left for the hospital. Mile couldn't see any reason why not, since the officers in charge had not stopped Trenton Sales from checking people out who had been in the big house, had allowed shoppers the opportunity to pick up their packages before they left the premises, leaving their names, numbers, and addresses. Cursory looks through the bags, and people were waved away.

"I'll have to check through your bags," Mile said.

"Of course," said Jane, hoping that there was nothing in the bags retrieved with Tim's tickets that would startle either one of them.

Cautiously Jane lifted out newspaper-wrapped parcels from Tim's shopping bags. She hoped her envious eyes didn't give away that these superb Weller vases did not belong to her, had not been her find. She caressed them and carefully swaddled them once more in newspaper.

Mile didn't make her unwrap everything. She helped Jane carry the four large bags and three boxes out to the patrol car.

Knots of green shirts stood talking, some smoking cigarettes outside the house. No one knew what to do. Almost all of the shoppers had filed away. Police officers covered the doors, walked through the edges of wood along the property line flashing beams of light along the ground, through the trees.

"Poor Trenton Sales," Jane said.

"Yeah. A murder can really dampen shopping enthusiasm," said Mile.

Poor Braver is what I should have said, Jane thought, but knew her heart wouldn't have been in it. Who was Braver anyway? He and Louie were Richard's thuggons, according to Tim. Who had Braver been fighting with up in the coach house? What could they have been fighting over? An AA meeting. That's what she thought she'd heard, AA or OA. Was one of them an alcoholic? Alcoholics Anonymous? Overeaters Anonymous? There was nothing but junk up there. Even Jane, with her need to pick up totally abandoned goods, had seen nothing that needed rescuing up there.

She had to tell Oh. This observation was important. Just like the picker's newspaper she had found in Jack's recycling. It said something loud and clear. Well, loud anyway. The fight was over something else, not a tug of war over some piece of glass, some jewel, some painting. It had to have been something else.

Richard carried an inhaler. Albuterol. Asthma.

Just like her son. How many times had she watched Nick run up and down a soccer field, playing midfield for a frantic coach who yelled nonstop. "Where are you, Mr. Wheel? You should be here." When Nick followed his commands, the coach would yell, "Why weren't you over there? Go to the ball. Play your position! Don't turn your back! That's your ball, Mr. Wheel!"

At halftime, Jane would run over and toss an inhaler to Nick, who would take two puffs and toss it back. The coach never acknowledged her presence or the fact that Nicky was panting and wheezing, playing his lungs out on that field. Jane always felt sick by the time the game was over. Nick would toss his gear into the back of the car and ask to stop for a drink or an order of fries, but never seemed angry at the coach, never as furious as Jane thought he had a right to be. He would only shrug if Jane told him he played a good game. "I was slow in the first half," he might say, and then would ask Charley if he had noticed when he dribbled around an opposing player. What was it with those boys who could shrug off injustice so easily?

Was it Richard breathing on the steps? Pushing her into the wall with his body, sucking the air out of the stairway in greedy gulps?

Officer Mile was talking on the phone and monitoring her radio, turned low, as she drove Jane toward the hospital. She abruptly turned south instead of north though, and when Jane looked at her, she held up one finger, gesturing for her to wait for the explanation.

"Mr. Lowry insisted on leaving the hospital," Mile said, when she put down the phone. "He has a slight concussion, a bruise, and a few stitches over his eye. Detective Oh okayed his leaving as long as he was accompanied by an officer. He'll be at your house in a few minutes. We're all to wait there for Detective Oh."

At her house, Jane hugged Tim and fussed over what to get him to eat, to drink.

"Nothing. Unlike you with a concussion, I am going to behave. Just let me stretch out on the couch and you bring in your packages to show me." Tim gave her the quizzical eye and she nodded, reassuring him that she had picked everything up.

Jane piled the packages in the living room, then went into the study to check the answering machine.

Jane? Jane? It's Dad. Don't worry. Everything is still fine with me. I tried to call Tim to tell him we were sorry. I saved the story in the paper for you. It's too damn bad. Call us, honey.

Tim was lying on the couch unwrapping the glasses in the box. Jane checked her watch. It was only ten-thirty, not too late to call home.

"Dad," Jane said, feeling relief course through her all over again. No cancer, not this time. "You weren't sleeping, were you?"

"Nope, watching the weather, feeling lucky."

"You must be so happy. Did you call Michael?"

"Honey, we hadn't even told him there was anything to worry about. Thought we'd wait until we found out. Lucky, isn't it, that we didn't have to put him through that."

"Lucky," Jane agreed, feeling the familiar envy of her brother, always protected, always important, always younger.

"Dad, on the answering machine you said you called Tim to tell him you were sorry. Why?"

"Hasn't he called you? I thought you'd be the first person he'd talk to."

"He's here, Dad, in the next room. I'm not sure he knows what you're talking about. I don't."

"That friend of his committed suicide, Janie."

"David Gattreaux killed himself? That's impossible . . ."

"No, his friend who lived with him last year, helped him out in his business, Phillip."

Phillip. The love of Tim's life.

"What? Where?" Jane stopped herself before asking the cosmic "why" or the grittier "how" since her father wouldn't know the answer to the first question and she wasn't sure she wanted to hear the answer to the second.

"Found his body in a shed on the old state hospital grounds. Been there since last fall. Just says that the death was ruled a suicide."

"Oh, god, I'll have to tell Tim," Jane whispered. "It is so not the right time."

"Be hard to find a time that is right, honey. Didn't mean for this to fall on you."

"I know, Dad."

When Jane returned to Tim and Mile, she was still undecided about what to say. If she asked Mile to leave, it would make everything even more momentous. There was never going to be a right time, an easy time.

"Tim," she began, stopped when she heard Oh knock and call out through the back screen door.

Officer Mile went to let him in, followed by a panting Rita, who had stood by her side at attention since she had come in.

"Tim, before they get back in here . . ."

"These glasses are perfect for the wedding. See the pastel stripes?"

"It's about Phillip."

Tim looked up. His face, bruised and stitched, was as blank as he could make it.

"My dad called and left a message about how sorry he was for you. I just called him and he told me, it was in the paper today, the Kankakee paper."

"What? What was in the paper?" Tim whispered.

"Phillip committed suicide. Some construction worker found his body."

"When?"

"I don't know exactly, but they think he had been there, where they found him, since last fall."

Jane had come over to the couch and sat by Tim's side. He had raised himself on one elbow and was looking childlike in his curiosity. His eyes round, his mouth half open, waiting with the next question. Jane suddenly missed Nick so urgently that she felt a physical ache in her side.

"Tim, I'm so sorry."

Jane stroked his arm as he lowered himself back onto the couch and closed his eyes. She thought about the two of them together, such good friends, such a complete couple. They'd finished each other's sentences like old marrieds. They'd teased each other, bragged about and for the other. Phil had been the first friend Tim had ever introduced to Jane that she hadn't been jealous of, hadn't held back friendship while she waited out the fling. Tim and Phil hadn't needed to exclude her or anyone else to be alone. Phillip respected Tim's old friendship with her and gave it room. He had a generous heart.

When Phillip had disappeared without a trace, moved out one weekend when Tim was at a flea market downstate, Tim was devastated. He had torn apart the house and shop looking for a note, an explanation. He had even called the police, but they had gently, if somewhat patronizingly, told him there was no evidence that he hadn't just left of his own accord.

"Not police business," the officer had told him.

"But he's a missing person," he had told Jane later over the telephone. "He's *my* missing person."

Now Tim, already battered, was sucking in air as if he had been punched again, a much lower blow.

Detective Oh cleared his throat and Jane looked up, wondering how long he and Mile had been standing in the doorway.

"A bad time has been made worse?" Oh asked softly.

Jane knew Tim couldn't speak. She looked up, her own eyes filled with tears.

"A friend of Tim's, a friend of mine, too, was found in Kankakee. We just heard."

"Was found?"

"His body was found. My dad called. He said the paper said suicide. Several months . . ."

"Yes, I know the case," Oh said. He gestured to Mile and they entered the room.

"What case? How could you know about Phillip?"

"The body was found last week, and when he was identified as a friend of Mr. Lowry's, Detective Munson called me."

"Why?" Tim asked hoarsely.

Oh seemed to weigh his words. He looked at Tim for a long time then looked at Jane.

"Because he suspected you had something to do with Mr. Gattreaux's murder, and when your friend Phillip Mayhew's body was found, I think he was hoping to show me that I had been wrong about you. That you, and possibly Mrs. Wheel, were capable of murder."

"No," Jane said, incredulous.

"Yes. Munson is not an atypical detective. Goes right to the most logical explanation and works at proving it true.

Believes the worst is possible of anyone. Nothing personal, Mrs. Wheel."

"You don't believe that though?" Tim asked.

"I believe that murder is seldom logical and that the worst is possible of anyone. Also the best. That, too, is nothing personal."

"Do you know how they determined that it was suicide?" Jane asked.

Again Oh looked at them both, deciding whether or not they really wanted the answer he was prepared to give them. He nodded slightly before speaking, as if getting an affirmative answer from some inner voice.

"One set of footprints, Mr. Mayhew's, led to an old toolshed by the river, completely out of the way, never used. He had a combination of pills, alcohol, and household poison, and seems to have taken precautions in the order of dosage, so that he would not vomit out the mixture. He had covered himself with blankets, an old tarp. He had brought a down pillow. He had a few mementos with him, a book and some photographs. There was a tape player and some tapes. He apparently played Mozart and the Talking Heads as he carried out his plans. He wrote a note."

"The photographs?" Tim asked at the same time Jane said, "A note?"

"One photograph was his mother and father and sister from 1952 or 1953, standing in front of a house decorated for Christmas. The second was one of the two of you standing in front of your flower shop, Mr. Lowry. Also decorated for Christmas.

"The note was quite brief. It was on a Post-it note stuck

to the tape player." Oh read from a small notebook, 'See, I made myself comfortable, just like I promised in the letter. "Don't cry for Me, Argentina." I love you. P.' "

Tim sat up slowly and rubbed his eyes, forgetting for a moment about the stitches and looking both pained and puzzled when he touched the bandage.

"What letter?"

Oh cocked his head to one side and turned up his palms.

"I never got any letter."

"I'm working on that."

"What do you mean?" Jane asked.

"Did Phillip Mayhew know Mr. Gattreaux? Was he working as a picker or a bidder for you when Mr. Mayhew was your partner?"

"Yes, Phillip met him somewhere. At a party, I think. We were looking for help. I hired him to work in the store when Phillip was out of town visiting his sister's family. After Phil got back, I started using David to bid for me at auctions. A few months later, Phillip left."

"Did the three of you socialize?"

"I think we went out for drinks a few times. We had a little party when we decorated the store for Christmas . . ."

"Yes?" Oh prompted, when Tim's voice trailed off.

"David took that picture. We decorated the store early, on November first. Took out the pumpkins and the gourd lanterns and got the holiday lights and greens up in one day. Phil left a few days after that."

"Charley and Nick and I were there," said Jane. "We went over to the tavern and got brandy from my dad to make real eggnog. It was about fifty degrees, way too warm for it, but we pretended like we were freezing and posed for pictures. Remember, Tim? We put that fake snow on our coats and said we'd use the photo for our Christmas cards?"

"You never send Christmas cards."

"But we always intend to," Jane said.

"Do you have those pictures, Mrs. Wheel? Those Christmas card photos?"

"Yes." Jane scanned the living room and Oh, Mile, and Tim followed her eyes as they read the room, left to right. Bookshelves lined the fireplace wall, filled with art, pottery, books, and small scenes, clutches of figures grouped around objects. One shelf held small chalk Indian figures and buffalo huddled around a fire, colorfully painted by Cub Scouts in 1958. Crudely carved wooden dogs lived on the shelf above. A wheeled wooden laundry basket that Jane had purchased at a convent sale was heaped with Pendleton blankets and souvenir pillows. A tower of vintage suitcases reached almost to the ceiling with original leather name tags dangling from their handles. Jane studied the stack. She stood on tiptoe to read the old tag on the case second from the top. She dragged over a solid oak box with a carved-out handhold, also from the convent sale—used by a nun, she imagined—as a safe stepstool to reach the high classroom bookshelves and used it herself to step up and extricate the case from the tower.

Oh looked over her shoulder as she set the case down and saw that the identification tag said, PHOTOS AND CARDS, PERSONAL FAMILY CORRESPONDENCE, SEPTEMBER TO JUNE 1999.

Jane opened up the valise and took out an envelope marked Kankakee, November, and began fanning through photographs.

"I am in awe, Mrs. Wheel, that you would be able to find something so quickly in this..."

"Yes, Detective Oh? In this...?"

"Collectors' paradise?" he offered.

"Here are the photos from that day. There are only five."

Oh sat down next to Tim on the couch, and Mile went around to the back to look over their collective shoulders as they passed the photos.

Charley and Nick hanging hammered tin cones from an enormous tree. Charley and Jane toasting with what appeared to be eggnog in pressed glass punch cups. Behind them an elegant punch bowl displayed on a table laden with ornaments and evergreen boughs, candles blazing from silver holders of all heights and shapes. Charley, Jane, and Nick peeking out from a huge wreath they held in their mittened hands.

"That's the one I would have used, if I had remembered to send cards," Jane said.

Tim and Phillip standing in front of the store, grinning widely, with their arms hanging loosely around each other's shoulders.

"This is the same pose David took. We were going to send out cards, but after Phil left..."

The final photograph was David Gattreaux, Tim, and Phillip standing in front of the store.

"Nicky took that, I think," Jane said. "I didn't send you a copy, because..."

"Because I wouldn't like it?" Tim asked slowly, holding the photo up directly in front of his face, squinting under his bandage.

The photograph of Tim flanked by two men, now dead, would be disturbing in itself, without the content that Tim was now forced to absorb. In the picture the three men were standing under a display of a life-size, vintage, mechanical Santa Claus, caught in this photo with his arms outstretched, opened wide. Tim was happily grinning into the camera, his head leaning slightly toward Phillip, who was also grinning but his eyes were locked on David, who was holding up two fingers behind Tim's head. David was clearly inviting Phillip in on the joke with a mocking smile. Under the watchful eye of Santa, David looked wicked, Tim angelic. Phillip, in this photo at least, looked as if he had chosen naughty over nice.

Tim passed the photograph to Oh, who looked at it for a long time. No one spoke. Then everyone spoke.

"Mr. Lowry, did you ever suspect . . ."

"Timmy, a photo is a only moment . . ."

"It's just a fucking photograph . . ."

"I'm going to check on Rita." When Officer Mile said this, a beat later than their own words, all three turned around to look at her. "She's been barking for a few minutes now," she said, explaining as she headed off to the kitchen.

"Mr. Lowry, do you think there had been a relationship between Gattreaux and Phillip?"

Tim stared straight ahead.

"I have reasons for asking, Mr. Lowry," Oh said gently.

Tim did not look at him when he answered. Jane tried to follow his eyes as he talked, to see what he was staring at, but knew she'd never find it.

"Phillip loved me. He was a more restless soul than I was, always wondering what lived behind every door. When we went to house sales, I would pick out what we bought, he would wander around and speculate about what the people were like who lived there, what it would be like to be them," Tim said, looking at Jane and smiling, very far away.

"He was like Jane," Tim said, nodding, as if realizing it for the first time. "He collected the lives while I collected the stuff."

Officer Mile came back, followed by Rita, who continued to look back over her shoulder and growl.

"Something out in the yard, sir. She was at the screen door, scratching and clearly agitated. I threw on the lights and checked around the house. Probably an animal, maybe a raccoon in the garbage."

"Let's be on the safe side, call for a car to check the neighborhood. Let's watch the house tonight."

Tim continued, unaware that anyone had spoken.

"I don't think Phillip really liked David. I don't know anyone who really liked David. But he was attractive like a bad boy is attractive: dangerous, selfish, conceited, handsome. Phillip might have been curious. You know . . . what would it be like to live there instead of here? We'd been together four years; he might have been tempted. Or bored," he added sadly.

"No, Timmy, you're right. Phillip loved you. I know he did. Sometimes, people just get . . ." Jane trailed off.

"Curious?" Tim said gently.

"Yes, curious." Jane stood up abruptly and announced she'd make coffee and left for the kitchen.

"I'm sorry, Mr. Lowry, you've had a terrible night. I haven't even asked you about your encounter with Mr. Braver at the sale."

"Who?"

"The man you argued with in the coach house. The man who was killed?"

"What are you talking about?"

"The man whose body we found next to you in the coach house at the sale. He was likely killed by a blow or blows to the head, probably with an ax handle. He was lying beside you."

"Somebody was killed? I don't remember him. I didn't see anyone in the room. I remember thinking that I wanted to unfold the rugs in the corner and I was going to do that; then I heard footsteps behind me and men's voices. That's it."

"You didn't see anyone else in the room?"

"No, I hadn't even turned around yet when I passed out. I don't even remember feeling anything. There was no pain until I came to."

"Do you remember seeing the ax in the room? Where it was in relation to the rugs?"

"No ax, no tools, no nothing. There were some broken wooden crates and the rugs. I didn't see anything in that room."

"You're sure you didn't see or pick up an ax?"

Tim shook his head. "I'm certain."

Jane came in carrying a tray with coffee and a plate of chocolate-covered graham crackers.

"What's the big deal about the ax?" Tim asked, glancing over at Jane.

"The murder weapon. You were holding it, dear. Cream?"

17

It took some time to convince Tim that someone had been murdered in the coach house, that he had shared the floor with a dead body, that he had been holding the alleged murder weapon. But he wasn't worried about the implications of being found with the ax.

"Any moron who watches TV would know to stick the weapon into my hand," he said, and Jane had nodded knowingly at Oh. He didn't bother to talk about his own innocence, to fear that he was a suspect. He simply didn't believe that it had happened. "I'm telling you, there was no one in there, and there was nothing to fight over. Just junk."

"That's what I wanted to tell you, too," said Jane. "There was nothing in there to interest anyone. I was thinking the same thing; that it wasn't a fight over anything in the room."

"How about Mr. Lowry? He was in the room."

Tim began rubbing his head. "Yeah, that's the ticket. Two guys walked in and thought I was so hot that they began fighting over me, accidentally whacked me, then one whacked the other too hard, panicked, but before he split, gave me an ax handle to remember him by."

"You were already in the room. Let's discount the 'you were so hot' theory for a moment. If these gentlemen were arguing, one of them at least ready to fight, perhaps to the death, why would they enter a room where there was a witness and a roomful of witnesses just outside the door, that one or both would have to parade past in order to get away. The Hendershott estate is a big piece of property. Woods, outbuildings, at least two tool sheds that were unlocked and in sight of the coach house. Could they have been following you, Mr. Lowry?"

"I had been in the corner going over a rug with a flashlight. The overhead was too dim, and I thought it might be a good one. I'd been in there a long time by myself. When they came in, they were arguing already."

"Are you sure they weren't after you?" Jane asked. "Something you'd found? Everybody was mad at you bastards for getting in that early admission line. That reminds me, why didn't you tell me you were going to the sale, that you had an early invite?"

Tim smiled, was surprised he remembered how, then shrugged. "I can't stand that guy Richard. I just thought it would be fun to show him you didn't need him to get you into a sale."

Detective Oh cleared his throat. "So you're certain the two men entered without knowing you were there?"

Jane poured refills all around and settled into an old, stuffed, horsehair chair, plumped a pillow, and hugged it in front of her. Tim sipped coffee and nodded.

"There were some people in the outer room of the coach house, in the living area," said Oh. "Two of those people remember seeing Mr. Braver and another man go into the backroom. However, their descriptions of the second man do not exactly match. They agree that he was large, but they do not agree on hair color or age. They both think he was wearing blue jeans and a dark T-shirt, a description that fits almost every male at the Hendershott sale."

"Almost," said Tim, smoothing out his own tan pleated pants. His white linen shirt had been removed at the hospital and taken by the police. He was wearing a pale green V-necked surgical shirt that he had begged from the first-year resident who had unsuccessfully prevented him from signing himself out.

"Mr. Lowry was in the corner examining the carpet. Enter the two men wanting a private place to talk," Oh said, looking at Jane. "Maybe this wasn't about things at the sale. Maybe they did come in to argue privately and didn't see Mr. Lowry?"

"Yes," said Jane. "Then they notice Tim. They don't realize he's in dearlerland, a whole other planet, examining the rug and not hearing whatever it is they're saying. They think of him as a witness. One of them, maybe Braver, whacks Tim from behind. The other one, angry at Braver for something already or angry at him for hitting Tim, strikes him with the ax, then puts it into Tim's hands. How's that?"

"Isn't that a little extreme? No one checked to see if I was dead? The other guy murders Braver over this mistake, a painful one for me, but why didn't they both just run off?"

"They were already arguing when they entered the room. Besides, the lights went out," Jane said. "Whoever was arguing with Braver took him in there, knew the lights were going out, and that was the signal to murder him. He had to knock Tim out so Tim wouldn't be a witness. And he had to get away down the steps while it was still dark."

"Very good, Mrs. Wheel. But the master switch for the electricity in the coach house is located in an unlocked cabinet in the stable area. There were at least twenty people roaming through there. No one saw anyone behaving suspiciously around the cabinet. If the murderer had an accomplice who was timing the blackout, he or she would have been standing there, checking their luminous dial watch, ready to switch the power back on, then melt into the chaos, people accusing others of taking their bags and boxes in the dark." Oh paused. "At least that's what my wife said happened when the lights went back on. She was in the stable and noticed no one over by the fuse box, before or after the lights went out."

"Richard or Louie," Jane said sadly. "Damn, I knew it was a mistake to start dating." Jane got up and walked over to Rita, who still sat at Mile's side. "I'm sticking with dogs."

"So this is basically solved? Three thugs, then there were two, right?" Tim asked, his eyes closed.

"No, not quite. Richard Rose was in the house. We can't place him in the coach house. We can't even place him in the barn where he might have given an order or sent someone upstairs. According to three witnesses, he was measuring the ballroom floor, talking the measurements into a tape recorder."

"But he has asthma, we saw his inhaler."

Tim opened his eyes, and he and Oh both looked at Jane.

"The man who pushed past me on the steps was breathing heavily, gasping for air. An asthmatic, right?" Jane asked. "Richard."

"You are a clever girl, Nancy Drew," Tim said, "but I can throw a monkey wrench into that."

"Please," said Oh.

"Asthma's the picker's disease. You don't have it yet, Jane, but if you keep it up, you probably will. You sift through enough boxes of moldy books, go through enough boxes of flood-damaged yearbooks and photo albums, open enough tins of dust-encrusted buttons, plow through enough piles of vintage nighties buried in an attic trunk, and you'll start sneezing and wheezing like everyone else. Know how your dad always says that lung cancer's the saloon-keeper's disease? Well, asthma's the picker's disease." Tim illustrated his talk by reaching into his left pocket and pulling out an albuterol inhaler. "Even I have succumbed."

"Go to sleep. I'll come back tomorrow," Oh said, nodding to Jane and Tim. "Is there a car out front?" he asked Mile.

"Yes and another covering the neighborhood."

Rita stood up and stretched, trotted off into the kitchen for water. Oh asked Jane if she minded if they closed the windows and locked them.

"We'll suffocate."

"Just on the first floor, a precaution. Your house is so easily accessible." Oh looked around at all the windows, wide open to the cooler night air.

Tim did not get up from the couch when Jane walked Oh and Mile to the front door.

"Did you check to see if either Louie or Braver was in AA or OA? If they were arguing about a missed meeting or something?"

"Lock the door after us, please."

"It's worth checking out, don't you think?" Jane persisted.

"Not an OA meeting, Mrs. Wheel. A meeting with Oh. Mr. Braver and I had an appointment for later in the evening."

*　*　*

Jane walked Tim upstairs and made him comfortable in her bed, turned on the air conditioner, and covered him with the Amish quilt he always tried to get her to sell to him.

She stroked his arm and fussed over his eye while he mumbled, drifted off to sleep.

"Phil loved me. I'm sure of that."

"Me, too, sweetie." Again, Jane was reminded of Nick. She wanted it to be Nick here, tucked in and safe. Then she could throw herself on top of him and protect him from love and the loss that follows, from greed and jealousy, from hate and violence.

"What about mystery and adventure, excitement and discovery?" Charley had asked once, when she had told him just what she wanted to lock Nick away from. "Don't you want him to feel thrilled? At least once?"

At the time, Charley had persuaded her. Yes, she wanted adventures for her boy. Yes, he should climb the highest mountains, swim the deepest seas. Yes, he should fall in love and give his heart and feel it crack like an egg when that love fell away. Then he would rebuild that heart, stronger and deeper walled; and when he met the true love of his life, it would be ready, worthy. Isn't that what they, his parents, had done? Yes, he should live, her son, their son. He had been eighteen months, still chuckling in his crib when they had discussed this. Then Charley had taken her to bed. And yes, he reminded her when they made love that she had taken a chance on him, on them. Yes, then she had been persuaded.

Right. Then a few years down the road, you lean your thrill-seeking, adventurous self over a butterflied leg of lamb at a stupid-ass neighborhood progressive dinner with its forced congeniality and hail-fellow-well-met bullshit; and pretty soon you're kissing a neighbor you don't even respect, let alone like, and hearts are cracking like eggs all around.

What did Charley think of all that open-hearted adventure now?

Try as she might, Jane couldn't turn this into Charley's fault. He had so little to do with this mess she found herself in that she could barely make out his outline on the horizon behind her closed eyes. She could conjure Nick, and he would be a force of energy between her arms. She could feel his shape and sense the heat from his trim little body. But Charley stayed far away. She had sent him there. She'd assigned this role to him.

After the party, when the rumors started, Charley came to her and asked if she was having an affair with Jack.

"And if so," he had said, always the professor making up the test question in such a way that he would receive the most complete answer, so he would know everything in his students' heads, "are you in love with him?"

It wasn't even an essay test for her. Short answer all the way. No and no. Or no and are you kidding? Yuck and yuck. Any of these would have done. All she had to do was say no, look into Charley's eyes and say, I was just curious. I just didn't back away. Curiosity.

Charley would have been disgruntled, miffed, he would have huffed and puffed around the house a bit. He would have thrown out hypotheticals like, what if he was curious about Cindy Crawford? Or a *Playboy* model? Or Barbara Graylord? Then they both would have started laughing and it would have been over. Mostly over. She would still have had to draw him slowly back to her. She would need to have been the penitent, head bowed. She would have had to become the grateful wife, the reassuring wife, the devout wife. It wouldn't have been hard. She was sorry. She was grateful. She loved Charley.

"Sorry-Grateful." That was a song on a record Jack and Sandy played all the time. *Company*, a Sondheim musical about marriage. Sandy and Jack called it their song. "Sorry-Grateful."

But Jane threw the test. She failed. She didn't give the answers, no and no. She didn't answer at all. When Charley asked about Jack, about the rumors, about the kiss in the kitchen, she simply stared right back into those well deep brown eyes, set in those weathered creases that she loved to touch when he smiled. She wanted so badly to see his eyes relax into that familiar, lovely release, but she couldn't answer no.

She had asked herself thousands of times why she had refused to ease Charley's mind. She hadn't been flirting with Jack at all. She disliked the man, didn't she? He was everything she despised in people, the reinvention of middle-aged self that she mocked and derided: the deceit and surface glamor that she hated about her own job and hated when it crept into her own life. The only connection she had to Jack was the *Daily* jumble, the Sunday crossword, and his occasional interest in what she purchased at weekend sales, hardly the kind of attraction that leads to an affair. But she had let Charley stand there, waiting patiently for her answer, prepared to do the right and honorable thing, no matter what she said. But she didn't say anything. She stared at him, mute, until he walked out of the room.

Why didn't she throw herself into his arms? Charley would have behaved so decently. Maybe that was the problem. She didn't deserve decent. Maybe she knew the only way she'd be punished would be if she did it herself?

There was no one to talk to about this. The women who worked for her and with her were young and smart and tough. They didn't dillydally. They wouldn't understand why she hadn't told the truth, especially when the truth was the right answer. She could be honest and moral and virtuous. Just tell Charley that she was drunk. It was a whim. A nothing. An accident. A curiosity. No one went to hell for being curious. There was Eve, of course. But she didn't necessarily go to hell.

"She just got kicked out of paradise," Jane said aloud, standing at the kitchen sink. She had left Tim sleeping and come down to rinse the coffee cups and make sure Rita had a full bowl of water. It was hot and airless downstairs and Rita panted painfully, sprawled on the kitchen tile.

"Want to come upstairs with me, girlfriend? We'll crank up the air in Nicky's room and get some sleep, okay?"

When Jane straightened up, she felt, before she saw, that something was wrong. She didn't hear any floorboards creak or any clothes rustle. She didn't sense that disturbance of air when another body is closer than it should be. She didn't feel the hair on the back of her neck stand at attention. Jane was aware of a visual disturbance. Something was rearranged in her kitchen.

Her house was a series of tableaus. They changed weekly, depending on what she found for herself, what she bought for Miriam, what she bought for the unknown client who wanted it but didn't know it yet. She was used to arranging and rearranging, falling in love with some small icon, then packing it up in bubblewrap and sending it off. But she was aware of a change in the kitchen that she hadn't made. Something was different.

When Tim had made lunch, he might have hung the towels differently? No, they were in order. Small embroidered terriers doing chores, side by side, one with THURSDAY across the top, and the cleaner, less wrinkled one, with a cross-stitched FRIDAY slung over the sink. Flowerpots lined one windowsill. Ball jugs and pitchers in the same order she had left them. Sale information clipped to the refrigerator door with a giant magnetic clothespin was undisturbed. Tiredness was weighing down her shoulders and blurring her vision. Tomorrow she would read the kitchen, left to right, and figure out what went where. But now she had to sleep at least a few hours before the sun rose. She waved to the dog who rose and, leading with her tongue, panted over to Jane's side.

"If I weren't so tired, I could figure this out, Rita." Her voice dropped to a whisper. "Somebody's been eating my porridge."

10

Jane's eyes opened wide at 6 A.M. She had only slept three hours, but her inner Friday estate sale clock rang loudly in her ear. It had been ringing for a long time. Six would actually be too late for most of the better sales. She knew if she slipped into shorts and rushed over to the McDowell sale in Kenilworth, she would find cars already lining the streets, pickers sleeping in their front seats with dented Baby Bens beside them. Scraggly Dave would have been there with his clipboard at 3 A.M. taking names on his numbered list so that when the McDowells opened the door to give out numbers at 8:30 for the sale, which would begin at 9, there would already be a tent city established, a homesteader's claim on the front lawn. Pickers would have already roamed the yard, peered into the windows with flashlights, checked the alley, and pawed through the garbage.

Jane had refused to be seduced by Dumpster digging for a long time; but at a sale last month, she couldn't resist the piles of basement and attic debris that an overzealous sales team had precleaned out of an old Evanston estate. She had given Nick breakfast and seen him off to school, come to the sale late, drawing a high number. She began roaming restlessly, following one of the book guys she recognized, and within thirty seconds of seeing the garbage mountain in the alley was cozily sitting next to him picking through boxes of old maps, notebooks, dusty clothing. She came away with two thirty-year-old Christmas candles, openmouthed choir boys, MIB, or at least they looked mint-in-box; however Miriam would be the one to judge if candles, even collectable ones like these were desirable after sitting in a damp basement for three decades. She also found some torn textbooks from the forties and hauled them to the car, hoping that some of the illustrations might be worth lugging the books home for.

She lay in bed, reflecting on the sales she was missing, the closets and basements and attics and Dumpsters that held the secrets only she could find. One of her many junking fantasies revolved around the broken jewelry box, the cracked vanity case. When she was ten, she had owned a pink leatherette, velvet-lined, multipartitioned jewelry box. Nellie, cleaning ruthlessly one morning, discovered that it had a broken hinge, dumped out the contents, and threw it away.

"It was broke," she had said, and shrugged when Jane had screamed, running to the alley and finding the garbage already picked up. Gone.

It wasn't only that Jane had loved the box itself, a gift from her grandmother. Nor was it that Jane knew the hinge was fixable and the box otherwise in perfect condition. It was the secret compartment. The box had a false bottom that lifted with a pink ribbon, invisible unless you knew it was there. Jane had kept her most special necklace in the secret compartment. She also kept school pictures of her three best friends and a note from Danny H., who said he liked her new haircut. That secret compartment had been one of the few places her mother's X-ray eyes had not penetrated.

At every rummage sale Jane would pick up the discarded jewelry boxes, knowing that someday she would find one with a tiny ribbon tail in the bottom, and she would lift it to find treasure. Even though it would not be the lucite heart with a red velvet rose embedded inside, it would be someone's treasure. And Jane would guard it for them, adopt it as her own.

Rita had no time for Jane's daydreams. She nudged her with her nose, with her whole head, to get up and open Nick's bedroom door, closed against the stifling heat of the hall and the downstairs, locked and shuttered on police orders. Nick's air conditioner hummed along, turning Jane's arms to goose-flesh and challenging her to dare remove the covers to run across that icy floor. Even Rita in her brown fur coat looked a little blue.

"Okay, yes, yes, I'll go."

Jane wrapped her son's baseball comforter around herself and ran to the door. The warmth of the hallway, the air so heavy with heat, held her, stopped her in her tracks, and made her feel trapped inside cotton gauze. Tim was coming out of the bathroom at the end of the hall.

"It's not the heat *nor* is it the humidity," Tim said, his toothbrush still sticking out of his mouth. "It's the temperature change that'll kill you."

"How's the head?" Jane asked, watching Tim try to brighten his eyes and quicken his step, but seeing the heaviness, the weight around his eyes and ankles.

"Still throbbing to let me know it's there. Let me just check something with you. I'm going to recite a list of things and you make a noise, honk, when I say something that isn't true, something I hallucinated, okay?

"I got hit in the head with an ax. A guy got killed next to me. Phillip killed himself. The police now have a motive for me wanting David dead. I am one stupid and doomed motherf—"

"Beep, beep," Jane said gently.

Jane and Tim were each showered, dressed, and downstairs making coffee and buttering toast by 7:30. Tim took Jane's sale page for the weekend off the refrigerator. She had clipped out six classifieds for conducted house/estate sales, about fifteen for garage sales.

"We're too late for the two house sales this morning. Why didn't you wake me for the McDowell? They have pretty fair prices."

"Honey, you got axed last night; thought you just might want to sleep in."

Jane passed the blueberry preserves to Tim, who was running his fingers down the garage sale ads.

"These in map order?"

Tim knew that when Jane made her tape pages, she tried to put them in a sensible driving pattern. She nodded.

"Earliest one is 9:30. Let's go."

Tim saw Jane hesitate and knew she was composing a heartfelt, if overly sentimental speech about Phil and their relationship and how she knew he was hurting. Jane, unwilling to sentimentalize her own relationship with Charley, stubbornly standing alone in her silence and confusion, would now heap all of her emotion on him, her dear friend, who wanted nothing more than to stay as aloof and brittle as she had been throughout her own chaos.

"Darling, I love you, but I'm warning you now. For every mushy thing you say to me about Phillip, I'm going to stir your heart with a probing remark about Charley. *Comprendez vous?*"

Jane nodded grimly and ran her fingers through her hair, shaking her head and reflexively checking her earlobes to see if her red Bakelite hoops were still in place.

"I will heal slowly and as completely as I am able," Tim said, "one garage sale at a time. Okay, baby?"

Jane was counting her cash and giving Tim directions to find the wrapping material they could throw into the trunk in case they found glassware when the phone rang.

Jane and Tim both said aloud, "Screen," and listened for the answering machine to pick up.

Yeah, it's Richard. Sorry about the way things turned out last night. Not a great first date. But I think seeing how there was a murder and everything, maybe we should just wait till things are on track, you know, solved or something, before we see each other. I don't know, seems like the right thing, out of respect to Braver or something. I'm going to Florida for a while anyway. Sorry. Bye.

"Oh, my god, I'm dated and dumped within twenty-four hours. That's got to be a record."

"Don't be naive. Blind dates come into view and the intended will pretend he's someone else, that he was just sent to say the 'date's' malaria is acting up. People can be dated and dumped in a matter of seconds."

"I don't believe that."

"And at least someone got murdered on your date. I mean that is a pretty good excuse. Better than 'I'm not sure we have enough in common.'"

"Actually, we have murder in common. Richard hit me

with a doorframe last Saturday when I found Sandy. He was at the auction and bid against David. We're at the frigging sale with Braver. How much more do you want in common?"

"Two questions. Did you actually like the guy? And when did you start saying 'frigging'?"

"No, but I wanted to. I wanted him to be someone different than anyone I knew, someone who understands how to value . . . but that's not the point. If I am going to be dating again, I wanted to be the dumper, not the dumpee. Question two: when Nick started listening to rap and I told him certain language should not be said, let alone chanted in our house."

"And he pointed out certain hypocrisies . . ."

"Yeah, yeah, let's go now. Then I want to get back home and go through those buttons you bought for me at the Hendershott sale."

"When did I say they were for you?"

"Last night."

"I had a frigging head wound."

Jane's garage sale list always started with the most promising sale. Choosing number one began with a winnowing process. First, she eliminated all sales that promised "lots of baby clothes and childrens' toys." Second, she passed on all sales taking place in newer housing developments or subdivisions unless they carried some intriguing tag like "getting rid of Grandma's sewing stuff," even though she knew that might be a con. One empty plastic sewing basket from Kmart mixed in with all the ersatz Tupperware and artificial flower arrangements might be the extent of Grandma's collection, but you never knew. Jane had found some pretty amazing tins of buttons marked fifty cents, sold by a daughter or granddaughter, happy to be rid of the musty-smelling junk. Third, Jane eliminated all sales that identified and described newer furniture and or "Asian" or "Oriental" treasures. She disliked other people's souvenirs of Eastern travel and found that most households who brought back poorly carved folding screens and faux ivory knickknacks were not likely to have any vintage tablecloths, American pottery from the thirties and forties, or Bakelite buttons.

Today's first sale was either going to be fabulous or a sucker punch that would knock the wind out of them briefly before they hopped back in the car and raced to number two. Tim read while Jane drove efficiently to the south end of Evanston.

```
Forty years accumulation. Moving to Florida,
Must sell all. Two complete sets china. Complete
silver table service. Kitchen and bedroom linens,
blankets, coverlets, and quilts. Misc. household.
Rugs, drapes, lamps. Cleaning out clothes from at-
tic and basement. You sort through. Tools and yard
equipment. Sewing machine, quilting supplies.
Wife selling knickknacks; husband selling stamp
collection. Make offer and send us South.
```

"A little too good to be true, don't you think?" Tim asked, chewing the end of a pencil, his own notebook and lists out on his lap.

"Maybe. But the address is on a street with lots of small bungalows, and it might be just as folksy as it sounds. Did you catch the clue in the china and silver that it might be good?"

"What are you talking about? It doesn't even mention what kind of china."

"Yeah, but if she has two complete sets and all her silver, she probably doesn't have children or at least daughters who have picked through the stuff. It's all there, Timmy. All the aprons and dish towels and crocheted pot holders and..."

"Easy does it, hon. Is this how you get every weekend? Hope springing eternal with every classified?" Tim shook his head. "No wonder..."

"No wonder?"

"Nothing."

"No wonder Charley left? Is that what you were going to say? I thought we weren't going to talk about our..."

"Easy, Jane. I was going to say, no wonder you ended up buying so much junk. You know, expecting the best from every sale, so you buy something to make it seem worth it, to make it as good as it sounded. Like trying to make that creep Richard into your soulmate. Man, are you jumpy." Tim patted her leg. "Calm down."

"Sorry," Jane said, "I overreacted." She turned onto Madison Street and started scanning house numbers.

"Jeez, no wonder Charley left," Tim said, as Jane parked behind a maroon pickup truck, scraping her tires against the curb.

The ad wasn't a con. A sweet, white-haired woman stood at the garage door shaking her head at the eight people waiting for her to open up.

"You're all up so early," she said. "I'll get started."

Jane did scoop up some buttons, three tablecloths, and two crocheted, strawberry pot holders, but got delayed looking through old high-school yearbooks and missed some inexpensive quilt tops. Tim bought a beautiful set of unmarked forties china.

"Just good everyday stuff," the woman had said, pointing out the serving pieces that went with it.

Digging in a box under the picnic table, Jane pulled out a pair of wall plaques that took her breath away. They were bunches of grapes, variegated purple yarn crocheted over bottle caps, with green-wrapped, wire, corkscrew vines and a greenish brown crocheted stem.

"My grandma," Jane began at the same time the woman said, "My mother made those."

"How much?" Jane asked.

The woman shrugged. She took one of the pair from Jane's hand and fingered the bottle caps. "Do you have the ones your grandma made?"

Jane thought of how she had begged Nellie to ask Grandma for them. "They're the only thing I want from Grandma's house, the only thing."

Nellie had made a face and asked why she wanted that old junk.

"Because they're what I looked at when I sat at Grandma's kitchen table. I liked them. I loved them. I just want them. Please."

When her ninety-two-year-old grandma died, Jane was on location in London. Charley called her and sadly told her not to come home.

"But it was my grandma," Jane started, but Charley interrupted.

"The funeral's already over, Janie. Your mom didn't want to bother you. They just had a small service and mass and none of the sisters called their kids until after it was over."

Jane had cried for a long time, alone in her London hotel. She knew her mother's reasoning. Grandma was old, had died quietly at home as she had wanted, and the grandchildren, scattered around the world didn't need to be bothered. There was no emotion wasted in her mother's family. Instead, it was stored up like the canned goods and toilet paper and laundry detergent that her mother hoarded in their basement. Nellie and her sisters gave a whole new meaning to Depression-era kids.

It wasn't just food and clothes and shelter that was dear to them, guarded fiercely, it was tears and laughter and admissions of love. She always pictured her grandfather, stone-faced and silent, listening to a Cubs game on the radio until late afternoon, then eating toast and going to bed. He was always asleep by 6 p.m. Charley once asked Nellie why Pa went to bed so early, and Nellie shrugged and said she guessed it was because of the "Depression." Charley thought for years that Nellie's family was acknowledging bipolar disorder until Jane explained that her mother just meant it was a habit left over from when he worked two jobs, janitor at the church by day, railroad lineman midnight to eight.

"The ones my grandma made got thrown out when her house was sold," Jane said, wrapping the wire curlique around her little finger.

"Take these," the woman said. "I'll throw them in with the pot holders. My mother made those, too."

"Don't you want to keep some of them?" Jane asked.

"Nah," she said, and shook her head. "It's your turn to keep them now."

* * *

Tim couldn't accuse Jane of too much sentimentality at the sale since he engaged the husband in a long discussion of stamps and collecting paraphernalia that Jane recognized as pure kindness. Tim was no more interested in beginning a stamp or coin collection than she was in collecting Beanie Babies.

"It was just so clear that he wanted to talk about it all with someone," Tim said, looking out the window.

The next sales, easy drives that zigzagged their way back to the north end of town, Jane's neighborhood, were uneventful. Despite the promise of "old tools" in one and "vintage gardening equipment" at another, there was just the usual pile of last season's clothes, romance novels, narrow belts, worn pocketbooks, and gag gift items that someone, somewhere, thought would be just right for a fortieth or fiftieth birthday. Sad collections of consumer detritus washed up on the middle-class shoreline of folding tables and garage shelves.

By sale six, Tim begged to go home. His head ached and he was having a bad plastic reaction, getting a polyester rash, coming down with the fondue pot flu.

"I thought fondue pots were back in," Jane said, turning north on Asbury and heading home.

"For a minute. During that minute we bought all we ever needed at one rummage sale. They're like rabbits, those things. Put two on a shelf, turn out the lights, come back in five days, there are seven."

Jane turned onto her block, wondering how she could ask Tim about Phillip. She wondered who would make arrangements for a service. Was there a family that Tim needed to talk to? What was the status of the shop? When would he open again? Did he remember anything more about last night? She saw someone sitting on the front porch and was surprised to find her heart rising, thinking it was Detective Oh with more pieces to the puzzles that were tumbling out of their boxes at her feet.

But Detective Oh didn't smoke cigars.

"Jack?" Jane carried her two plaid shopping bags up to the porch and struggled to get her key out of the pocket of her shorts. Tim transferred the box of china to his own car parked out front then followed Jane up to the porch.

"Out shopping? So early?"

Jane noticed Jack had commandeered a maroon ceramic flowerpot saucer for an ashtray and was clipping a cigar with a small silver cutter. Next to the makeshift ashtray was a grande something from Starbucks.

"Working, Jack. This is what I do now."

"You could have gotten another advertising job, Janie. For Christ's sake, I told you to go see my friend Tod, the headhunter. He could get you set up in two shakes. You didn't have to become a junk dealer." Jack put away the cigar cutter and nodded at Tim. "What happened to you, Lowry? Discovered by an angry wife or did you just walk into an antique door?"

"Jack," Jane said, holding her arm out in front of Tim instinctively, protecting him.

"Sorry again for your loss, Jack. You seem to be holding up well." Tim took Jane's key and bags and opened the front door.

Jack followed them into the house holding the *Chicago Tribune*. "You too, Tim. Sorry for your loss."

Jack held up the paper. It was the metro section, folded

into a square. He pointed to a small article whose headline read, BODY FOUND ON DOWNSTATE HOSPITAL GROUNDS RULED SUICIDE.

Tim took the paper from Jack and went into the kitchen.

"You've only met Tim a few times. Any reason you're so rude?"

Jack ignored the question. He looked around the living room, scanning the bookshelves, the mantel. He opened the door to the corner cupboard and stared hard at the miniatures on each shelf, the few teacups salvaged from her grandmother, a small pair of Roseville candlesticks. He wandered over to a standing sewing box and opened the lid. He tried to look casual, like a customer browsing through a shop, but it was clear that he was on a mission.

"What are you looking for?" Jane asked, putting down the rest of the bags on the dining room floor next to the still unopened Hendershott sale parcels. "Maybe I can help."

Jack just smiled. He continued to walk the living room, picking up the flowerpots on the round corner table and turning them over, one by one. He looked at Jane, reading her from left to right, just as he had the corner cupboard.

"Any new finds? Anything special lately?"

Jack's voice sounded perfectly even and controlled. It was so level, in fact, that Jane felt frightened. This robotic Jack was far more menacing than the blustering yuppie neighbor, always ready to share the cost of his new car, his new golf clubs, always ready to tell you who you should get to seed your lawn or tuck-point your chimney.

Jane thought she heard Tim talking on the phone in the kitchen. No. He was lecturing Rita about spilling her water dish. She wanted him to come back. There was something different in Jack's walk, his big fingers wrapped around the unlit cigar, that unnerved her.

She told herself that it was only Jack, harmless Jack. Harmless to her anyway. Despite what her father thought, despite what Charley said, she wasn't going to panic. Sure, it's always the husband, but Jack wasn't her husband. She could handle him. This was Jack. She had kissed this man, for heaven's sake. What was the big deal?

"What are you looking for?"

"I'm not looking for anything, Janie," Jack said, and sighed. "Maybe peace of mind." Jack dropped the cigar into his pocket and ran his hands over his face. "I think I'm going crazy, that's all."

Crazy made sense. His wife had been murdered. Grief made you crazy. It had only been a week. She looked at Jack jiggling back and forth from left foot to right. Guilt made you crazy, too, didn't it?

"I need something normal, Jane. I used to love hearing you describe everything you bought. Just talk to me, tell me what you bought last Saturday, last Sunday. Tell me about all this stuff."

Jane motioned for Jack to follow her into the kitchen. She poured him iced tea, but he asked for the early morning coffee left in the pot over ice. He hadn't been sleeping, he said, and was living on as much caffeine as he could tolerate. Jane filled his glass, then found a tin of biscotti, a client gift from last Christmas.

"Still sealed, this ought to be okay," she said, prying off the lid and inhaling the rich chocolate.

Jack began scanning the kitchen, just as he had the living room.

"Those pitchers, are those new?" he asked.

"Nope, one was from a garage sale years ago and the rest are all from flea markets. Those ball jugs are impossible to find as unknowns anymore. Every month a shelter magazine reveals a new area of collectibles, which makes every price tag go up. Or a new magazine starts altogether. Pretty soon, there'll be *Ball Jug* magazine, devoted to the collectors of twentieth-century kitchen water pitchers."

"If a magazine comes out called *Ball Jug*, it won't be a shelter magazine, sweetie," Tim said, walking into the kitchen and helping himself to a biscotti.

"Sorry I was so . . ." Jack let himself trail off.

"Yeah, me too," Tim said, nodding at Jane who held up the iced tea pitcher. "With lemon."

"Jane was telling me what she bought lately," Jack said, sipping his iced coffee. He made a face. "How about this coffee? How old is this?"

"I got those plates last week," she said, ignoring the dig at her too strong coffee. She was used to that criticism. She pointed out some tablecloths, a few aprons on pegs by the window.

The flowerpots she found at the demolition sale last Saturday lined the kitchen window for now. They were too crowded to stay there, but she hadn't found them a new home.

"I got those last Saturday out in Lake Forest. They were the last things left in the house. It was funny because I missed a box of flowerpots earlier then found these in an empty cupboard in an empty house."

Jack stood and walked over to them, waved his hand over the row of pots. "These were all in the box?"

Jane nodded as Jack began turning them over, leaving them upside down on the kitchen table. Then he began moving them around, like walnut shells in a carnival con game.

"Jack, you'll chip the rims."

"Sorry."

He shook his head and moved them more gently, moving his lips slightly as he studied the bottoms of the pots. When he seemed satisfied with the arrangement, he folded his arms and looked at them left to right.

When he looked up and saw Jane staring at him, he seemed confused. He turned and saw Tim, still in the doorway.

"Timmy, I . . ."

Timmy? Jane and Tim exchanged looks. Jane knew that Jack had only met Tim a few times, called him about furniture, but never made a purchase. Tim looked as confused as she felt.

"I don't know why I said that before. I am so sorry about David."

"You mean Phillip," Jane corrected.

"Yes," Jack said, "yes, I mean Phillip."

"Did you know David, too?" Jane asked, moving closer to Jack, who backed up toward the kitchen table.

He shook his head, his eyes remaining far away. Jack gestured toward the newspaper he had given Tim, now lying on the table.

"The article mentioned, you know, everything. Phillip working at the flower shop where, you know. David Gattreaux's name. Phillip. Tim . . ." Jack said, shrugging, "you need a scorecard for christ's sake."

Jack had grown pale, but seemed now to be regaining color. He even smiled at Jane, nodding at the flowerpots he had lined up.

"Nice."

Then he turned and exited the kitchen through the dining room. Only when they heard the front screen door close did Tim move from the doorway toward Jane and the flowerpots.

"What the hell was that about?" Tim asked.

"I'll tell you what it wasn't about," Jane said, standing over the kitchen table, looking down.

"It wasn't a condolence call about Phillip," Jane said. "Did you read this article?"

"Skimmed it," Tim said. "I don't really want to go through all those details again right now."

"Then you can read this article. There aren't really any details. Just that Phillip had worked at the flower shop. Nothing about the murder," Jane said, pointing to the line as she read.

"No mention of David Gattreaux?"

Jane shook her head and started to say something, but one of the flowerpots caught her eye.

"That bastard did chip it."

The Shawnee flowerpot, upside down, was leaning to one side. Jane picked it up and inspected it but didn't find any nicks.

"Look how crooked this is, though, Tim." Jane put it back on the table, upside down, and the saucer did seem to be slightly sliding off to one side.

"Honey, it was made as cheap pottery, not fine porcelain. You're the expert on this junky stuff. I thought you said that's what gave it its charm . . ." Tim said, his voice trailing off as he studied the paper instead of the pottery. "Oh, fuck me," he whispered softly, putting the paper down.

Jane had picked up the Shawnee pot and was gently tugging at the saucer. Now she looked up at Tim.

"Didn't I tell you that David had some sugar daddy that he was bragging about? Someone he bought for and went off for weekends with?"

Jane nodded.

"Guess what David bought for him as a present?" Tim asked, rubbing the bruise on his temple. "A silver cigar cutter."

"Jack," she said.

"That's right, Jack. So much for the alleged gaydar. I didn't sniff him out at all."

"Jack," Jane repeated, still holding the flowerpot and looking toward the other kitchen doorway.

"Yeah, I guess I don't know everything in my field of expertise either," Tim said. "Talk about your off-kilter pottery. What are you . . . ?"

Tim looked off in the same direction and saw what Jane saw. Jack was back. Not the pale and confused Jack who had been sniffing around the house a few minutes earlier. This was the cocky and resolute Jack. The efficient businessman who saw a problem and had determined how to solve it.

"Hey, Janie," Jack said, pointing his finger first at her, then at the flowerpots. He walked in and took the pot from her hand and set it back on the table with the rest of the five. "Do this jumble with me."

The attached saucer bottoms read, Shawnee, McCoy, Bauer, the fourth was unsigned but had a raised number 21, Morton, Brush.

Jack smiled at Tim and Jane and shook his head. "It's like a code, isn't it? If you wanted to give someone a secret message that this was the right box?" His eyes were so glassy, they seemed to brim with tears.

"The right box for what, Jack?" Jane asked, her voice thick.

"Where is the box, Jane? You don't throw anything away, do you? Not even the cardboard box these came in?"

"No," said Jane, "it's in the garage with all my packing stuff."

"A code like this, with initials, that's the kind of thing you'd do, right, Jane? The kind of thing a girl like you would do, yeah?"

Jane looked at Tim, who raised his eyebows and indicated that she should probably agree to whatever Jack said as he edged himself toward the door.

"Fucking games. Stay put, Lowry. You need a decoder ring to talk to some of these assholes." Jack stared at the Shawnee, a celery-colored glazed pot with a Greek key design around the rim.

"Oh, Jack," said Jane softly. She felt her heart drop. Jack had done it all right. He had committed murder or arranged a murder and that horrified her. But her heart was plummeting at this minute, she knew, because he had ruined a perfectly charming piece of '40s pottery.

"Why did you go to all this trouble?" She picked up the flowerpot and turned it over. She twisted the attached saucer as if it were the lid of a jar and it came off cleanly in her hand, a dollop of tacky glue still stuck to the bottom of the pot. A key dropped onto the table.

"The back door," Jack whispered. "Who knew that Sandy left it unlocked all day anyway?"

Jack picked it up, slipped it into his pocket. When he

withdrew his hand, Jane thought he had pulled out his cigar. She was about to remind him she didn't allow smoking when she realized she was looking at a gun.

"Where's the box these pots came in, Jane? You said the garage?"

Jane nodded and moved closer to Tim.

Jack waved both of them in front of him. "Let's go find it, kids."

Jane walked directly to the cardboard box. It still held the newspaper used to wrap the pots, so Jane could reuse it when she packed up various pieces for Miriam. Jack signaled for her to bring it to him. He ran his fingers along the bottom of the box. They heard the pop of the bottom cardboard flap loosen and saw Jack smile as he withdrew a thick sealed envelope.

"Since I had to get the key, might as well take the money back. I was going to let it go, you know? I got what I paid for anyway. No need to be greedy, but what the hell? Waste not, want not, right, kids?"

"You left this box for Braver, didn't you, Jack? That's why you had to know what sales I went to. It was supposed to look like I put it there, right?" asked Jane.

"That's right, darling. It was supposed to look like you left it there. You weren't supposed to find it and take it home."

"No one would think that I . . ."

"Jane, you were just a supporting player here. A cover for me, a little smoke for the police, and a little sacrificial lamb to—"

"You can't kill anybody, Jack," said Tim.

"I bet that's what so many people will say about you.

I'm really sorry about your friend Phillip, Tim. I'm especially sorry that it's made you so despondent. So suicidal. So crazy that you'd kill yourself and take your best friend with you."

Jane could hear a low buzz but could not figure out where it was coming from. By the time she recognized it as Rita's growl, Rita herself had crept out of the house. Unlike a movie star dog, cued to go for the throat, or bring the villain down as soon as he showed his evil heart, Rita was a more cautious canine. Protective, but trained. She continued growling but clearly was not ready to jump on Jack. She continued the menacing sound from behind Jane's legs, awaiting the command.

"Looks like you'll take out man's best friend, too. You are one grief-crazed guy, Tim."

"Jack, why do you have to kill us? We don't really know anything. How can we hurt you?"

"Oh, I don't know. The more you think about it—how I know David Gattreaux, for example—the more questions your suspicious little minds might come up with. Besides, I don't always keep an extra house key glued into a flowerpot, sweetie; and if asked about that, I wouldn't want you to lie for me, even if you are my mistress. Tidier to just say good-bye."

"Nobody believes I'm your mistress."

"Yes they do, darling. Barbara, Charley. Enough people to make sure they were looking in your direction while I was heading out in another one. I thought it would satisfy Sandy's curiosity. She'd believe I'd fallen in love with little Jane and just kick me out, but . . ."

"What kind of gun is that?" Tim asked.

"A collector to the end, yes? It's a sweet little pistol from the forties, the kind of gun a guy in a Raymond Chandler novel would pack. The most amazing thing is that it belonged to your dear friend Phillip. That's why you have it now. All the more poignant that you use it to kill your grief-stricken self and your little friend who tried to stop you. Phillip waved it around in front of David one night, who was as sticky fingered as they come. He promptly stole it and gave it to me as a little token of affection. I knew it would come in handy, but not this handy."

Tim took Jane's hand and squeezed it.

"Don't be scared, it's going to be all right," Tim said quietly. "Detective Oh is on his way."

"What an appropriate token of affection, coming from David Gattreaux," said Jane.

"Right. And you're going to find gold coins at a garage sale, Lowry. Detective Oh is in Kankakee today. I called this morning and found out he's conferring with Munson this afternoon. From what my people tell me, nobody's going to have to ask Munson twice to believe you murdered Gattreaux."

"But you did it, Jack?" Jane asked.

"I'd have to stand in line to get at that little two-timer . . ."

Rita's growling had gotten increasingly louder and now erupted into a series of sharp barks. She was straining to attack, desperate to be given the okay. Jane kept trying to give a subtle hand command, a go-ahead wave that would cause Rita to lunge at Jack's throat. Mile had shown her some hand commands and told her to speak with authority. She had forgotten every last gesture. The only signal she had seemingly mastered appeared to be sit/stay.

"You won't be able to convince anyone I killed myself if you have to shoot me like this," Tim said, stepping in front of Jane and walking toward Jack and the gun. "Can't make me hold it to my head if you have to stop me right now."

Jack, agitated, moved to the side of Tim, trying to get a clear aim at Jane. Tim kept waving Jane to stay behind him, and Rita scooted herself behind Jane. They moved in this odd little conga line toward Jack, who hadn't expected to be challenged. He backed up, knocking against a shelf of glass flower frogs and Russell Wright plates that Jane was planning to pack for Miriam.

The combination of breaking glass and Rita's barking was probably why Jack didn't hear Oh and Mile push through the back door into the humid garage. Jane and Tim hit the ground and Rita, hearing and seeing something from Mile, lunged at Jack, who fell back whimpering.

"Now you act like Rin Tin Tin," Jane said to Rita, letting Tim help her up. "And you, when did you become such a hero?"

"Since I saw the fake gun I had bought Phillip at a Hollywood prop auction in that dickhead's hand."

"You bought the gun where, Mr. Lowry?" asked Oh, carefully using his handkerchief to pick it up off the floor in front of Jack Balance, where it had fallen.

"An auction of movie props. At least five years ago. I gave it to Phillip, and he carried it on Halloween when we went as ... as detectives."

"Nick and Nora Charles?" Jane whispered in Tim's ear.

He nodded and said to Oh, "It wouldn't fire. They told

me it was just a prop; that some mechanism had been removed."

Oh opened the gun and checked the clip and nodded. "I believe this gun is in working order. It probably only needed ammunition. It appears that Mr. Balance knew what to do to make this into a deadly weapon," Oh said, handling the piece carefully.

"You are a licensed gun owner, right, Mr. Balance?"

"I want to call my lawyer," was Jack's only answer.

19

Everybody had known Jack did it, Jane was thinking, as she washed her face and hands. She let the cold water soak the washrag and placed it on her face, pressing the cold water into her cheeks, her eyes, with the heels of her hand. Dad. Charley. *Even I knew Jack did it*, she thought, *if I had let myself believe it*. She replayed getting knocked out in Jack's garage, knowing he was lying about carrying her upstairs to the spare bedroom. She remembered the picker's classifieds she found in Jack's recycling. He had been following her last weekend. Waiting to plant that stupid box of flowerpots at some sale she had attended. He did it and was trying to pin it on Jane. How did he think he could get away with that?

Jane came into the kitchen as Oh was explaining things to Tim.

"Jack didn't do it," he said, "not exactly."

Oh was washing his hands at the kitchen sink. Tim sat at the table, a glass of ice cubes placed in front of him. He had wrapped one in a cloth napkin and was massaging his temples and the back of his neck. The bandage around his stitches was soaked and nasty looking. The heat and grime of the garage had left their mark.

"Jack did do it, is that what you said?"

"Actually, no. Jack Balance tried to hire someone to kill his wife, but that person did not, could not, do it," said Oh.

"What about that envelope? Tim, did you tell him about the envelope? And the flowerpots?"

Oh pulled the envelope out of his own pocket. Written on the front of it, in Jane's handwriting, it said, "Thanks. A pleasure doing business with you. J."

"You wrote this, correct, Mrs. Wheel?" Oh didn't wait for Jane's answer. "Something you left at their house, the keys to the Suburban, perhaps?"

"He collected this stuff from me so he could frame me for hiring someone to kill Sandy," Jane said angrily.

"Yes, and pretended that you and he were having an affair so people would not suspect that he had another secret life; one that he concealed very well."

Oh looked at Tim for confirmation. Since finding out that the gun was real, in working order, Tim hadn't spoken. Now he barely looked up from the kitchen table where he began methodically fitting the broken pot and saucer together over and over.

"Mr. Balance had lamented to his neighbor, Mrs. Barbara Graylord, how obsessed you were with him, how jealous you were. He was sure that after she saw you kissing at the party, she would spread the word quickly," Oh said. "And I believe she did. Last Saturday, when we questioned her after finding Mrs. Balance, she couldn't wait to describe to me how she had walked into the Balance kitchen and watched you lean into Jack, and how his eyes had locked on hers and he had given her a 'What can I do?' kind of panicky look. She was very dramatic."

"Maybe he could convince Barbara Graylord I was in love with him, but who would believe I orchestrated the murder of his wife? It's too complicated."

"Homo-Baroque," said Tim softly.

"What?" Jane asked.

"We don't have everything put together yet, but we know Mr. Balance was planning to start a whole new life. He had already moved much of his money and business. He changed his name when he left his home for college, but he still had the social security number and identity of his birth. He had a bank account and business under that name. He had a passport, too, and presumably would have left the country as Jack Balance and returned as Rivers Marsden, which was, in fact, his real name.

"Mr. Balance used your collecting habits to map out a plan, Mrs. Wheel. He liked to collect antiques himself, right, Mr. Lowry? You had some dealings with him?"

"Yes, he came down to auctions occasionally, asked me to bid on things for him, keep an eye out."

"You told me he never bought anything," Jane said.

"He didn't. I must have been his advance scout; then he'd have David buy for him when I wasn't using him."

"That's what David meant when he said there were other starfish in the sea. Jack was his . . ." Jane let her voice trail off.

"Fish," said Tim.

"And Sandy knew, didn't she?" Jane asked Oh.

"Yes. She apparently talked to her father, even though he isn't capable of understanding her anymore. When she visited, she sat and confided in him aloud just as she would if he was still lucid."

Jane and Tim both looked puzzled.

"His attendant, Emma, was in the next room, listening to all the conversations. We visited Mr. Mason to question him about Mr. Balance's business, and he was unable, of course, to tell us anything. Emma, though, was starved for conversation."

"But Jack didn't kill David," Jane said. "It was the day after Sandy . . . He couldn't have even gotten away from the house."

"No, Mrs. Wheel, he didn't kill David. We believe the same entrepreneur who killed Mrs. Balance killed Mr. Gattreaux."

"Who's that? You said that the person Jack hired didn't do it."

"Yes, but the person he hired gives us the clue. The person he hired was supposed to pick up the cash in the envelope and the key in the flowerpot."

Oh walked over to the flowerpots still turned upside down on the other end of the table. He moved the now broken-off saucer to the first position.

Jane walked over and stood in front of the flower pots. She ran her fingers over the raised lettering on the saucer bottoms.

"Jack said it was a jumble, but it's easier than that, isn't it?" she asked. "Just an acronym? Shawnee, McCoy, Bauer, is Sandy Mason Balance. Twenty-one is for July twenty-first, last Saturday, and Morton, Brush. Mortie Braver."

"Excellent work, Mrs. Wheel," Oh said. "The box was left at the house for Mr. Braver, but he didn't find it at the demolition sale. His cold feet got colder. He told his boss he was sick and left the job."

"So that leaves Richard and Louie . . ." Jane started, "and I remember now . . . Louie didn't want me to get that box."

"Cousin Louie knew what Braver was up to, and as soon as he saw the box knew what it was and figured he could take the cash. Louie figured that Balance would just assume Mortie Braver took the money and didn't do the job. Double-crossed him. Louie didn't plan on doing the killing though. That happened when he got to the house to look for the money in the flowerpots in the Suburban, but the truck wasn't home. He didn't even realize that you would empty the truck at your own house first. The back door was open, and he went in and found Mrs. Balance," Oh said sadly. "That's when he decided to earn his money."

"He ripped off the button so you would think I killed Sandy?" Jane asked.

"Braver believed you were involved. He had told Louie that. Jack referred to his boss who gave the orders, a woman friend. Jack was playing a game here, acting out a script. He had told Braver he wanted a souvenir to prove it was done, that his friend collected Bakelite. Pulling off the button was Louie's touch since he hadn't found the money and was going to have to prove he did it to collect."

"When did he take my saw?" Jane asked.

Oh cleared his throat. "This is such small comfort, I'm sure, but it wasn't your saw, Mrs. Wheel. Louie used Mortie Braver's saw. That was another reason why Braver wanted to talk to the police. He thought he would be framed for the murder. He did, after all, agree to the terms at first."

"But you showed me the toolbox and my saw . . ."

"Was missing, yes. Jack Balance noticed that you left your toolbox, took it out, and removed the saw: thought it might incriminate you, throw us off course just enough. More smoke, as Mr. Balance would say."

"How do you know all this? Braver got killed before he met with you, right?" Tim asked.

"Louie came in this morning. He confessed to killing his cousin Mortie; and the more we questioned him, the more he told us. The fight with Mortie wasn't supposed to end with a murder. Louie is quite upset about that. He's confessed nonstop all morning. Mr. Rose hired a lawyer for him who couldn't get him to slow down, let alone stop talking about Mrs. Balance and Braver."

Jane walked over and picked up one of the flowerpots, turning it in her hand. "How did Jack think this wouldn't be traced back to him? Even my dad said it's always the husband."

"Sounds like he thought he could be gone by the time the smoke cleared," Tim said. "He put you into the mix, made it seem like you might have found the guys to hire. You were the picker, the one who knew these kinds of creeps."

Oh nodded.

"If Mr. Gattreaux hadn't been murdered, we might have believed Mrs. Wheel was more involved. The second murder threw everything off. If the murders were connected, and I always believed they were, it certainly took Mrs. Wheel off the shortlist."

"Jack wanted the appearance of an affair with me so no one would suspect he was gay, right?" Jane asked.

"Probably. It was simple enough to play at. Even if he couldn't work things out to get rid of Mrs. Balance and place the blame on you while he escaped the country, the charade wouldn't have been wasted."

"But he even got someone in New York to dress like me?"

"Not just anyone," Oh walked over to the briefcase he had left in the kitchen doorway and pulled out the sketches he had shown them at the same table a few days earlier. "Any ideas now who that might be?"

Tim almost laughed. "I can't believe I didn't see it before."

"David," Jane whispered.

The sketch seem to take on a entirely new character. What had seemed a charming, Hepburnesque smile, now took on the ugly smirk of David Gattreaux. Jane could barely stand to look at it, those gorgeous silver bracelets around his bony wrist. She knew she should feel sorry for this man. He was a fellow human being, and he had been murdered. Brutally murdered. But he seemed now to take on a much more villainous role. She still didn't understand why he had been killed.

"We're still working on this. Louie has not told us what happened with Mr. Gattreaux, but he promised that after a discussion with his lawyer, he'd tell us everything," Oh said. "His attorney seems frantic.

"I'm not sure how or if it ties in with his murder, but I will tell you both that we do have some information about Gattreaux. We did some checking in Kankakee at some of the places he frequented. He was not well-liked. After he had sexual relations with people, and he did sleep with both men and women, he told them he was HIV positive."

"After he slept with them?" Tim asked.

Oh nodded. He took out a faxed sheet, curling at both ends, and handed it to Tim.

"I don't want to forget the reason we came. It was to bring this letter found at Mr. Gattreaux's apartment. Detective Munson faxed it to me. Although I'm quite sure the letter was intended for you, Mr. Lowry, Munson is under no obligation to give it to you. I thought you might want to read it."

Jane knew it was the letter Phillip had left for Tim, the letter that explained it all. Jane tried to read Tim's face as he read the letter and saw the small smile, then the pain that creased his forehead, lined his mouth. Phillip had been his true love, that's what Tim always said. Jane might be a soul mate, but Phillip was the one who had his heart. And Phillip had earned it. He was as quiet and thoughtful as Tim was clever and flippant. They were kinder and braver and smarter when they were together. Jane liked to think that during their best times, she and Charley were like them.

"It appears that Phillip was not immune to David's charms," said Tim softly.

"Or to David's curse," Jane said.

"Well put." Tim wiped his face then continued to stare at the letter, memorizing it. "He said it was easier to go this way, on his own terms, not tempting me to be with him again, not asking me to care for him. I knew it. I just didn't know it all."

Detective Oh waved his hand when Tim offered him the fax.

"I can get a copy if I need one. That is yours."

"So why would Louie kill David?" asked Jane. "What was the motive there?"

Oh shook his head. "That is still the mystery. It's easier to see why he would kill his cousin, Mr. Braver, who had made arrangements to talk to us right after the Hendershott sale. And according to the officer who answered his phone call down at the station, he was most upset about the dog."

Jane and Tim both looked at Rita, asleep now at their feet.

"Yes, Louie loved their watchdog, but Braver felt he wasn't tough enough and beat him to make him tougher. When Braver called to offer information, he also reported his dog missing, said he hadn't seen it since his cousin had left with her in the truck. Braver thought Louie had stolen her and set her free."

"What's her name?" Jane asked, rubbing her bare foot over the top of Rita's head.

"I wrote it down somewhere. Some collectible name. I'll call you with it, but it probably doesn't matter. I believe now it's Rita."

Detective Oh stood up and called to Mile, who had remained at the front of the house.

"There is more to work out and discuss, but I think it's time for me to go to the station and deal with Mr. Balance and his lawyer. We traced much of the Balance property sales to Rivers Marsden; and when we followed Marsden's identity paper trail, it led us back to Mr. Balance. He still had contacts in South Dakota, still had family he spoke to even though he kept it from his wife and friends. Louie filled in some of the information about purchases Balance had made, large pieces of furniture Richard Rose's company had procured for him."

"But David? As evil as David was, I don't know why Louie would have killed him," Jane said. "What did Louie have against him?"

"There was no money in it," added Tim.

Oh shrugged. "Not that we know of right now. Mr. Gattreaux was widely despised. Someone might have been willing to pay to get rid of him."

Oh promised he would be back later, assured them that Jack's lawyer would not be able to get him out that night. Jane walked with Oh to the front door as Tim slumped down into a kitchen chair.

The mail was in the box and Jane stepped out on the porch to get it.

"One real mystery of Gattreaux's character is why he said all that about HIV to his bed partners," Oh said, shaking his head at Jane, "since he wasn't HIV positive."

20

Tim took a long shower upstairs while Jane showered downstairs in the bathroom off the study. When they met in the living room in bathrobes and slippers, Jane felt almost happy in spite of herself. They were clean and alive. Today that seemed like a lot.

Jane ordered a grilled vegetable pizza; Tim tossed a salad. Jane poured Cokes over ice, and they set all the food down in front of the television, ready to turn something on, anything, so they wouldn't have to think too hard or feel too deeply.

They spoke very little while Tim commandeered the remote, going from station to station until he found a sure bet for both of them.

"Tim," Jane began, "how did you know that Oh would show up?"

The *Antiques Roadshow* distracted her with its snappy theme, and Tim and Jane both started singing, da, da, da . . . da, da, da, laughing at the absurdity of their day and now night.

"You know who I have the biggest crush on?" Jane asked, picking off an onion ring from her pizza and chewing it slowly. "Leigh Keno. He is so into the furniture, and so happy for the people who bring it in."

"How do you know you have a crush on Leigh? Maybe you have a crush on Leslie. How can you tell them apart?"

"Right. You're right. I have a crush on both. It's good to have a crush on twins; there's always backup."

Jane put her feet on Tim's lap, and he began massaging them. She wanted to tell him what Oh had told her, that David was not HIV positive, just because it was so evil and so cruel and so creepy. She didn't want to know it by herself. But Tim was the last person she could talk to about it. Phillip was gone and nothing would bring him back. It wouldn't help to know that David Gattreaux had sent him into that spiral on a whim.

Instead she asked Tim again, "How did you know Oh would show up?"

"Just a bluff," Tim said.

Jane poked him with her foot.

"Really. Just the way Helen Corning would have done it for Nancy Drew. A stall."

"Did you have any idea about Jack? About him being gay?"

"I'd like to say I did, but I didn't. I guess if I ever had a sense he was family, the fact that he seemed to be chasing you threw me off."

"Family?" Jane asked.

"Yeah, family of man, you know. Nice partners' desk, eh?" Tim leaned forward. "Look at Leslie. He's going to wet his pants."

"That's Leigh. I'd like him to drool over me like that."

"Never happen. Guy like that has to have an early American something to salivate over—you'd have to be at least a hundred years old to get him going over you."

"With my original finish."

"And hardware."

"Tim, I want you to stay here forever, but I have to ask, to prepare myself, when . . ."

"Tomorrow. Noonish. We can hit a few sales first if you feel like it, but it's time for me to get back home."

"I'll be so lonely." Jane withdrew her feet and sat up, realizing how empty the house would be tomorrow night.

"When do Charley and Nick come home?"

"Nick should be here the second week in August. Charley might stay at the site longer; then he'll come back to his apartment. He moved out before he left for the dig; you know that."

"He'll move back in as soon as you ask him."

Jane picked up the pizza box and took it into the kitchen. She picked up the classifieds to bring to Tim so they could make a morning plan. She quickly looked over her shoulder out the window. What was it about the kitchen that gave her the shivers? Probably the flowerpots lined up back on the shelf minus the broken Shawnee.

Detective Oh had stopped by later in the afternoon to tell them again that Jack would not be out on bail; there was no need to worry. Louie would remain in custody. He had signed his confessions to Sandy's murder and the accidental killing of Braver. He and his cousin had walked into the back-room of the coach house arguing over what Louie had done. Braver was insisting that he would meet with Oh and tell him everything. Even though Tim wasn't paying attention, didn't understand what they were saying, Louie and Braver didn't know that. Louie, in particular, thought they might have incriminated themselves, so he went over and whacked Tim on the head. Braver yelled at Louie and Louie hit Braver, a little harder than he had intended.

"Louie claims he was working alone, that the lights going out was a happy accident."

"Very happy. How would he have gotten out unseen if they hadn't gone out?" Jane asked, then added, "Of course, if he didn't mean to kill Braver, he wouldn't have had to plan an escape. Does Louie have . . . ?"

"Asthma? And emphysema. For years. In fact, he's a very sick man. His lawyer told us he was recently diagnosed with lung cancer. Inoperable and, so far, he's refused any type of treatment. No chemotherapy or radiation. Odd man," Oh had said, "acts like a soldier waiting to die, sitting up straight in his cell."

Oh had talked to Tim for over an hour, confirming details of Jack's antique queries of Tim and other antique dealers in the Bourbonnais Mall. It appeared that Jack was laundering money from some of his bogus companies and filtering much of his income to Rivers Marsden, who was on the verge of becoming a very wealthy man. And one with impeccable taste in antique furnishings.

Jack had reinvented himself once. Jane wondered why that hadn't been enough. Detective Oh had shrugged and said it was hard to tell exactly.

"Maybe he was restless, just curious. Midlife crisis gone mad."

After Oh left, Tim had raised one eyebrow and whispered, "See where curiosity leads, my dear."

* * *

"Do you want some ice cream?" Jane called in to Tim.

"If it's chocolate something."

Jane brought in a quart of Cappuccino Chip and two spoons.

A woman on television was gushing into the camera over the good deal she had gotten on an art glass vase, and Tim and Jane both shook their heads. "Fake," they said together. The expert confirmed their analysis, pointing out the fresh signature, the poor quality of color and detail.

"A couple of things are still bothering me," Jane said. "First of all, why did Louie want this money if he was dying of cancer?"

"Why not? Live out the rest of his time in style? Wasn't afraid of any risks. What's the worst that could happen?"

"Just seems off somehow that Louie and Braver are the guys Jack would get involved with. They don't seem that smart or ambitious to get involved in murder, even if it meant lots of money."

"Braver wasn't smart or ambitious. That's what got him in trouble. He said no."

Tim took the carton and finished the ice cream.

"Besides," said Tim, "if Jack wanted to kill Sandy, what kind of guys would he get involved with? Horace Cutler? Barbara Graylord's husband? He needed thugs, right?"

"And the initials on the pottery. That just seems too silly, too affected. Why would they go to all that trouble?"

"Associates the payoff with you, the flowerpots. More smoke from Jack. He thought it was a feminine sort of thing to do, I guess. And it sure spelled Braver out as the killer."

"Circumstantial. Not real proof. And Louie didn't confess to killing David."

"No, but Oh seemed to think that he would. He wanted to talk to his lawyer before he discussed that." Tim picked up spoons, napkins, the rest of the dinner debris, and started toward the kitchen. "Probably wanted to work out some kind of deal. Plea bargain."

"Listen to you. 'Plea bargain,' " Jane said, following him into the kitchen.

" 'Circumstantial,' Nancy Drew? Since when did you become such an expert?" asked Tim.

"You know, Nancy Drew said that all you need to solve a mystery is an inquisitive mind and two good friends," said Jane, giving the kitchen counter a final wipe and turning off the light over the sink.

"You can actually quote from Nancy Drew?" Tim asked in mock horror.

"Worse. I'm quoting from *The Simpsons*. Lisa said it once," Jane said, smiling. "Then you know what else Lisa Simpson said?" she asked, starting up the stairs.

"What?" Tim asked, following her. "What'd Lisa say?"

" 'At least I have an inquisitive mind.' "

Jane and Tim woke up at 5 A.M. and drove directly to a conducted house sale that was opening at 9. Tim knew the book guy, Claude, who slumped behind the wheel of his beat up Chevy van and handed them a clipboard. They were numbers three and four.

"Be back at eight-thirty for their numbers, man," Claude said, already closing his eyes and sliding back down in his seat.

"Rumor must be out on some good books here. Claude had to have left Urbana at one-thirty to get here."

After Jane and Tim ate a leisurely breakfast at a pancake house, they hit three early opening garage sales. Two were in Skokie, and at the second one, Jane picked up a sewing box that looked like it hadn't been opened in thirty years. Cub Scout patches from 1956, waiting to be sewn on a uniform, sat in the bottom under unopened packages of lace trim and rickrack.

"Do you think he quit the troop?"

"Because his mother didn't sew on the patches? Come on. He quit because it was a fascist, intolerant, gay-bashing organization. No one quits because their mother doesn't sew on their badges."

Jane decided not to tell Tim that she quit Brownies when her mother said she couldn't attend the Flying Up ceremony. It was supposed to be in the church, right after they had their Juliette Lowe Tea. Jane had thought they had meant it was going to be a low tea instead of a high tea because they were just kids in Kankakee. Mrs. Gordon had explained to them that Juliette Lowe was the founder of the Girl Scouts and they would have this tea party for their mothers; then all the Brownies would cross an imaginary bridge and become Girl Scouts. When Mrs. Gordon asked whose mothers were attending, all the girls had raised their hands, even Louise Malvin, who wore the same uniform blouse to school for months and who everybody whispered about, saying that she mustn't have a mother. Even Louise was producing one for the Flying Up. Mrs. Gordon had looked at Jane so sadly when she explained that her mother had to work. At home, Jane begged Nellie to come, told her how important it was. Don had told her to go ahead and take a cab over to the church. He would pick them both up at five. Nellie had shaken her head, clamped her lips together, and refused.

Jane didn't tell her parents she quit Brownies; she just stopped going to meetings and they didn't remember to ask about it. When she was a teenager, her dad had told Jane he thought her mother was afraid to go to events like "teas." She was afraid they would be too fancy, that all the other mothers would know how to act, how to talk to each other. Jane had forgiven Nellie then, deciding that she could understand embarrassment and fear. But to this day she kept her Brownie pin deep in her jewelry box; and when she searched out a gold chain or a pin, she saw it there, a reminder that she hadn't flown up.

Jane bought the sewing box, a package of coasters that said, THE FOUR SADDEST WORDS/EVER COMPOSED/SURELY MUST BE/THE BAR IS CLOSED and a wooden rolling pin with red handles.

"You collect rolling pins now?"

"Miriam will give me five dollars for it. It was only fifty cents. She can sell it for ten or twenty. Martha Stewart had a feature on her show and in her magazine on building a display rack for old pins, so you know they're only going to get hotter and hotter."

The house sale was good for Tim. He found a stunning empire table and a breakfront that he made arrangements to have delivered to the store. He already had customers for them, Jane knew. It was like shopping with a big brother who got twice her allowance and saved it up instead of blowing it on bubble gum and wax lips.

In the basement, Jane was going through a box of old

maps, when she noticed a large wooden crate in the corner. It was nailed closed and she asked one of the workers what was in it.

"Friend of the owner came and packed up some stuff. He's a big collector. Took all the McCoy vases and flowerpots, some Bakelite jewelry, and bunches of old postcards. He's sending a guy for it later."

Jane turned the card attached to one of nails. Richard Rose.

"Do you know if Richard Rose was here today?"

"Last night, I think."

On the way home, Jane told Tim about the crate tagged by Richard.

"It's creepy, isn't it? All my stuff?"

"Jane, even people who don't collect anything collect McCoy and Bakelite. Only a complete nut would think the competition over that stuff was personal. And you don't collect postcards, do you? I thought you stayed away from that stuff?"

"I like old calendars and maps, but no, I don't usually collect old paper. Too much dust and mold. Nicky's allergies."

"See? Not so creepy?"

"He lied about going to Florida, though."

"That's being a creep, not being creepy. You know, just being a guy. Besides, maybe he has to stick around for Louie, you know, answer questions. Didn't Oh say Richard had gotten Louie the lawyer?"

Jane helped Tim load up his purchases, and by noon he was ready to head to Kankakee.

"Here's a thought," Tim said, shutting the trunk of the Mustang. "Maybe Richard Rose bought those things for you."

"What are you talking about?"

"You're an attractive woman, Jane. Don't blush. Not always so bright, but some men like that in a girl. Richard might be planning to woo you."

"Woo?" Jane asked.

"You're very woo-able," Tim said, kissing the top of her head. "Don't underestimate your charms."

"I'll miss you so much."

"I'm an hour away. Before the boys come home, I'll go to Ohio with you. It's time I met Miriam. Then I'll know who I'm competing with for your services."

"You've never asked me to work for you before, Tim."

"I thought you shouldn't be in the business, but it looks like you're not leaving it, so you might as well join me."

Jane was delighted to be asked, although she knew she wasn't quite ready to leave Miriam.

As he finally walked out to his car, there was lots of waving and kisses into the air. Tim held her close and whispered fiercely, "Be careful, will you? You're all I've got now."

Jane nodded, hugging him, her head buried in his chest.

Then Tim was gone.

Jane went in to give Rita some food and water, glanced up at the clock, and froze. One week ago, right around this time of the afternoon, Louie had killed Sandy. Is this how she was going to mark time now? Counting the weeks from Sandy's murder?

Better to keep busy. Jane swept up the broken glass in the garage and began packing boxes for Miriam. She'd call UPS on Monday and get this place emptied out. When she went into the house for water, she noticed Rita was giving her attentive growl at the front door. The mail carrier was coming up the walk.

"Easy, Rita, that's a friend."

Jane flipped through the flyers, bills, lapsed subscription notices. At the bottom of the pile, she found a postcard. She barely glanced at it, wanting to savor her communication with Nicky. She got her water and sat down to decode her son's cramped handwriting.

You don't even collect ephemera, do you? Stay out of my business.

Jane turned the card over and ran her thumb over its linen finish. A familiar pastel-tinted scene. Beautiful.

PAINTED CANYON AT SUNRISE.

She got up slowly and walked into her kitchen. That's what was missing. The postcards from last Saturday were still propped up on the bookshelf, leaning against the cookbooks. Except the one in her hand. The one that grew more and more animated as her hand began shaking.

She moved to the phone to call Oh. Voice mail. She was taken aback. How do you leave a message like this?

"Detective Oh? Jane Wheel. Louie's lying; I can prove it." She spoke quickly, her voice shaking. She asked him to meet her for a complete explanation. Jane read him the address from the phone book and hung up. She called Rita and quickly bundled her into the car. Jane wanted to get there first. She knew exactly what she was looking for.

Richard Rose's shop was enormous. In fact, it wasn't a shop, didn't pretend to be. It was a warehouse. Three floors of mantels, columns, iron gates, lawn sculpture, crates of old bricks, bins of nails, screws, hinges. Great baskets of doorknobs, locks. One giant expanse of wall was covered with windows, all sizes, shapes, and styles, hung against the exposed brick wall.

"Not really much of a view, huh?"

Jane jumped. She had walked in the door from the parking lot, leaving Rita in the backseat with the window halfway down. She had wanted to bring her in, her champion, but Rita whimpered and cowered in the backseat. She was a smart dog, but she couldn't read the newspaper. She had no idea that Braver's death notice had been in the paper that very morning and he wouldn't ever again spring from this building to beat her.

"I'm Sparks. What can I do you for?"

Sparks was a large, bearded man. Sixtyish. Gray ponytail spouting from under a yellow John Deere cap. He had a red T-shirt pulled tight over his immense stomach, and Jane read, I AIN'T OLD, I'M VINTAGE.

"Cute shirt," Jane said, smiling and hoping her upper lip wouldn't start to quiver as it usually did when she was nervous, lying, or forcing herself into amiablity.

"I made it up myself," Sparks said. "I sell a lot of 'em at flea markets."

"Is Mr. Rose, the owner, here?" Jane asked, looking around. Why weren't there any other customers? "I called him last week about some doorknobs," she added, thinking she remembered that Nancy Drew said you should add specifics when you were lying.

"Doorknobs?"

Nope. Nancy must have said to keep it simple.

"Richie didn't say anything about anybody coming in for doorknobs."

Very simple.

"But he ain't here anyway. Told me I didn't have to open up today, just be here for some deliveries," said Sparks. "My cousin died a couple of days ago." Sparks shrugged in what Jane saw was a kind of mourning gesture for him. "He worked here and we're all sort of discombobulated."

"I can imagine," Jane said, genuinely sympathetic. She was feeling a little discombobulated herself.

"I didn't put the sign out, but left the door open. Customers make the time pass better." Sparks pointed out the open sign while he was talking.

The sign itself was simply OPEN stenciled in red on a piece of barn board, but its presentation was sensational. The board was hung around the neck of the biggest mannequin Jane had ever seen. It was a fifties-looking male, over seven feet tall, shoulders, head, hands, all proportionately huge. Just the painted part in the giant's hair must have been over fifteen inches long.

"Came from a Big and Tall shop that got torched. Impressive, huh?"

Jane nodded, feeling a bit more like *Jack and the Beanstalk* than *Nancy's Mysterious Letter*. Sparks was so happy to have company, he didn't seem to care about the fact that he didn't know about her doorknob order. He had, in fact, forgotten her inquiry about Richard.

"Richie's going down to Florida, so I'm in charge today, I guess. Our cousin just got killed, so . . ." Sparks trailed off. "What can I do you for?"

It dawned on Jane that she didn't need an elaborate cover-up with Sparks. Someone in this outfit had dropped a few too many doorframes on this guy. He might have a vocabulary that included "discombobulate" but his shortterm memory didn't extend past two syllables.

"I'm just shopping. Antiquing," Jane said, upper lip steady. "Any furniture here? Or smalls? You know pottery and all?"

"Sure, sure," Sparks said, nodding. "Cases up on the next floor filled with stuff . . . Richie's got an eye. Got lots of pretty statues and vases. Jewelry, too."

Pointing to the staircase at the far end of the floor, Sparks sat back down heavily on a dilapidated couch. Jane noticed a small black-and-white television balanced on a crate tuned to a baseball game.

"I got to wait for deliveries. You go up and look around. Take your time. There's lots of pretty stuff."

Once his eyes returned to the ball game, Sparks forgot all about Jane. He didn't look up from the television as she crossed the immense first floor to the staircase. She kept turning to check on him. Was he going to call Richard? Wasn't he going to watch her, make sure she didn't try to steal anything?

Apparently not. Jane walked up the stairs and emerged into a wonderland of the old, the curious, and the exquisite. Case after case displayed pottery, jewelry, silver. The same wall that had held the decrepit window frames on the first floor, here showcased stunning watercolor landscapes, many signed by artists that even amateur Jane recognized. The first floor was a rehabber's Home Depot, filled with grunge and kitsch and filth as well as the occasionally significant architectural gem, while this floor was as fine a showroom as one might find at Sotheby's.

Jane stopped at a group of cases centered under a skylight. The sun shone down on the pieces inside and illuminated them, annointed them as religious vessels. Jane could identify the makers of some pieces in this case from similar ones she had seen in Tim's shop, but most she knew only from books. The most stunning display of American Art Pottery she had ever seen. One shelf alone seemed to contain nothing but Fulper—no vase or bowl worth less than a thousand dollars. Jane hadn't memorized the price guides, but she had a keen sense for what she could not afford. Most of the great artists of the Art Pottery movement were represented and she wandered openmouthed, aware of the quiet, the sunlight, and the magnificent showcasing of these pieces. She realized she was walking on tiptoe, had unconsiously assumed her museum-going manners. She realized that this was where she was, a museum. None of these pieces was marked with a price. Occasional small white cards with descriptions and dates, artist names and brief histories, but no prices.

No museum guards, though. Why was this floor open at all when no one was up here keeping an eye on customers? She gently tried one of the cabinet doors. Locked. But a glass cutter could quietly, easily give her access to any of the fine pieces here. There were no visible wires running through the glass. No alarm would sound if she could just reach in and . . .

Of course, she wouldn't ever steal. She was certain she wouldn't do that. She moved on to another set of cases and lust rose within her so quickly, so violently, that she was sure she had become feverish. These cases, tall display tables, the type that one might find in a natural history museum displaying rocks and mineral collections, were filled with Bakelite. The bracelets were thick, chunky, carved, and richly colored bangles. Next to the bracelets, there was a display of tiny, carved pieces. Pins? She leaned over to look at a strand of graduated beads, each blood red sphere intricately carved in a geometric pattern, and stopped herself from literally drooling on the glass. Jane laughed aloud and tried the top of one of the cases. The windowed lid lifted easily. She longed to slip on a bracelet, a five-color laminated, two-inch-tall, ribbed bangle. She smiled at the colors ... red, black, butterscotch, green, and the pale yellow referred to as creamed corn. It was her ideal bracelet, the one her Bakelite dreams were made of. Too perfect to touch.

Instead she let her hand wander over to the smaller pieces and picked up a creamy yellow, deco, line-carved ring. It was both delicate and substantial, the color of sweet butter. She slipped it on to the ring finger of her right hand and admired it. It was a nothing, a twenty-five-dollar piece of Bakelite in the middle of thousand-dollar bracelets, dangle pins, and necklaces. Maybe Tim was right, hounding her to move up. In the middle of Tiffany's, would she only be tempted to steal a signature blue box? Why did the ring call out to her so strongly? It might have come from a dime store or her own grandmother's junk jewelry box. But it suited her hand, she had to admit that. She loved the way it made her fingers seemed longer, her whole hand strong.

She left it on. She would try to get Sparks to sell it to her, even though there weren't any prices in this case either. Again, small cards with descriptions. She didn't have any reading glasses, so leaned forward until her nose almost touched the glass. Next to these small pieces were dates, a few names. Coded descriptions?

A small, dark green vase, maybe six inches high, seemed out of place in this case. It was laid on its side and Jane could see that it wasn't Grueby, which she might have guessed at first glance. The mark on the bottom was what? She squatted down level with the case and got as close as she could. Was it Hampshire? What was it doing there anyway? It was chipped and certainly stood out from the other mint pieces in this case.

"You look like you belong downstairs with the broken window frames, baby," she muttered, moving along. She was troubled by more than its odd placement in the case. Where had she seen that little vase before?

Then she saw what she had come for. What Nancy Drew might have found in the bottom of a locked desk drawer she had to pry open with a hairpin or discovered behind the face of an old clock, Jane saw lying right in front of her. Mixed in with the jewelry was a three-quarter-inch sew-through button, a creamy swirl laminated to black. A yin/yang Bakelite cookie resting on a small card with "July 21" printed on it. Jane felt every hair raise on her body, an icy finger of fear touch the back of her neck.

She knew that when she could get her feet to move, when she could walk to another case, she would find a group of flower frogs. One would be made of carnival glass, resting on a card that would have a neatly printed July 22 as an identification tag.

Sandy and David were now a part of this macabre collection of Richard Rose. She looked down at her hand. Who had belonged to this ring? She began rotating it on her finger as she headed for the large desk at the back of the display space, the apparent business center of the warehouse.

When she put her hand on the phone, she wasn't even surprised to feel a large, callused hand clamp down over hers.

She didn't try to scream or cry out in any way, she simply kept her voice level and turned to face Richard. "Decide against Florida?"

"Too humid this time of year," he said, smiling that goofy vacant grin that she had found rather charming at the demolition sale. Last Saturday he had seemed so simple and uncomplicated. Now she saw the glazed look, the anger behind the smile.

Walking her over to the display case where Sandy's button lay, Richard held both her small wrists in his grasp. He released them in front of the case, put his arm around her, like they were any couple browsing, except for the viselike pressure he kept on her shoulders, and asked, "Do you like my stuff?"

Jane nodded. "Yes, very much," she managed to say, trying to keep a normal tone.

"That idiot Jack. Said he could pin everything on you and get you out of my hair for good. That's why I gave him my best guys. That stupid, pretty-boy, rich kid. That was why I took the fucking job. Because Jack said he could get rid of that little bitch who buys up all the flowerpots and all the buttons and all the stuff my stepmother collects and asks me to send her. Please, she says, send me this like in Martha's magazine. Did you see that on the Collectibles' Show? Send me that. And she pays such stupid prices for the crap. She's wrecking things, I told Jack. It's Jane Wheel and Martha Stewart and the fucking Antique fucking Road fucking Show. It's those stupid women and those fucking fags that are ruining this business."

With every sentence Richard had been squeezing her harder, staring into the case as he talked. Now he let her go, opened the lid, and straightened the small vase, turned it so the chip did not show.

"Why did you kill David, Richard? What did he do?"

"That bastard bid against me on those doors. I wanted those doors. I needed them. I saw them and I wanted them. Louie was going to go after him; but I said no, I'd take care of that pretty boy. Louie's dying and he said he'd take care of everything for me before he went. That's what my dad told him to do, take care of everything. That's what he did. Took care of Braver, that little toad."

"But he didn't take care of Sandy, did he?" Jane asked softly.

"Louie couldn't bring himself to do it, didn't really want to kill anybody. Braver said he would, wanted the job, but couldn't find the money, couldn't find the box of flowerpots, and got scared."

"I found the flowerpots," Jane said, inching away from Richard.

Richard grinned. Jane remembered admiring that smile, those teeth, the first time she met him.

"I let you find the flowerpots," Richard corrected her. "Didn't matter anyway. Louie and I were going to take care of business."

"So you went to Sandy's house to find the box . . ."

"No," Richard said, "I went to Sandy's house to kill her for Jack. For money. A lot more than he was going to pay Braver."

Richard started fussing with the bracelets, turning one just so, sliding a card back into place near a carved and pierced red bangle.

Jane was now six feet from him. He still stood between her and escape down the stairs. If she screamed, Sparks might hear but would he care? He was just another of Braver's cousins, another of Richard's guys. Maybe now, though, there were some customers downstairs, rehabbing couples browsing through the doorknobs and moldings in their Saturday clothes, just waiting to rescue someone about to be killed by a crazy Bakelite collector?

"I sent Sparks to lunch and told him to lock up, Jane," Richard said, holding up the laminated bangle she had so loved. "Did you see this one? Great, isn't it?"

Jane looked over into the case where he was busy touching all the pieces, wondering when he would notice that she was wearing the Bakelite ring. She finally recognized the vase.

"That little green vase was the one in the box of flowerpots that I saw at the first house sale. You bought the flowerpots from that woman at the house sale."

"Louie bought those. Vase is chipped though. Jack needed a Shawnee for some stupid puzzle with the vases. Part of his plan to involve you, get rid of you. But I've got a way to get rid of you that's much better than his."

Richard took out a gun, a much more realistic one than the vintage piece Jack had held, but, as Detective Oh had pointed out, looks weren't everything. Jack's gun would have shot them, and Jane was quite certain that Richard's would also do the trick.

Jane saw that Richard was touching all the pieces in the case compulsively with his free hand. He was licking his lips and blinking rapidly, keeping only one eye on her as he looked around at all his things.

"Something's missing," he said.

Jane clenched her fist, turned the carved part of the ring inward and covered her right hand with her left.

"I'm getting bored with all that pottery I've got at home, Richard. Why don't you take my flowerpots? You can have them. I've got some McCoy vases and some good jewelry at home. Let me give them to you."

Richard twisted his mouth. He wanted to see the vases, Jane could tell, he was so hopped up. Jane couldn't tell if his behavior was caused by taking too many illegal drugs or not taking enough prescribed medication, but she could now see he was out of control—rabid.

"McCoy pottery, Richard, and I've got a Weller vase that Tim gave me for my birthday."

Richard was blinking even more rapidly. Jane saw he was sweating heavily, but that was understandable. He wore a big pocketed barn coat, and it was nearly ninety degrees outside. He slid out of the coat, shaking it off. The coat clattered as it hit the floor, something sliding out of the pocket. A saw. Jane's beautifully proportioned little saw that Miriam had given her. When had Richard taken it? The night of the Hendershott sale when he must have taken the postcard? No. In Jack's garage when he hit her with the shovel. She hadn't seen her toolbox in the truck, but the police had brought it up to show her when she was in the guestroom. Richard had been putting it back, but he had taken the saw.

Richard had killed Sandy. Louie was willing to confess because he was going to die anyway. Louie's job was to take care of Richard and that meant take the blame. Richard was the one with the fury to kill. Richard had hit her with the shovel and carried her upstairs. Jack probably said they still needed her, needed to confuse the cops, try to pin the murder for hire on her, but it was already unraveling then. Poor Braver. Poor Louie.

"I'm sick of all my stuff, Richard. I'll give it all to you. I've got buttons, a big tin from the Hendershott estate. Tons of Bakelite. Let me go and get them, Richard."

"Shut up," Richard shouted, "just shut up." He raised the gun. "I can have all your stuff anyway, you idiot. Right after Sparks shoots you. Sparks takes care of me and my stuff just like Louie. You're a thief. Sparks thought it was suspicious that you didn't come down, then . . ."

Jane looked at all the objects on the shelf above the case next to her. Vases, candelabras, urns, nothing that would make a weapon equal to a gun. She reached out and grabbed the neck of a lamp. Not just any lamp, she knew. She held the base and shade in front of her.

Jane knew this lamp. Eighteen inches tall, mushroom shape, leaded-glass inserts in the shade, and she could read the stamped vertical mark, FULPER.

"If you shoot me, you'll shoot your lamp."

Richard froze.

Jane tried to see if the tag hanging from the lamp had a price written on it or if it was part of his museum collection. Priceless. She was sure it would be worth about nine thousand dollars if it was on the market.

"Put the lamp down," Richard gasped, his breathing rapid. Shallow. "I can shoot you anyway," he said, barely audible.

"Even if you get me and miss the lamp, I'll drop it. It will smash into a million pieces," Jane said, backing around, circling toward the stairs.

Richard still held the gun, but rummaged in his jeans pocket and pulled out an albuterol inhaler. "You . . . wou . . . n't."

"Yes, I would. I collect junk, remember. Cheap stuff, remember? Fulper, shmulper, this baby crashes."

Jane held the lamp in her right hand and with her left, grabbed a pitcher by its handle off the shelf next to her. She didn't have to check the mark on this: light blue on cream, oranges on trees, dark blue spout and handle; one of Tim's favorite's.

"Newcomb, Richard," Jane yelled, "Newcomb, shnewcomb, it's going to crash."

Richard couldn't get the inhaler to his mouth. Eyes rolling back and gasping, he crashed to the floor, his gun sliding past Jane's feet.

At the top of the stairs, Sparks huffed and puffed, his face radiantly happy.

"Look who I just busted out of a car in the parking lot, Richie," he said, "it's McCoy."

Rita sat obediently next to Sparks, waiting for Jane to put down the lamp and pitcher and give her the hand signal for whatever she was supposed to do next.

SUNDAY

Richard Rose was not only a crazy murderer, Jane learned, he was also a crook. His architectural salvage business took many special orders. If you wanted a certain set of vintage door hardware, you just went to Richard and he worked tirelessly to find it. The only thing is, he often found it on someone else's door and removed it around midnight when the family was away at Disney World.

"Did you ever read *Oliver Twist*, Mrs. Wheel?" Detective Oh had asked, after the paramedics and police had taken off with Richard in the back of an ambulance.

Richard's "people" were the grown-up, mean and hardened version of Fagin's pickpockets from *Oliver*. He'd send them out at sales with instructions and shopping lists, and they came home with the goods or else. Sometimes they were the early birds and got all the best worms, and sometimes the good worms had to come out of other peoples' cars and trucks and shopping bags.

The picking business had gotten so crowded, so overworked by the nouveau junquer, that it had driven Richard, a pill-popping nightmare of a model son, into a kind of flea market madness.

"Fished out," he allegedly yelled from the back of his

303

pickup truck at passersby at the Kane County flea market last month. "These waters are fished out!" he had screamed. Louie had dragged him down and gotten him away just as the police arrived.

Richard had narrowly avoided arrest on assault charges twice in the past year when he attacked opposing bidders after auctions. Charges went unfiled when Louie, on Richard's behalf, offered a generous payment for pain and suffering, invoking the name of his father, Richard senior, who had been a relentless bargainer, a cajoler, a legendary figure who could sweet-talk a housewife's wash off the line.

"He couldn't remember the last time he had slept," Detective Oh told Jane later, after interviewing Rose at the hospital. "He was remembering back week by week, sale by sale, and got as far back as mid-May without recalling one stretch of sleep."

"He seemed a little edgy," Jane agreed, pouring coffee for Oh and Mile at her kitchen table.

"You were right to be so suspicious of Louie's involvement with David Gattreaux's murder. He couldn't confess to it because he didn't know how it had happened, or when. He had been with Richard at the Balance house, couldn't bring himself to go in. Waited in back, in the alley; said he cleaned out the truck while he waited for Richard, who was happy to provide him with all the details for his confession," Oh said.

"That's why I found the classifieds back there," Jane said. "They weren't Jack's, they were Louie's."

"Yes, he was Richard's godfather, had promised his father he would take care of him," Oh said. "I don't think his father knew how bad his amphetamine usage was or just how much caretaking he was asking Louie to do."

There would be paperwork and courtrooms down the line, but Oh assured Jane that the week-long nightmare was over. She could rest.

Jane believed him. She had slept soundly, Rita, nee McCoy, sprawled next to her on the bed. When she woke at 5 A.M. on Sunday morning, she decided not to go to any sales. She didn't need or want anymore stuff. Not this day. Richard had killed people over stuff, silly objects, shiny toys. It had driven him crazy. She needed to cleanse herself, prove that she was not lost in any of the madness that had emerged this week. It was time to get her life in order.

She showered and straightened out her bedroom, hanging up the clothes draped over the exercise bike. She even made her bed and weeded out magazines, tossed out catalogues, and stacked the bedside reading material.

Downstairs she got out a large calendar and marked off available dates for an Ohio trip with Tim. All business, she packed items for Miriam. She cleaned out the refrigerator and jotted down things she needed to replace before Nicky got home. She cleaned out her day runner and kept only the current and upcoming sale list.

As her last bookkeeping chore, she got out a business-size envelope and tucked twenty-five dollars cash into it. She printed, FOR BAKELITE JEWELRY, neatly on an index card, tucked it in next to the bills, and addressed the envelope to Richard Rose's store. Sparks would probably use the cash to buy his lunch, but her conscience was clear. Clear enough. She twisted the creamy Bakelite ring on her finger. It was a beauty.

When she looked at the clock, she saw it was only 7 A.M. Restless, she looked at her list of the Sunday sales highlighted in yellow. She thought about all the people already standing in line, standing on tiptoe to see in the windows, chatting cautiously with the person next to them, fearful of mentioning what they liked, what they collected. What if the people ahead of them heard and decided they had to have it, too? People like Richard, obsessed with whatever someone else wanted? She thought about her dad, who had once told her, ever so gently, that she would never be able to fill up the empty places inside of her with stuff. It would always take more and more stuff.

"Yeah, there's the stuff," she had told her dad, "but it's more than that: it's the gold rush, the hunt; it's the searching."

Again, Jane looked down at the classifieds and read the familiar tease—*Wear old clothes, a full basement and attic. We haven't even unpacked all the boxes. Killer stuff!*

She headed for the car.

Read on for an excerpt from Sharon Fiffer's latest mystery

DEAD GUY'S STUFF

Available in hardcover from St. Martin's Minotaur

_____

How do you know, Jane Wheel wondered, not for the first time, whether or not your rituals, your own little signature gestures, are celebrations of your individuality and part of your own quirky charm or if they are neurotic tics, proof positive that you suffer from obsessive-compulsive disorder?

For example, at estate sales, as Jane warmed up once inside the house, immersed in the possessions of another, she began humming, sometimes quite loudly, as she thumbed through books, rifled drawers, ran her fingers around the edges of bowls and rims of glassware. Humming seemed innocent enough.

What about the constant checking for car keys in one pocket, checkbook and identification in another, and cold cash in a third? Her fourth pocket, upper left, held a small notebook and tiny mechanical pencil that advertised: GOOSEY UP-HOLSTERY—TAKE A GANDER AT OUR FABRICS. Under the slogan was the telephone number WELLS 2-5206. Natural enough to check your pockets in a crowd. She did pat them in a special order, but that was probably something to do with muscle memory or neurological instinct. Right, left on the bottom; right, left on the top. Perhaps left-handed people who checked their pockets moved left to right, top to bottom. She would keep an eye on her friend Tim. He was a lefty.

It was 9:00 A.M. and Jane had just received her number for the sale. Doors would open at nine-thirty, so she had some time for her presale voodoo in the car. She patted her pockets, swallowed a sip of her now lukewarm coffee—after all, it had been sitting there as long as she had, two and a half hours, waiting for the numbers.

Pulling out her little notebook, she checked her list. She had a small sketch of a Depression glass pattern that a friend had asked her to look for and several childrens' book titles that Miriam, her dealer friend in Ohio, was currently searching for. God, she didn't want to have to fight the book people, but Miriam had said condition didn't matter on these. Miriam had a customer who was after illustrations and would remove them from damaged books that the real book hunters would cast aside. Both Jane and Miriam had shuddered at that. They were both strongly against the adulteration of almost any object, unless of course it was already in tatters and one could feel noble about the salvage. A thoroughly moth-eaten coat from the thirties could have its Bakelite buttons removed. Bakelite buckles and clips that had already been damaged and jewelry already broken or deeply cracked could be refashioned, but by god, Martha Stewart, keep your glue gun away from intact buttons and beads.

Jane's list had the other usual suspects. Flowerpots, vintage sewing notions, crocheted pot holders, bark cloth, all her favorites. She was also hunting old Western objects—linens, blankets, lampshades with cowboys and Indians, horse-head coat hooks. Tim's sister had just had a baby boy, and Tim was already planning the upgrade from nursery to toddler's room and had settled on turning this small corner of a sub-urban colonial into a set from *Spin and Marty*, the dude ranch serial from the original—the one that mattered—the *Mickey Mouse Club*.

Jane had only five minutes to write down her Lucky Five. At every house sale, to pass the interminable waiting time, Jane tried to guess by looking at the outside of the house what the inside would hold. She wrote down five objects, and if they were all in the house, she allowed herself an extra fifty dollars to spend for the day. The game didn't exactly make sense, she knew, since if she won, she lost: fifty dollars. But playing the Lucky Five was so satisfying.

She studied the compact Chicago brick bungalow, lo-cated a few blocks from Saint Ita's Church. The front side-walk had cracked, and the brickwork on the front steps was in disrepair. The classified ad had said "a lifetime of posses-sions," "a clean sale, a full basement," and the most delightful tease of all, "we haven't even unpacked all the boxes."

Jane listed the Lucky Five: Ice-O-Matic ice crusher (with red handle); a volume of Reader's Digest Condensed Books, including a title by Pearl S. Buck; a Bakelite rosary; Pink Coates and Clarke seam binding wrapped around a 1931 "spool pet" card.

Jane looked at her watch. She needed another item fast, and she was blank. She punched at her cellular phone.

"Yeah? Talk loud."

Jane could hear a lot of people in the background. Tim must already be inside some sale or at least scrambling for a place in line.

"I need one last thing for my list!" Jane screamed.

"An advertising key ring with a five-digit telephone number!" Tim screamed back.

The phone cut out and Jane unplugged it from the lighter and locked it in the glove compartment. It was almost time. She patted her pockets and drained her coffee. Parked just ahead of her was that nasty woman who had once sent her on a wild goose chase, told her about a great sale, and when Jane got to the address it was a vacant lot. Donna, Jane had named her, for no particular reason other than the fact that she liked her enemies to have names.

Did Donna have a lower number? Would she beat Jane through the front door? So *what if she does*, Jane told herself. She would race through the house with blinders on, allow no distractions, and beat Donna and everyone else to the treasures.

She would make a beeline down the stairs of this sweet brick bungalow on Chicago's northwest side and be drawn magnetically to the current object of her desire—whatever it was. She would know it when she saw it. Maybe a '40s brown leather Hartmann vanity case with intact mirror and clean, sky blue, watered silk lining. Jane would snap the sharp locks that would fly open with a clear pop and find the case filled to the brim with . . .

With what? This was the good part, the gut-wrenching, heart pounding, nerve-racking question. The speculation. The suspense. The mystery of it all. It was why, whenever she went to house sales, flea markets, garage sales, or rummage sales, she tried to come home with at least one box, suitcase, basket, or container filled with unknown stuff. Buttons, pins, broken jewelry, office supplies, fabric scraps, photos, maps, a junk drawer with a handle was what she wanted to carry home and sort through at her own kitchen table.

When a friend once asked her why she bought so many locked metal boxes, so many jammed suitcases, containers that required crowbars, chisels, screwdrivers, picks, and brute force to open, she shrugged. What kind of a person resists a grab bag? Especially when it costs only a dollar or two? Who doesn't want to own a secret?

Charley, her-not-nearly-estranged-enough-but-nevertheless-maybe-soon-to-be-ex-husband, likened her sifting to his own methods in the field searching for fossils.

"We not only collect the bones, we collect the earth around them. We need to know about the plants, the insects, everything that provides us with clues as to how the creature, whatever the particular creature we're excavating, lived," he said, explaining to their son, Nick, the vials of soil that lined the crowded desk in the den where he often worked weekends, despite the fact that he no longer officially lived in the house.

"Like what Mom does with her buttons and stuff, but . . ." Nicky stopped himself from even forming the whole thought. He might be only twelve years old, but he possessed the cautious wisdom of the child hoping for the reconciliation of his parents. He was savvy enough to stop any remark that might smack of a value judgment on their respective work. He certainly didn't want his mother's relatively new "professional picker" status to be put under his father's microscope.

"But what?" asked Jane, who had been eyeing the bottles of soil herself, thinking that the caps looked like they might be black Bakelite.

Nick shrugged his shoulders and looked at Charley.

"When we're in the field, we're looking for answers to big questions about life on earth, and when Mom is in the field, at an estate sale . . ."

"Yes, Professor?" asked Jane, coming to full attention. "What is *she* doing?"

"She's observing how one person or one family operated during their day-to-day lives," Charley said smoothly. "She's gathering the debris of popular culture of the thirties, the forties, whatever. She's keeping field notes on what people saved, what they deemed usable or beautiful. She observes what is still held by our society to be valuable and cycles those objects into the world as artifacts on display at the contemporary extension of the living museum . . . the flea market tables and antique malls of the Midwest."

"Nicely done, Charley," Jane said, ruffling his uncombed hair.

Nick felt his heart rise, attached to a small, hope-filled balloon. His father would give up the tiny apartment five blocks away from their house and move back home full-time. Nick would not need the doubles on shin guards, basketball shoes, and school clothes that so many of his friends kept in their two separate bedrooms. So far, he had not needed a bedroom at all in his father's shoebox studio. Charley just came over three or four times a week and most weekends to work, eat, sleep, hang out. Nick's friends assured him it wouldn't stay that way, all loose and friendly. Pretty soon, they warned him, things would get ugly, doors would be slammed, locks would be changed, and suitcases would be packed. Furniture would most definitely be rearranged.

No, thought Nick. He might only be twelve years old, but he saw how his father looked at his mother while she was watering her plants or dusting her old books or spooning coffee into the pot. He watched Jane follow Charley with her eyes as he crossed back and forth to the large reference books on the dictionary stand in the den. Sure, Nick was only a sixth grader, but he watched television, read books, played video games. His parents were still in love.

Earlier that very morning, she had left Charley sleeping peacefully on the couch in the den when she tiptoed out the front door into the still darkness. Now, sitting in her car, she read over her "wants" lists, both her own and the ones she kept for Miriam in Ohio and Tim in Kankakee, and reviewed the Lucky Five. Tucking the notebook back into its proper pocket, she let her mind wander. She watched the latecomers scurrying out of their vans and trucks to snag a numbered ticket from the roll on the porch of the house, whose contents would soon enough be scavenged and scattered to the four winds, and pondered her "separation" from Charley.

A marriage, she thought, trying to open an old-but-new-to-her Bonnie Raitt CD she had found, still sealed, at a garage sale just last week and stashed in the glove compartment, is a lot like this packaging. Even if you manage to open the wrapping, get a fingernail under a corner fold and make a start, the transparent wrap clings so tenaciously to the plastic cover that it's nearly impossible to get to the music inside. If she and Charley did manage to separate and listen to what played beneath, around, and under their marriage, would they run back to the comfortable togetherness they had shared for fifteen years or move on to a new and unsteady beat?

Enough pondering. Hearing the sound of car doors slamming, Jane dropped the still-unopened CD on the seat. Down the street, one door had opened and, as if they were all connected by an invisible wire, each early bird had followed the leader. Dealers, pickers, and bargain hunters opened their trucks and vans and stretched, making their way to the porch, where the busybodies who always bossed everyone around were already checking numbers, lining everybody up.

Donna was two numbers ahead of her. Seven to Jane's nine. How had Jane let that happen? She didn't really know her, this small, speedy woman with a crooked mouth and pinball eyes that darted from your face to your purse to whatever object you were holding in your hand, this woman who sent you off to phantom sales.

"What do you do with those buttons?" she had yelled at Jane once at a rummage sale, and Jane had been so taken aback, both by being spoken to at all and by being asked a direct question about the functional value of what she was buying, that she had simply shaken her head and shrugged. Being questioned about a purchase could ruin the moment so thoroughly that it never even occurred to Jane that it would be fun to shop with a partner. To have to discuss why the fabric squares and rickrack looked so appealing, to have to explain why one salt-and-pepper shaker appealed, but not the other, to have to convince someone that people really collected mechanical advertising pencils and that a shoebox full of them marked two dollars made perfect sense? The horror. The Donna of it all.

The doors opened and the first fifteen were admitted, handing over their tickets and entering the house like a greedy pack of dogs. Jane heard a man's voice behind her, angry about the number system. She turned to look at the source.

"Nine o'clock the paper says and nine o'clock we're here. What's the deal? Who you gotta . . . ?" Jane turned around and tuned out the voice. *Another new guy,* Jane thought, *Where do they come from? Aren't there enough dealers and pickers now? Can't we just close the tunnel and say, Sorry, full up?*

Jane paused in the small tiled entry and tried to take in everything at once. The living room on her right held the tables with plates, glasses, stemware, and some pottery figures. A case next to the all-business card table with calculator and newspapers for wrapping the more fragile objects held finer jewelry, pocket knives, and small artifacts of eighty years on earth, sixty years in one house. Hat pins, tape measures in Bakelite cases that advertised insurance companies, their four-digit phone numbers recalling a time when one phone line was all anyone ever needed and the possibility of running out of numbers, creating new exchanges and area codes, would have been a joke pulled from a bad science fiction novel. Inside the case were several sterling silver thimbles, which gave Jane hope that there would be buttons. A seamstress hoarded buttons and rickrack and old zippers, tucked them away into basement drawers, and stuffed plastic bags full of them into guestroom closets. That Coates and Clarke seam binding might be right around the bend. In the corner of the cabinet were three gold initial pins from the 1940s. Jane stretched to read them, then realized she would not have to make up a name and fit it to the initials, "RN." *A nurse,* Jane thought. *Perfect. Clean, well organized, good linens.*

All this information and conjecture took no more than five to seven seconds to gather, while Jane got the lay of the land from the tiny foyer. She shook herself out of her reverie on the house's owner and took off in search of stuff.

The kitchen. Jane grabbed a seven-inch Texasware pink-marbled plastic bowl from a box under the table and held it up to the worker standing at attention, pencil in one hand, receipt book in the other. "Fifty cents?" she answered to Jane's wordless question. Jane nodded, and the woman scribbled it down, starting Jane's tab.

Before she left the kitchen, Jane snatched up the oversized oak recipe file. She collected the wooden boxes sized for 3 × 5 cards, sorting buttons and gumball machine charms into them, but this box was more than twice that size and it was overflowing with handwritten cards, yellowing newspaper clippings, and stained cardboard recipes that had been cut from Jell-O and cracker and cereal boxes.

"Six?" asked the worker, barely looking up.

Jane thought the tag on the box said ten, but it was hard to see, and she didn't have two free hands to fiddle with it, so she nodded. Six was probably too much, but if the tag said ten, it was a bargain, wasn't it? The kitchen was so satisfying, filled with the kind of well-maintained but used and loved vintage items that spoke so convincingly to Jane's soul. Take me home, they all said, loud and clear. At least that's what Jane heard them say as she hustled through the kitchen. A souvenir of Florida spoon rest, hand-crocheted pot holders, tiled trivets that some child had labored over in the crafts room of summer camp. An ice crusher! Not an Ice-O-Matic, though, and Jane never cheated on the Lucky Five.

This was a forties to fifties household where the mother probably stayed home with the kids, baked cookies, and packed healthy sack lunches. Jane's thoughts lingered on the sack lunches, remembering back to elementary school meals in Saint Patrick's Grade School cafeteria. The food had been unrecognizable and inedible. She'd begged her mother to allow her to bring lunch, but Nellie, ever the practical woman and only occasionally the empathetic mom, had been thrilled with the modern addition of a cafeteria where students could buy a hot lunch. Nellie would no longer have to slather peanut butter and jelly on Wonder bread and wrap up chips and fruit every night.

Realizing she could skim off one more chore from her already too filled night of housework after nine hours work at the EZ Way Inn, Nellie refused to listen to the complaints about slimy macaroni slathered in ketchup, unrecognizable chunks of meat in a gluey gravy over slippery instant mashed potatoes. Not wanting to waste time with the lengthy explanation of how tired she was at the end of a long day of cooking, serving, and tending bar, Nellie didn't bother to explain the reasoning behind her decision.

"Eat the hot lunch . . . It won't kill you," she'd said.

Jane, forgetting all about lunches, brown bag or otherwise, hummed as she walked carefully down to the basement, ducking her head and stowing her finds into a large plastic totebag that she carried with her to all sales. Thoughts of Nellie might have sneaked into the kitchen with her, but Jane refused to take her along as she continued through the house. Donna was still going through kitchen cupboards, and although Jane feared her rival would be the one to find the blue Pyrex mixing bowl that would complete the set that sat waiting in Jane's basement, she knew it was pointless to stand behind Donna and watch her. Better to strike off in a new direction. Better to sniff around in the basement.

She noted that her assessment of the owner, a nurse, had been correct. Objects did seem clean and well packed, neatly organized on crude, built-in shelves in all four of the spotless basement rooms. There was a little storage area off the laundry room that looked dusty and promising for boxes of unsorted odd dishes and holiday decorations, but Jane decided to scan the shelves left to right, top to bottom in each of the rooms first.

She moved off to her right and found herself in the middle of First Aid Central. Boxes and boxes of gauze bandages, sealed bottles of disinfectant and saline solutions, rolls of tape were stacked floor to ceiling. Two women, neighbors or friends from the sound of their conversation, were already in there, one of them cramming rolls of paper tape into a wicker shopping basket.

"Was the owner a visiting nurse?" asked Jane, breaking two of her rules—asking a question and getting distracted by the owner's history instead of the owner's stuff.

Both women looked at Jane, not surprised at all that someone might want to chat during the feeding frenzy of a house sale. Yes, they were Mary's friends and neighbors, amateurs, not dealers or professionals.

"No, not Mary. She was a nurse a long time ago, but it's her granddaughter who's a visiting nurse, gets these supplies. Mary just wanted them not to go to waste."

Jane nodded, enjoying the contact with Mary through these two old friends.

"Mary saved all of everybody's things. Her husband's stuff is in that other room, and he's been dead for nearly thirty years."

Jane tried to keep an appropriately sympathetic expression—after all, Mary's husband *had* been dead for thirty years—and not show the callous joy she felt when she pictured some of the vintage clothes and office supplies that might be in the adjoining room.

"Was Mary's husband a doctor?" asked Jane, spotting and seizing a buttery leather doctor's bag on the floor.

Both women laughed and the one who seemed to be in charge of talking for the pair said, "Oh no, dear. Bateman owned the Shangri-La."

When Jane shook her head and shrugged, the silent partner whispered, "It was a tavern. Bateman was a saloon keeper."

Jane hoped the women didn't think her rude, but she turned away almost immediately. She couldn't move quickly enough into the "Bateman" corner of the basement. A saloon keeper! Eureka! Pay dirt! Gold in them thar hills. If she had the flexibility of an animated cartoon character, she would have kicked up her heels and leapt into the next room. She sighed with pure rapture when she saw the similarly organized and shelved remnants of thirty years in the tavern business, all of it clean, boxed, folded, and tagged.

Jane wiped the corners of her mouth with her sleeve, just in case she had inadvertently drooled.

Don and Nellie, Jane's parents, had operated the EZ Way Inn in Kankakee for forty years. A ramshackle building across from the now-closed stove factory that had given the town so much employment, so much prosperity, the EZ Way Inn was as charming on the inside as it was tacky on the outside. Don had never been able to talk Gustavus Duncan, the owner, into selling the building.

For forty years, Don had paid rent on the flimsy shack, shoring up and improving the interior, praying that a heavy wind wouldn't blow it all into kindling overnight. Don always called himself a "saloon keeper," considering that to be the most honest description of what he did. He never gave up though. Each first of the month, along with his rent check, he extended the offer to buy. Four hundred and eighty offers finally worked their magic. Last month Gus Duncan had finally caved.

Don had called her, his deep voice trembling with excitement.

"I'm buying the place, honey," he said. "I guess now that the factory's been closed for twenty-five years, old Gus decided nobody's going to give a million to mow down the EZ Way and make it into a parking lot."

Jane hadn't asked if it was still a worthwhile investment since her father had lately talked about retiring at least once a week. She didn't want to do anything that would temper his excitement about this deal, this sale that would give him so much joy. She would leave that up to her mother, Nellie, who had been throwing cold water on Don's plans for thirty years.

"Now I'll be a tavern owner instead of a saloon keeper."

"Pay raise?" Jane asked.

"Pay cut, but I get a bigger office," Don said, describing the building improvements he was planning.

Nellie had told Jane last week that the carpentry was done and they were planning on having a grand opening next month.

By next week, the painting and plastering and pounding would be finished, and Don had promised Jane that she could come in and decorate. That is, she could decide where the beer distributor's big calendar and the bulletin boards where Don posted the golf league standings and the bowling league scores would hang.

Jane had been planning some surprises though. She had

found some great vintage signs, old beer advertising trays that could be hung, even an old high school trophy case that she figured could stand in the corner for a display of Kankakee photos and tavern memorabilia. She had collected Kankakee postcards for years, made inexpensive copies, and enlarged them to make a Kankakee River montage that she couldn't wait to show her dad.

And now she was smack dab in the middle of a tavern memorabilia collector's dream. It was only twenty minutes into the sale and a small-enough house that the first twenty or thirty shoppers were her only competition. Because the other basement rooms seemed to be filled with vintage tools and a radio workshop—she spotted some great-looking Bakelite cases sitting on one of the shelves and another room had racks of spotless vintage dresses and hats—most of the dealers were keeping busy and out of Jane's way.

There were several neighbors, Jane now realized, milling around the basement, whispering about Mary and Bateman. Her two new friends from the medical supply storage corner had followed her, and one of them now pointed to a group photo, framed on the wall.

"That's Dorothy and me right there, the year our bowling team won the league." The more talkative of the pair took down the photo and held it close. In it, twenty women were grouped around a huge trophy. They wore silk bowling shirts, with individually sewn letters spelling SHANGRI-LA across the front. The black and white was so clear and well-preserved that Jane could read DOROTHY stitched over the pocket of the laughing woman with blonde curls and OLIVIA over the pocket of the much younger version of this now gray-haired fount of information.

"She looks like a movie star," Jane whispered, all notions of the plump, kindly nurse sending extra medical supplies to Third World countries disappearing and being replaced with a bad girl, B-movie starlet pouting in front of her martini at the Shangri-La.

"Mary was a beauty," said Dorothy. It was the first time Jane had heard her speak in a voice louder than a whisper. Ollie was clearly the talker.

"Still is. I bet she gets a husband by Christmas," Ollie said, and they both giggled.

Jane had found a kind of laundry cart or wooden dolly, a crate on wheels, and was loading it up while they talked. When she saw that they didn't want the bowling photograph—both said they had copies at home—she stuck it into the crate and kept filling. Boxes of old advertising shot glasses, Bakelite ashtrays, and a motherload of dice, decks of cards, and coasters.

"A husband?" Jane asked. "She isn't . . . she didn't . . ."

"Nursing home. Fell and broke her ankle and Susan, a visiting nurse and her own granddaughter, thinks she ought to live somewhere other than her own house," said Ollie.

"It's an assisted-living apartment, Ollie, and it's very nice," corrected Dorothy. "Susan can't care for her full-time, and she wanted her to be safe."

"Holy Toledo!" said Jane, using just the kind of archaic exclamation that her son, Nick, was trying to eliminate from her vocabulary, at least around his friends, and just the kind of expression that endeared her to Dorothy and Ollie.

"Punchboards," she told them. "There must be a dozen in this box. All sealed with their keys in the back."

The peaks and valleys of a childhood spent waiting in

the tavern for your parents to end their day when the bartender arrived at six are few and far between. Waiting was mostly a plateau.

But the highest point, the peak that defined a mountaintop, was the day Don set out a new punchboard, a one-inch-thick piece of pressed particle board punctuated with a grid of foil-covered holes waiting for you to insert a key punch and push through a tightly rolled cylinder of paper. Was there ever a more satisfying activity? Pay your quarter, study the board for clues, cross your fingers, choose your spot, push the key hard through one of the holes, puncture the foil, force the paper out onto the bar, unroll, and read the numbers. Jane remembered that fives were usually lucky. A sequence with fives or multiples of fives was a winner. A box of chocolates, usually chocolate-covered cherries, was the prize, and there were few customers left at the EZ Way Inn by six o'clock who had anyone waiting at home who they wanted to surprise with a box of candy.

Bored stove factory workers, whiling away the time until the loneliest hours of their day were gone, would pay Don, Nellie, whoever was at the bar, a dollar and signal for the punch board to be brought over. Then they'd crook their fingers at Jane, calling her over for good luck, and ask her to punch out a winner. If she did, she got to keep the candy, a whole box for herself; and if she lost, she still got the glorious pleasure of punching out those tiny paper pills of hope. Don had once referred to a customer who played the board incessantly as having "gambling fever," and Jane hadn't known what he was talking about. Gambling was sweaty men in a backroom rolling dice, wasn't it? Or tuxedoed James Bond types at a Baccarat table, yes?

No, Don had told her. He described gambling fever, and she recognized her own symptoms—the tiny beads of perspiration that broke out on her upper lip, the intense need to swallow, and the fullness in her chest when Vince called her over and threw down a dollar. That moment of tension and release when he told her to punch out some winners, that satisfying fit of the key into the punchboard . . . that was gambling.

Jane held JACKPOT CHARLEY in her hands. Twenty-five cents could win you a dollar and a chance to punch out a jackpot winner, another five or even twenty-five dollars. ALL AWARDS PAID IN TRADE it read. Don had always had candy punchboards, but here in Bateman's corner of the basement, Jane ran her hands over money boards, radio and television prize boards, and a small, round MORE SMOKES board where you bought a punch for a nickel and a winning number got you five packages of cigarettes.

Jane snapped back to the present. She looked at Dorothy and Ollie, who had become energetic helpers, putting leather dice cups and Bakelite dice, boxes of glass jars, bar towels with SHANGRI-LA embroidered in rainbow colors into her makeshift shopping cart. Jane had been a picker only a few months. Timid and still distracted by the owner's history, she had often let the owners' property, what she was really at a sale for, slip away. She had to make a quick decision and the right offer. Prices were low in this room. Clearly the sales team expected to get their money from Mary's fabulous vintage clothes and the "smalls" upstairs.

Bateman's old inventory was nickel-and-dime compared to the stuff in the rest of the house. Because this was a separate room with a door, a sales representative stood with a clipboard and pencil, ready to add the cost of the odd shot glass to your ticket. Jane hoped this was an owner, someone in authority and not just a helpful friend of the sales team, wearing an apron for the day just for the opportunity for early bird shopping.

Jane went up to her and talked low and fast. "I'll give you three hundred dollars for the whole room." Jane hesitated only a second, then upped her ante, "Five hundred and we tape it off right now."

Jane had never made such a bold offer. She had seen rooms sold though. Once she had been at a sale during the last hour and tried to go into a bedroom, getting tangled in some string across the doorway where a Donna type had barred entry with her body and waved her away. "I bought this room; it's all mine. See the string? I own the room."

This sale had only been going on twenty-five minutes at the most, and clearly this was a last-hour offer. Its appeal was the figure. Three hundred was a fair wholesale price for everything in this corner room, and five hundred was a fair retail price. Jane knew she would have to get the saleswoman's full attention. One of the other helpers was distracting her, telling her about some man who had tried to slip her a twenty to get to the front of the line. "Can you imagine?" she was saying. "Thought he could just buy me off? The people in line would kill me if I started taking tips like that."

"Look, Lois," Jane said, reading the name tag on her apron, "I'm a decorator and I'm doing a recreation room as a vintage bar. You're not going to get that much money for all this stuff even if you sell everything here individually for your asking price. And you know you're not going to get the tagged prices on all of it."

Five minutes later, Jane offered Dorothy and Ollie their choice of some of the Shangri-La souvenirs or cash if they'd help guard the door while she carried Mary's neatly taped boxes and bags out to the old van she and Charley still shared. They were terribly excited over meeting a real interior decorator and waved away any notion of payment.

"Mary'll be tickled pink when she finds out the Shangri-La is going to live on in some rich person's basement," said Ollie, and Dorothy nodded. In a moment of pure picker's rapture or the hallucination of gambling fever, Jane hugged them both, then proceeded to use Dorothy's roll of paper tape from the medical supply room to seal off the space. Crisscrossing the tape over the door frame, Jane sensed something familiar in the scene. What did this remind her of?

Shaking her head at someone trying to duck around her, she said, "No. Sorry, I just bought the room." When she turned and glanced over her shoulder, it only increased her giddy delight to see Donna slinking backward over to a sale's employee and complaining about a whole room being sold so early. *Let her whine,* Jane thought, *it will only make the sales people mad and less willing to bargain with her.*

She finished taping from the outside, sticking a sold tag on the center of the tape. She nodded at Dorothy and Ollie, who were both surprisingly strong, more than up to the task of pushing the boxes to the doorway for Jane to haul. Looking back at the older women framed by the strips of tape, she realized what it all reminded her of: a crime scene. She had just bought herself a crime scene.